WHEN PHILOSOPHERS WERE KINGS 12-23-03

Ron,

Merry
Christmas!

Steven M Best

WHEN PHILOSOPHERS WERE KINGS

Steven M. Best

SUNSTONE
PRESS

SANTA FE

Cover graphics by Stephen Johnson

Sunstone books may be purchased for educational, business, or sales promotional use. For information please write: Special Markets Department, Sunstone Press, P.O. Box 2321, Santa Fe, New Mexico 87504-2321.

FIRST EDITION

1 3 5 7 9 10 8 6 4 2

Library of Congress Cataloging-in-Publication Data:

Best, S. M. (Steven M.), 1951–
    When philosophers were kings / S. M. Best.—1st ed.
    p. cm.
    ISBN: 0-86534-362-4
      1. Wisconsin—History—Civil War, 1861–1865—Fiction. I. Title.

PS3602.E79 W48 2003
813' .6—dc21   2002042664

 Published in SUNSTONE PRESS
Post Office Box 2321
Santa Fe, NM 87504-2321 / USA
(505) 988-4418 / *orders only* (800) 243-5644
FAX (505) 988-1025
www.sunstonepress.com

In memory of
Norma Jean Bachman and Donna Jean Best.
Their lessons helped me through
thirty years of debilitating illness.

ACKNOWLEDGMENTS

ONE CAN HARDLY WRITE HISTORICAL FICTION WITHOUT CONCERN FOR preservation of truth. Yet, it is the story between the lines of written history that captured my imagination and motivated my writing and telling of this story. That is, after all, the challenge of the novelist. We will never know what these people really thought or how they acted, but I have tried to present their personalities in keeping with what is known about the family nearly one-and-a-half centuries later.

The Best family genealogy and biographies have been researched for over a half-century by a group of dedicated family members, thus providing a rich source of information. From these sources, I have endeavored to present a dramatized story, true to the lives and times of the people. Dorothy Petry and Ethyl Rybarcyk provided me access to their private collections, without which, I would never have been able to envision this story. Other people contributed indirectly by sharing their information with them, including: Norma Jean Bachman, Doris Beach, Don and Marilyn Best, John and Beverly Best, Janice Healy, Col. Wm and Judy Johns, Ralph and Darlene Kelly, Louana Best-Lamb, Randy Palmer, and Duane I. Smith.

Early family researchers such as Laurel Mussman, Irving C. Best, T.C. Wimberly, Archie Crothers and Xena Carman collected information or wrote significant memoirs, passing the family legacy onto their children before going to their final rest. Sarah BORTON Best wrote a detailed letter to her sister following the war, which outlined the roles played by various family members in the war, as well as the impact those events had upon them. Ruth, daughter of John Nelson Best, wrote a ten-page letter to her brother Walter in 1901.

Erwin, Ruth, and Kenneth Crothers took me to the area cemeteries, pointed out the locations of the original family farms and Indian campgrounds, provided some oral tradition, area histories, and a copy of: Reminiscences, Sophronius S. Landt. Portage history was researched by Edwyna Curry and Karen Kappenman. Fred Galley described the character of the town in its earliest years. Information, photographs, and documentation regarding Dr. Thomas Best's family was provided by Geraldine and Daniel Draney of Lincoln, Nebraska. Special thanks to Steve Anderson, Dee Grimsrud, Frank Idzikowski, Lynnette Wolf, Jim Blackwell, and Jim Ogden for additional research assistance. Kevin Dier-Zimmel provided the research for the Battle of Paint Rock Bridge and the Unit surrender at Chickamagua. The song, Pawn Your Soul, was written by my good friend and former traveling companion, Douglas Bremicker ((c) 1969, all rights reserved).

I would also like to thank the U. S. National Archives in Washington, D.C., the U. S. War College Library, the National Park Services at Americus, GA, Perryville, KY, Murfreesboro, TN, Fort Oglethorpe, GA, the Wisconsin Veterans Museum, the Public Libraries of Neligh, NE, Portage, WI, Cobb County, GA, the University Historical Archives of Athens, GA, River Falls, WI, Dallas and Northeast, TX, and the Historical Societies of WI, Chippewa Valley, KS, and NB.

Map artwork was done by Sonja Kallstrom. Donna Best, Nicholas Best, Annika Best, and Ryan Johansson gave clerical assistance. Martin Best, Ellen Pine, Jerry Goodmanson, Gary Fricks and Tonia Best enthusiastically helped with proof reading. Nancy Baxter of Guild Press read my first draft and gave meaningful suggestions. Greg Zeck of the University of Minnesota, and Susan Malone, of Malone Editorial Services, guided me through the long critique and editing process. But none of this would be possible without the cooperative and understanding spirit of my wife, Paulette, who encouraged me through a seven-year process of research and writing.

Bests of Big Spring and Portage [1]

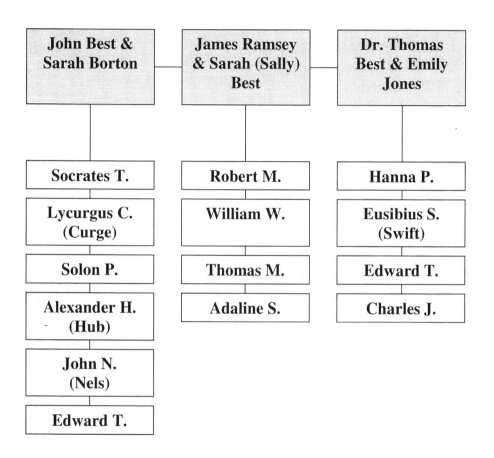

John Best & Sarah Borton	James Ramsey & Sarah (Sally) Best	Dr. Thomas Best & Emily Jones
Socrates T.	Robert M.	Hanna P.
Lycurgus C. (Curge)	William W.	Eusibius S. (Swift)
Solon P.	Thomas M.	Edward T.
Alexander H. (Hub)	Adaline S.	Charles J.
John N. (Nels)		
Edward T.		

---

[1] Only family members living in Wisconsin at the time of the book are listed

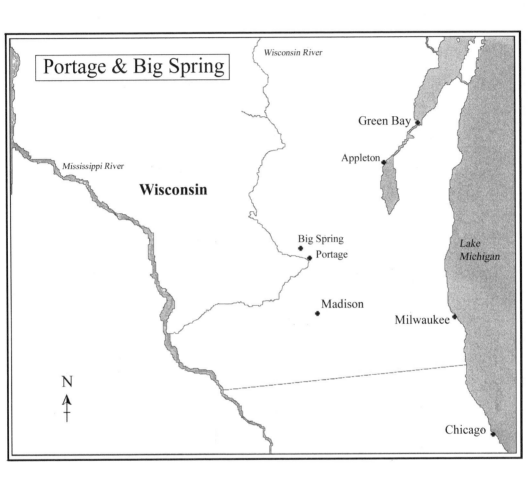

PROLOGUE

I N THE NINETY-FOURTH YEAR OF THE GREAT EXPERIMENT, FIRE RAINED FROM the sky and struck a small island in Charleston Harbor, South Carolina. Distant watchers thought it strange that such a small piece of ground, so thoroughly encompassed by water, could kindle a flame capable of consuming an entire nation. But panic and passion knew no reason, and amidst such forces the people floundered. Dogmatic politicians and fastidious scholars in the North decried the inflammation, calling for volunteers; while equally elegant Southern aristocrats vowed to fan the flames.

So it was in the summer of that year, when generals' minds turned to war and young men's hearts grew cold, that rivers of men surged down the hills, through the cities, and out into the valleys below. Rivers of gray and rivers of blue thrust forth into the tempestuous rage of two opposing floods. It was as though they had never considered the words of the philosopher, Socrates, penned by Plato:

"Until philosophers are kings, and princes of this world have the spirit and power of philosophy, and political greatness and wisdom meet in one, and those commoner natures who pursue either to the exclusion of the other are compelled to stand aside, cities will never have rest from their evils, no, nor the human race, as I believe, and then only will this, our State, have a possibility of life and behold the light of day."

ONE

"A just man harms no one."

—Socrates

April 14th, 1861, Daingerfield, Texas

SOCRATES BEST STARED IN STARK DISBELIEF AT THE NORTHERN REGISTER spread out on the long oak counter top of the local livery. His course, dry, callused hands crumpled thick creases through the paper's borders. He had heard the news on the street, but found it impossible to believe. In front of him lay the words that the Confederacy had fired on the Federal Garrison at Fort Sumter, barraging the stone walls of the island fortress until its commander surrendered.

Socrates closed his eyes, took a deep breath, and sighed. Why such dark shadows over Texas? And where was the *Form* in this? Had to be here. Someplace. He never would have brought Ellen to such a distant land, had he not first sensed that inner voice—envisioned a greater destiny. It had all seemed so clear then, but now there were so many reasons to doubt. The words of Aristotle flowed gently through his mind: "He causes motion as an object of desire, and the heaven which is moved, moves everything else."

Yes. There would be good in this too. Everything ordered by the *one who knows*. Time would prove it.

Socrates folded the newspaper and placed it under his arm. A group of men stood between him and the door, every eye staring intently at him. A few were town folk. The rest were rough-cut and crusty, the kind always brawling in saloons, or sleeping it off in one jail or another. Two he knew from his earliest days in Daingerfield, Billy Morris and his uncle, Buck Malneck.

Morris, a short, stocky redhead, often picked fights in school. The reason didn't really matter, he could always find one. Buck, on the other hand, was long and lean, his high black Stetson lengthening his appearance as he strutted through the streets of Daingerfield like a rooster on parade. Shortly after

Socrates and Ellen had arrived, Buck came from Missouri with his sister, Jane, and nephew, Billy. Buck's brother-in-law had been killed in Bleeding Kansas while raiding a town of abolitionists, and Jane had come to make a fresh start here, a desire Buck hadn't really taken to heart. He didn't want Billy to forget the pain the abolitionists had brought—not ever. Having a Yankee for the nephew's teacher ground salt in Buck's wounds, driving him over the edge. As soon as Billy was old enough to ride and shoot, Buck pulled him out of school and headed back to Missouri. Socrates hadn't seen either of them for nearly four years.

Redheaded Billy spit as he fired off a challenge. "Well, what-da-ya think of yer precious North now—seeing as they's getting their butts whupped?"

"Yeah!" said Buck. "Whupped good!"

Socrates bit his lower lip, scratched his scalp through its thin brown mane, studied the angry faces. A couple had children enrolled in his school and should have known better, but they just stood quietly by, watching and waiting. He was on his own. A shiver ran down his spine. He started doing what any self-respecting teacher did best—talking. "Now just hold on to your britches there, Buck! Firing on a garrison is one thing, and all-out war, well, that's another."

Buck's face wrinkled into a sneer. "Damned Yankee. Comin' down here all cocksure of yourself, butt brushin' the young folks, breathing your stinking abolition into their heads. Tell me, schoolteacher, how does it feel to do the Devil's biddin'?"

Socrates shook his head hard. "What's the matter with you, Buck? The rest of you, too. Haven't I been with you long enough? Nearly five years. Sure there's been some hard times, but I've done my best to get along with everybody. Haven't I? Besides, I never talk politics with young ones. Too busy teaching school and working my farm."

A tall, round, fat fellow with a wide-brimmed hat leaned forward at the waist, his scraggly brown hair falling forward to frame his bulbous face. "That mean you'll fight for Texas?"

Socrates shifted his feet. "Is *that* what the town brought me here for—to fight—or to farm and teach?"

The fat man kicked a keg of nails. "That's the problem with you Yankees—you's either for Lincoln or ya don't wanna get involved with nothin'!"

Buck spat a wad of moist tobacco onto Socrates' lower pant leg and boots, his gaze slowly wandering up Socrates' frame, until he stared straight into Socrates' eyes. "Way I see it—ain't no one can be neutral. There's a difference 'tween right and wrong—a big difference! Any pimple-nosed school boy knows that. Yer gonna have to decide where you stand."

Socrates' stomach shrunk into a tight knot. Had to reason with them. Make them see. "Look. You heard what Sam Houston said. The North has ten times more industry than we've got in the whole Confederacy. They've got more people too—folks who don't go off like some hair trigger every time there's a bump in the road. They live where it's freezing most of the year and possess strong wills—hard wills—forged in weather worse than anything you've ever seen—and they've never turned back. If they come to fight, it won't be for a planting season. A war like that could last years. You want to fight like that? Watch your friends die?"

"Shoot!" said Buck, spraying tobacco and spittle. "Y'all hear that? He's always askin' questions he thinks he knows the answers to. But listen to *him*! We shouldn't fight the Union boys cause they's all bigger, stronger, and live where it's cold! Well! What kinda talk is that? Houston's a coward and you sound just like him!"

Socrates slowly shook his head. "The absent are always wrong. Aren't they, Buck?"

Buck's jaw worked its way forward, pushing his lower lip out. His beady eyes narrowed. "What's that supposed to mean?"

"Means you shouldn't talk a man down when he's not here to defend himself."

"Shoot! I wish Houston was here right now so's I could say it to his face. Listen. I don't care if they got ten men for every one of us. One Southerner's worth more'n ten Yankees any day. Ya hear?"

Socrates straightened his nearly six foot frame, coolly stared straight into Buck's eyes. "I hear you all right, but words won't mean much when the band starts to play, and cannon fire fills the air."

"Teachers—think you know everything."

"No, Buck, I don't know everything. Never said I did either. But I have a couple friends who fought in Mexico, and they said talk doesn't mean a thing when your butt puckers and your body starts making water. *That's* when you'll find out what you're talking about; but then it'll be too late."

Buck's eyes nearly bugged out of his head. "Faced more guns than you *ever* will, teacher."

"Don't listen to him!" said the fat man. "He's just a coward—coward and a traitor. Let's hang him."

Shouting their agreement, the others pressed in.

"Dear, God," said Socrates. As they grabbed him by his coat, he lurched forward, twisted his upper body, and craned his neck, veins bulging under the strain. Long, rock-hard arms pumped back and forth. He twisted frantically, but to no avail. They had him.

A shot rang out.

The angry men stopped. Sheriff Will Peacock stood outside the open door. He was slightly older than Socrates' father, silver haired, weather-skinned, and wrinkled; hardened by multiple decades of farming, Indian fighting, and law enforcement. Behind a small cloud of smoke his hand pushed a blur of metal downward, leaving his pointer finger resting on the dark wooden handle of a silver Colt pistol holstered at his belt. The Colt was a .44 caliber, the kind favored by lawmen around Texas, and capable of blowing a hole through a man the size of a Bing cherry.

"You boys wouldn't be taking the law into your own hands now, would you? This here's my town, and I don't like folks thinking they can do whatever they please in it." His fingers danced over the Colt handle.

"But he's a Yankee!" shouted Malneck. "He should be hung."

Peacock cocked his silvery head. "That true, Socrates? You taking the Union side?"

"No. I came here to teach. Not to fight. If I have to do anything I can make powder, but I won't be joining either army if it means I have to carry a rifle. I won't do it."

"Hear that?" said Peacock. "Plenty of powder'll be needed for our army. Seems Socrates can do his share by making it for you boys, then he can still teach school. Now since this matter's settled, why don't you all get on over to Wheatville? Will Shepherd is forming some cavalry there. I'll bet he could use a few more hot heads."

Buck's beady eyes bulged. "No! Sheriff, we're hangin' him."

Peacock's left-hand yanked Buck's hair so hard, the back of his head nearly broke the oak counter top. The lawman's Colt pistol appeared just as fast, its cold steel barrel pushing straight up Buck's nose. "You better not argue with me, Buck, or you'll be blowing snot out of the top of your head. Understand?"

Buck nodded emphatically, eyes wide.

"Good! Then there won't be any more discussion on the matter." He slowly returned the pistol to his holster, patted it for emphasis while staring down the others, then let go of Buck's hair. With one sweep of the hand, he ushered the group out of the building.

The portly man turned at the doorway and scowled. "One thing's for sure, I ain't sendin' my children to no school what's taught by no Yankee spy."

"Yeah!" shouted another. "I ain't giving one dollar of my money to no Yankee neither."

Socrates turned and walked out, past Musgrove and Pouns Dry Goods store, past the Post Office and the larger buildings used for Chapel Hill College and Sylvia Academy. Beyond those stood only one-story wood buildings and the old, black, log cabins that lined the dirty little street. Off to one side was the spring, though it looked more like a water-filled ditch. The word around town was a battle had been fought here, back in '30, when this territory was claimed by both the Mexicans and the Americans. Later it ended up as part of the Republic of Texas, but long before the Tex-Mex thing was ever settled in San Jacinto, the United States sent a Captain Daingerfield into the area with a hundred men. They were camped around this spring when the Redskins attacked. Daingerfield's crew won. Daingerfield lost his life, and the people of the area later named the town in his honor. Wonder what the captain would have made of this mess? thought Socrates—what side he'd take?

Sheriff Peacock caught up with him. "That's a tough bunch. Hope they didn't get to ya."

"The herd? Nah. At least I didn't think so until they pulled that rope down. Then I about crapped my drawers. I'd hoped folks would cool down some by now, but this Sumter thing's really got 'em going—worse than I've ever seen."

"You think this is bad? Should've been here when the Moderators and Regulators were feuding back in '41. Now *that* was something."

Socrates thought back to the stories he had heard from the older settlers, how President Lamar appointed Peacock as Sheriff and gave him free rein to clean up the mess. Blood had been shed from one end of the County to the other that year. "I heard you took a few down before it ended."

"More than a few, Socrates. More than a few. Had to. Texas was drawing every kind of low-life scum that could scratch its way out of the Louisiana sloughs, or crawl itself across the western plains. Why, back then Daingerfield was just a few dirt-floor cabins scarcely fit for pigsties. I took no pleasure in what I did, but it put an end to lawlessness around here."

"At least until now, Sheriff. Now—well—they've just got to cool down, got to think this thing through."

Peacock grunted as he walked, kicked a small rock down the street. "Oh. I doubt they'll ever cool off much. Texans're a rare breed—mixture of Mexicans, settlers, ranchers, merchants, cow pokes, misfits, and drifters. It's only the last two ya have to worry about, especially after they get some forty-rod lightning into them. Then those boys'll get on their high horses over just about anything."

"And with Darby preaching secession like it was religion, and other slavers pumping them full of liquor, they're up on their high horses all right."

Peacock stopped walking and turned to Socrates. His fingertips ran over his rough-whiskered face as he spoke. "I suppose we can't blame Mr. Darby. He's probably the biggest slave holder in this country—figures he's got more to lose than anyone. Can't let *that* happen without a fight."

"I know," said Socrates. His shoulders drooped, and his gaze fell upon his own brown leather boots nearly scraped white from the jagged edges of iron stones that littered what seemed like every square foot of the highlands around Daingerfield. "It's just—people—property? Don't seem right folks fighting for that."

"Don't give that no never mind. There's plenty of good folks here. It's just they get all passionate when it comes to their state's rights. To many, this trouble with the government reminds 'em of their problems with Santa Anna and the Mexican rule. Probably wouldn't have accepted statehood in the first place if they hadn't thought they could pull out whenever they wanted."

"I know. Cotton croppers come with slaves, and that's a fact. I'd just hoped the idea of war wouldn't take root. It didn't have to be this way."

Peacock nodded. "You're right. And a good third of Titus County agreed with you in February, but across the state there were over forty-six thousand votes cast for secession. Hell, that's over seventy-five percent of the vote! But secession's one thing, and fighting the Federal Government, now that's a horse of a different color altogether. I can't help but wonder how many of those folks're having second thoughts about now."

Socrates chewed his lip and shook his head. "I think Texans like to fight."

"Ha! You're right about that. If Santa Anna and his whole army couldn't make them back down, I don't suppose the Union's gonna."

The two started walking again. "I just don't want to get involved," said Socrates. "Ellen and I, we've got family in the North—friends too."

"That puts a pretty big fly in your ointment."

"Don't I know it? I may not care much for making powder, but I will if that's what it takes to stay out of the fighting."

"And you won't have to leave Ellen."

"Yeah," said Socrates softly. "Funny, she was just starting back out of her shell—getting back to normal. Now I'm afraid all this talk of war is going to send her right back into herself. But I can't stop teaching. I still have three students."

"That all you've got left? Hardly seems worth your while."

"Think so? What if I could train one young man to realize his potential—to hold an office with truth and justice?"

Peacock smiled. "An honest politician? That'd be something. Might change politics altogether, but I'm afraid it'd take a lot more than one."

"Well," said Socrates with a grin, "I've got three."

"And if all goes well, they'll still be here when the war gets over. If not, you won't have wasted your time. Look. I know it's none of my business, but why don't you folks just go back north 'til then?"

Socrates smile faded. "It's kind of complicated, Sheriff, but there's two reasons. First, when I went away to college, Pa thought I was a ringer for the ministry."

"So? Many are called—few are chosen. Isn't that what the Good Book says?"

Socrates stopped again, searched Peacock's aged eyes. "That's the *heart* of the problem. I was doing great until I discovered more current theology—the idea that man had God within himself, could control his own destiny. My namesake—the Greek philosopher, he had it right: 'One Form of the Good, over all.' And there were fresh ideas coming out of Harvard—ideas that dared answer hard questions—like why Jesus said, 'Ye are *all* gods'."

"So you rejected the old man's religion?"

Socrates stopped and tilted his head. "Guess you could say that, but I never thought of it that way. Just figured he was sore since he couldn't be a minister and I could, but wouldn't. When I discovered theater he about hit the roof. After that it seemed like we couldn't see eye to eye on much of anything. Not in Ohio. Not even in Wisconsin. All it took was one last pack to break that mule's back"

Peacock shook his head. "Funny how Old Man Strife can stalk a pair 'til the time is ripe. Seems like I've seen it a hundred times. If it doesn't slither its way between father and son, it's between brothers—or worse yet, husband and wife. Never knew my Pa. He joined the Northwest Army back in 1812—massacred at Detroit before I was even weaned. Maybe it was a good thing, then again, maybe not. Guess I'll never know. Still, often find myself wishin' I could've met him, could've at least talked to him once. Just wasn't in the cards."

The two started walking again, this time in silence. They passed the edge of town and approached a gray stand of woods made up of one hundred foot tall hickory trees, and the smaller, rounder post oak and blackjack oaks. Like groups of men with no apparent order, they stood around in small clusters that thickened and spread out into the surrounding hills, known to the locals as the Daingerfield Mountains. The hickories had already popped their leafy bunches through their buds, giving some hints of green, while the oaks had yet to sprout their curve-cut leaves. This stand was unique since it sat on the edge of a forest that had seeded its way diagonally through the valley hundreds of years before, crossing the Big Cypress River from northeast to southwest. It formed a thirty-to-fifty mile timber belt that separated the short-leafed pines and scattered oaks of the Coastal Plains, from the higher black land prairie grasses of Comanche Plateau in the north central part of the state. Beside the stand of trees was an open field with a small, well-built, three-bedroom house on it. Socrates' home.

Peacock stopped and turned toward Socrates. "Listen. If those boys give you any more trouble, or if there's anything else I can do, just let me know."

Socrates stopped and exhaled. "Thanks, Sheriff. I guess it'll just take some time to sort all this out."

Peacock nodded, then turned and went his own way. Farther down the street Socrates could see his son, Gus, running after some other seven-year-olds. Might as well let the boy play. He needed to talk to Ellen alone.

Inside Ellen rocked, her long black hair draped over her narrow shoulders, her blue eyes sparkling like delicate blue sapphires—the baby's mouth busy suckling at her breast. Occasional sucking noises were interrupted by tiny grunts, followed by little farts, muffled in woolen blankets, and Socrates found himself not wanting to interrupt the peaceful scene. Still, he knew it would be better if she heard the news from him. He forced a smile as he started to cross the room, stopping halfway. "Ellen, I'm afraid there's been some bad news."

His words were soft, but clear, yet she ran a gentle finger over little Willie's face as though she hadn't heard a word.

He took a step closer. "Looks like there's going to be a war for sure. The Confederacy fired on the Federal Garrison at Fort Sumter. Texas is raising an army. Could be an all-out fight."

Ellen's face flushed. "They've thrown the apples on the table?"

Socrates thought of the stories he'd read to her so many times. For once, Homer didn't seem so exciting. "Yes."

She turned her soft blue eyes to him. "You won't have to join them, will you, Socrates? I don't know what I'd do if you had to go. Why, with Mama and Papa gone, I'd be all alone with our babies. Promise you won't leave me."

A sharp pain pricked his chest. Her long depression after losing both parents and then her little girl weighed heavily. Loneliness swept over him. How far his family was from them. Over a thousand miles. And the parting had been hard. "You mustn't worry. I've arranged to make powder for the soldiers so I can still teach school." He looked away from her, staring through the window at the cows in their pen. "That is, if anyone'll bring their children. Seems like some of these folks see us as Yankees—think we've suddenly become their enemies. Guess they plum forgot we came to make our home here, too."

"They're just a pack of fools," hissed Ellen. "Talking about their right to property and keeping slaves—as if those poor black people were nothing more than animals. Many of them don't even own a slave! What're they getting so upset about that they want to go off and get themselves killed for it? Maybe if they'd lost their mamas and papas—or little baby girls—they wouldn't be so quick in going off to war."

Socrates swallowed hard. "I know, but it's more complicated than that. These people don't want the government telling them what they can own. They think each state should make its own laws, that the Federal Government should mind its own business. They're afraid it's getting too big for its britches and they'd rather fight than let anyone tell them how to live."

"Maybe they should just forget all that and look at it simple." Her thin brows arose, eyes alight. "Then no one would have to die."

He could find no rebuttal to her child-like faith and stood silent.

"Let's go home, Socrates, back to Wisconsin. You can make up with your father. I'm sure of it now."

The pain in his chest dropped into his stomach like a red hot poker. "No. If he wouldn't accept you as my wife then, he won't now."

"But you don't *know* that. A lot of time has passed and things are different now. You could at least try."

The intensity of his anger, the fire in his belly, surprised him after all these years. "No! Pa was wrong and he has to admit it. Besides, we have a lot of property here. It's taken us years to put this spread together. We can't just get up and go—leave it all behind."

Her eyes went wide. "This spread! This spread? You speak of our land as if it were a place of majestic beauty—arrowed pines, placid pond, virgin soil, hickory nuts at our fingers. Look around! This isn't Paradise—or Walden Pond either. It's a big farm with a lot of timber, sandy soil, good drainage, and good water; but only a few acres will do us any good if no one's willing to help us work it."

He stared at his infant son, still nestled in her arms, said softly, "Ah, that's where you're wrong. You are looking at what is while I am seeing what will be. This conflict won't last forever. Once the Federal Government sends its armies, the people will wake up and see they were wrong. Everyone will forget about the past and get back to business. Then we'll be sitting pretty."

Ellen trembled and drew in a deep breath. The hard lines of her oval face softened, before disappearing altogether. She shrugged her shoulders. "Well. If we can't go north, maybe my brother could come and stay with us."

"Does he want to?"

"I don't know, but I received a letter from my sister Isabella today. She says that Ben is in Illinois. Says he doesn't seem to have any direction since Mama and Papa died. I pray for him every night. You know how precious he is. I was thinking, maybe he could come and stay with us for a while. It would do him good to have family around, and he could help you make powder and harvest our corn."

Socrates chewed his lip, stumped. Certainly he could use Ben's help, but something bothered him about the idea. How long could this war last? What could it mean to them? And what if she had another reason for bringing Ben here? He tried to think of it from her viewpoint. Taking the sleeping baby from Ellen, Socrates settled Willie in the cradle, gently pulled her from the chair, and wrapped his long arms around her little frame. Her full breasts pressed against him. His arms tightened their hold. "It's become a lonely world for you since your folks died. Hasn't it?"

She pressed her face into his chest.

"It's all right, Ellen. If you want Ben here, that's fine with me."

Her head lifted and her round, blue eyes cleared like pure sapphires. "Really?"

"Yes. You know I love your brother almost as much as you. He'd certainly lighten things up around here, and I could use his help. Write and see if he can come before winter. He's probably signed onto a farm for now, but summers are long here. Even if he comes in the fall, there'll be plenty of work for him to do. And if things get worse, he can help us move north, maybe to Missouri. 'Til after the war."

April 14th, 1861, Big Spring, Wisconsin

Edward Best gripped the reins of the feisty mule team, while his father, John, and brother Nels, picked up bunches of hay and tossed them onto the wagon bed. The brothers shared gray-blue eyes and sandy-brown hair, but the eighteen-year-old Ed was thinner than his twenty-year-old brother and had a darker complexion. Brother John's name was actually John Nelson Best, but everyone called him "Nels," which helped distinguish father and son. Their father was old and slightly bent, which was the only way these two brothers would ever catch their father's height. He had stood nearly six foot at one time, but was now rapidly approaching the five foot eight inch level of his two youngest son's.

Long, thin tufts of white cirrus streaked the spring sky, while a flock of wild geese, covering nearly half the sky, ca-honked its way northward in a broad, multi-layered V. The hay the three gathered remained from the early snowfall the previous year, and was now being salvaged to feed the livestock. From these forty acres of high ground, Ed could see all the nearby woods dotting the landscape. Oak and birch pleasantly contrasted with alternating strips of pasture that stretched out like long green rugs laid in every possible direction. He leaned back into the reins of his over-eager team, and spotted a wisp of a man racing on horseback toward the barn. Even at that distance he recognized the dark hair and beard of his second oldest brother, Lycurgus, whom everyone simply knew as "Curge."

"Look! Pa," said Ed. "Curge is flying like a swallow in the wind."

John straightened and frowned. "What's gotten into that boy? Nels, hold these mules."

Nels stepped over and snatched the mules' bridle as Pa turned in a huff. The wagon's wheels had bored deep ruts into the soft ground, pushing up little walls of mud that he easily hopped.

Curge pulled his horse up sharply. Ed strained to hear their conversation, but a light breeze broke up the words so he couldn't make sense of them. His father wagged a knobby old finger at Curge. Ah, the reproving words his brother must be hearing. Horses were important to Pa and he never allowed the boys to abuse them, which to Pa meant anything over a canter.

Curge turned his horse and trotted back down the road. Pa turned to face the boys, cupped his hands, and shouted for them to bring the hay wagon into the barn. What was going on? His father had already headed toward the house, so Ed nodded to his brother, who helped him swing the mules around, then lofted the reins to drive the beasts forward. Just as the team came alongside a pile of manure, Ed jerked the reins, sending Nels' feet straight into the mess.

"Hey!" shouted Nels. "Watch where you're going."

Ed smiled, raking his fingers backwards through his thick brown mop. "Hay? Hay's for horses!"

"Don't be a wise acre—and keep this thing on track."

"Sorry," said Ed, stifling a laugh.

Up came another pile and Ed jerked the reins again.

"That's it!" cried Nels. He reached down, grabbed a handful of manure, formed it into a ball, and launched it directly at his brother's face.

Ed ducked just in time to miss it, but as he straightened up a second turdball struck him square in the crotch. "Give! I give!" he shouted. "You got my family jewels!"

"Call *those* jewels? Them's no jewels."

"Hey! Don't insult my particulars."

"They're particular, alright, particularly small."

Ed lifted his head and thrust it toward one side, then turned his attention back toward the reins. "Giddayup," he shouted, and Nels offered a satisfied smile before pivoting back toward the barn.

After the hay was stacked and the mules released into the corral with the horses, the boys walked to the well and pumped water, rinsing the mud from their boots. Another flock of geese winged their way overhead.

"Think what they say about them honkers is true?" asked Ed.

"Them being the souls of unbaptized babies?"

"Yeah."

Nels squinted through cool, gray eyes, his light brown hair dangling over his fair-skinned forehead. "Doesn't seem likely, God making them wander till judgment day. Nah. Just a story."

Ed turned back to the pump and the cleaning of his boots. "Nels, why you suppose Pa never steps in manure?"

"Huh? Now what are you talking about?"

"You know—works right beside us—clod hops over everything—never gets dirty—and just look at us."

"For starters, he don't throw no turds."

"That's not what I mean. Even on a good day we're covered with mud and manure from the belt down."

Nels stared ahead for a moment, then turned his gaze toward the ground and shook his head. "Don't rightly know, Ed. Never really stopped to think about it. *Doesn't* seem natural. Does it?"

Ed shook his head. "Sometimes I think he could work this whole field in his Sunday prayer-meeting clothes and it wouldn't make any difference one way or the other."

"I know. Looks like we went hog wild in a pig pen, don't it?"

Entering the back door, they took off their boots, washed-up, changed into clean pants and shirts, and came to the dinner table. Their mother and father were already seated, concern embedded in their aged faces.

"What did Curge want, Pa?" asked Ed.

"Just hold your horses, son, we'll get around to that when the others get here."

Ed drilled Nels with a quizzical expression, but Nels just shook it off. Pa never had the entire family get together, except when something really big happened, like some kind of family crisis.

Within the hour the back door slammed again and again, announcing the arrival of the other brothers. The first to enter was Alexander, or "Hub", as the family called him, accompanied by his wife, Ellen. She was petite, dark haired, dark eyed, and quiet. He was a huge, barrel-chested farmer and schoolteacher, with light brown hair, a double chin, and a continual smile.

Then came Solon, a tall, brawny blacksmith, light of hair and soft in complexion. His wife, Elizabeth, had long dark hair neatly thrown back, held by an intricate wooden comb with hand-carved designs, the kind the Indians made and sold around Big Spring, but her countenance was dismal, eyes red and glossy from crying. She'd come to Big Spring from Bowling Green, Ohio, where her parents lived, and she always seemed homesick.

Curge, and his wife, Angeline, arrived last. Beneath his thick, brown hair he looked haggard. She was as tall as he was stoic, and somewhat rigid in carriage, yet with a certain regal quality, a trait that Ed's father claimed was the result of being raised the daughter of a Pennsylvania judge. Curge was the shortest of all the brothers, cheeks sunken beneath a thick brown beard, from fighting dysentery all winter.

Pa spoke as soon as they were seated. "Curge says the Rebels fired on Fort Sumter. Lincoln's calling for seventy-five thousand volunteers to serve three months. Wants to put down the insurrection and preserve the Union. Governor Randall already promised him a thousand men. Your Cousin Swift and his rifle company at Portage are going to offer their services. The whole town is turning out to show their support. The volunteers may be leaving as early as Sunday, so Doc wants all of us to come over for their town meeting."

Ed looked at Nels, then at his father. Excitement charged the air. "Can we join, Pa?"

His father's cold stare slapped him hard, while a look of deep, maternal concern embedded itself in the soft wrinkles and gentle face of his mother. "What?" she demanded. "Isn't it bad enough we already lost little Rosewood? Are your lives worth so little you'd throw them away? I'm not going to sit idly by and watch you boys go traipsing off to war just to get yourselves killed. Remember those boys who fought and died in Mexico. They're all gone now— like Humpty Dumpty. There's no bringing *them* back!"

As she paused, the stiff, lifeless image of Rosewood came to Ed's mind. He remembered his older brothers dropping the little pine box into the ground when he was five. It was an image he wished he could forget, but never could.

"What makes you think you have to go?" she continued. "There's plenty of boys your age to fill the ranks. Don't have to volunteer. Besides, we need you to work the farm. You know how long and hard these winters are. Takes all we can raise in the short summer just to get us through winter." Her eyes were deep gray pools, welling up and overflowing.

Gloom descended upon Ed, as if he alone had brought this irrevocable sadness upon his mother. The war seemed like an answer to a young man's prayer, an opportunity to break the boredom, show he was a man. A wondrous and adventurous idea. Why did she have to go and make him feel bad about it? Then his gaze fell upon Angeline, her brown eyes sadly questioning, her regal face masked in sorrow. Embarrassed, he averted his gaze, only to see Sol's wife on the verge of tears. Her countenance formed a sad lament, like that of a condemned man pleading for mercy.

"Ma's right," said the gaunt Curge. "We've plenty of work right here and there's hardly enough time for harvesting our crops the way it is. With Hub and me teaching, and with Sol blacksmithing, we don't get enough time to work our own claims. Who's gonna pick up your slack if you leave."

"President called for men to serve," said Nels. "People'll think we're afraid if we don't volunteer—or worse, they'll think we're a bunch of copperheads. Besides, we voted for Honest Abe 'cause we believed slavery wrong. We'd be hypocrites if we didn't stand up against the Confederacy now."

The brothers nodded.

Ed glanced at his mother. She appeared much older in the kerosene lamplight, hair cast in gray, velvety pale skin deeply wrinkled. And like Solon's wife, she too looked betrayed and on the verge of breaking down. Her tearful gaze drifted from face to face, until those gray eyes fell upon Ed, cutting through him like a Swede's saw, as if asking—Do you know what you're saying? Do you know what it is to die? Haven't I taught you better? And then there was this gnawing sensation, this knowing that she could read his mind, judge his inner thoughts. It was maddening, like the time he had stolen his brother's pocketknife, and she kept asking him who did it, as though it were impossible to suspect anyone else. And he lied, over and over, trying to convince her without success. At first he'd merely wanted to cover his sin, avoid punishment. But then something else took over, and he found himself desperately wanting her to believe in him, to believe he could never lie, that he was something better than he really was. So he kept on lying, denying the truth again and again, until he saw in her icy gray eyes that she knew he was lying, and would never stop asking until he admitted it. *That* was the kind of power his mother had in her eyes, a force that now announced her disappointment and heartache as loudly as horses scream in a thunderstorm.

Pa cleared his voice, breaking Ed free from his mother's hypnotic grip. His father looked around the table until every tongue was silent and every eye upon him. "Nels has a point," he said in a deep, bass voice. "We're behind the president and shouldn't be shirking our duty to the country. But Curge is right too. We have responsibilities at home. We've got to weigh one against another. Set our priorities straight. If Mr. Lincoln is correct, he'll probably have all those enlistments filled within the month, and this thing'll be over in no time. If so, we won't need to get involved. Remember, this won't be like fighting the British or some other invading country. It'll be more like fighting within our family. Our own legislators are divided over these issues. Let's give the three-month army its chance. See if this'll be resolved without having to leave home. If it can't, I reckon there'll be plenty of time to show where we stand. Let's not act without thinking clearly—lest we regret our decision later."

Ed heard a rush of air as the taut facial muscles of his mother softened. Pa had a way with words that could lead the boys to reason soundly, even in the midst of confusion, and Ed observed a faint smile at the corners of Ma's delicate mouth. Then Ed noticed that his father was not so exuberant, as if not convinced of his own words. What was he thinking? That the war would be longer? That Ed and his brothers would have to fight? Sarah must have caught it too. The slight traces of smile vanished, replaced by deep-furrowed lines.

Later, when the familiar chatter had died and the back door slammed its final slam, Ed lay in his bed, imagining what it would be like to fight with the Portage Light Guard. Nels was already asleep, a faint, shrill, high-pitched whistle sounding from his nose every few seconds. But Ed could not. His mind raced as he imagined what a real battle might be like.

The gentle, soprano voice of his mother sounded from the next room. "I heard from Ellen again. Socrates' school is shut down, and some of the people there are fired up against Yankees. Why don't you ask him to come home?"

Silence settled in. Ed tried to imagine his father's blue eyes. The hue of Pa's eyes always told his mood. They could be light as the morning sky, or dark and cold as dusk

"I never told him he had to leave," said Pa.

Dark as dusk, thought Ed.

"Didn't have to" said ma. "You told him living with Ellen was the same as adultery. How could he live with you around, always knowing you think that of him? Can't you see what your approval means—how hard he worked in school just to please you?"

Silence again. The floor boards squeaked, but no footsteps ensued.

"Well, say *something*."

"What can I say? He's denied the faith—living in adultery. Can't turn my head to that. Everything he's learned is for naught. Greek governmental philosophy has become a basis for theology. Unitarianism. Ha! John Knox would roll over in his grave."

"But you've always venerated the Greeks and their writings."

John's voice grew even louder. "Still do. But I haven't embraced pagan gods or mixed philosophy with theology. It's Plato's Republic I hold close, not pantheism. What the Greek and Romans built were great physical feats. Not lasting ones. Alexander didn't just conquer the known world, he discovered that one could never hold his conquest without becoming one with it. Socrates analyzed things, turned the search for knowledge from the physical world to the virtues of human character. He recognized that a man was divided, mind, body, and soul, and that each needed to be strengthened in order for the whole to be complete. Lycurgus discovered that the strength of Sparta's defense was not in the soundness of its walls, but of its men. Solon did away with Draconian Law. Don't you see? I wanted our sons to remember those lessons, to couple sound republican principles with sound Christian doctrine. *That* is what I've put my faith in—the idea that the highest form of government, together with the highest form of religion, will build a lasting empire of good. Not the integration of philosophy with theology!"

Ed lay silent in his bed, thinking of the Greek stories his father had told, and the ones his older brothers had read to him when he was a child. But all that ended when they moved from Ohio. In Wisconsin every minute of the day consisted of one labor or another. Year round they milked, churned, and fed livestock. Spring hurried by with hoeing, plowing, and planting, while the summer was spent weeding, haying, and harvesting. Fall brought more haying and harvesting, but then came endless days of canning. Once winter hit, you could only pray you'd saved enough money, canned enough fruit and vegetables, and stored enough hay and oats to keep the people and animals alive until the next harvest. Otherwise the bank would end up owning your land. Everything you'd done would be wasted.

Ed started to fall asleep when he heard his mother say, "I've never been to much school, John. You know that. But there's some things never been written in those fancy books of yours."

"Like what?"

"Like the feeling I have in my gut for our boy. John, Socrates is in trouble."

"Like I told you before, there's nothing I can do."

"Yes there is. You can write him—tell him you forgive him—accept him despite all your differences."

"Agree to disagree? No. He must first admit he's wrong."

TWO

"Let us consider the problem together."

—Socrates

April 19th, 1861, Portage, Wisconsin

INNUMERABLE CARRIAGES, WAGONS, AND HORSES LINED COOK STREET IN portage when the Best family arrived in three wagons about mid-afternoon. Ed looked around and smiled at the little metropolis located between the northerly coursing Fox River and the southerly flowing Wisconsin. The earliest French traders recognized this strip of land as a vital link between the lucrative Great Lakes trading port at Green Bay and the countless river trade routes used by the Indians of Minnesota, Iowa, Illinois, and southwest Wisconsin. By 1828 the Federal Government also came to recognize the importance of Portage, not for trade purposes, but for its strategic position in quelling Indian uprisings. Thus it commissioned the building of Ft. Winnebago, and in 1829 a young Second Lieutenant by the name of Jefferson Davis delivered those plans, acted as quartermaster, and helped oversee the building of the fort, which was completed in 1832.

Then, over two hundred miles of military wagon road was built to connect the new fort with Ft. Crawford at Prairie du Chein and Ft. Howard at Green Bay. To that end, the soldiers of those forts worked for three years, carving a path through the wilderness, and felling trees to form cord roads over swamps and marshes. A local company then began digging a canal to connect the Fox and Wisconsin rivers; but that effort was now bogged down in cost overruns, political quagmire, and newly found competition with the railroad. Despite the failing canal project and the fact that Ft. Winnebago was now abandoned, the city of Portage had become a thriving trade center with nearly three thousand residents.

Ed surveyed Cook Street. To the right, a large brick wall with a broad sign said, "Charlie Shays." That building now housed the local H. Wood

Mercantile Store, which traded in everything from furs and food to farm and building supplies. From there on down the street ran a long row of cream-colored, two-story brick buildings, interspersed with a few one- and two-story wooden buildings. The fresh, cream color of the brick edifices gave the street a unique, light, bright appearance. At the end of this block was DeWitt Street, and on the other side of that intersection stood the four-story Pettibone Block building. Its first floor alone housed both an intricate maze of cubicles where different merchants came to show and sell their wares each week, and an entire ballroom known as Pettibone Hall. Beyond the Pettibone building sat the three-story Colombiana County Court House, its Romanesque arch serving as a landmark of sorts, and farther beyond it, the two-story, brick Armory. Along the second story of every building ran an even row of tall, thin windows, squared at the bottom and either squared or arched at the top, their continuity broken only by an occasional alley or one-story building. Behind those stood the many large warehouses and industrial buildings of Canal Street that skirted the Wisconsin River. The structures on the left side of Cook Street were similar to those on the right, and beyond them little white cottages spread out in every direction.

The sight of horses, buggies and wagons parked at each end of the street, reminded Ed of the many log jams he had seen on the Wisconsin River while accompanying his father to the nearby lumber camps the previous October. Those were lively nests, made up of Swedish, German, and Irish immigrants, many of whom had left their families in Europe until they could save enough money to purchase some land of their own. Such hard-working men bought much of the maple syrup John Best and his sons made every fall, thus providing a good supplement to their meager farm income.

Ed liked being around the lumbermen with their powerful muscles. He never tired of hearing their stories, listening to their accents, or watching them cuss at each other in foreign languages. And while he couldn't understand a word, their angry tones and mean expressions said it all. But during winter one didn't need to travel to those camps to find this brand of entertainment. While most towns in this part of the country shrunk beneath the frigid blasts of the season, Portage swelled. And since the lumber camps closed during the coldest months, the lumbermen had few places to go besides Portage. That kept the sheriff busy breaking up drunken brawls in the many taverns, investigating shootings, and looking into all sorts of trouble. Sometimes Portage seemed more like a wild west town than a Wisconsin trade center. But spring had arrived and the lumberjacks were gone. Everyone gathering here today had come for one purpose, to support their President by commissioning the Light Guard.

Ed helped his father secure the wagon at the end of town before the family made their way to the Armory, where Aunt Emily awaited them. The spurring breeze ruffled her dark curls and bonnet strings around her angelic face, an image of serenity. But that illusion shattered as Emily greeted them with a troubled smile and an emotional embrace. Her Chestnut-brown eyes pooled around the corners.

"I am so glad you all could make it," she said. "I'm not sure who is more excited, the doctor or his son, but they'll both be delighted to see you're here. We saved some seats in the balcony where it's a little warmer and not so crowded."

They followed Emily up the stairs to the U-shaped balcony that spread out across the back of the Armory's hall and forward along its sides. In the center, they found twelve empty seats in a long line. Beside the row sat a large man in a dark suit, with a black head of hair flowing straight back from his widow's peak. His silver-streaked, full, black beard framed a square jaw and handsome face that flashed an overanxious smile toward John and Sarah as they approached.

"John, I'm so glad you could make it."

"Wouldn't miss it for the world, Doc," replied John as he ushered his sons and daughter-in-laws past him and into their waiting places.

Ed knew that his father had always been close with his younger brother, Dr. Thomas Best. After all, John was only eight when his father died, and the baby brother's birth washed away so much sorrow, it seemed right to everyone when Grandma named the infant Thomas, after his father. John took a fatherly attitude toward his brother, reassuring him in his studies, encouraging him to follow his interest in science. And Ed always smiled at the stories of the two having to remove a couple of "new residents" from the local cemetery during the night. Doctors needed to study, but no one wanted to think of such activities as wholesome, so the aspiring medical students went about such endeavors under cover of darkness, just as the classic artists had many centuries before. By the time Thomas was well established in medicine he had become the family leader, and in 1849 he took his wife, his children, and his mother from Deerfield, Ohio to establish a new home at Portage. That same year his sister's and John's respective families followed, establishing their homesteads nearly twenty miles west of Portage.

Alongside of Doc and his children were his sister Sally Ramsey, her husband, James, and their family. Smiles erupted as cousins greeted cousins.

"Hey! Sol, where've you been?" asked big Bob Ramsey. "And where's Elizabeth? I can't believe she'd want to miss this!"

Will Ramsey, Robert's lanky younger brother spoke in turn. "Is that Curge? Well, bless me. You still teaching school and tormenting those young children? My, my, those poor boys and girls must *hate* school by now."

Their youngest brother, Tom, and their thirteen-year old little sister, Addy, smiled politely but said nothing, glued to the goings-on down below.

Emily took her seat beside her brown-haired daughter, Hanna, the oldest of her children. Hanna flashed a polite smile at her cousins before turning her attention back to the lower floor.

Shortly after Ed sat down, Hub and Curge arrived with their wives. Ed combed his fingers through his hair, reached into a jacket pocket, and pulled out a burr he'd been keeping for just such an occasion. Quick as a magician his hand went out. He stifled a grin. No sooner did Curge sit down than he came shooting back up. "Yow!" His hands reached back and pulled out the burr while everyone looked on. "Where'd this come from?"

"Oh," replied his wife. "Probably followed you in on your coat tail. You men! Always so careless."

"But—but," he stammered.

"Oh, sit down and stop making a fool of yourself."

Curge sat down, while Ed chuckled to himself, anxiously drumming his fingers on his knees. The hall buzzed with excitement, the voices blending into one solid rumble. Mayor Richmond pounded his gavel on the wooden podium at center stage, and the hall suddenly hushed at the sound of a drummer tapping a steady beat. Heads turned and necks craned to see the Portage Light Guard march neatly in two columns through the back door and into the hall. Each man wore a dark gray coat with matching gray cadet hat, like that of a toy soldier. A short black-leather bill protruded in front, with a thin black-leather strap rising above it. A single row of gray cloth buttons extended half way down the front of the three-quarter coat, while a white cloth belt, with leather pouches and shoulder harness crisscrossed the torso, and finally beneath the gray coat hung black trousers. The entire uniform was neatly trimmed with red thread. Each man cradled a musket in his right hand, the barrel resting back against his right shoulder, bayonet pointing heavenward.

The clatter of their shoes stamped the wooden floors in perfect unison. The men marched side-by-side, dressed right and covered down in a perfect order of rows and columns. The first men reached the open area directly in front of the stage. With the crisp command, "Column split!" the two columns turned sharply in opposite directions until one continuous line was formed, and the command, "Halt!" was heard.

The hushed audience of friends and relatives gazed at the soldiers, and the men faced forward. A handsome gentleman marched down the empty aisle with two officers directly behind him. The trio halted in front of the center stage, clicked their heels in unison, and turned to face the back of the Armory.

Ed drummed his fingers faster on his knees. What I'd give to be one of them, he thought. Every one is beautiful. And they're men, real men—just like I'm gonna be.

"That's Captain John Mansfield and his two lieutenants," Emily whispered to Sarah and John, as Sally and Jim, seated behind them, leaned their heads forward. "He's a lawyer who's taken over the command of the guard. The other two are Lieutenants Vaughan and Hill."

Sarah nodded. "He certainly is a good-looking man. And he organized all this?"

Emily shook her head. "Actually, someone else organized the group and did much of their drilling, but Mr. Mansfield was elected captain. He's so popular with the men, very courteous, well-spoken, and fearless, too, I'm told. I met him early this month when the guard made its first public appearance at a social and ball. It was grand."

The voice of Mayor Richmond boomed through the hall. "Ladies and gentlemen, I'd like to call a meeting to order if all the town board members are here."

The city council and town board members arose from their seats, stepped over and around legs and feet with a litany of "excuse me's," until each had made his way out into the aisle and up to the stage.

Upon reaching a chair behind a long wooden table, a tall distinguished gentleman said, "I nominate Mayor Richmond as president of this meeting."

There came a second, a chorus of ayes followed and Mayor Richmond pounded his gavel, shouting, "Motion carried! And I nominate the honorable Mr. Abbott as secretary. All in favor say aye." Another round of ayes filled the air and the Mayor continued, "The motion is carried! Now the board will appoint a committee of three to draft a resolution for our boys. In the meantime captain Mansfield wishes to address the community."

Captain Mansfield stepped forward. "On behalf of the Portage Light Guard, of which I am privileged to be captain, I would like to thank all the people of our community who have so graciously helped us. Many of you are not aware that Wells Butler provided our uniforms. Others have given their time or money to help us create a company fund and our own unit colors. We will be forever grateful for your kindness and support."

"Now I feel our moment of decision is at hand. Everyone knows Fort Sumter has been fired upon by the Confederacy and that President Lincoln has asked for volunteers to end the rebellion in the South. Our own Governor Randall has asked for a thousand volunteers to be the first regiment responding to the call. You men have spent weeks drilling and training under Mr. Abbott and myself for this very purpose. Now you must decide if you are up to the task of fulfilling Governor Randall's call. If not, you should turn in your muskets and uniforms so better men can use them. Now I ask you once and for all time, will you go with me and end this bloody insurrection? If so, answer by saying 'aye'."

Without hesitation, forty men shouted, "Aye!"

"Good," replied the captain with a smile. "I will send this telegram to Governor Randall immediately, to let him know that the Portage Light Guard graciously offers to tender its services on his behalf. Would someone please run this telegram to the telegraph office and see that it is dispatched?"

Two boys ran up to the officer. Mansfield looked at one, then the other. Finally he gave it to the younger boy and turned to the older one saying, "Let him take it. We may need you later in the Light Guard."

The older boy nodded happily, then returned to his seat while the younger one ran to deliver the message. The band played as the captain led his men outside where they formed into straight lines. The crowd poured out of the building, lining both sides of the street. Then the citizens shouted and cheered as the Light Guard marched down the street and into Pettibone Hall.

Inside, the Mayor stood at center stage and made a resounding speech, reading the resolution the committee had written. "Whereas, the government of the United States, which has existed for more than seventy years and under which its citizens have enjoyed a greater degree of happiness than any other people in the world, is now threatened to be overthrown by traitors. And, whereas, the President of the United States has called for volunteers to aid in sustaining and enforcing the laws. And, whereas, the citizens of Portage city and vicinity propose to respond to the call. Therefore, be it resolved that we respond with pleasure. We pledge our fortunes, our honor, and, if need be, our lives in the defense of our government and the maintenance of the laws of our land. Be it resolved, that in the great contest before us we will recognize but two parties: the Union and Disunion party. That we will render all of our assistance to aid the one and destroy the other. And finally, let it be resolved that we recommend the sum of $1,000.00 in providing for the support of families of those who volunteered, and such further sums as may be necessary for the support of those families."

While the audience cheered its approval, the band played *The Star Spangled Banner* and everyone joined in singing, then came cheers, laughter, and more cheers.

The boy who had taken Captain Mansfield's message to the telegraph office ran in, waving a piece of paper above his head. Mayor Richmond took out his spectacles, placed them on his nose. A smile appeared, gradually spreading until every one of his teeth showed.

"I have a cablegram for Captain Mansfield which is of great importance to us all. It says, and I quote, 'Your company accepted for Second Regiment, subject to call of Government. Stop. Proceed with enrollment of men. Stop. Instructions by mail. Stop.' It's signed: Governor Randall."

"Hurrah!" the people shouted.

The band played and everyone danced with joy. Along with everyone else, Ed felt alive and vibrant. This was history in the making, and the names of these principal characters would be written by sages and poets for generations to come. The thought made him delirious with excitement, his enthusiasm generating more energy than he'd ever felt. He was proud that his cousin was going, that all these men would go and fight, that they would bring home the victory.

His father and brothers went out the front door and soon returned with musical instruments. Solon and Nels tuned their banjos, while John worked on his guitar. Within minutes the three joined in with the band. Ed thought of getting his guitar and joining them, but he felt too care-free for sitting in one place. Another thought crept into his mind as two large bowls were placed upon a long table and quickly filled.

He inched toward the one filled with hard cider. The children and women always drank from the other. And so had he until now, but no one was paying attention to such things here. In the space of ten or fifteen minutes he managed to down three quick glasses without anyone noticing. He found the sweet but slightly metallic taste quite palatable. Working on his fourth, he noticed the hall taking on a surreal appearance. Everything seemed so beautiful, so wonderful. To find anything wrong here would be impossible. The band had never sounded better nor the people more majestic, and Ed felt this uncontrollable, overwhelming sense of love for everyone.

He searched the crowd for the one face he most hoped to see. Lila De Vitte had golden, tight-spun curls, and emerald green eyes. Many a day he had wasted his lessons, stealing glimpses of her, and wondering what it would be like to kiss such a beautiful girl. But he had always been too shy, never able to speak directly to her. Somehow in this magical moment he felt the certainty, the confidence that if he asked her to dance, anything was possible. His feet never stumbled as he threaded his way through the crowd, and before he knew it he stood directly in front of her, her face beaming.

"Would you dance with me?" he asked, and she quickly nodded.

He'd never danced with anyone other than family, but in a short time he relaxed, pulling Lila closer to him as they stepped around the floor. Around and around they went, dance after dance, until Lila stopped to fan herself. "My. My," she said. "It certainly is hot."

"Can I get you some cider?"

She smiled and nodded.

As he turned to walk away she caught the back of his shirt and pulled him close enough to whisper in his ear, "I'd like the same as you had."

Ed's jaw dropped. Pushing out his chest, he moved across the room and filled two glasses with cider, then hurried toward the back of the room where he'd left her. She downed both glasses without stopping for air, then sent him back for more. Those went down in the same manner before she whispered to him, "Couldn't let you get too big a head start on me. Now could I?"

Her eyes sparkled like precious gemstones set in gold. She took his hand and pulled him out the side door, and he eagerly followed. This night was getting more magical by the minute. Once outside she turned, causing him to catch her in his arms. "You never kissed a girl before, have you, Ed?"

Ed blushed.

She leaned forward, the silver moonlight accenting the soft lines of her face. "Would you like to kiss me?"

As he nodded, he felt her push her body directly against him, saw her lips moving toward him, felt her soft warm chest rise and fall against his. He closed his eyes as his lips met hers. Fire filled his lungs. Her lips moved forward, then backwards, as if playing with a fish on a line. Ed felt himself losing control, following her moves like an eager apprentice. For thirty minutes they kissed against the outside wall of Pettibone Hall, and then her lower abdomen pushed forward, touching him in a way no one had ever done before. The fire in his chest nearly exploded into his loins. His right hand moved to her breast. She pushed him away. He stood there in the moonlight, panting in confusion. A voice called from the doorway, "Lila. If you're out here, Pa says it's time to head home."

"Got to go," said Lila. "I'll see you at school." She turned and walked back into the hall.

Ed watched her vanish. He wanted to see her real soon, and not at school. A minute later he started toward the door, where he saw his friend Bill Day. Wherever he was, and whatever he did, it seemed like he was always smiling, and right now his teeth glowed in the moonlight. "Where you been, Ed? Been looking all over for you. Come on. I've got something to show you."

Ed followed him down the alley past other kissing couples until he came to the back of the building. Several young men stood in a circle, some with hands in pockets, others holding drinks. Ed recognized John Gaffney from Lewiston, a stocky fellow whom he'd never liked. John was an Irishman, strong as a bull, and confident to the point of boastfulness. He delighted in telling wild stories to the other young men who followed him, for they soaked up his words like dry sponges. He often used rough speech and course manners, two habits not tolerated in the Best home. On the other hand, he had a reputation for handling teams of animals with great skill, anything from mules to oxen. Around that area, those were valuable skills.

Beside Gaffney stood Gary Bellford, a big oafish bully whom Ed despised. Next to him were George Clark, Sophie Landt, and Will Ellis, three friends from Big Spring. Of them from Big Spring, Landt was the most formidable, standing nearly six feet. On the other side of them were a couple of Light Guards, their cadet hats looming high and ominous in the moonlight. Filling out the circle were two boys from Briggsville that Ed had seen around town.

"This here's Corporal Shanghai Chandler," said Bill Day, pointing to one of the Light Guards.

A full mustache flowed into a neatly shaven goatee beard. Dark brown hair as thick as anyone's Ed had ever known framed a handsome face. Every young man and boy in the county knew of Shanghai. His real name was Julius but he preferred Shanghai, a name he had picked up while writing for the local papers. A package of vim and vinegar charged with endless energy, his antics around town were legendary.

"Ed Best. Pleased to meet you, Corporal," said Ed as he reached out his hand.

Shanghai's hand met his half way as he replied, "Any relation to Swift?"

Ed pushed out his chest. "First cousin."

Shanghai pulled out a metal flask from the inside of his coat, twisted off the top and said, "Swift is one plucky soldier. To Swift." He took a swallow and handed the flask to Ed.

Ed could feel every eye on him as he echoed, "To Swift," and took a big swallow. His first taste of whiskey burnt from the base of his throat all the way down and through his stomach. "Whew! That's got a lot more punch than hard cider."

"No kidding, Best," laughed Shanghai. "Hard cider can't hold a candle to good whiskey. Nothing better than good food, fast horses, sharp whiskey—and wild women."

"I think I've been tasting a little of each tonight."

Bellford stepped up beside Shanghai, deep lines furrowing across his forehead. "If you're talking about Lila Dim-wit, that stupid whore can't hardly be no wild woman."

Ed stared hard. "What do you know about it?"

"I saw you go out the side door. She's just trying to get me jealous. Believe you me, you ain't tasted anything me and half the other boys in this town haven't had. Just two weeks ago she wanted me to marry her. Started crying and everything. Tells me she's gonna be a straw widow—like I'm supposed to believe I'm the father! Not me. Been too much seed planted on the other side of those blankets."

Ed steamed.

Shanghai slapped his knee. "How would you boys like to play a little game I learned down in Chicago? Seems like you'd both be of the mind for it about now."

"What is it?" asked Ed, glaring at Bellford.

Shanghai stepped into the center of the circle, where he drew two parallel lines an inch apart. "This is a little game the coloreds taught me—and believe me—they can play it! Best, you stand behind this line, Bellford, you behind the other." He paused while the boys moved into positions facing each other. "Now, Bellford, you say whatever you like to Best—the biggest insult you can think of. Best, then you take your shot. No matter what either one says, you can't go over the line. First one to step over the line loses."

Ed realized what Shanghai was doing, and might have begged off, if he hadn't hated Bellford so much. But right now he wanted a piece of him bad. "Go ahead."

"Okay. Donkey-breath," snapped Bellford.

"Oooh! I'm so hurt—being called donkey-breath by somebody who's butt-ugly."

Bellford's jaw dropped open, then tightened up like a bulldog's mouth. "I'm ugly? I'm ugly? If I had a dog that looked like you, I'd shave its ass and make it walk backwards. "

"At least I ain't afraid of my own shadow."

"And I ain't dumb enough to get myself tied to no hen-pecker's apron strings—like some jackass I know!"

Ed felt his face flush. "Stupid ox!"

Bellford's back went up. "Hey! I ain't hard up enough to chase no straw widow!"

Ed felt chicken skin run up and down his arms, stopped his foot just short of the line, then dug in. "You lie like a Butcher's dog." Then he remembered something he'd heard whispered once or twice before.

"Your mother's a slut," said Bellford.

Ed laughed. "And yours drinks like a fish."

Bellford's feet slid forward in the gravel, his large hands shaking. "Your old man is a crook," he stammered.

"Where's your mother now, Gary? Drunk as David's sow I'll bet."

Bellford swung straight at Ed's face. But Ed side-stepped the punch and threw a headlock just like his brothers had done to him a hundred times before. He jerked Bellford's weight straight over his back and dropped the boy to the ground beneath him, letting his own rib cage fall heavily into his opponent's chest. That took the fight out for a second, but then Bellford arched his back and flailed wildly.

"Give him Jesse," shouted Bill.

"Come on, Bellford," urged the stocky Gaffney.

Ed looked up, hoping they would break it up now, but judging by their cries of amusement they weren't about to try. He had a bear by the tail and couldn't let go. He pushed his hand toward his shoulder with his other arm, increasing the pressure on Bellford's skull, harder and harder, like a walnut cracker, he could feel the fight going out of the big slob now.

"Give?" he inquired. But Bellford was stubborn. Ed tightened the vice again, thought he heard a whimper. He knew it wouldn't last more than a minute longer. He'd been on the other side of this hold too many times. Bellford would have to give.

"What do you think you're doing?" someone shouted behind him. Two strong hands clenched Ed's feet and pulled him away from Bellford. Ed held the headlock for another moment, then relinquished it as he was dragged along the ground, through the circle, and away from his nemesis.

Ed twisted around in time to see his brother Solon throwing those feet and legs aside like pieces of rough lumber. He sprang to his feet in anger but the burly blacksmith pushed him back to the ground as though he were nothing. "What do you think you're doing?" Solon demanded again.

"I was just tanning Bellford's butt," yelled Ed.

"No you weren't!" scoffed Solon. "You were gonna get yourself killed. Bellford's twice your size. Have no business fighting him. You're just the baby of the family. Get it? And I'm not the one who is gonna tell Ma that her baby got all messed up in some back alley."

"He was holding his own," said Sophie.

"Shut your trap, Sophie, you've got no business in this. Ma's already lost one baby and I don't wanna be around if she loses another."

Ed charged head first into Solon's midsection and bounced off it like he'd hit a rubber wall.

Solon clasped Ed by the nape of his neck, twisted his collar tight, and led him toward the back door of Pettibone Hall. "Come on," he said, "You're getting cleaned up and going home now, before you get in any more trouble."

April 30th, 1861, Daingerfield, Texas

Socrates bent over and slowly took a seat on the corner of his desk. He'd given a lot of thought to what he was going to say. His three remaining students sat quietly waiting, George, the tall one, Aaron, the light-haired one, and Andrew, the quiet one with coal-black hair. These, the brightest of his students, had already finished their basic studies, and might have gone on to a larger college than Chapel Hill, had they the means. Their eyes were brightly fixed upon Socrates.

The tall one slowly, tentatively raised his hand, but Socrates nodded it back down. He needed to keep control. Couldn't let this get of hand. Had to smile. Put them at rest. "Well," he said with a wide grin. "There's been a lot of news around town. News I think we should talk about. But, we've got our final test coming up next week, too. So I thought it might be good to combine our review of philosophy with the events of late. What do you think?"

The boys' eyes brightened as they fast shook their heads.

"Good. We are obviously confronted with an issue. An issue that we will be forced to make decisions about. So let us look at the argument from the eyes of the objects of our studies—the philosophers themselves! Aaron," he said to the blond, "define the question at hand."

"Why war?"

Socrates threw his head back. "Why? Why is the question of an immature mind!" He turned to the tall one. "George, define the question."

George straightened his long skinny frame in the little oak chair, nervously rolling his fingers over his desktop. "Well. Reckon the question is if we should go fight the Yankees. I guess."

Socrates nodded. "We - meaning yourself, your fellow students, me?"

"Well. Yeah. I reckon everyone—'cept the women and old folk."

Socrates let his eyes widen. "Indeed. And what stand might the Sophist take on this question?"

The boy's shoulders relaxed as he smiled. "Think he'd find it a good idea."

"Based on what reasoning?"

"Well. He could win the spoils of war—and become a hero."

"Aha! A hero like Achilles. Anything else?" The blond boy's hand shot up. "Aaron?"

"He could organize a company, become a leader of men—like Mr. Austin. After we win the war, he might even become governor."

"But what if he were wounded—or even killed? What then?"

The boys' gazes darted quickly from teacher to fellow students. Aaron shook his head. "That wouldn't be good."

Socrates pointed to the black-haired boy, whose dark eyes stared back without wavering. "Andrew, what do you think?"

"Sophist wouldn't risk the military, unless he could be a high officer. He'd be more likely to sell powder and shot, or food for the Army. He'd want to better himself without gettin' killed."

"Good," said Socrates. "And if he could argue both sides of the war?"

Andrew spoke without expression. "He'd make money off both sides."

Socrates nodded. "He could. And what of my namesake? George, what might he have said?"

George's intense brown eyes rolled inward, then sparkled. "Where a man takes up his stand, because it seems best to him or in obedience to his orders, he is bound to remain and face the danger, taking no account of death or anything else before dishonor."

Socrates bolted upright. "Excellent quotation. But, is there any other that might apply?" Aaron's straight blond hair bounced as he raised his hand. "Aaron?"

"That no evil can harm a good man, in this world or the next."

"Excellent! Another excellent quotation. "But what of the deeper questions? Gorgias said, 'It is no easy matter to remember the past, consider the present, or divine the future.'" Socrates looked around as heads bobbed. "Then tell me, Aaron, for I'm zealous for your wisdom, what form might the Socratic argument have taken?"

Aaron blinked. "That it would be the proving ground for courage?"

"Ah!" said Socrates, throwing his hands wide in the direction of Aaron. "The virtues—justice and courage enter the argument. And as the great Socrates once said, the just man harms no one, so how could he justify such courage as warranted?"

"Because it's a social virtue, an obligation to one's brother?"

"Wonderful, Aaron, you are hitting on the basis of virtue! 'The mind of the universe is social'—Marcus Aurelius. Hence, we live in a brotherhood of rational beings. But what if our brotherhood is irrational? What then? Are there other arguments to turn this wheel?"

"Property rights," said George.

Socrates deepened his voice. "Yes. And what property?"

"Federal garrisons on Confederate land," said George.

Socrates shook his head. "We already have them, so what is left to fight for?"

The boys whispered to one another, hands flying in wild gestures. Finally they turned to Socrates and waited.

Socrates stood erect and paced the front of the room. "I think my namesake would find this a good point to ponder. Remember, 'We shall be better men if we inquire than if we do not—that is a belief for which I will fight in word and deed.' Now, spend the week philosophizing, working out your Socratic arguments for your final exam. What could serve us better?"

The boys smiled at one another. It wasn't often they were allowed to do their exams at home.

Was he getting too soft? Too easy? Somebody had to think this thing through. He hoped they'd ask questions of their folks. Lots of questions. He gathered his books into a pile as the boys went out the back door. The white form of a postal envelope protruded from one end. Ellen had asked him to mail it for her on the way to school, but he hadn't. He lifted his finger to his mouth and moistened it with his tongue, before gently pressing it along the line of the seal. In a short time he repeated the process, then slowly unsealed the envelope and pulled out the letter. It was addressed to her sister in Milwaukee.

Dear Isabella,

I can hardly contain myself for the desperate fear in my heart. As I told you before, the people here are determined to fight rather than have Lincoln take his chair over them. I have never seen such a pack of fools, and this matter at Fort Sumter proves what I've been saying all along. Socrates' school is all but shut down, and every opportunity for a job with the railroad has fallen through. There was a time when I thought his dream to come here divinely inspired, but now it seems more a curse. He won't leave it, and whether it be for his anger with his father, the value of our property, or the few remaining students, he will not say.

Oh, how I wish I could be there with you, to see your children, and for you to hold mine. With mama and papa gone, we children are all that is left to each other. I have written Ben and asked him to come help us, as there is a sudden shortage of young hands, and I hope, together, we might impose upon Socrates to return to Wisconsin. The long winters there, which once seemed too long for a body to endure, no longer weigh so heavily upon my convictions. What is the good of a warmer climate, when the distance now separating us leaves our hearts barren and cold?

Say hello to Frank. I will try and write Baby soon, but am overwrought with the fiery trial which now tests our faith. Always know you continue in my thoughts and prayers.

Your loving sister,
Ellen

Socrates gently refolded the letter and slowly slipped it back inside the envelope. A fire blazed in his chest. He stared at the back of the room. The classroom was built completely of wood, mostly hewed lumber from soft pine, whose knotty boards and thick resins filled the air with an intoxicating aroma. He drew a deep breath, flooding his senses. He loved it here. Always had. Didn't matter if they had money or not, they could make this place go. Why couldn't she see?

His mind wandered to the picture of his namesake's last day, of his wife and children seeing their father one last time, and him sending them away so they would not have to watch him die, Plato's words:

"So died our friend, of all the men I have known, the best and most just."

The latch on the door at the back of the room clicked, and two elderly gentlemen slipped through to greet him. Socrates immediately recognized the two senior elders of the Presbyterian Church. They had called him here to teach, following the initial success of their girl's academy. The taller of the two always did the talking, while the other merely followed, flashing an unflappable grin that revealed a near-perfect set of teeth.

The tall elder took off his hat with an air of formality. "Socrates, we've come to ask you to speak for us at church Wednesday night. On the matter of slavery and the Bible."

Socrates sat back on the corner of his desk. "With Jefferson Davis leading this new Confederacy, I'd think that a mute subject."

The tall elder's tired eyes went wide. "Absolutely not! We have freedom of speech. And abolition is still worthy of debate."

Socrates nodded. "Maybe. But there's a few folks around here that won't think so."

"True. But you don't have to speak for outright emancipation. We have a minister from Missouri coming down to represent that argument. We just want you to raise questions nobody would ever think of. You know, like you always do."

The fire in Socrates chest turned into an outright inferno. Ellen wouldn't like this one bit. Better not do it, he decided, but his head nodded instead.

"Splendid," said the taller elder. "See you there tomorrow night."

Socrates felt them shake his hand, watched the broad smile flash all those perfect teeth, and wondered at what he had just done.

THREE

*"The good man will not be a common thread in
the fabric of humanity, but a purple thread
—that touch of brilliance that gives
distinction and beauty to the rest."*
—Socrates

May 1st, 1861, Portage, Wisconsin

THROUGH THE COURSE OF A SINGLE MONTH SWIFT BEST HAD EXPERIENCED a cascade of excitement. Now deep in sleep, he dreamed of endless dancing in the grandest ballroom of Portage, Pettibone Hall. In the midst of his dream, he felt honored. It had been easy for him growing up the eldest son of a local physician, but not necessarily rewarding. The people of the community always treated him with respect and his outgoing personality won him many a friend. Even the girls were often enamored with him, but all too often, only because of his father's status. But *this*—this was *different*. He was winning their respect and admiration because of what he was doing, and not because of who his family was. Crystal chandeliers sparkled overhead as young ladies dressed in their Sunday best eagerly awaited a turn to dance with him. Look at them, he thought, they *love* me. Lord, how they love me.

The image dissolved as two large hands shook him awake. Rubbing his face briskly, he pulled himself up, and peered through a dreamy mist. Downstairs his mother's voice rang. "Onward Christian Soldiers, marching off to war—"

His father stood over him, silver-streaked beard glowing in the light of the window.

"Time to get up, Eusebius," said Doc. "Guard'll assemble at the station soon. Your breakfast is ready. Better get it while it's hot."

Swift screwed his fists into his eyes. "Why'd you call me that?"

"Eusebius?" Doc said softly. "It's your first name."

"Was yesterday, too, Pa, but you called me Swift then."

Doc nodded. "Yes. But today you are Eusebius—a man with a Divine mission—a destiny."

Swift's thoughts returned to the stories his father and mother had read him in his youth, stories from the History of the Church. Its author, Eusebius, was a fourth century bishop, librarian, researcher, and orator. And although he lived in Caesarea for most of his life, he aggressively collected information, carefully chronicling his sources into a ten book history. By the time Swift was twelve, he could recite the lists of martyrs for his parents, and knew most of the book by heart. It was the stories of the Great Persecution that captured his imagination early on. But as he grew and matured, he became more and more mystified by the chronicler's many notes, references to Josephus, Africanus, Origen, Justin—stories of the disciples—their martyrdom told amongst the endless lists of those who gave their lives for the faith.

Such stories brought to mind a glowing picture of the saints John had written on the island of Patmos:

"And white robes were given unto every one of them; and it was said unto them, that they should rest yet for a little season . . . ."

At times Swift wondered what it must have been like to know Jesus, to walk with him, talk with him, dine with him—to hear the sound of his voice carrying the Divine Word. Sometimes he wondered about Eusebius, what the library of Caesarea must have looked like, how many volumes it held, and how many laborers worked there. Did it still exist? Did it possess the letter from Jesus to Abgar the Toparch, King of Mesopotamia, or had they only copied it from the records at Edessa? Often he wondered about the martyrs, their families, their friends. Wondered if he could endure such suffering for his faith. Soon there would be no more wondering. The battle lines were drawn, and righteousness would be put to the test.

He took a deep breath, and pushed his arms straight in front of him. Stretching, he pulled his arms until they were even with his shoulders. A series of popping sounds traveled down his spine as he bowed it forward, pushing out his chest like a barnyard cock. He let out a loud yawn as a blast of air rushed out and his chest deflated. I'm ready, he thought. Ready to bring down this rebellion. "Thanks, Pa. Could've slept all day."

Doc sighed. "Such a different mission than I envisioned for you. And you only a year away from graduating law school."

"Maybe so, Pa, but you've always said life doesn't often let one choose his fights."

Doc dipped his head and stroked his silver-streaked, black beard. "Yes. That's right. Anyway, better not be late for assembly or you'll be considered a deserter. After everything this town has done for you boys, you'd be the laughing stock of the county." The last words of his sentence trailed off into a whisper.

He's holding back, thought Swift. He waited, silent.

Doc looked away, then back at Swift. "There's something I wanted to tell you, Swift, before you go."

"Yes."

"There's a lot of talk around town, folks telling their boys they should never darken their doorway again if they don't fight well."

Swift smiled wide. "Don't worry, Pa. The *Lord* is *my* shepherd."

Doc's dark eyes narrowed. "That's *not* what I mean. What I mean is, it's sad how people pile shame on a man, enough to ruin him, right or wrong, if he doesn't do what they think he should."

Swift pushed out his jaw. "I've got no time for cowards, Pa."

"But would that be so bad, to turn away if you were outnumbered, outgunned? I know you want to defend your country. I also know that your mother and the woman's abolition league have had strong words about God's righteous right hand in this, but I want you to think."

Swift thought of the many copies of *Uncle Tom's Cabin* stacked at the Methodist church, copies the members purchased and disseminated free of charge throughout the county. He'd read it three times before his mother would relent. But when she came home with the swamp tale about Dred, the runaway slave, even though Swift gave it his best, he couldn't get through it even once. The thing just dragged along until he finally put his foot down. "Mother, I got the message in Stowe's first book. You *don't* need to rub my *face* in it."

Swift smiled inwardly. Now she'd see the truth of his commitment.

Doc continued, "Is that all this war is about? It's hard to know when everyone's parroting each other and no one's thinking for himself. Where are the doves? Hiding their faces in the sand? Or aren't the newspapers reporting what they say anymore?"

Swift was quiet. Didn't his father want him to go? Were the ones staying home right? No. *That* wasn't right. Couldn't be right. This was a *holy* war. No less than the Crusades of old. "What do you mean?"

Doc squinted, his face a mixture of aged lines and confused emotions. "Just want you to know that maybe we shouldn't be so hard on those who see things different from us. Some of the things I was most certain about when I was young, I now know are wrong. It could be the same way here."

Swift thought of Eusebius' translation of Genesis 12:

"I will bless them that bless thee, and curse him that curseth thee: and in thee shall all races of the earth be blessed."

"No. This *is* right—to retain a righteous government over *all* the people—to protect inalienable rights." He took a deep breath, lifted his hand to scratch his head and stopped. "You think I'm going to run, Pa?"

"No. It's not that. It's just, well, when you find yourself in a dangerous place I want you to remember: there'll be plenty of time for fighting, and I'm sure you'll be brave in whatever you're asked to do. Promise me you won't do anything foolish—won't go sticking your neck out like some fool chicken too stupid to fear the ax."

Swift let the rest of his air out. "I hear you, Pa. I won't take *any* risks I don't have to. I promise. It's just, well, I only hope that when the bugle blows, I'll stand my ground and not disgrace you; won't bring shame to your good name."

Doc's facial muscles tightened. "You could be *killed*, Swift. This is more than just a game, more than just pride, glory, or dishonor. At least use some horse sense."

The way his father said "killed," struck Swift hard, conjuring up the images of three dead babies buried nearby. The memory of his deceased infant brothers and sister hung momentarily in his mind, faces pale and questioning. Then he remembered his mother's tears, the awful wailing of her and his sister. "I'll be all right, Pa. I'm *not* a child."

"I know, Swift, but in some ways you are. You've yet to know true love, or hold your firstborn—haven't yet tasted the best things life has to offer. There's so much you haven't experienced—things that'd make you love life, esteem it so highly you'd guard it with all you have."

Swift rolled his fingers. "I do, Pa. But why are you telling me this? It's the Rebels you should be worried about."

Doc laughed, then his eyes glossed over, and the old, whisker-framed face took on an expression Swift had never seen before. "One more thing, Swift, I'd like you to carry this with you." He handed Swift a circular gold medal on a long gold chain.

Swift stared at the image of a knight on horseback, his lance driven deep into the breast of a dragon. "Your Saint George, Pa, I can't take this!"

Doc put his hand on Swift's. "You must. You see, George was the last one persecuted for his faith in England. He ended the nightmare for everyone in his land. If you must go, I pray this slavery thing will be finished once and for all." Doc removed his glasses, wiped a tear from his eyes, looked away.

Swift continued rolling his fingers, wishing the moment would end. He turned his head, looked out the window where he spotted people moving on the street below—not with any clear direction, just scurrying about wasting time, waiting for the final send off. He could almost feel their excitement, but his father's somber mood was interfering. After a minute, Doc stood up and offered a half smile. His dark eyes pooled again. "I'll see you downstairs."

Swift turned back to the street, to the waiting crowds, all there for him and his friends. A surge of exhilaration coursed through his veins. The Light Guard had drilled for a month, developing a precision and exactness that thrilled the people of the city—even impressing the soldiers themselves. He could almost hear the German Society choir and all the people singing *The First Gun is Fired* and then *The Red White and Blue*, could hear that eminent speaker Emmons Taylor saying, "We offer our men as a barrier between our beloved land, and the treason which seeks its destruction."

And Emmon's Taylor had spoken other words, words so strong they defined his cause beyond measure, leading Swift to commit them to memory. Now they surged through his mind with an energy all their own: "The institutions we enjoy are ours only in trust—they are sacred heirlooms confided to our keeping for those who are to come after us. We would have you remember that the battle you are fighting is not only for our beloved land, but for *all* mankind. We would have you remember that you bear with you our hopes, our hearts, our prayers.

Swear it, soldiers, that our institutions, strengthened by this very trial, shall be established firmer than ever before. *Swear it* that the scorpion secession shall be surrounded with a circle of fire. *Swear it* that the Rattlesnake Flag shall never float above the Red, White, and Blue. *Swear it* that treason shall be *swept* from the land, though it cost every drop of blood in every Confederate State. *Swear it* that this rebellion shall call upon the rocks and the mountains to cover it, and that the gates of Hell shall not prevail against our America. *Swear it!*

For if your cause is lost, all is lost. The *Union* is lost—the *Constitution* is lost—the *future*, with all its radiant glorious prospects are lost. *Liberty* is *lost*." Such words moved Swift beyond measure, but Captain Mansfield had brought them to a rousing conclusion, when he said: "Light Guard, this is *our* banner from the fair of the city. I have assured them that with *your life* its integrity and honor shall be maintained. If I have expressed your sentiments and determination, up, and cheer the banner!" And Swift answered that call with every fiber of his being, leaping from his chair and cheering so loud that his ears rang for twenty minutes afterwards. What a night it had been! Such memories. Such sweet, savored memories.

After breakfast Swift and his company assembled in the center of town, where they received shiny, pocket New Testaments and a short benediction by one of the local ministers. They were then formed into two columns and marched through the cheering streets to the railroad depot, where the men halted before a waiting train. There Captain Mansfield stood, bareheaded, uniform spotless, sunlight reflecting off the brass hilt above his sword. Two rows of golden buttons ran up and down his dark blue coat like so many soldiers marching in place. His dusky hair parted into neat waves that rolled away from his crown, and his thin dark eyebrows and thick, broad mustache framed a delicate white face.

By his outward appearance he seemed a gentleman incapable of war, but set deep were coal black eyes that looked straight through a man, as if gazing far into the distance with unstoppable determination. Swift had only seen that look in one other person—their local sheriff, a man highly respected for his ability to bring about justice. In Swift's mind such a look erased any doubt of Mansfield's conviction or courage. This man, the best leader in the entire county—a mighty man like King Arthur—was theirs, all theirs. They couldn't lose with him leading.

The locomotive swooshed and pumped. Mansfield's baritone broke through the noise as clearly as a church bell breaks the silence of a quiet Sunday morning. "Guards!"

"Guards!" echoed his officers and sergeants.

"Attention!" The men snapped their heels together as one, backs stiff, heads straight, muskets at their sides. A few passengers exited the train amidst a quiet crowd. "First column, left turn—march! Right turn—march!"

Swift followed the column directly onto the train. Within minutes he leaned out a window and waved to his family. As the train pulled away, he turned and sat down, grinning at his friends with delight. Lieutenant Sam Vaughn, a former shoe salesman at Portage, sat across from him. Vaughn's receding hairline made his forehead seem larger than the rest of his face. Thick dark curls of hair covered the top of his ears and a dark mustache above his lips gave him a look of distinction.

Swift was working for the Wisconsin State Register, a Portage newspaper, when he first met Vaughn. The lieutenant was then the Clerk of Courts for two terms and encouraged Swift to consider a career in law, which he did until the Light Guard was formed. Meanwhile Sam had left politics to sell shoes, a vocation that suited him well. He was a natural salesman. "You know, Swift," he often said, "selling shoes is about the easiest job I've ever had. Unlike politics it's surprisingly easy to please people. After all, everyone needs shoes."

Swift lifted his left shoe and pointed at it with a wry smile. "Now we'll see how this buffalo leather wears," he said, "when we do some real marching!"

Vaughn threw his hands up, disavowing responsibility in the matter.

A few seats ahead of him, Charles Dow, another writer from the Wisconsin State Register, bounded down the aisle in civilian clothing playfully pushed and shoved by Shanghai and some of the other boys seated along the aisle. Charlie was tall, with long thin arms and a full, reddish-brown beard that matched his neatly combed hair. The other men laughed, while slapping him with their hats. Charlie seemed intoxicated the way he howled and bounced around the car. He turned toward Swift and his friends.

"Yahoo!" shouted Charlie. "Vaughan, you sorry excuse for a shoe peddler. Who let you in the Guards—the Confederates? Ha!"

"No way, Dow. I've been training and drilling since the Guard was formed. Have good right to be here. What are you doing, getting something to write in that lousy rag we call a newspaper?"

"Didn't come here just to write. I came to fight. Just like you fellas. I finally got Ma to realize I could serve two purposes, writing for the paper and killing Rebels. Shoot! You didn't think I was going to let you have all the fun did you?"

Everyone congratulated Charlie for joining. His round baby face normally wore a smile but at this moment it took on a solemn expression. Slowly removing his hat, he held it over his heart and half bowed his head. He stood silent for a moment, scanning the anxious faces before him. With a sheepish grin he declared, "With a few regiments like this, I do believe we could send the whole Confederacy swimmin' for Algiers."

Mid May 1861, Portage, Wisconsin

Ed Best stumbled as he caught his foot on a piece of sidewalk planking, in the waning light of eventide.

"He's drunk as a beggar," whispered Bill Day.

"I beg your pardon," Ed slurred. "I am not drunk."

"I've got him," said the burly Sophie Landt. "This way."

Ed felt himself pulled along, watched the passing shadows of the side alley beside Pettibone Hall where young couples paid little attention to him, lost in their own pursuits. The three stopped at the back of the alley. Ed leaned against the wall and straightened himself. "I'm gonna get Bellford tonight," he said.

Sophie leaned forward and smiled. "Sure you are, Ed."

Ed nodded. "Saw him on the street. Said he'd meet me tonight. Time I finished him and showed everybody what I can do." Ed turned a sad face toward Sophie. "You don't think I can beat him. Do you?"

"Of course I do, Ed. Saw it with my own eyes."

"Darn straight. Except I didn't win 'cause Bellford didn't give. Would've if Solon hadn't stuck his nose in. Well! Tonight I'm gonna." He stared hard at Sophie, now ignoring him.

"What're we gonna do with him in a fight?" said Bill. "He's had too much hard cider to fight anybody."

Ed smiled, amused that they were talking as if he wasn't present.

"I know," said Sophie. "And if Gaffney shows up with Bellford we're in deep muck."

Bill reached over to the roof of an old shed, pulled off a cedar shake, unbuttoned his shirt, and slipped it inside.

"What are you doing?" said Sophie.

"If I'm fighting Gaffney, I'm not losing any lunch to his haymaker."

Ed laughed.

"Come on," said Sophie. "Let's get Ed inside, see if we can get some coffee in him."

After two cups, Ed was sobering pretty well. The redheaded John Gaffney stood on the other side of the dance floor, but no sign of Bellford.

"I'm going to dance," said Sophie. "Keep an eye on him."

Ed kept smiling, first at Sophie, then at Bill Day. After a couple hours Bill was dancing with his lady friend, the board looking flat and silly in his shirt, while Sophie wheeled around the floor with his girl. Ed moved slowly toward the hard cider, filled a glass and drank, then filled and drained another. Everything seemed to be going well until he started thinking about his humiliation with Bellford again. "That tears it!" he said, and headed out to the back alley. He stood outside sobering for at least ten minutes before he remembered what Bellford's brother had said to him on the street that day. "Your girly friend is pregnant for sure. Three boys from town went out to claim the baby as their own, but Mr. De Vitte already sent her packing to some aunt's in Chicago. And Gary! He took a train to Rockford to join the Illinois infantry with his cousins. Won't be coming back until the war is over. Find somebody else to fight!"

But Ed didn't want to fight anyone else. He wanted Bellford, wanted to give him the same pain he felt, to defend Lila's honor. Wanted to be a man. The more he thought about it, the angrier he got. Madly he paced the alley, building up pressure like steam in a boiler until something inside him snapped. Whirling, he turned to the back wall of Pettibone Hall, put down his head, and swung his fist into the building. One of the bones in his forearm cracked. Excruciating pain charged up his arm and exploded into his brain. "Aaagh!," he groaned as he ran around in little circles. His hurried footstep found a hidden hole in the alley floor, twisting his ankle and sending him headlong into the mass of bricks.

Everything around him went far away for awhile. But then a sudden headache pounded like a hammer on hard steel, followed by a sick throbbing in his right forearm. Turning toward the wall he threw up. Strong hands lifted him and walked him into the building. Merciful fingers washed the huge bump at the top of his head that suddenly burned with fire. He winced and felt cleansing tears roll down the corner of his face.

"Bellford," said Sophie.

"But he left for Illinois this afternoon," said Gaffney.

Ed could see the faces pressing in, their expressions questioning, seeking the answer to this riddle. "Don't remember a thing," he mumbled. "Not a thing."

May 22nd, 1861, Daingerfield, Texas

By the time Socrates arrived at Cumberland Presbyterian Church, a large crowd was gathering. Buck Malneck was there, dressed in a fine gray uniform. Now a member of the Titus Rangers, he would soon be leaving with his unit. His long frame bent forward eagerly helping an elderly woman around a mud puddle and up the stairs. He seemed so gentle and kind at the moment, his attention riveted on the lady's footsteps. Socrates quickly worked his way around him without being seen.

The first man to greet him inside the door was Sam Pouns, part owner of Musgrove and Pouns Dry Goods Store, and mayor of Daingerfield. Sam flashed a quick smile, took Socrates' hand, and shook it violently. "So sorry about the trouble in town. Peacock told me all about it. You know most people don't feel like that. We want you to stay. Need a good teacher. Need to keep Chapel Hill going. Spent nearly ten years keeping it alive, and we're not about to lose it."

Socrates nodded, then followed as Sam led him through the crowd, to the altar, and up to a podium that stood between and slightly behind two church lecterns. Two elderly gentlemen stood there, dressed in black suits and talking lightheartedly to the elders of the church. Sam quickly introduced the two to Socrates as the keynote speakers, Reverend Barnes, and Reverend Pope. Straws were drawn, and it was determined that Barnes would go first.

Socrates offered a short welcome to the members and guests of the congregation, asking them to hold all questions until both speakers had presented their viewpoints. He then introduced the two ministers, who stepped into their places in their respective lecterns. Each man's eyes gazed straight into the audience—as if seeing but not really seeing. Socrates lightly pounded his gavel, and nodded toward Reverend Barnes.

Barnes put his hands on the sides of the podium and smiled. "Ladies and gentlemen, I thank you for the opportunity to discuss this difficult, sometimes perplexing issue, in a spirit of Christian cooperation and truth. Our beloved Southern states have seceded from the Federal Government that was formed barely a century ago. It has been divided over many issues, but perhaps none so volatile as those surrounding the topics of slavery and property rights."

He lifted his hands straight in the air, then gently let them fall upon his Bible. "Many nights I've spent awake, praying and searching the Scriptures, asking God's guidance in understanding. I cannot claim to speak for God. Nor should any man. For no other shall stand in your place on the day of judgment. Each must answer for himself.

I would like to begin by reading Exodus chapter 21, verses 20 and 21:

'And if a man smite his servant, or his maid, with a rod, and he die under his hand; he shall surely be punished. Notwithstanding, if he continue a day or two, he shall not be punished: for he *is* his money.'

Clearly God shows in these verses that a slave is the property, the money of the man who owns him. He has a right to use him, trade him, and discipline him as he chooses. Furthermore, various reasons are given that demonstrate why men and women have been sold into slavery. Some made poor financial choices. Others were taken captive in war. In the case of Israel in Egypt, God sent a time of testing to strengthen his people before conquering Canaan. Once Israel conquered the land, she was sold into slavery for her many whoredoms—for repeatedly following after other gods. Others, such as the Gibeonites, willingly submitted themselves as slaves rather than fall in battle before the God-given power of Joshua's armies. Such willing servitude is clearly shown in Deuteronomy, chapter fifteen, verses sixteen and seventeen:

'And it shall be, if he—that is your servant—say unto thee, I will not go away from thee; because he loveth thee and thine house, because he is well with thee; then thou shalt take an awl, and thrust it through his ear unto the door, and he shall be thy servant forever.'"

Barnes stopped and scanned the audience. "Slavery has existed since the earliest of times. Abraham clearly bought and bred slaves within his own household. Nowhere in the Scriptures does God either forbid or condemn it. Instead he gives clear direction regarding their treatment. It appears to me that the issue at hand should not be whether slavery is to exist or not, for such world matters are beyond our scope. Therefore, let us look at Exodus chapter twenty to see how we should treat our slaves, in accordance with God's mercy and love, and at what points a slave owner has gone too far in disciplining—"

Socrates leaned forward over his podium, stretching his lower back muscles as much as he could without being too obvious. Barnes' words flowed through his mind as he peered at the audience. Socrates had discovered in college that he could listen to a lecture, observe other things around him, and absorb it all at once.

Some of the longest standing citizens of Daingerfield were there, Dr. Grey, Mr. Willis, Mr. and Mrs. Rogers, the Connors family. All had lived here twelve years or longer. Buck Malneck sat stiff and rigid, his sister's hand in his own. Mr. Darby was there too, listening intently, eyes riveted to the speaker. Socrates felt a wave of compassion for this man, who's daily commerce, tobacco farming, was inextricably entwined with the use of slave labor. The dilemma he faced as a Christian were many, though somewhat obscure in the light of Old Testament writings. Socrates liked the way Plato had described it:

"This is the climax of popular liberty, when the purchased slaves are no less free than the owners who paid for them."

A polite round of applause marked the completion of Barnes' dissertation, and then Reverend Pope began. As he did, he held his hands together over his Bible, fingers straight, as if praying. With each issue, he opened his hands and spread his arms wide, before returning them to their prayerful position. "Thank you for such an excellent presentation on the proper care of slaves, my dear friend. I must begin by saying that these are important elements of Scripture regarding the rights and care of those under our stewardship. Indeed, it's true that slavery has been known for the entirety of recorded time. Yet, the same can be said of murder, adultery, theft, disobedience to parents, and many other elements that God provided instruction for within the Old Testament. There are, however, some important Scriptures which you've overlooked."

"Perhaps it should be noted that in Israel a slave was free after serving six years—not unlike those of our forefathers who came to this new world as indentured servants. Indeed, if any man in Israel was a servant and unable to gain his freedom, he would certainly be set free in the Year of Jubilee, when every kinsman slave was freed and all family property returned. He and his children would not be bound as slaves for eternity. Furthermore, under our new covenant, has not God said that in Christ there is neither slave nor free? Let us first turn to the arguments my colleague has brought out from Exodus chapter twenty-one."

Socrates turned to Exodus and read silently along with the speaker, but his mind drifted. College. So many nights without sleep. So many hours of translating. The Septuagint. Greek—such an exacting language. So much work. He'd loved the Greeks, though. Epic poetry. Mathematics. Philosophy. But nothing they wrote in law matched the Old Testament. Divinely inspired. Had to be. No man could write so objectively, so wisely. The great Socrates, himself, understood. No one did wrong willingly, if he understood the good of the soul. Virtue is knowledge, but the soul has to possess it first. Otherwise there was nothing. No insight. No virtue. Nothing. Were they that different— the teachings of Socrates, Plato, Aristotle—Jesus? Could the great Socrates have helped prepare the way of the Lord?

A clap of applause jerked Socrates back to present reality. Now it was his turn. A wave of nausea swept through him with the thought he had not been listening, but he stretched himself to full height, took a deep breath, and smiled. "Thank you Reverend Pope. Our two distinguished speakers have indeed given us much to think on. Perhaps we should give them another round of applause." Socrates waited as the congregation and guests applauded again, this time with more enthusiasm.

When the clapping died, Socrates turned to the audience. "For those of you who do not know me, my name is Socrates Best. I teach at Sylvan Academy, and also work as an associate professor at Chapel Hill College, where I provide instruction in philosophy, Greek, and homiletics. Our local elders have asked me to pose some questions regarding the presentations of our distinguished speakers. So if I may, I would like to begin with our first speaker."

"Reverend Barnes, both you and Reverend Pope have given considerable attention to the twenty-first chapter of Exodus. Yet neither of you mentioned the fact that these rules are posed regarding Hebrew servants. In other words, they are kinsmen of the same race and religion. Are you saying that Negroes are of our same race?"

Barnes frowned. "Physically? Of course not. But as my distinguished colleague said earlier, in Galatians, the third chapter, Paul writes: 'There is neither Jew nor Greek, neither bond nor free, neither male nor female: for we are all one in Christ Jesus.'"

Socrates smiled. "So these rules actually cross over to the New Testament as rules for how to treat one's Christian brother?"

Barnes' oval eyes rolled inward. "I think that would be safe to say."

"And there is no standard of right behavior toward a slave who has come from a heathen nation?"

"I can find none."

Socrates let his eyes go wide. "They are *property?*"

"I make *no* apology for Scripture."

"And God doesn't care how we treat them?"

Barnes shook his head fast. "I *never* said that. Even an uneducated man knows better than to beat or misuse beasts of burden, for in the long run he will get less work out of them. Besides, in Ephesians, the sixth chapter, it is written, 'And, ye masters, do the same things unto them, forbearing threatening: knowing that your Master also is in Heaven.'"

Socrates scratched the top of his head. "And a Negro is a beast of burden?"

"I didn't say *that* either."

"But they *are* property?"

"Indeed."

"And if this property runs away, it should be returned to the rightful owner when found?"

"Of course."

Socrates leaned forward, unfolding a wide smile. "Then how do you explain the words of Deuteronomy, chapter twenty-three, verses fifteen and sixteen?"

Barnes leaned over the lectern, rapidly flipping pages.

Socrates read aloud. "You shall not give back to his master the slave who has escaped from his master to you. He may dwell with you in your midst, in the place which he chooses within one of your gates, where it seems best to him; you shall not oppress him."

Barnes ran his finger over a page, then slowly lifted his head. "Perhaps it means we're to keep him safe and well cared for, until his master comes to find him."

"Is *that* what it says?"

"No. But it could be reasoned—"

"Ah," said Socrates, eyes wide again. "Then we don't rely *completely* on Scripture, but on *reason*."

"Yes."

"What if one finds it reasonable to misuse his property, while another does not? Where does society intervene with what it considers reasonable laws?"

Barnes shook his head. "I'm not sure. Those would be matters for discussion by legislative assemblies."

"Of course," said Socrates. "Matters which our Confederacy would say are best settled within each state. Yet, when states differ on such matters, and someone else's property flees to another man's farm, shouldn't he be given sanctuary according to the verse I've just read?"

Barnes nodded. "It certainly could be read that way."

Socrates turned toward the other lectern. "Reverend Pope, what would you say?"

Pope smiled and nodded. His fingers straightened, hands coming together. After a few seconds, he slowly opened them. "Our reasoning should be based on New Testament teaching, with a respectful look to the Old Testament. It is, after all, the basis of all civil law." His hands closed in a prayerful position.

Socrates scratched his head. "I see, but I don't quite understand. Are you saying New Testament teaching takes precedence over Old Testament law?"

"Absolutely."

"And the essence of such teaching is?"

Pope opened his hands and held them palm up. "The indwelling presence of the Holy Spirit—our counselor and teacher."

"The same Spirit who came upon the apostles on Pentecost?"

"Yes."

"And all the apostles had this same Spirit?"

Pope's hands folded together again. "Absolutely. The same Spirit who empowered them to heal the sick, raise the dead, and write the Scriptures. You question the inspiration of the Scriptures?"

"No," said Socrates softly, looking around the audience, and scratching his head. After a time, he turned and looked directly at Pope. "But there's still something I don't understand."

Pope threw his hands out to his side. "What?"

"If Paul, who had written instructional letters to churches all over the Roman Empire—if he had God's Spirit on him when he wrote Philemon—and if God was against slavery—why didn't he order Philemon to set Onesimus and all the other slaves free?"

Pope's hands dropped slowly to his side. "I don't know. And *neither* do *you*."

"You're right," said Socrates with a smile. "Neither do I. Simple questions seem to avoid the simplest answers." He turned to his audience. "Ladies and gentlemen, let's have one more round of applause for our distinguished speakers. They have given freely of their time tonight. And, hopefully, have helped us better understand the difficult questions before us."

When the applause stopped, Socrates added, "If any of you have questions you'd like to ask, our distinguished speakers have agreed to stay and talk with you."

Men and women alike stood and pressed forward to speak with the two ministers, while Socrates picked up his Bible and turned to leave. He barely made it to the front of the altar before a well dressed gentleman stepped up and gripped his hand. It was Darby, the man some said owned more slaves than anyone in the entire country. Socrates felt his stomach turn. Good God, he didn't want a fight.

Darby smiled wide. "Good job, Socrates. Never realized you were on our side. Who'd have thought? Had me going for a spell, but then you did it. Set those abolitionists straight. Way to go. New Testament. That was the way to get them. Great job."

He pumped Socrates arm until Socrates finally wrenched it free. "Uh, thanks Darb, but I've got to go." Stepping around Darby, he made it half way to the door when the two deacons met him, their faces set in stone.

"Socrates!" said the tall one. "We wanted you to raise questions, not humiliate our speakers. What on earth were you thinking?"

"Sorry," said Socrates softly. "Didn't mean to, but can we talk about this another time? Got to go." When the two didn't move, he stepped around them and moved further down the aisle, only to find another slaver watching and waiting. Sheesh! Another one? Can't get out of here.

The man was holding his hat in front of him with both hands, eyeing Socrates' every step. "What you said," said the man without expression. "Well, it got me to thinkin'. Those reverends, I agree with both of 'em. And I treat my Negroes good. Always have. But I can see other things now. Things I couldn't see before. Maybe Jesus showed us the way. Maybe we should use reason—set the captives free. Even so, how can I? They got no place to go. Raymon, my head servant, when this whole abolition thing started, begged me not to send him out. Says he's got no home. No place to live. Nothin'."

Socrates nodded. "And if you had a grown child, and it was time to send him off to school, but he's afraid, what would you do?"

"My boys aren't of age yet, but I guess I'd do what any good father does. Pay his school. Room and board too. I'd try to explain how the world works, how he has to make a living. Walk him through the best I could. But I can't do that with every slave! You realize what that would take—the time—the money? How could you expect me to?"

Socrates shook his head. "Didn't say you had to do anything. Just asked a question. Look, I can't talk any more. Got to go."

The man's wife stepped directly into Socrates' path. "Wait a minute," she said. "If he lets our slaves go, who's gonna take care of me? Mommy and daddy told me a proper lady must have servants. Whose gonna work our fields, cook our meals?"

Socrates stared at her pouting little face, shook his head, opened his mouth as if he was about to speak, and darted past her.

Sam met him at the door, grinning from ear to ear. "Never met anybody who could say so few words in so little time, and get so many people mad. Socrates, I'd say you have a rare gift."

Socrates shrugged. "Come on, let's go before the herd sins against philosophy a second time."

Camp Randall, May 14th, 1861

The thundering cannon blast shook the soldiers' billets, followed by the voice of Sergeant Marsh hollering. "Get your sorry butts out of bed." Swift sat up and looked at his pocket watch. Five o'clock. Men in long johns climbed down from their bunks in various states of wakefulness. The lengthy dormitory had been used to hold animals for the Wisconsin State Fair until the Second Regiment was formed. Now, instead of pens for livestock and farm machinery, the building was filled with wide bunks stacked one atop the other, running the entire length of the barn. Each bunk left just enough room for two men to sleep side by side on straw mattresses.

Swift's gaze fell upon the straw. His first night sleeping here, he and his friends suffered an all-out attack by Rebel fleas, but the men boiled clothes and took vinegar baths until they eradicated every last one. Just the thought of it now made him itch. He hoped to never see another flea.

After morning exercises, drill, and breakfast, he and his friends fell into formation on the parade grounds. All the fences and outdoor pens once used to hold the state's prize livestock had been cleared to make a place for the regiment to drill. In the huge area, acres and acres of long grassy plains rolled over the finest pasture land he'd ever seen. Sparsely scattered around the fields were a few oak and pine trees that offered little shade. Across this open space the Regiment stood in formation, companies side by side, their sergeants and officers standing before them. What had started as three companies was now ten companies of forty to seventy men each.

Swift's gaze wandered, exploring the extent of his peripheral vision. Look at us, he thought. We're beautiful. What Rebels could stand before such an army and hold its ground? Must be the grandest army ever formed. "Regiment—" the executive officer's command sounded, followed by the echo of the captains relaying the command to their individual units. "Company—"

"Attention!"

Hundreds of heels slammed together in unison, as the men stood stiff, hands and muskets at their sides. Out of the corner of his eye Swift watched one man salute, while another returned it and stepped forward to speak. It was Lieutenant Colonel Peck, the acting regimental commander. He was spit and polish, a West Pointer in every sense of the word.

"Men, it has been reported that some of you are creating disturbances in the city of Madison. As a result, I am imposing restrictions to avoid further disruption of the community. As of today you will not leave this camp unless you have obtained the correct password from my office. Anyone caught attempting to leave camp without proper authorization will be placed in the stockade on bread and water for one week. I expect no more ill reports on the behavior of the Second as long as I am in command. Is that understood?"

Hundreds of men thundered in unison, "Yes, sir."

"Good. Now to the other matter at hand. The regiment will not be called into three months of service as previously believed, but for three years. Those of you who have already signed your enlistment papers will be given another opportunity to do so. Anyone not wishing to extend his commitment will be allowed to return home. Captains, you will spend the remainder of the day drilling your men." Colonel Peck turned on his heels and marched away while the executive officer shouted a new series of commands.

Captain Mansfield spoke to Sergeant Marsh who then directed the men through their drills. "Forwaaaard—march. Column right—march. Column left—march. Right flank—march. To the rear—march."

As he marched, Swift wondered at the Colonel's words. No Rebel army could last three years. Not against this army. Not against God! The Psalmist had written:

"Why do the heathen rage, and the people imagine a vain thing? The kings of the earth set themselves, and the rulers take counsel together, against the Lord, and against his anointed, saying, Let us break their bands asunder, and cast away their cords from us. He that sitteth in the heavens shall laugh: the Lord shall have them in derision. Then shall he speak unto them in his wrath, and vex them in his sore displeasure."

Swift shook his head at the thought of the Almighty, of his rage, of the Israelites standing in the shadow of a smoking mountain, feeling the earth tremble as the Lord thundered. They'd cried out in fear, begging Moses to ask God to stop. No man, they said, could hear God and live.

Swift felt the call stronger than ever. It was the call to fight, like the mighty men of old. And before him was a regiment of like-minded men, nearly a legion strong, who drilled in precision by company. To him, this was the army of the Almighty, beautiful in every way. One command and everyone obeyed. No arguments. No confusion. Just the way it was ordained to be, before Adam and Eve messed up in the garden.

Noon brought a welcome break from the steady drilling. Swift and his friends proceeded to the mess hall and sat down for lunch in a heavy sweat. A young man with a red Beloit patch on his shoulder, and shiny golden hair, frowned as he scanned the Light Guards. "That Peck is a real piece of work."

A second Beloit man, with a coal black mustache and dark curly hair, sat behind the blonde. He smiled, nodded. "He's a West Pointer all right, right down to his shiny boots and arrogant mug."

Swift couldn't believe his ears. It was as though Emmons Taylor, that great Wisconsin orator who had addressed the Light Guard before leaving Portage, were repeating his speech, and his words charged into Swift's mind.

The institutions we enjoy are ours only in trust—they are sacred heirlooms confided to our keeping for those who are to come after us.

Charlie Dow made a fist around his fork and stuck it hard into his meat. "Peck's doing his job. Can't be having problems with the people in town if he's going to run a camp. Enlisted men getting into trouble means poor discipline. That reflects on his leadership. Until Colonel Coon gets back, he's responsible, and that's fine with me."

The blond flushed crimson. "He's so stiff, looks like someone stuck a ramrod up his butt. Who does he thinks he is to tell us what we can do on our time off? If I want to go to town, then I will."

Swift pushed his jaw forward, shaking his head hard and fast. "How are you going to do that? You won't get past the guards at the gate without the password, and no one's ever gotten over the fences around this place."

The black-mustached man leaned forward. "Don't need no password to get out those gates. Signed on for three months, not three years. I'm getting out while the getting's good—before they try to make some kind of life-long soldier outa me."

Swift's mouth dropped open. "We're here to stop treason, to preserve the Union. How can we defeat the Rebels if we can't agree among ourselves to serve as long as it takes?"

Shanghai, arose. "That's right."

The blonde's face wrinkled. "Long as it takes for what?"

"Long as it takes to quell the rebellion!" said Swift as he rose to stand beside Shanghai.

The blond looked around the room before turning back to Swift, then gave a wide grin. "You mean to kill those Southern gentlemen who left the Union? You're right. They must be stopped. After all, they bombed Fort Sumter and killed a whole Union horse. We'd better do something before they attack our pork supply. Ha! Ha!"

"This ain't funny," shouted Lieutenant Vaughn. "We're talking about our country."

"That's right" said the black-mustached man, rising to stand beside the blond, "and about its constitution. I read at school that New England wanted to secede back in the twenties. They strongly considered it before deciding not to, but there was a lot of support for it. Seems they considered the right to secede as one of their own constitutional privileges. How come it doesn't work both ways?"

Swift felt his eyes bugging, face burning like fire. "Just a few months ago I was in law school, and maybe I'm not a lawyer yet, but I do know a few things. Nobody has the right to fire on the government, nobody. So this isn't just about secession anymore. And what did you join up for in the first place, if you weren't going to fight?"

"Good question," said the black-mustached man. "Guess I figured we'd just show up and the show of force would change their minds. I mean, who would want to fight a dragged-out war? Or who'd be *that* stupid?"

"I would," Vaughn said, as he arose to stand with his friends, "to stop a rebellion and keep our nation strong. That's *not* stupid. That's *smart*."

"And I," echoed Shanghai.

Swift hesitated. The Beloit man's question had stung him. He knew nothing of the North talking secession. What was he trying to do, keep them off balance by talking about issues that happened before they were born? Everyone was behind the Union, the governor, the mayors, the people, everyone. Only copperheads could speak such treason! He eyed the dissenters as if he could stare them into submission, shame them into right action. "You can all go back home if you want," he said, "but I came here to put down the rebellion, and I'm going to fight whether it takes three months or three years."

Charlie Dow and Lieutenant Vaughan nodded.

The blond Beloit man softened his expression. "What do you think they want three-year enlistments for anyway? This war won't take longer than a battle or two. What'll we do then? Serve in some outpost in Minnesota or Dakota country? Not me! I think they're just using this Rebel thing as a trick to get more men to fight the Indians, or fill their forts on the Oregon Trail. Anyway you look at it, it smells fishy. I'm not sticking around to see what Peck and those other officers are up to."

Shanghai was usually of a light spirit, but now his long face flushed crimson. "As far as I'm concerned, you're a bunch of cowards. We haven't even seen the enemy and you're ready to run home with your tails tucked between your legs. Ow, oww, owww! Ow, oww, owoooo," he continued as they walked away, but they didn't even look back.

Shanghai turned toward Swift. "Come on, Best, let's have some fun."

Swift and some of the other men followed out the door, laughing every time Shanghai repeated his dog impression. The group walked around the building and started toward their quarters, when they came upon a cow grazing outside the mess hall.

Walking up to the hefty beast, Shanghai yelled, "What are you doing here, Private Cow? Don't you know you're supposed to be drilling with the rest of the boys? What's that I see on your face, Private Cow? Is that a smile? That better not be a smile I see on your face! Do you understaaaand, Private Cow?"

The cow rolled her huge round eyes at the young man.

Vaughan and Best laughed hard.

Shanghai continued. "Private Cow, you better stand at attention when I talk to you! Do you hear me? Oh! So you're a difficult one. Are you? Extra drill will shape you up. Private Cow, to the rear, turn!" He shouted the order loudly. The cow chewed her cud. "I said about face! All right, you shirker, we'll just have to make you."

Shanghai snapped to attention, made the sharpest right turn Swift had ever seen, and marched three steps forward before stopping to execute two successive left turns, which brought him directly to the rear of the cow. "This is how you make an about turn, Private cow." He grabbed the cow's tail and tried to pull it around, but the unwieldy beast stood hard. "Give me a hand you guys." Best and Vaughan took the cow by its horns and pushed. A number of other soldiers gathered around. With a growing audience, Shanghai hollered louder. "Right turn. Left turn. About turn." The three soldiers grunted and turned the cow with each order. The audience was now laughing so hard, some of them could barely stand.

"Hey!" said Shanghai. "I have a great idea."

Swift waited, catching his breath. "What's that?"

"You know those Milwaukee boys who are always drilling on their off times?"

Swift nodded.

"They're just over the crest of this hill. Forwaaard—march!" He snapped the order and the three soldiers led the beast along, their audience following and laughing every step of the way. From the top of the hill Swift spotted the Milwaukee boys doing their manual of arms below. "Right shoulder—arms! Present—arms! Order—arms!" Their officers barked the commands loudly and the rifles snapped smartly into place.

Swift waited to see what Private Cow's drill sergeant would order next. So did everyone else.

"Charge, bayonets;" shouted Shanghai. "Double-quick—march!"

At the sound of his command the entire group let out a deafening yell. The terrified cow started forward, at first reluctantly, but gaining momentum on the downhill slope, it lumbered forward into a cow's version of an all out gallop. Ahead of them the lieutenant of the Milwaukee Company heard the commotion and looked to see hundreds of pounds of live beef charging straight at him. The great horned beast must have looked like some ferocious monster as it appeared out of nowhere to attack these unsuspecting troops. The frightened lieutenant's eyes darted about as he and the men with him ran every which way.

One of the cadets tossed his musket at the monster as if to stop it, but the musket's strap caught on its horns, making it crazy. It wheeled about, shaking its head, charging anyone who dared come near it; but the beast couldn't shake the rifle from its horns.

"Corporal Chandler," said Best, snapping to attention, "We won't be needing those Beloit boys. Private Cow has run off the adversary and captured one enemy musket."

"By Gaaawd," said Shanghai, "we better draft that cow before some fool goes and eats it!"

FOUR

"One cannot live pleasantly without
living wisely, unearthly, and justly;
nor can one live wisely, unearthly, and
justly, without living pleasantly."
—Epicurus

June 1, 1861—Daingerfield, Texas

SOCRATES STRETCHED HIS LONG RIGHT ARM ACROSS THE GLISTENING BLACK back of his favorite foal, pulling the brush back through its hair, while gently stroking the underside of its neck. She was a spirited one, reminding him of his first girlfriend, Maggie. When he was fifteen, he thought Maggie O'Donnell was the sun, stars, and moon. But she wouldn't wait for him when he went off to college, and by the end of his first year of school, she was married and heavy with child. For the better part of two and a half years he immersed himself in self pity, finding solace for his bereaved heart in the writings of Shakespeare, especially Romeo and Juliet. Despite the prolonged mourning season, he did ultimately come to peace with his loss, when, several years after returning home, he passed her on the street, almost not recognizing her massive form, unkempt dress, and unwashed hair. But her shrill, high voice was impossible to deny as it yapped at the little man walking beside her, in the same manner that a tethered Terrier nips and yaps at passers-by. In the glimmering light of one moment, his terrible misfortune transformed into a glorious deliverance. Ellen was his wife now, and Maggie, well, she was just a memory.

"Socrates," Ellen called from outside the barn door. "There's a couple of men to see you."

"From the railroad?" he asked without looking up.

"Don't know. They wouldn't say. Just that it's a private matter."

"Tell them I'll be there in a minute." He finished his work with Maggie, all the time wondering who the visitors were. He had written to the railroad, hoping he could get a job with them until the war was over. They paid well, and since the Army was dependent on the railroad for transportation, he figured working for them might quiet the complaints of the local hotheads. Or could it be the school board? They'd promised to talk to the people around town about the importance of learning. Promised to pose the question: "What good will a new country be to anyone if it's children are illiterate?" He figured that would set the hook, but several months had passed and no word had come.

Hopeful, he entered the back door of his house, but the faces that greeted him in the parlor were unknown to him. "Herr Best," said a short, dark-haired man standing beside a taller, bald-headed fellow. The man's speech was thick and guttural, every w sounding like a v. "My name is Jacob Mueller, and this is mein friend, Gustaff. "We were wondering, could we speak to you outside—in private?"

Neither man carried a gun, and both appeared peaceful, so Socrates nodded and led them to the barn. He stopped just inside the big doors, and without closing them, turned and faced his visitors. "What's this about?"

Jacob shifted his weight from foot to foot, then slowly lifted his head and looked at Socrates. "My friend and I are from the Red River area. I have a cousin in Daingerfield. He told me you're from Wisconsin."

"That's right."

"We came from Wisconsin too. From Milwaukee. And we're looking for men like you, men who voted against secession."

"People loyal to the north," said Gustaff with a broad smile.

Socrates chewed his lower lip, felt his stomach sink. "What for? The Peace Party already lost the vote."

"We're starting a secession movement too," said Jacob, dark eyes shining. "We will secede from Confederacy."

Socrates eyes went wide "You crazy?"

Jacob kept smiling. "No, mein friend. Confederacy was formed on right to secede. They cannot deny us our right. Not without denying themselves."

"And we have eight continuous counties that voted against secession," said Gustaff, spreading his hands to show some form of measurement completely lost on Socrates.

"We are forming a Union League among loyal citizens," said Jacob. "We have hundreds of members from Red River all the way to Cobb Creek, near Gainesville."

Socrates' scalp tightened. He scratched his head and chewed his lower lip. The northeast border counties had voted against secession, some by a margin of two-to-one or better. But three of those were small, only casting a hundred votes or so; and some of the others were nearly split down the middle. That left only three or four counties that were strong Unionists, and those were full of German immigrants from the north. In a way, they were secluded from the rest of Texas, separated by a language barrier that many of them had refused to cross. Some towns even printed their newspapers in German, an act that enraged many Texans, though Socrates doubted either of these men knew it. "You think Texas will go along with this?"

"They can't say no," said Jacob.

"It would make them the laughing stock of the world," said Gustaff.

Socrates turned and started to walk away, remembered his namesake's words, "Let us consider the problem together." He turned back. "You're wrong, Jacob, for one big reason. You think Texans give a hoot about what the world thinks?"

"They must," said Jacob. "How else could they fight the North? They have no industry. They are counting on British help."

Socrates put both hands on his hips. "Jeff Davis might, but not some of the young hotheads. You know what they say? They say, 'Why wait to kill a Yankee when you've got one next door?' Or better yet, 'The sooner we start the killing, the quicker it'll be over.' If you put the law on *their* side, we'll be in deep muck."

"No matter," said Jacob. "God is on our side, and only the impious man would believe otherwise."

Socrates shook his head. "The impious man is not he who abolishes the god of the multitude, but he who attaches the opinions of the multitude to God."

Jacob's eyes brightened. "Plato? Perhaps we should speak of Protagoras. 'Man is the measure of all things'."

Socrates laughed. "You question my piety and quote an agnostic who could reach no decision regarding the existence of any God?"

"The same could be said of your Plato. He was, after all, a reprobate."

Socrates looked away, sensed this conversation was going nowhere.

"We will secede," said Jacob, "just as West Virginia did. And if Texas will not recognize us, we will assert our allegiance to the Union, and apply for military assistance."

The sinking feeling in Socrates' stomach widened into a gaping hole. "Then what? President Lincoln makes some magical army appear out of nowhere and invades Texas?"

"He is already calling for volunteers," said Jacob.

69

"Maybe," said Socrates, "but there can't be more than a hundred miles between Richmond and DC. Don't you think he'll protect Washington first?"

Jacob's gentle, round face straightened into a firm, hard stare. "Lincoln is no fool. He will not save Washington to lose the rest of the country. There will be an army in the West, and when it comes, we will offer supplies, our knowledge of the land, even our lives."

Gustaff nodded. "Will you join us?"

Socrates looked away, chewing his lip. Hair-brain scheme. A philosopher had to think. Couldn't get embroiled or he'd lose objectivity. "I don't know. I'm just a teacher. Never killed anyone."

Jacob smiled. "Nor have we, mein friend. But information can be more valuable to an army than another rifle."

Socrates shook his head. Hair-brain? Insane! "Be a spy? I don't know."

Jacob's face hardened. "When this is over, history will tell of what we chose to do here. Only you can decide what it will say of you."

Socrates' gaze met Jacob's. His eyes were a soft hazel color, like those of a black cat Maggie once owned, and the likeness made Socrates wonder if she still did. Then a quick, bright light flashed from somewhere within, and in that moment, Socrates glimpsed something pure and whole. Not hard and critical as he'd expected, but soft and compassionate. He looked away, embarrassed. "I'll need some time to think."

"Of course," said Jacob. "And I trust the words of this meeting will stay between us?"

"Are you kidding? If they don't, we could all hang."

After the men left, Socrates remained in the barn, pacing from one end to the other, wondering what his namesake would do. Platonic dialogues came to mind, one after another: "Virtue is knowledge"—"The virtues are one"—"A just man harms no one"—"Better to suffer than commit injustice." Everything in him seemed to say war was wrong. But his namesake had fought in war, and bravely at that.

Socrates stopped and kicked a wooden bucket hard against the wall. Milk splashed in every direction. "Well. That was stupid," he muttered. Walking over to the wall, he picked up the bucket and stuck it back under the cow he had milked earlier, pumped out what little milk she had left, and headed through the door. Ellen stood outside, waiting.

He put down the bucket and started to put his arms around her, but she pushed him away. Her face was something less than angelic, chilly blue eyes cold as iron. "Who were those men?"

Socrates shook his head. "Don't ask."

Her eyes went wide. "What? The county is fixing to go to war, strange men come to our door and talk in private to my husband, and I'm not supposed to ask who they are?"

Socrates forced a smile, raising his hands waste high, palms up. "You remember Pandora's box?"

"Of course."

"And you trust me?"

Ellen nodded.

"Then take my word for it. I'm not opening this lid for anyone."

Ellen's eyes went wide again. "Not even your wife?"

Socrates shook his head slowly, leaning forward and staring deep into those sapphire eyes. "Especially for you. I must protect you."

"Protect me! Protect me? Sometimes I'm not even sure you know I exist. You're always in such *deep* thought—about *what* I have *no* idea—and *if* I should interrupt those sacred meditations, I'm greeted with anger. Anger! As if *I've* done something terribly wrong."

Socrates looked at the ground. "I'm sorry. Never realized—"

"Of course you didn't. How could you? Always off in your own world."

Socrates felt the burn of humiliation run up his spine and flush his face. He put his arms around her again. This time she didn't resist as he pulled her close to him, but her unanswered question stood between them like a brick wall.

June 24th, 1861, Baltimore, Maryland

The boards beneath Swift's feet rolled up, down, and side-to-side as the train lost momentum, a sensation he had become accustomed to over the past week. Each time the locomotive slowed, the cars rose and fell with every pitch of the tracks. Sergeant Marsh passed by, his face white. "Fix bayonets!" he shouted.

The last few days had been a whirlwind of excitement for the Wisconsin volunteers. Their regiment was filled with companies from one end of the state to the other. In some of the companies, as many as half the men went home rather than enlist for three years. The Cadet Rifles from Beloit were cast into such strife over the government's demands for longer enlistments, that they were sent home and replaced by a company of Milwaukee riflemen. But with the news of more openings, other men came, eager to fill out the ranks and become members of one of the first formed regiments from Wisconsin.

The Belle City Rifles, Oshkosh Volunteers, Dodge City's Citizens Guard,

Dane County's Randall Guards, Grant County's Grays, Janesville's Volunteers, and the Iowa County Miners' Guard were all absorbed into this regiment that now numbered around a thousand men. And just as they had come from all areas of the state, they wore uniforms according to each group's tastes. Some wore blue, some gray, and each uniform had different badges, stripes, or other patterns to set them apart.

Swift eyed his sergeant quizzically. Up until now the train ride seemed like a holiday sent from Heaven. Loved ones from home and hundreds of people from Madison came to give them a rousing send off from Camp Randall. So many pretty girls and beautiful ladies kissed him that Swift had begun to wonder if he should stay home after all. But that was only the beginning of the celebrations. Every town swarmed with cheering crowds, praising them for their bravery in going and wishing them Godspeed. Janesville rendered a great reception, but it was nothing compared to what they found in Chicago, where tens of thousands turned out to see the Illinois volunteers join the men from Wisconsin. Swift couldn't even put a guess on the number, but Charlie Dow estimated it at forty thousand.

And so it had gone, through Laporte, Indiana, and Elmore, Macedonia, and Bellsville, Ohio, every stop a magical encounter with the American people, until they arrived in Pennsylvania. Its countryside heralded high rocks and majestic, rolling mountains, but its larger cities seemed cast in a cloud of darkness. Pittsburgh, the worst, was a cold, smoky place, covered with ash and soot. After that, Harrisburg was pleasant and receptive. But since leaving there, burned bridges and twisted tracks marred the countryside, and Union soldiers encamped around every railroad bridge. Even the countryside seemed ominous, farms and barns decrepit, crops meager, people dressed in rags. Words of the Psalmist came to mind:

"God setteth the solitary in families: he bringeth out those which are bound with chains: but the rebellious dwell in a dry land."

He felt as though he were in a different world here—a world covered in darkness, the shadow of death. This was the battleground for the nation, the place where the Union would be preserved or divided for eternity. Thus, Swift was already feeling vulnerable when Sergeant Marsh gave the command to fix bayonets. His voice cracked as he asked, "Have the Rebs gotten this far already?"

Marsh paused, studied the car and its anxious faces. "Been some reports of civilian rioting and disorderly conduct. Be on guard—and keep those barrels pointed straight up so you don't go slitting nobody's britches. Understood?"

A chorus of "Yes, sir," and "Yes, sergeant," sounded around the car, as the soldiers fumbled with their bayonets and slapped them into place. It wasn't precision military, but Marsh turned and pushed his way toward the next car.

Swift looked out the window into the blackened sky over Baltimore. The light of the full moon glimmered across rooftops, skipping from church steeple to church steeple. Aside from the locomotive's long thinning puffs, the night's black canopy hovered naked above. The train ever still, buildings rushing by. The sky's countless flashpoints dancing from treetop to treetop. Some peaked here and there through the leafy branches of a tree, only to vanish momentarily before reappearing amidst another.

A shrill whistle sounded. Wheels screeched on steel rails, metal rods rattled, distant bells clanged, and iron wheels thumped. As the train stopped, the men filed off, rifles held in front, bayonets reflecting silver moonlight. They formed into ranks and waited for a second train. The remainder of the regiment had fallen behind, and was nowhere to be seen. Sergeant Marsh hollered, "Stand at ease!"

The boys milled around for nearly three hours. Some put down blanket rolls and knapsacks, taking the opportunity to get some sleep. A large crowd gathered from the city, mingling with them, asking questions, and talking about home.

A well dressed young man with light brown hair stopped a few feet from Swift, as though waiting for permission to speak. "Hi," said Swift.

"Hello," came the soft baritone reply.

Swift felt himself relax. "What are all you folks doing out here in the middle of the night?"

The young man offered a half smile. "Just come out to watch the Yankee troops go through. Seems it's what the whole town's been doing today— watching train load after train load. Can't hardly believe we've got that many men willing to fight Americans."

Swift tightened, shifted nervously. "Can't let treason go unpunished."

The young man's half smile faded into a look of amusement. "Treason? I'd hardly call secession treason. They're only fighting for their state's rights. You know. Just want to be on their own. That's all."

Swift's jaw went forward. He thought of the sermon Reverend Langley, a Virginian by birth, delivered at the M. E. Church of Portage just prior to the Light Guard's departure. The text of the sermon was from Jeremiah, "A wonderful and horrible thing is committed in the land." Swift's hands tightened into fists. "Not treason? Then what do you call bombing a federal garrison?"

The young man's icy look lingered. "It wasn't federal land. They'd withdrawn from the Union."

Swift frowned. "What for? So they can go on beating their slaves?"

"*That's* not the question. The question is, What right does the Federal Government have to obstruct justice in sovereign states—property rights and the like?"

"Property rights! Property rights? You mean to tell me they'd destroy the unity of the entire country just so the South can keep people as property? What state in one nation under God would do such a thing?"

The brown haired boy looked away. Moonlight danced on his eyelashes, making them look long in the night shadows, almost feminine. After a minute of silence, he turned his head and looked back at Swift. "You know, you wouldn't even be standing on this ground if it weren't for Lincoln. People around here are ruffled about it."

Swift's eyebrows arched. "Ruffled about what?"

"Ruffled about throwing our mayor and his cabinet in jail. That's what."

"What?"

"Yeah. Lincoln did that all right. Threw the whole bunch in jail, so they couldn't mount any support for secession. The president talks high and mighty about constitutional rights for nigras, but doesn't seem to mind violating the rights of good, God-fearing white folks."

Swift was tired, hungry, and thirsty, and these words sounded foreign—impossible to believe. Worst yet, they came from the mouth of an obvious traitor, one who couldn't see the need for a strong Union. Such a man would never understand why the rest of the country hated the egregious crime of slavery. His mind searched for just the right answer to the question, but his tired brain only pushed out thoughts that ran together in confusion. Then it came, a simple but logical answer. "What about God-fearing black folks?"

The Marylander's forehead wrinkled in a way that pulled his scalp forward, causing his ears to wiggle. "You don't know them darkees—never lived with 'em. They're not like you and me. Can't be. Won't ever be God-fearing people."

Swift put his arms out, palms up. "How could they be when the only Christians they see are on the other side of a whip?"

The young man turned his gaze away, as if trying to come up with an answer. He shrugged and walked away. A young lady came by with a basket of food and offered some, but Swift declined. Sergeant Marsh had ordered the men not to take any food or water from the people, and now Swift knew why. It could be poisoned.

Finally the second train arrived, and the entire regiment was formed into ranks. With all present and accounted for, the regiment turned right and marched through the streets of Baltimore. Colonel Peck, dressed in his finest uniform, rode on horseback beside his men. The regimental band played some hearty music, and Swift found himself marching in time to its lively beat. People filled the streets and sidewalk as the regiment approached the heart of town.

The crowd seemed restless and angry, casting an air of trouble over the scene. Swift gripped his musket in anticipation of a fight.

One of the men in the crowd shouted, "Three cheers for Jefferson Davis!" which was followed by a good number of hurrahs. Then another voice cried, "Three cheers for General Beauregard!" and the crowd continued cheering and shouting names—most of which Swift didn't recognize. His blood boiled.

Sergeant Marsh whispered loud enough for his men to hear, "Just let one of them come near us. We'll give them something to remember us by."

"They're plug ugly," said Shanghai.

"Killing 'em might just beautify the town," added Charlie.

Swift watched the moves of the crowd, more aware of the musket and bayonet in his hands than ever before. Anger swelled within, turning quickly to hatred. The Psalmist's words quickened in him: "Why do the heathen rage, and the people imagine a vain thing?" His fingers squeezed the stock of his rifle. He'd come to put down the rebellion, not thinking it had spread this far.

Everyone around him a potential enemy, he sensed the pistol and knife at his belt. Felt their deadly power. Wondered if he would have to use them here. The cheers for Jefferson Davis were insults. Slapping at his ears. Provoking him and his comrades to defend their cause. He sensed the ease of loading and firing at these arrogant Rebels, but it seemed as if that was what they wanted. Swift gripped his rifle tight. Grit his teeth. Marched forward. Anxious for the next command. These people would not be assaulted without orders.

The taunting continued until a company of policemen arrived on the scene and pushed some of the unruly crowd back. The regiment marched over a mile to a place where loud voices cheered for the Union and Abraham Lincoln, but others cried, "How dare you Yankees desecrate *my* Maryland?" Some cursed them for carrying the Union flag. There were obvious rabble rousers—running up and down the street. Shouting obscenities at the Union. Cheering Jeff Davis and his Confederacy.

"Wish I had some boiling water to throw on these Yankees!" a man shouted. A stone hit Swift in the back of his shoulder. Others thumped the ground around him. The sound of pistol fire broke the night air. Swift ached to use his weapons. Restrained himself. Surprisingly the majority of the people were actually peaceful, even approving. Ladies and gentlemen waved handkerchiefs, cheering a hearty welcome. But many of the Confederate supporters were loud. Their vicious attitudes magnified their presence.

An elderly gentlemen in a gray suit and top hat stepped out beside the marching men. "Don't pay any attention to those boys. They're errant cowards. They know you could easily kill them. You'll get through here all right."

The kind words had a settling affect on Swift as he marched. When he passed the next corner, several hundred men and women singing "*The Star Spangled Banner*" further heartened him. When the Regiment reached a second depot, the men stood at ease while cars were added behind a locomotive. What was happening to his country?

Swift stared warily at his friends. "Can't believe those traitors, standing in the middle of a street and cheering for Beauregard."

Charlie drank from his canteen. "I know. Maybe they're more confused around here. The closer you get to a pig sty, the harder it is to smell the pigs."

"That's not it at all," said Lt. Vaughn. "Around here they think the war is about abolition, not preserving the Union. Slaveholders think the government is trying to seize the property they've paid good money for."

"But the President called us to put down the rebellion, to save the Union," said Charlie. "They've fired on a federal garrison. He's not saying anything about the slaves."

"Maybe he can't," said Vaughn. "Maybe he's afraid."

"Afraid?" shouted Swift. "If he was afraid, he wouldn't have declared war and called out an army."

Vaughn's high forehead wrinkled in the moonlight. "I'm not talking about being afraid to fight. There's greater things to fear than that."

Swift stared in disbelief. "Like what?"

"Like being afraid of dividing the country more than it already is. There's no guaranty we'll win this war. And there's still plenty of slave holders in Pennsylvania, Ohio, Indiana and Illinois. Maryland too. If the single issue of the war is slavery, maybe all those people won't be so eager to support the President. What would he do then? He can't keep arresting duly elected civil servants who oppose him, not like he did here. The people won't stand for it. Courts neither. I'm sure of that."

Swift pushed his jaw forward. "I don't care what you say, I'd support the president and fight the Confederacy no matter what. Both causes are right, and that makes us twice right. The Lord is on our side, and we'll win. Mark my words." He turned to Charlie Dow for support, only to find a blank stare on his friend's face. "Darn it, Charlie, aren't you gonna say anything?"

"He's got a point there, Swift. Maybe the President's out on a ledge. Politics can be real funny."

"Well! That stitches it. Never thought I'd hear my own friends talking treason. You two go on and believe what you want. Me, I'm for Lincoln."

Vaughn stepped over and put his hand on Swift's shoulder. "Didn't say anything against Lincoln. We're here for him. There's deeper issues. That's all."

Swift stared at the ground. He was tired and hungry. Didn't feel like talking. "Cursed country's falling apart," he mumbled. "Friends too. Can't wait to get out of here."

July 1st, 1861, Daingerfield, Texas

Socrates sat on the porch swing in the fading sunlight of late afternoon and laughed. Little Willie giggled and splashed water out of his round metal washtub. Ellen had brought the tub, a small table, and one-year-old infant out to the shade of a Post Oak, just a few feet from the water pump. She tried to wash him there, but every time she ladled up more cool water, he roared with laughter and splashed it all over her. Finally she ladled it straight over his head. His round blue eyes swelled in shock. His hands went straight up at his sides, and he looked about to cry, but when his mother started laughing and pointing at him, he took to laughing and splashing her all over again. Gus ran around the tree with a stick, hiding and shooting imaginary Indians.

It was hot and humid—much too hot for working hard in the late afternoons and early evenings. With all the rain that fell here in March, April, and May, the place steamed until late August. Socrates had heard it could rain a lot here, but he'd never expected fifty or sixty inches a year. Considering the fact that September, October, and November were dry enough to drain every high-ground creek and run in the area, a roaring river could miraculously appear after five or seven-inch rainfalls that often came without warning in the Spring and early Summer. And all of that water somehow managed to make its way back into the June and July air, choking the life out of anyone foolish enough to work into the late afternoons. He'd learned early on that a body could get more done if he rested during this time.

Beyond Ellen, Socrates saw Sheriff Will Peacock turn his horse off the road and ride slowly toward the Best house. His gray-spotted Appaloosa looked almost black in the long shadows of early dusk. Gus aimed at the Sheriff and made shooting noises from the tree. A knot formed in Socrates' stomach. He'd always been on friendly terms with the Sheriff, but Peacock wasn't the sort of man to stop and socialize. He had his own farm six miles south of town, and between farming and keeping the law, little time was left for such things.

Peacock tipped his hat as he passed Ellen. "Afternoon, Mrs. Best. Mind if I set with your husband a spell?"

Ellen lifted Willie with one arm and toweled him down with the other, smiled, and said, "Course not, Will. Already had supper, though. Can I get you anything?"

"No, thanks." He stared at the ground for a moment, then looked up and added, "We'll need some privacy."

Ellen's face went ghostly white. She carried the baby under one arm, pulled Gus down from the tree with the other, and headed straight into the house.

The knot in Socrates' stomach tightened. Peacock dismounted, tied the reins to a post at the side of the porch, then, with a big smile, reached into his saddle bag and pulled out a bottle of wine and two tin cups. "Know you don't cotton to corn whiskey, but I thought a bottle of French wine might hit the spot."

Socrates felt a rush of air escape as his stomach uncoiled. His face relaxed into a smile. "Right nice of you, Sheriff."

"Will, Socrates. How many times do I have to tell you? Just call me Will."

Socrates shook his head. "Don't want to disrespect your office."

Peacock laughed. "I told you, you can call me Will. So how would that be disrespectful when I done gave you permission?"

Socrates shook his head again. "Don't know, Sheriff. Just doesn't seem right is all."

This time it was Peacock who shook his head. "Come on," he said laughing. "Let's get the cork out and try some of this fine wine."

After several cups, and a good hour of talking about various neighbors and their crops, a slight breeze picked up, pushing a strong odor in from down river. "Woo wee!" said Peacock, puckering his lips. "Is that Conner's pigs I smell?"

"Could be," said Socrates. "Then again, could be just about anyone's. Must be five times more pigs around here than milk cows and cattle."

"Ha!" said Peacock as he swept his hand across the valley. "Say what you like about farmers around here, but don't never ever say they don't know how to raise hogs. Especially those Tennessee and 'bama boys."

Socrates laughed. The mellow buzz in the back of his head felt good. "Long as they can remember which one they married."

Peacock howled. "Could you see me telling some learned judge that some poor, dumb farmer just butchered his wife and took his pig to bed?"

"He'd probably say happens all the time in Alabama!" said Socrates, and he laughed until his sides ached. It was a long time since he'd laughed like this, since he'd laughed 'til he cried, and he didn't want it to end, but after a while, a peaceful calm descended upon the two.

"Well," said Peacock. "Pigs are one thing and sheep, now there's another. You know, I once worked for a man takin' care of his sheep. Got so I could tell every one apart. Even liked some more than others."

Socrates smiled. "Cows can be sort of like that—'cept I think they're more bovine."

Peacock stared expressionless across the yard. "I remember one sheep in particular got a tumor on its leg. Man I worked for said I had to cut off the leg, or it'd kill the sheep. I asked him why he didn't just butcher it. Said he wouldn't eat mutton that came from a sick animal. Wouldn't ask anyone else to either. Even quoted the Bible on it." Peacock stopped, ran his fingers through his white whiskers, and looked in the direction of the barn. "I cut the leg off that ewe, thinking it would be good for nothing. But she learned to walk on three legs. Even gave birth to a whole bunch of lambs. So many I lost count."

Socrates chewed his lower lip, sensed Peacock was about to make a point.

"It was something like that for me when President Lamar asked me to stop the feuding between the Moderators and Regulators back in '41." He turned and looked into Socrates' eyes. "Know who the Moderators and Regulators were?"

Socrates nodded. "Heard there was a bunch of trouble on the eastern border, bad land contracts, cattle rustling. Regulators were formed to stop it."

"Yep. 'Cept Charlie Jackson was the leader of the Regulators, and he was a fugitive from Louisiana Justice. Shoot! It was like hiring the fox to watch the hen house. Didn't take long for things to get out of hand, then the Moderators were formed to stop the Regulators." Peacock ran his fingers through his beard. "Gave a whole new meaning to vigilante Justice. Hundreds of men fighting, burning down houses, ambushing each other, even shooting folks in the back. It was such a mess that Sam Houston said the whole state should turn their backs and just let them finish each other off." He turned and looked at Socrates. "You know Potter's point out on Lake Cado?"

Socrates nodded.

"You know who Bob Potter was?"

Socrates nodded again. "Signed the Texas declaration, didn't he?"

Peacock shook his head and looked away. "He was much more than that, Socrates. He was a lawyer in North Carolina before coming to Texas. Served two terms in their House of Commons before he was elected a United States Congressman. Was serving there when he caught a couple fellows screwing around with his wife." Peacock turned and looked straight into Socrates eyes again. "I heard he cut those two boys' dingers off so they couldn't do it again—but the proper folks out East couldn't appreciate it. Fined him six hundred dollars and stuck him in jail for six months." Peacock's aged eyes sparkled as his smirk spread into a full grin. "Hell. If that'd happened in Texas, we'd probably have made him governor!"

Socrates laughed. Felt the wine again. "Isn't that the truth?"

Peacock nodded, turned and looked at his horse. "Regulators rode up to Potter's place, caught him fleein' out the back, into the lake. Shot him dead and left him in the water for the fish to feed on." He looked back at Socrates, his voice just above a whisper. "I'll tell you, it broke my heart to take his widow out there and get his body. Damn. I wept with that good woman. Wept good and long. Took years to bring peace to those counties." He leaned closer to Socrates, narrow eyes ablaze. "Today there's a cancer in Texas. Could be worse than the one we had in '41."

Socrates' stomach coiled again, working itself into knots. His mind raced, trying to think of an appropriate philosophical saying, some wise word of the Greeks, but nothing came. He bit hard on his lower lip and nodded, afraid of what the next words might be.

Peacock stopped, pulled out a pouch of tobacco and rolled a cigarette. "I tell you, Socrates. I don't give two hoots about this secesh thing. You know that. But Texas has made her stand, and being a loyal Texan, I reckon I'll stand by her." He paused, flipped the top of a matchstick with his thumbnail, watched it light up. The flame gave his coarse face an eerie glow as he took a long drag and let it out. "There's talk around town that some folk in the northern counties are forming some kind of Union League. Heard anything about that?"

Socrates looked away.

"Thought you might. Listen. Never liked killin' Texans. Moderators or Regulators made no difference. My job is to uphold the law, and I'll do it, whatever it takes. Even if I have to cut the leg off some fool lamb."

An acid burned in Socrates' stomach. He stared hard into the dark shadows of dusk, wishing he could hide in them.

The sheriff stood and stretched. "Well. It's getting late. Guess I'd better head home before it gets any darker."

"Thanks for the wine," said Socrates, voice trembling. He wished to apologize, to explain, but couldn't find the words. Instead, he quietly watched Peacock step down from the porch, mount his horse, and ride away, all the time wanting to rise and see him off proper, to say thanks or goodbye or something, but his knees were weak, mouth dry, so he just sat on the swing and waved.

No sooner had Peacock disappeared than Ellen stepped out onto the porch. The shadows of her face formed long, hard lines. "What did he mean cut off a leg?"

Socrates shook his head. "I don't know."

Her voice cracked. "You must."

"No. I don't."

Her glare burrowed into him. "What about those men who came here?"

"I *told* you I can't talk about that," he snapped.

"What does it all mean?" She asked, pleading.

"I don't know. I only know one thing."

Her sapphire blue eyes beaded up, tears forming in the corners.

Socrates looked away, her sorrow squeezing him, constricting his chest, making it hard to breathe. "This war's gonna be worse than I thought," he whispered.

"Worse than Mexico?"

"Much worse than Mexico."

She sat down beside him on the swing, put her hands on his, and waited until he looked her in the eyes. "Then why don't we go home, where we'll be safe?"

"Socrates took her hands, held them firmly in his. "Two reasons, Ellen. First, this *is* home. Second, with all the trouble in Missouri we've been reading about, I'm not exactly sure where safe might be anymore."

FIVE

"There is a time wherein one man hath
power over another to his hurt."
—Ecclesiastes 8:1 (ASV)

July 21st, 1861, Virginia

IT HAD BEEN A DREARY MARCH FOR THE SECOND REGIMENT, FILLED WITH NEARLY three weeks of disappointment and frustration. The Union army pounded the Confederates back at Germantown and Centerville, bringing great joy to its men. With the enemy armies almost continually in retreat, no one doubted this conflict would soon be over. For days Swift awaited his chance, but rather than stand and fight, the Rebels adopted the lowly tactics of felling trees across the roads. And though the Union won virtually every engagement, the Second had not yet found an opportunity to prove themselves. They always arrived after the enemy was routed, or waited in reserve while enemy cannons trained on them. It was maddening fire, one that tore them up, while they could do nothing in return.

Swift and his friends were more than ready to fight when his sergeant awakened him at two o'clock on this morning. The words of Emmons Taylor charged through his mind:

"We would have you remember that the battle you are fighting is not only for our beloved land, but for all mankind. We would have you remember that you bear with you our hopes, our hearts, our prayers."

Within the hour, the entire regiment started down the road to Richmond. The countryside opening like a morning flower as the sunrise poured its colors over the landscape. It was a beautiful land, covered with low rolling hills of green that slapped like waves against patches of brown and green oak forests; but in a few hours the air grew hot and humid. The column veered from the right side of the road into the woods, where it formed battle lines.

Swift hadn't slept for the past three nights. On the first he feared a night attack, while harassed by accursed mosquitoes that buzzed and whined in his ears incessantly. The second night started the train whistles. Hour after hour they spoiled the still night air, their sounds carrying from far behind the enemy lines. It was most unsettling—the sound of Confederates coming by the thousands—and then the tens of thousands. He was sure there would be a fight today—a big fight.

A steady Boom Boom Boom shook the ground as the artillerymen on the turnpike fired their cannons, spurring the words of the Psalmist:

"The earth shook, the heavens also dropped at the presence of God: even Sinai itself was moved at the presence of God, the God of Israel."

Swift waited in a heavy sweat. On the other side of the turnpike the Union regiments formed into a long line, while others in the woods directly before and below him, fired across the river into Confederate skirmishers. The enemy returned the fire with equal passion. Off to the left, perhaps a quarter mile away, a column of Union soldiers ran across a field, moving into position behind the Confederates on the river. As they approached, he recognized them as the soldiers of General Hunter's column. Too late, the Confederates realized they were being flanked. They stopped firing across the river, turned, and charged across the field at the Union men flanking them. Little puffs of smoke turned into a huge white cloud amidst the popping sounds of a thousand rifles. Hunter's men drove them back only to be attacked again. Swift was elated. The Union boys were claiming new ground.

On the edge of the road behind him, three teams of horses and artillerymen cursed and shouted as they worked a huge cannon through some brush and out onto the road. After several minutes, they managed to get it set up and firing. Heavier and more powerful than the other pieces on the field, it quaked the ground beneath Swift's feet, spurring more words of the Psalmist to mind:

"The Lord thundered in the heavens, and the Highest gave his voice; hail stones and coals of fire."

"Lieutenant Haynes's Parrot rifle," said Dow.
"They call it 'Lincoln's baby-waker,'" said Shanghai.

Swift laughed. It seemed an appropriate name for a twelve foot long, black, rifled iron tube that fired thirty-pound, bullet-shaped shells. Even on two wheels it was a monster to move, but when fired, it issued a terrible sound.

"Forwaaard—march!" shouted the sergeants.

Swift moved in a long line that soon left the cover of the woods. Officers on horseback waved their sabers, urging them forward.

"Double-quick—march!"

The battle line ran at a steady pace, each man maintaining his interval so the line would be unbroken. Metal cups and eating utensils clanged amidst their heavy packs, as they followed to the right along the Union side of Bull Run. The men's skin boiled beneath the prickly wool uniforms.

"Can we drop our packs?" begged Shanghai in a half shout.

One of the officers turned toward the red-faced soldiers, drenched in sweat, and galloped off toward Colonel Peck. The Colonel rode some fifty yards ahead of his men, so eager for battle, he was apparently unaware of their plight. In a minute he'd turned his mount and ordered a halt. Men threw blankets and knapsacks to the ground in a disorderly clump, happy to be relieved of them.

Swift sat on the ground, and crossed his legs. "Thought I was gonna die with all that stuff on my back."

Shanghai nodded.

Swift looked around. "Any chance we'll eat? I'm starved."

Shanghai wrinkled his forehead. "Not when there's a battle to fight. Looky there. I'd love to dive into that river. Hey! Maybe I'll soak my feet after we chase off Johnny Reb."

Swift smiled, eager for his first fight. Sergeant Marsh strode down the line, checking his men. Seeing the rucksack and blankets thrown helter-skelter over the ground, he shouted, "How will you know what belongs to you?"

Packs and blankets were quickly restacked into neat piles along the meadow. One man was chosen to watch over their belongings, while the others formed battle lines again. Within minutes the regiment double-timed to the ford across Bull Run, where they halted beneath the welcome shade of some tall trees. Artillery and small arms fire continued downwind from both sides of the river, as the men moved out of the shelter of the trees.

"Hey, Shanghai," Swift said with a chuckle, "looks like you'll get to soak those sorry feet of yours after all."

"Yep," said Shanghai. "You and me both."

"Roll up your pants!" shouted Marsh.

Swift laid down his musket and rolled his pant legs before entering the cool water. A shower of artillery shells fell in the forest he'd just left, sending a splinter-filled wind that pushed him from behind. The fury of every thunderstorm he'd ever known crashed around him. Fear gripped his heart. He looked around frantically. No cover, nothing to hide behind in the middle of this little river. More shells fell in rapid succession. Their blasts ripped trees to pieces, sent limbs and splinters flying into the water before him. A man screamed in the woods. Had the shell hit the guard they'd left behind? The voices of other men came, crying aloud, shamelessly. Terrified, injured, maybe dying. Goose bumps flew up and down his arms. Another Union Regiment had been caught in those woods. He prayed as he plodded through the cool, rushing water, heart pounding. "Oh! God, please don't let me get caught out here."

The Run's rocks tricked his feet. He nearly turned his ankle twice. Out of the water, a bluff laden with loose sand caved beneath him. He fought to keep his footing. Dodging little scrub-pines, he pressed upward into the bottleneck, pushed hard from behind against the backs of his friends. Moving like cattle in a chute. Legs and feet tangled, sending him onto his left hip and nearly sticking his rifle barrel into the sand. A hand reached out. He took it. Its power delivered him from the web of limbs. Regaining his footing, he smiled faintly at the rugged face of Sergeant Marsh, then plodded up the bank. Some places were so narrow, the regiment could only proceed in single file, causing more men to plow into each other and fall into the sand. But the herd had its own momentum, pushing ever upward. At last they topped the rise amidst a shade of trees that offered momentary relief from the blazing sun. Swift bent over and put his hands on his knees, gasping, pressed forward by those behind.

"Maintain your lines, men!" shouted Lieutenant Vaughn.

"Re-form!" bellowed Marsh.

Swift fell into place. This was no longer a herd. It was an army, an army of Badger men.

A couple of Union soldiers marched past with a Rebel at the end of their rifles. "By God, we're whipping 'em again!" someone shouted.

"Forward!" ordered Lieutenant Vaughn. "Double-quick—march!"

The regiment double-quicked across a grassy plateau, which ran about a hundred yards, then dipped down a hill onto another grassy plateau. Far across that field, several hundred yards away, stood a stately Virginia house, where Federal troops marched toward the sounds of battle. They looked so good, so powerful, so proper that Swift felt like cheering. Then the line of blue men went over the edge and disappeared. His regiment would be next.

As Swift ran across the fields, the earth dropped away, only to rise again in a low, smooth incline. Topping it, he realized he was running along the edge of a hill that rolled down and away to his right, coursing around to the place where the other Federal troops had disappeared. Beyond the Virginia house, he could now see gently rolling hills of green, separated by lush green valleys. The body of a Union colonel, mangled from a cannon explosion, lay in the grass to his left. He turned his head from the gross site, only to see multiple stretchers of men being carried up the hill from the distant battlefields. He counted ten, then fifteen, but they just kept coming, an endless stream flowing uphill—driven away by the force of battle. He spotted General Hunter's men again, fighting in that valley where it opened up on a level with Bull Run. They were firing at the Rebels, now routed and fleeing toward a patch of woods. He prayed as he ran, "Oh. God, don't let us miss the battle again," but then he remembered the sounds of the men crying near the river. "Lord, don't let *that* happen to me."

Swift sensed his line holding its form despite double-quicking for two hundred more yards. He was over the edge of the plateau and feeling the heat of the run, when his eyes first beheld the lower ground ahead. Sacks, blankets, canteens and muskets covered it. Dead bodies lay everywhere, strewn about in a hapless, random order. He hurdled a dead man, then a horse—almost lost his footing when his foot came down on a canteen. The line was now ragged, but still moving forward. His wool uniform scratched and stifled beneath the insufferable heat.

The ground leveled onto a second plateau. He kept running, stopping to rest near a small road that wound by the stately Virginia house.

General McDowell rode by with his staff, oblivious to the ragged skirmish line.

Shanghai grinned through a pool of sweat. "The general looks like he's out on a Sunday ride."

Best nodded, too winded to speak.

Colonel Sherman rode over. He looked thin—almost gaunt—eyes darting wildly. "Well done, boys, we're whipping 'em good."

Those words caused a rush of excitement, and though Swift had yet to fire his musket, at that moment he didn't feel quite so hot and tired. As the colonel rode away, Swift's gaze fell upon several more corpses lying in the grass. The faces seemed frozen in time, locked eternally in immeasurable pain.

He instinctively looked away, but their images followed him, recalling the sounds of screaming men back into his mind. He silently prayed for courage.

As if in answer, the fear left the moment he heard the voice of Sergeant Marsh hollering, "Get rid of anything you won't need in battle."

Swift unloaded what little extraneous equipment he had left. He drained his canteen in lusty gulps before discarding it, then dropped his mess kit, which jangled as it fell. His cartridge boxes and rifle were covered with sand, requiring closer attention. If not clean, they wouldn't work—certain death for an infantryman. He pulled a handkerchief from his pocket and wiped the sand from his rifle. It was loose and came off easily. Satisfied, he brushed off his other equipment and fell back into the skirmish line.

The regiment marched across the road, passing a church, and formed a battle line facing southeast. They had been away from the artillery since crossing the river, but the sounds of cannon fire, rifle fire, and explosions drew ever closer as the men advanced again at a double-quick. A Union regiment from New York, called the Fire Zouaves, came alongside of them. They wore dark baggy pants and bright red jackets. Shredded uniforms and a few bandages evidenced they'd been the ones caught in the woods earlier. The two lines joined like fingers touching at their tips, before running down a long slope amidst the explosions of cannon fire.

A shell whistled so close that Swift felt the wind from it. Its explosion threw up dirt and debris behind him. He picked up speed, thrilling in his freedom from gravity. He was outrunning the explosions. In a short time he reached the cover of a small woods at the bottom of the hill, where he stopped again to catch his breath. Panting, sweating, and glad to be alive, he turned to see Shanghai gasping for air.

"You okay?" asked Swift.

"Huh? I'll be fine just as soon as I get me a shot at those Reb artillery boys. Don't like them hurlin' those cannonballs one bit."

"Me neither. Seems like we're safe here though. At least we can get our breath before killing 'em."

Shanghai laughed.

The Fire Zouaves marched away. Where were they going? The woods here provided a haven from the cannon fire, a welcome shelter from fear. Cannon shells hummed their strange lament, and rifle bullets zinged above the trees, unable to drop into the little knoll. Remarkably, the regiment appeared to be intact. That they had made it this far with negligible losses, made Swift feel light, almost giddy. Yet, at the same time, the tension stabbed, gouging away his confidence. A few men giggled and laughed like bride's maids at a wedding, while others ran out of the cover and back up the hill, amongst the crashing bombs, to fill some canteens in a mud puddle. Voices from the knoll cheered them on, but Swift's voice couldn't join them. This was a madman's world, a circus of clowns amidst a rain of hellish thunder.

A soldier sprinted out of the trees and up the hill. Coward, thought Swift. But the man stopped at an unexploded cannonball, pried it from the ground and rolled it down the hill. He kicked the ball around like a child at play, bringing even more cheers from the men. Swift laughed hard until he noticed some of his comrades being helped back up the hill. They'd been injured, struck by flying debris and shrapnel as they came down. A few bodies lay around patches of broken earth, limbs scattered where cannonballs had exploded, ripping them to pieces. *They'd* not be going home again. More words of Emmons Taylor charged his mind:

"Swear it, soldiers, that our institutions, strengthened by this very trial, shall be established firmer than ever before. *Swear it* that the scorpion secession shall be surrounded with a circle of fire."

At the top of the hill, another regiment formed and marched down it in ranks. Cannonballs exploded all around. A shell blew through the color bearer, leaving a bloody hole where his head had been.

"Holy smokes!" shouted Shanghai.

Instantly, the unit's flag was snatched before it could hit the ground. At the same time, the other men closed ranks and continued without stopping. Swift shouted hurrahs for all he was worth as others joined in the salute.

Colonel Coon rode up on his steed with a banner in his hands and shouted over the explosions, "Follow me!" The regiment sprung to life. Men cheered as they jumped to their feet and marched away in two columns.

Leaving the protective knoll, cannonballs whistled overhead. On the regiment's right, the Fire Zouaves fired and charged up the closest hill. They were met with a hail of bullets that sheared their ranks, followed immediately by a Confederate cavalry charge. Mounted Rebels lanced the Union infantrymen with spears, then hacked them with swords before they could reload. What would it be like to lose an arm? A sudden whack and then nothing—or pain so great one couldn't' bear it? The sounds of men screaming in the woods echoed again. God, he wished he were home. But Swift couldn't think that. Had to get out there and *fight*.

No form of lines remained on the hill as horsemen charged wildly through the ranks. The few remaining Zouaves turned and sprinted for the protection of a patch of trees, with the Confederate cavalry close on their heels. A good number of infantry made it to the shelter, where they reloaded and fired again, cutting down the charging horsemen. The cavalry turned tail and galloped away.

Another New York regiment took its turn to charge the hill as the Wisconsin volunteers moved out. But instead of joining the New Yorkers as Swift had hoped, his regiment marched around and behind them, purposely avoiding the hill. Couldn't two regiments overrun the hill where one could not? They were so near, so close to the fight that he felt like a coward marching away. He looked around confused, hating marching away, hating cowardice, or was he just afraid of *being* one?

The regiment moved along the valley to a place where a little brook flowed. Swift ran with his friends to get a drink. Falling to the ground, he dropped his hands into the stream, then stopped in revulsion. The water ran red, but his head was on fire and his body trapped, caged within this woolen uniform. He looked down the line, watched the other men drinking, put his head down, and cupped up as much as he could drink. The smell was awful. It tasted worse—like the morning taste after a bloody nose in the night. He held his breath as he drank his fill, then moved to the shelter of a fence line where the turnpike crossed a road. Wounded Yankees stumbled down the hill in droves. The cavalry had cut them to pieces just as they had the Fire Zouaves. One man walked with eyes bugged out, his arm neatly sliced off above the elbow.

"Good Lord!" someone shouted, and Swift turned in time to see several horses gallop down the hill, their riders dead, but mounted. Panic gripped him. His bowels cramped into a hard knot. Oh, God, not now. Please not now. He flexed his buttocks, squeezing them together as hard as he could. The sphincter was open, ready to explode, but he wouldn't let it, couldn't let it. Was it the water or the fear? "God," he prayed, "don't let me be afraid." The cramps stopped as quickly as they had begun.

Lieutenant Colonel Peck, wearing a bright red shirt like the fiery red jackets the Zouaves wore, rode up to Colonel Coon and fast exchanged words. It was impossible for Swift to hear what was said over the clamor of the nearby battle, but a moment later, Peck turned to the men and shouted, "This way, men! This way!"

The regiment followed across the turnpike to where a small bank on the side of the road momentarily sheltered them from Rebel fire. As they marched, Swift turned to see the hill they had passed. Another regiment charged at the same place the others had. The sound of rifle fire and artillery explosions intensified. The first line was mowed down halfway up the hill. Swift turned away just in time to avoid stepping on a wounded man. He'd been shot in both arms and the abdomen, and he stared at Swift with a look that showed no sign of awareness or recognition. His shirt was red with blood. He was dying. Perhaps they'd all be dying soon.

All along the road lay dead and wounded soldiers. They had sought shelter here, some to die, others to wait for relief. Men were groaning, crying, talking out of their minds, all the while resting their wounded bodies on those of their dead friends and enemies. Blood ran everywhere. The tension mounted. Fear urged him to run away from this place. He knew it was right. Knew it was wrong.

He tightened his grip on his rifle, fixing his focus on Colonel Peck. The man rode as though he didn't notice the suffering humanity along the ground. Ahead, Union soldiers ran away from the battle in total confusion. Smoke flowed down the hill—blocking his vision—covering everything.

Peck raised his sword. "Right face!"

The column turned right, forming two long battle lines.

Swift stood in the first line. His throat dry—the taste of blood lingering. The Confederates defended this hill with artillery and rifle fire from all sides. Best's regiment merely reinforced a different assault site, and would be the next to attack. No one spoke a word.

An explosion of rifle fire came from the hill above the protected ridge they had just marched through. Riding through a hail of bullets came Colonel Coon.

"Hurray for Colonel Coon!" shouted Charlie.

A few joined him, but Swift and the others just turned and stared through a fog of smoke, straight up the hill to where another regiment withered under intense fire. Unable to stand any longer, the defeated men broke ranks and ran downhill. The Badgers opened ranks and let them through, but the routed soldiers didn't stop to re-form.

"Looks like those boys'll run clear back to Washington," shouted Shanghai.

Swift's eyes narrowed as they ran away. And all the time they hurdled the dead and wounded, Emmons Taylor's words flowed:

"Swear it that the Rattlesnake Flag shall never float above the Red, White, and Blue. *Swear it* that treason shall be swept from the land, though it cost every drop of blood in every Confederate State."

Cowards, he thought. Can't be one. Can't disgrace my family like that. Never. Then he looked at the trail of bloody bodies he'd just passed. An urge to run swept over him. Will I die here? Knock it off! Can't think like that. The musket shook in his hands. He turned to face Sergeant Marsh and stepped back into the skirmish line. Every ounce of energy that had driven him here was now gone, replaced by an emptiness that permeated his entire being. His hands shook, knees weakened. He could die here and now. With that understanding came a curious review of all the things he hadn't said or done, letters he hadn't written. "God, I'm sorry," he whispered, but Emmons Taylor wouldn't stop:

"Swear it, that this rebellion shall call upon the rocks and the mountains to cover it, and that the gates of Hell shall not prevail against our America— *Swear it!"*

A Union general galloped up, face flushed and covered with sweat, gaze moving from man to man. "*Charge* that hill!" he shouted.

Lieutenant Colonel Peck turned to his men. "You heard the general. Charge!"

Swift's company was the second farthest on the left. He squeezed his rifle, stuck out his jaw, and ran up the hill. Adrenaline surged, heightening every sense. He hurdled a wounded man—then another—this one dead. Wounded and dying soldiers lay everywhere. The sun beat down. But the smoke ahead cloaked everything. He charged upward into the smoky madness, leaping over more downed men, rifles, and dead horses. The smoke grew thicker, nearly blinding him until he reached a small plateau where the air cleared. Atop the hill, a line of riflemen took careful aim at him and his friends. Memories of the New Yorkers being mowed down on the other side of the hill flashed through his mind. He hardened his heart. Amidst the firing of rifles came the black hail storm of a thousand bullets from Hell. Fifty-eight caliber shells tore through the air like big black marbles, mimicking the sound of huge bumblebees.

Captain Mansfield walked up and down the line shouting. "Give it to em, boys! Give em Hell! Down with their damned flag!"

Then the shouts of the Rebels on the hilltop above answered. "Kill 'em! Knock 'em down! They's sons of bitches! Give 'em no quahteh!"

Swift moved forward, stopping only to reload and fire, swept along by a mass of men and emotions that had traveled over a thousand miles to fight these Rebels. Bullets whizzed by his head. They no longer affected him as he fired. The fear had left him. He was now gripped by an insane urgency, an overwhelming passion to kill.

Through the smoky haze, the Confederate lines began to break. Some threw down their rifles, while others simply turned and ran. Only a small remnant remained. Victory seemed certain.

A sudden fusillade of fire came from the cornfield on Swift's left flank. He ducked below the shower of bullets, frantically working to reload his musket. The Wisconsin company between him and the cornfield lay decimated in minutes. The rifle fired so hot in his hands he could hardly hold it. His shoulder was badly bruised. But he continued loading and firing, using his handkerchief to pad the rifle barrel. Men fell all around him, crying, cursing, groaning.

Swift lifted his rifle to fire. A bullet tore into his right leg. Time ceased. Fire spread through his groin and left hip, like burning coals. He fell to the ground in what seemed like slow motion, clutching his groin.

Realizing he wasn't dead, he picked his rifle off the bloody ground and fired at the nearest Rebel some thirty yards off. This time he watched to see the man drop his rifle and clutch his head—falling dead. "The Lord rebuke you!" Swift shouted. "*He* is *my* sword and shield."

Lieutenant Hill stood above him, shouting at the top of his voice, "Give it to 'em!"

A bullet ripped through the lieutenant's shoulder, knocking him backward and to the ground. A man turned to help him. Another volley of bullets came from the cornfield, miraculously missing the two. The lieutenant stumbled down the hill as the soldier led him away.

"Yow!" yelped Charlie, grabbing the back of his neck.

Swift turned to see blood flowing over Charlie's hand and out of his mouth. Charlie wavered a little, then turned, weaving as though blind. The first sergeant pulled his hand and led him down the hill through the smoke and bullets, stopping every few feet to step over the dead, the wounded, the discarded rifles and other belongings. Cavalry on black horses burst out of the cornfield and charged the line. Sergeant Marsh hollered above the noise, "Shoot their horses!"

The lead cavalry officer shot Marsh in the mouth, knocking him down hard. But, with no sign of blood anywhere, Marsh pushed himself up from the ground. Growling aloud, he pulled his revolver and shot the Rebel officer straight in the chest. Sarge was unbeatable! Swift turned to see if anyone else had witnessed it, and spotted Shanghai crawling up the hill on his hands and knees, trying to get a better shot at the enemy. A regiment of Union reinforcements charged the cornfield, but mistaking the gray-uniformed Second for the enemy, they unleashed their first rounds of fire into Swift's comrades, causing them to scream, "Friends! Friends! We're your friends." By the time the Union reinforcements realized their mistake, they were charged by the black-horse cavalry, and driven back into what was left of the Wisconsin regiment. Swift reached for a cap at his belt and found none. In desperation he searched the belt of a dead man. It was full. He fumbled with it for a second before getting it on the rifle and firing.

Shanghai worked his way back down to Swift. "You wounded?"

"This is no wound. Just a scratch. Wouldn't be a fight if I didn't get *that.*"

"Come on. I'll take you down the hill."

"No. There's more Rebels. Shoot em!"

Bullets flew everywhere, and Swift grew more and more deaf from the ringing in his ears. He turned to see a bullet explode the box of caps at Shanghai's waist, which flared into a mass of blue and yellow flame. The entire belt fell to the ground with a smoking rip through it. As Shanghai bent sideways to pick up the belt, a bullet whizzed over his head, striking a sergeant behind him in the chest. The sergeant convulsed in a backward spasm, throwing his rifle directly into Shanghai's head, and knocking him out cold.

Swift found himself alone as his regiment pulled back. A sickening shudder swept through him. The remaining Confederates came out of the cornfield, charging after the Union boys. More of Emmons Taylor's words ran through his mind.

"If your *cause* is lost, *all* is lost. The Union is lost—the Constitution is lost—the future with all its radiant glorious prospects are lost. *Liberty* is *lost.*"

Every fiber of Swift's being wanted to stand and fight, but he couldn't. He was exhausted and dehydrated, racked with pain and guilt. He looked around the field, hopelessly searching for someone to carry him to safety. A few feet away, a young Rebel tried to stop his leg from bleeding, while he said over and over, "Mama! Mama! What's become-a-yer little boy? What's become-a-yer little boy?"

Other men were groaning, griping, crying. Some called for Jesus, while others cursed repeatedly. The dead sprawled everywhere. The only ones alive on the field were those who couldn't walk. Some were lying nearly immobile. Others thrashed about wildly from the pain they couldn't stop. The words of the Psalmist played in his head. "The sorrows of death compassed me, and the floods of ungodly men made me afraid." Ungodly men? Why were they calling for Jesus? Men in blue and gray. Men who dropped their rifles, grasping their New Testaments as death clapped its final grip on their mortal flesh.

Everything seemed clouded, as if the air was filled with smoke, but the firing seemed far, far away. He was failing from fatigue, sinking into an abyss, as he felt his face press into the grassy earth. Shanghai Chandler moaned nearby. "Who's got some water? Lordy, it's hot. One of you Rebs must have some water for old Shanghai. Ah! This one's got some."

Was Shanghai really nearby? Was Swift dead?

"Whoa!" shouted that familiar voice. "This ain't water. This here's whiskey! Why, Johnny Reb, I do believe this here canteen is filled with contraband. I'm afraid Corporal Chandler is gonna have to confiscate it."

Swift heard the gurgling sound of someone drinking and knew he wasn't dreaming. With every ounce of energy, he struggled for consciousness, willing his mind to think. This is it, my only chance.

"You were a plucky little soldier, Best."

The realization of being toasted as a fallen comrade stirred something deep within Swift. He summoned the strength to lift his head, just in time to see Shanghai reach out, grab his rifle and stand up. Shanghai steadied himself for a moment by leaning on his rifle. Swift could see him clearly now, though first as three distinct images, then as one. "Don't, leave me, Shanghai."

Shanghai turned fast. "Swift? Geez! Thought you were dead! Here. Let me get you down this hill."

Best felt himself being pulled up, felt the haze cloud his mind again, almost overwhelming him. Then everything became clear. Fully awake and alert again, he focused on the right leg hanging useless beneath him, pants red with blood. The two went down the hill like a very poor entry in a three-legged race at a church picnic, nearly falling over every obstacle. On the other side of the valley was the remainder of his regiment. Something within Swift cheered. The words of the Psalmist returned, bringing new comfort:

"You brought us into the net; you laid burdens on our backs; you let people ride over our heads; we went through fire and through water; yet you have brought us out to a spacious place."

"Rebs must have pulled back," said Shanghai.
"We won after all," said Swift.

The sun was relentless as the duo worked its way back over the dead and wounded.

"Your leg looks pretty bad."

"Nah," Swift muttered. "Just a scratch."

"That's no scratch. Can't put any weight on it. And you've lost a lot of blood."

"No worse than a cut finger."

"A finger! This ain't no cut finger." Shanghai shook his head in an unusual display of serious concern, but Swift said nothing, too busy concentrating on maintaining his balance.

They covered nearly a half mile before reaching the remainder of the regiment. The absence of the Rebels made it appear as though the Union had won. Men were bandaging wounded comrades or helping them away. Others walked around picking up belt buckles and the like, remembrances of their victory. But less than half the regiment was standing.

"I'm gonna set you here and get some water," said Shanghai.

"Fine with me," said Swift. "Can't take another step, and my throat's parched."

Shanghai walked away, while Swift turned to his bloody groin. He was prodding the wound when the most hellish sound ripped the air, like demons shrieking in concert, turning his attention to the hill above. Several regiments of fresh Confederate soldiers charged straight toward him. He glanced back at Shanghai, standing frozen, ten or fifteen yards away. Swift pulled out his pistol and shouted, "I guess I'll live. Shoot 'em!"

SIX

"For with what aim did he insult the gods,
and pry around the dwellings of the moon?"
—Strepsiades

August, 1861, Big Spring, Wisconsin

THE OPPRESSIVE HEAT AND HIGH HUMIDITY WITHIN THE BARN, WORE ON Ed Best. He lifted his straw-laden pitchfork into a small crib, where the milk cows feasted on it at their leisure. It had been a rainy week, leaving the August air so muggy that his skin itched. Sweat dripped in a steady stream from his chin onto his shirt. He hated working in the barn on these kinds of days, but Nels was helping Curge on his farm today, and Pa didn't believe in wasting time no matter what the weather. Why put off 'til tomorrow what you can get done today? That was Pa's motto.

"Come over here and give me a hand," said Pa.

Ed dropped his pitchfork hard, so its prongs stuck into the moist clay floor, then walked across the barn. The smell of hay and mold was so thick that it felt as if he had cotton stuck up his nose. In the shadowy light, he saw his father shoeing their old brown mare. She was a faithful old beast, but never had taken a liking to the idea of someone pounding nails through her hoofs. Her weight shifted anxiously from one leg to another. Ed walked around to face her, put one hand under her long jaw and one hand above her nose, gently stroking backward.

"There, there," he said. "Nothing to get troubled about. Pa's just giving you a new set of shoes. It'll be over in no time."

The sound of hammer on nail stopped, followed by a short silence, then came the digging and scraping noises. Ed knew his father was cleaning and filing the other hoof before shoeing it. Just a few more minutes. Wished Pa would let him take the cows back outside. He was dying in here.

"Pa, when you're finished, can we get these cows outside?"

"Too early. Still dangerous."

"But, Pa."

"Don't give me trouble, Ed. We'll put the cows out when I'm certain the lightning has stopped, and that's all there is to it. Henry Landt lost one of his best milkers this morning. One flash from the sky and that was it. Just like that. I'm not about to lose one of mine. Takes everything we've got to make this farm go, and I'm not taking any chances ."

Ed grumbled under his breath. "Ain't no talking to him once he's got his mind made up."

"What's that?"

"Nothing. Didn't say nothing, Pa."

"Then how come your lips were moving?"

Ed grew silent. Last night brought a display of thunder and lightning like nothing he had ever seen before. Throughout the morning little thunderstorms continued to roll over the countryside, cracking the sky with bright flashes of lightning and deafening claps of thunder. With Henry's prized milking cow as a warning, Ed knew his father's mind was set in stone. In a day or so, the storms would be gone, and he would be able to let them graze freely in the pasture. Until then, he'd just have to tolerate working in here.

The metallic sounds stopped on the other side of the horse, and Pa stood up and smiled. He always did that when he was finished with a job well done. Ed couldn't understand it. Shoeing horses and shoveling manure. What kind of living was that? How could he be happy with dirty hands all calloused? Anybody could do this. Ed was gonna be somebody, not just a farmer, something special, like Swift. Then everyone would know he was a man. Not a baby. Not a kid either. They'd know. Everyone would.

The news from Bull Run flashed through his mind. The Union Army had been whipped, and whipped bad. The picture of the indestructible Light Guard marching through the streets of Portage was so clear. Defeat was impossible. The Union might have been beaten, but not them. No way any Rebels could beat them. They were the best. Swift would come home a hero; and if the war would just hold on a little longer, so would Ed. Soon as he got his chance.

He trimmed the lantern and followed his father out of the barn. A steady, rhythmic squeak and the clopping sound of horse's hooves announced the approach of a wagon. Stepping out under the gray sky, he spotted Doc and Emily riding toward him in their buggy. Strolling across the yard, he smiled. Something was wrong. He knew it the instant he saw his aunt's mournful expression. His smile drained.

"Hello, Tom, Emily. What brings you out in this kind of weather?" Pa sounded like he was trying to be cheerful, but it was obvious he too had noticed something amiss.

Emily started weeping, and Doc's face flattened into wrinkles of grief. Ed felt a shrinking feeling come over him. Several times Doc started to speak, but his words choked off, and nothing came out. Finally, Doc spoke, his words hoarse and soft, carefully measured, like the little scoops of medicine he mixed at his pharmacy. "The list is posted, John. Swift's listed mortal."

Tom's words smashed down like a hammer on steel, harsh and painful. Ed shook his head forcefully. Impossible. The Light Guard was invincible. No one could stop them.

"Doesn't make sense," said Pa. "They were our strongest. Our best. Who could figure them getting whipped—Swift dead?"

"Nothing makes sense any more," said Doc. "I was sure the rebellion would be put down quick. Probably in a month. Maybe two. I thought our boys would send the Rebels packing and come on home in no time. Now—"

The newspapers had glowingly reported victory after victory. The enemy was on the run. The secesh Rebels were being brought to their knees for the preservation of the Union and the freedom of the slaves. Good was conquering evil. It was that simple. But this, this was insane! Yes, it was conceivable that the Union could lose a battle, but not the Light Guard. He'd seen them with his own eyes, marveled at their precision and power. His mouth hung open. Feeling stupid, he closed it.

"Papers say we could've lost two thousand men," said Doc.

Two thousand! Ed tried to imagine that many soldiers in one place, all dead. Couldn't picture it.

"Union Army's fallen back to Washington," said Doc. "Some say the Rebels'll take it soon. I don't know. Everything seems upside down."

Ed quietly vowed, "I'll teach those Rebs something. Just give me the chance."

September, 1861, Daingerfield, Texas

Socrates watched his son Gus stand on his toes as he leaned into the pump-handle for the third time. Cool, clear liquid poured out the spout and into a ten-foot-long, wooden water trough, where several mustangs lapped in thirsty gulps. Ellen's voice sounded from the front of the house. "Socrates, Gus, come see who's here!"

Socrates caught Gus around the waist and carried him into the house. Gus flailed and kicked until Socrates put him down with a loud laugh. Inside the room, Ellen stood beside a handsome young man, hat in hand, with a thick, black mop of hair, and a bemused smile. She leaned forward and looked into Gus's face. "This is your Uncle Ben. Remember him?"

Gus shook his head, studying the visitor with inquisitive blue eyes.

Socrates reached out his right hand and smiled wide. "Ben, good to see you."

Ben took the hand and shook it hard, then bent forward, and looked straight at Gus. "And look at you, Augustus, what are you now, six?"

"Seven," Gus said loudly.

"Sure you are," replied Ben. "And I bet you'll be cutting your eye teeth before long."

"I didn't expect you at all," said Ellen. "Why didn't you write and say you were coming?"

Ben grinned, two holes dimpling deep into his cheeks. "Got your letter. Figured by the time my letter'd get to you, I could be here. Drew my last pay, packed up my horse, and headed out. By the way, I brought you something." He took a dress fabric from behind and presented it. Her eyes lit up, and her smile spread until her entire countenance glowed.

"Ben, you shouldn't have. Must have cost you a month's wages."

His hazel eyes sparkled. "Nah. Mary gave me a good deal."

Ellen's sapphire eyes went wide, then narrowed. She wagged her skinny little index finger. "Mary, is it? Not the grieving widow, Mrs. Colrain? Now how did you find her on your first visit to Daingerfield?"

"Met your sheriff in town. Seemed like a nice fellah. Pointed me to a bath house. When I asked, told me I could find some materials in Mary's shop."

Ellen smiled, leaned back a bit, studying him. "She's nice—but all the ladies seem to think my little brother would make a fine husband."

Ben blushed crimson.

Socrates felt his forehead wrinkle. "Sheriff say anything else?"

"Didn't ask me where I was from, once he knew I'd come to see you. Just dropped a hint I shouldn't hang around town. Said the fever there was contagious."

"That what he called it?" asked Socrates.

"Yeah. Why? What did he mean?"

Socrates shook his head. "Don't know. Maybe Typhoid fever, maybe war fever. There's a whole lot of fever running around here lately."

Ben smiled. "No different than any other place. Whole country's talking crazy."

"Where do you stand?" asked Socrates.

"Don't know. Job is livestock, not politics. Personally I think Jeff Davis bit off more than he can chew. Word around Arkansas is the Rebels whupped the whole Union army at Bull Run. But if that was true, seems to me the war'd be over. I'm afraid they stirred up the hornets' nest. Just haven't gotten stung yet. Time'll tell."

Ellen frowned. "That's enough talk about those things. When are you going to find a girl and settle down?"

Ben blushed. His soft hazel eyes went blank.

Ellen put her hands on her hips and shook her head. Then a smile swept across her face again. "My *little* brother—"

"Come on, Ben," said Socrates. "Sit down and tell us about your trip. Haven't heard one of your stories for a long time."

Ben sat down at the kitchen table, where Ellen quickly set some corn muffins, which he devoured while he spoke. "This here's the best corn bread I've had since leaving Illinois. Didn't have a good cook there. Don't even think he could've cooked peccadillo, not that we had any that far north."

Ellen tilted her head, smile brightening. "So you left because of the cooking?"

"Nah. Work was hard, pay was low, and the foreman woke up on the wrong side of the bed every day. Then the boss's daughter started coming on real sudden like. I'll tell you, leaving that job was easier than rollin' off a hump-back mule."

Ellen smiled. "Was she pretty—like Helen of Troy?"

Ben grinned wide, eyes sparkling emeralds. "Well, she might've had the face to launch a thousand ships, but that girl was the *Whore* of Babylon, plain and simple. No, ma'am, wasn't tastin' no paradise apples with her. The way she threw herself around, could have had the French gout. I steered clear of them boomers." He paused, looked at Ellen who drilled him with hard blue eyes. "Hey!" he said. "I didn't show that girl no interest. Besides, what self-respecting man wants a Gomer for a wife? Ma and Pa raised me better than that."

"What's French gout?" asked Gus.

"Never mind," snapped Ellen. She shook her head at her brother. "Ben, let's not be down on the girls now. I've heard more than a few stories about *wild* cowboys."

Ben laughed. "Probably all true, but only sugar foot stories, I'd guess. Any cowboy dumb enough to spend time around a dance hall hostess, finds out he can't clap and ride a horse at the same time."

"I can," said Gus. "See?" He skipped around the room clapping his hands.

"That'll *do*, Gus," said Ellen. Then, turning back to Ben, "There'll be no more of *that* talk around here! Understood?"

Ben blushed and contracted his neck.

"And how was the rest of your trip?" said Socrates.

"Well. Real strange. Everywhere I went, seemed like people wanted me to take sides, join up for the blue or the gray. It was worse than being caught by hostile Indians in a box Canyon. Felt like an outsider in every town I stopped in, except one—a cozy little town in Missouri. Wasn't but one boardin' house there, and no one seemed to give a hoot about the war. I felt right at home until I started playin' cards with the other boarders." He stopped and scratched himself, twisted in his chair, lowered his voice, and dropped his head real low. "There I was, all set to gamble away the sun by sunrise, when I notice this nice lookin' gent across from me dealin' cards off the bottom of the deck. Before I could say anything, I see this other fellah stuffin' a couple cards up his sleeve. Well. Any fool with a lick of sense could tell this game wasn't worth its candle."

Ellen's eyes widened. "What did you do?"

Ben smiled, lifted his head, and leaned back in the chair. "Well. I turned to this comanchero sitting next to me, to see what he might be doing."

Gus leaned forward, round blue eyes wide. "What was he doing?"

"Oh. Not much," Ben said casually. Then he leaned forward, hazel eyes dancing from Gus to Ellen, and back to Gus again, "'cept playin' with this *big* knife!"

"How big?" asked Gus.

"Shhh!" said Ellen. "Let him tell the story. Go on, Ben. How big was it?"

"Big enough to gut a full-grown cow pony. And that wasn't the worst of it. That's when I noticed every one was packin' shootin' irons—everyone 'cept me that is."

Gus grinned. "Did you go get your gun?"

Ben's eyes went wide. "No, sir! About that time, I felt like Daniel in the Lions den—only difference was, this was more like a den of thieves from the hoot owl trail.

"But you could have taken them. Huh, Uncle Ben?"

Ben smiled a thin-lipped smile, shook his head. "A man's gotta know when to fish and when to cut bait, Gus. Me, I figured it was time to cut bait and run." He leaned back in his chair again. "Anyway, I did just what any self-respecting cowboy would do—excused myself like I needed to relieve myself out back, grabbed my saddlebags from my room, climbed out the window, and rode away."

Socrates frowned. "How much money did you leave on the table?"

"Not enough to get killed over, and that's all that mattered. Anyway, Adam's profession is lookin' better by the day."

Socrates stood and stretched. "Its good to have you here, Ben; and if it's Adam's work you're looking for, you've come to the right place. In fact, Gus and I've got a few chores waiting on us right now. But don't you worry about that. You just take some time and visit with Ellen."

"You sure? I'd be glad to help."

Socrates smiled. "No. It's been awhile since you two had a chance to talk. Relax and kick your feet up. I'll be back shortly."

Socrates pulled Gus out the door, closing it carefully behind them. "Your mama needs some time alone with Uncle Ben. You get over and get some feed in the cow cribs."

Gus's mouth and eyes went wide. "By myself? Thanks, Pa!"

Socrates smiled as he watched his son run off toward the barn. Walking softly around the corner of the house, Socrates leaned against the wall just beside the open kitchen window. Ellen was speaking. "He needs to feed the cattle. Gives him something to do other than making gunpowder, least 'til the harvest comes in."

Ben's sweet tenor voice carried clearly through the window. "Seems *different*."

"He is. Says he talks to God while he works, but I don't think he does. Philosophy. His whole *life* is philosophy. Says cities will never rest from their ills 'til the spirit of philosophy and wisdom are taught to our politicians. Talks about a *New World* government, and building it one by one. You ever heard such a thing? Like these local farm boys could make a difference."

Socrates felt a burning in the back of his head. Thought of Lincoln. He was just a farm boy. Wasn't he making a difference? Socrates leaned harder against the wall.

"I think he's bitter," said Ellen. "They've stopped him from teaching most of their children. Only has three students at the college now."

"Really? Doesn't seem like many," said Ben.

"It isn't, and the way folks are talking around town, he may not have those for long. Wonder if he'd really have come all this way for only three or four students."

Socrates felt an urge to speak out, to step into the window with a barrage of questions, to show them how little they really knew. But he had a creepy feeling, as if he'd been here before, knew what was about to be said, though the words escaped him. The messages of his namesake popped into his mind. "Birth is the process of forgetting." Had he lived this before—in another lifetime? Foolishness. Why would he live it again? Perhaps there was something to learn here—some essential element missed on another journey. A virtue. Something eternal. Could he be losing his mind?

Ben's words came soft and slow. "No one could have predicted this. Not his fault. Not the college's either."

Socrates felt himself exhale.

Ellen gave a loud sigh. "I know. But nothing ever hit him like that before, and I can't help feeling sorry for him. Guess he always threw his frustration into his work. Now he's got nowhere to go with it. There's been other things, too, people pressing him to take one side or the other. Even the sheriff stopped by for a talk."

Socrates' neck tightened. He'd been wondering what she'd heard.

"He wanted him to take sides?" asked Ben.

"I'm not sure. Talked about Moderators, Regulators, lambs. Couldn't make sense out of it. Don't think Socrates could either."

Socrates wondered what her expression might be like. Concern? Anger? He listened closely.

"Socrates doesn't want to kill anyone. And I don't want him to, either. This must be terrible for him. What are we going to do, Ben?"

A repulsive knot formed in Socrates' stomach as he realized she *pitied* him. Pitied him!

"You still have land and timber."

"Yes. But timber does no good without extra hands, and all the young men around here want to join the army. I'm worried—really worried. We're expecting another baby."

Ben laughed. "No kidding? Well. Congratulations."

Chair legs scraped the kitchen floor, followed by floorboards squeaking with the movement inside, as Ben's tenor voice spoke again. "Looks like I've come at just the right time."

Socrates stared ahead. Why hadn't she told him? This was his child, too. His stomach was one big knot.

Ellen's was now the soft, innocent voice of a little girl. "Ben?"

"Yes?"

"Talk to Socrates. He won't go to church with me anymore. Won't forgive his father, either."

"Don't know what good I'd be there, Ellen."

Socrates felt nauseated.

"Talk to him, Ben. Tell him what it was like for you when Papa died."

"I *could* do that, Ellen. I miss Pa a lot."

Ellen started to cry. "I wish," she said between sobs, "we could go back to Wisconsin. Go back and start all over."

Socrates hands formed into hard fists.

"Ellen, you sure? Those were some mighty tough winters."

Ellen's voice became desperate. "Yes. I'm sure. Socrates is never going to have peace. He's got to go back and mend fences with his father. I'm sure of it. If we sell everything we own here, and buy a nice farm in Wisconsin, we'll be a real family again."

"Sounds kind of good."

"Yes, it does," said Ellen, her voice a little lighter. "That's why *you're* gonna help me change his mind."

Mid September, 1861, Richmond, Virginia

Swift lay upon his bed, holding a golden medallion before his eyes. The wicked dragon stood physically defeated—pierced by George's long lance. Yet, somehow its visage seemed impudent—its face frozen in the same defiant grin Swift had witnessed on a hundred battlefield corpses. He turned it around, all the time thinking, praying, and thinking in an endless litany. The words of the Psalmist poured from his heart:

"Save me, O God; for the waters come in unto my soul. I sink in deep mire, where there is no standing: I am come into deep waters, where the floods overflow me. I am weary of my crying: my throat is dried: mine eyes fail while I wait for my God."

An elderly officer, dressed in a blood-stained gray uniform of the Portage Light Guard, walked through the doorway and across the second floor of the old brick factory toward Swift. Cots stretched out along the long walls on opposite sides of the wide brick room. Tall windows reached above the brick sills to a height of six or seven feet, allowing plenty of light to illuminate the little factory-turned-hospital. The officer somehow looked a little older today. "I'm glad to see you're feeling better, Swift. Was starting to worry about you."

Swift had experienced some bad times with his wounds. The bullet went through his left thigh, shattering the head of his femur, exiting his lower groin and entering his right thigh, from which it had been removed. Unfortunately, the left thigh bone was so badly fractured, it could not yet bear weight. But all those pains combined couldn't match the one in his soul. He forced a smile at the man who had become like a father to him, recalling the raging fever those wounds had wrought, remembering the doctor's poultices and cold compresses.

"I'm getting a little stronger."

"Are you, Swift? You cooperate with treatment all right. But is your *heart* in your recovery?"

Swift looked away. How could he tell this man the questions in his mind. God had abandoned him. Or had *he* failed God? Was he guilty of some secret sin, like Achan, who once brought disaster upon the Israelites? Swift hadn't visited the bordellos in Washington, like many of the other men, but he had listened closely to their stories. And though feigning disinterest, he *had* been interested—*had* listened closely—*had* been strangely aroused. Such hypocrisy could easily have brought defeat upon his friends.

It was not that the sins of others couldn't have made a difference, but that he had *known* better, and Scripture was clear that to him who has been given much, much more shall be expected. He had been instructed in the faith from childhood, understood the biblical concept of destiny, yet still had failed to diligently guard his heart. To compound matters, he was desperate for word from home, but no news came. There was nothing to lift his spirits or lighten his load, only the long, course cedar boards across the ceiling, the red brick walls, and those filthy windows. Hour after hour they stood, never changing, something like the thoughts in his head that ran over and over like a big water-wheel, goaded perpetually by the power of thinking. Why didn't his family write?

The doctor knelt beside the bed and put his hand on Swift's arm. "I'm afraid I have some bad news. The Confederacy has arranged an exchange of prisoners. They're sending me home tomorrow."

Swift felt a sudden surge of hope. "That's not bad. It's great! Hey! Will you take a letter home for me if I write one quick? I've sent several, but haven't heard anything. Don't even know if they know I'm alive."

"I'd be honored, Swift."

Swift pushed himself into a sitting position, while everyone who was able walked over to congratulate Dr. Lewis. As they did, Swift grabbed one of the two crude sticks he used to get around with, and moved to the head of his bed. He scribbled a quick note, and pushed it into the hand of the doctor, who received it without interrupting his conversation with the others.

"To think you're going home," said one of the men. "I can hardly wait 'til I see my folks."

A reflex spasm rippled across the doctor's gaunt face. "I shouldn't be leaving you. There's so much more to be done."

Swift pushed his jaw forward. "Yes. You should. Your leaving doesn't make us sad. Gives us all hope. Maybe we'll go home soon. Besides, you've done so much for us. You deserve to go home. Shoot! Lord knows I would if I had the chance." The others nodded.

"But I promised everyone I'd look after you boys."

Swift frowned. "And you have, Doctor. You could've left us like everyone else, when the Confederates routed our army. Why, I heard you disobeyed a direct command."

"I cursed those orders! To leave you boys in the condition you were in would have been the same as killing you. I could have no part in such a cowardly act."

"See what I mean?" said Swift.

"Anyone would've done the same."

"Anyone? Look around, Doctor. Where are they? They all followed orders to save their sorry butts. You're the only one who stayed. Amputating arms and legs. Plugging wounds. You wouldn't leave us. Even the Confederate officers respect you."

"That's because I happened to be treating one of theirs when they came in."

"No," said another prisoner. "I've heard them talk about you. They admire you."

The doctor looked about the room. "There's so much to do. I feel remiss in my duties, leaving you here without a proper physician."

"We'll be all right," said Swift. "Go home and tell our families that we're alive and well. And when you do, don't forget to tell 'em you saved our lives."

The doctor's hands went up. "I could never take credit for that. We're all in the Lord's hands. Whatever good I may have done has been by his grace. Besides, if I took credit for saving your lives, what would I do with the memories of all those boys who died? That's too great a burden for any man. I'm just a soldier doing my job, just like you."

One of the men stepped onto Swift's bed and shouted, "Three cheers for Doctor Lewis! Hip, hip, hurrah! Hip, hip, hurrah! Hip, hip, hurrah!" Swift felt his spirit soar, but somehow couldn't cheer, despite his gratitude. Without the physician's dedication they would probably all be buried somewhere along the Bull Run. But why had they lost? Was it the sin of one, or many?

Ed Best sat at the dinner table, Nels at his right, his father at the head on his left. A loud crash sounded in the kitchen. It was the second plate Ma had dropped and broken while making dinner tonight. "Haven't seen her *this* upset since we lost little Rosewood," Pa whispered, "and that was *clear* back in '48."

Ed didn't know whether to nod or not, so he did nothing. He kept glancing at Nels, who wasn't giving him any cues. Everyone at this table already knew when four-year-old Rosewood died. That was the year before they had come to Wisconsin, so Pa was probably trying to smooth things over. Problem was, it just made Ed feel worse than he already did. Ma came in carrying a porcelain bowl that clunked as she set it down hard on the table. Her hands now fumbled, shaking as she dished out boiled green beans. The steady ticking of the mantle clock seemed loud, only occasionally drowned out by the sound of her shoes knocking on the hardwood floor.

"Glory be," said Pa. "We've got three Bests to help old Honest Abe. Shouldn't be long before this war'll be over."

"Maybe so. Maybe not," Sarah replied coldly.

John cocked his head sideways, smiling at her. "Come on, girl. Our boys are going to fight. Have to stand behind them."

Sarah frowned, her gray eyes fixed on the food she was serving. "Maybe so. But it doesn't mean I have to like it, does it?"

John shook his head. "Well, no. But—"

Sarah stomped her foot on the hardwood floor. "That's enough, John, and I don't want to hear any more about it. Can't stop thinking about Swift, killed in battle, his body left out east. Hasn't even had a decent burial." Her voice trembled and her hands shook.

A knock came at the door, followed by the creak of it opening. Ed started to get up, being the closest. Who would let himself in like that, he wondered?

Doc, dressed formally in a black dinner jacket and top hat, entered. His dark eyes sparkled as he said, "Sorry to barge in on you, John, Sarah, but I just heard the most magnificent news. Drove my buggy all the way here to bring it to you." He smiled wide. "Swift is alive!"

Everyone sat in stunned silence. Sarah lifted her apron to her mouth, and took a deep breath. The boys looked at each other. "I knew it," said Ed. "Ain't a Reb alive could take down cousin Swift!"

"That's right!" said Nels. "Hasn't been one born yet."

John's cool-blue eyes were wide. "Why that's wonderful, Tom. But how—or what?"

"I just received a letter from Richmond, Virginia. Dr. Lewis, the surgeon for Swift's unit, brought it to me. Apparently when the Rebels overran Bull Run, he wouldn't leave his wounded. Took him prisoner, and he's been tending our boys since. Was just exchanged last week. Here, read it."

John Best took the wrinkled paper from his brother's hand and read it aloud:

"Dear parents:

By the kindness of one of our attending surgeons, who is about to return to New York, I am permitted to send a few lines. I am at the Richmond Prison Hospital, where I have been for something over six weeks. I was wounded through both legs, shattering the bone of the left leg, but I am getting along fine. I can walk around a little now, with the aid of a couple sticks. I have had my health all the while, and so long as I do, I can get along well enough. I wrote you a few lines soon after I arrived here, but do not know whether you received them or not, as a letter from here has to pass through a great many hands. I do not know what disposal will be made of us, or when you will hear from me again; all I fear is diarrhea. The weather is cooler here than it was, and I like it all the better, although it never has been excessively hot since I have been here. Give my best respects to all my friends and do not be under any unnecessary anxiety on my account.

Swift.

P.S. Tell Mr. Chrystie that his nephew, John Chrystie, is dead."

Ed's heart swelled as his father read the letter. The boy once lost now was found. It was just like a Bible story.

"Dr. Lewis," Tom continued happily, "says Swift may soon be home once a prisoner exchange can be arranged. He's petitioned them to give his case priority, but isn't sure they will."

Everyone was talking excitedly when Sarah burst out sobbing. She took in a rush of air, making a terrible Eeeeh sound, then sobbed again, her chest heaving. Pa put his arm around her, but she pushed him away, stormed out of the dining room and up the stairs to their bedroom. Everyone heard the door slam shut, followed by the sound of unrestrained sobbing, which reverberated throughout the house. John turned meekly toward his brother, who looked about anxiously.

"It's all right, Tom, we're delighted with your news. God has brought your son through the valley of the shadow of death, even beyond our hoping. Such a thing is a miracle, and we give thanks with you. Nels and Ed are going with Sol the end of this week. We'd appreciate your prayers."

Tom grasped his brother's hand. "And you will have them. I know what Emily and I have gone through these past months. We will not forget to make earnest supplication for you and your boys."

Nels and Ed looked sheepishly at their father as they listened to their mother continuing in her tears upstairs. Ed felt as if his heart had been dropped on the floor and stepped on. "Sorry, Pa. If we'd known we were gonna hurt Ma, we never would've signed up. Maybe we can go to Milwaukee, ask the sergeant to take our names off the list." No sooner had he said those words, than he wished he hadn't.

"That's big of you, Ed, but I'm afraid it wouldn't make much difference. They'd just draft you and you'd still have to go. This is a difficult time for everyone. Your mother'll work through her feelings. Then she'll support you, just as sure as she has everyone else who's answered the President's call. Just give her time."

The boys nodded, then started eating again. Ed was sure of it now. No rebels could ever stop him. The sound of his mother's sobbing grated his conscience. Why did she always have to go and ruin everything?

Early December, 1861, Daingerfield, Texas

The winter wind whistled through building breaks, kicking up sand and dust into Socrates' chapped face and stinging his sore eyes. It was a chilly wind for Texas, but nothing compared to the sub-zero temperatures of Wisconsin that could frostbite one's fingers with the slightest wind. Seemed ridiculous to be cold here, but he was acclimated to the warmer temperatures of Texas and more susceptible to its sudden drops, which sometimes could be as much as thirty degrees in one day. Holding two letters tightly in one hand, so they wouldn't blow away, he hastily worked the latch and entered the supply store.

John Miller, the tall, skinny, dark-haired storekeeper, stood behind the counter. His entire family had died here, leaving John like a ship without a rudder until his father's brother moved to the Red River area from Germany. The sudden presence of family brought him great joy for a time. But ever since the vote for secession, he was obviously unsettled, anxious, never offering more than a thin, nervous smile. "Help you, Socrates?"

Socrates rubbed his hands together. Two white-haired men were in the store. Socrates blew heartily into the center of a circle he made by cuffing his fingers. "Whooo! That wind chaffs."

Miller nodded, anxious eyes widening. "Winter can be darn right cold."

Socrates shook his head. "No one warned me it'd be like this. Never would've moved this far if I hadn't figured it'd get me away from the cold. Guess you could say it's my Achilles heel. Anyway, didn't come to complain about the weather. Need more potassium nitrate and sulfur. They in yet?"

"Yeah. Came yesterday." Turning around to the shelves along the wall, Miller reached down and pulled out a large, heavy canister, and handed it to Socrates. Then he reached down and pulled up two slightly smaller ones, placing them gently on the counter. "You'll need a hand with this. Should I get someone to help?"

"No. Ben's in town. I'll have him pick up those two before he comes home. Thanks for asking."

The two old men went out the front door, and Miller watched them move away through the window before turning back to Socrates. "My countrymen want me to tell you cousin Jacob is coming. There will be another Union meeting Friday."

Socrates wagged his finger. "Got to stop saying that, John. Sounds like being German is more important than being American. Gives folks a big reason to hate you."

"These *are* my countrymen! Came from the land of my father. And now they've come to live here, where I was born. They are twice my countrymen."

Socrates stiffened, felt his stomach contract. "I told you, I'm *not* getting involved."

Miller's face glowed with astonishment. "But you must. You're from the North."

"Which gives these people one more reason to hang me!" Socrates felt blood rush to his face, wanted to holler at the top of his voice and tell this fellow to leave him alone. Thought, "Let us consider the problem together," realized it was useless with Miller. Socrates took a deep breath and slowly let it out. "Look. I told you. Too many people know already."

"But we need someone like you, someone who can write and speak well." Miller's face grew hard, angry. "My uncle's family came to this country for religious freedom. They want to be part of America, not part of a rebellion."

Socrates took a deep breath and sighed. "A hundred years ago, that's all America was—a rebellion. Celebrate it every Fourth of July." He paused, chewed his lower lip, slowly shook his head. "Now we've got a rebellion from the rebellion, from which your friends want to rebel." He spread his hands wide, raised his eyebrows and smiled again. "Now why doesn't that surprise me?"

Miller frowned. "But we don't want to have anything to do with *this* rebellion!"

Socrates lifted the canister and started toward the door. "And I don't want to have anything to do with either one."

Miller hurried to open it, eyes pleading. "Would you reconsider?"

The cold air whipped in, chilling them instantly. Socrates turned, looked him in the eyes, and stepped back into the store. As Miller closed the door, Socrates put the cans back on the counter. "Look, friend. I've got four good reasons." He lifted his hand and counted off his fingers. "First, I've got two young boys. Second, my wife is pregnant. Third, my school is about shut down. Fourth, there's a shortage of hands to work my farm. By my figuring, that's enough trouble for one year, so I've done all the considering I'm going to do."

Miller dropped his head, then lifted his thin sad face. Socrates hated to see the man's disappointment, but no more than he hated the people pulling at him, as if he were a tug-of-war cord.

Miller's nervous eyes brightened. "Oh. Almost forgot, there may be trouble getting more gunpowder supplies."

Socrates narrowed his eyes. "Says who?"

"My supplier. Course, charcoal's never a problem, but sulfur and potassium nitrate are in high demand. If the blockade keeps up, could get darn near impossible. Thought you should know."

Socrates nodded. He quietly picked up his supplies and stepped out into the cold air again, where he headed for Mary's store to find Ben. If John's supplier ran out of powder, he and Ben could both be impressed into the Confederate Army. Socrates made up his mind that he'd return to Wisconsin before that. Wasn't a pleasant thought, giving up everything he owned and returning to face his father's rejection, but recently word had come that his

111

cousin Swift was a prisoner, and that three of Socrates' brothers had joined the Union Army. He wasn't the type to carry a rifle or handgun, and couldn't imagine killing anyone, but the prospect of fighting his own family was absurd.

After crossing the street, he stepped onto the plank sidewalk and entered Mary's store. Ben was there, standing on a chair, holding a long velvet dress along his front. Mary knelt before him with a mouth full of silver pins, working steadily along the lower hem. The picture reminded Socrates of his namesake's words in the *Republic*:

"He may pray, and intrigue, and supplicate . . . endure a slavery worse than that of any slave—in any other case, friends and enemies would be equally ready to prevent him, but now there is no friend who will be ashamed—such is the entire liberty which gods and man allow the lover."

Socrates had all he could do to keep from laughing, but Ben didn't even notice. He was telling another one of his tall tales. "I'll tell you, Mary. After escaping by the skin of my teeth from those Missouri boys, and then breakin' all them wild horses, I figured it might be a good idea to ride with someone I could trust. That's when I met Crazy Charlie. Indian who had so many wrinkles, he was the spittin' image of Father Time. Nobody could figure out how old he was. Well, I'll tell you, he had a way with horses like nothing I've ever seen—claimed he could outride old Slewfoot himself—a wager *I* wasn't about to take. Well! One day we stopped at a farm just north of the Texarkana border—"

"You buying a dress for yourself?" asked Socrates, eyeing him from head to foot.

Ben turned a sour face. "Thanks a bunch! My story was just gettin' good. And why do you have to go and say a thing like that? I already feel like I'm on the wrong end of the horse here."

Socrates kept looking him over, grinning wide.

"Look. I'm havin' this made special for Ellen's Christmas present, but don't you breathe a word of it to her."

The shiny red fabric changed shades as it caught the light at different angles. Ben's consideration toward his sister caused Socrates to swallow hard. He was generally so wrapped up in his work that he often forgot his wife's and children's birthdays, and had yet to give Christmas presents a thought. Fortunately, Ellen was a mate who didn't put as much stock in those qualities as his willingness to work hard and provide for his family. Even so, having Ben around could sure make Socrates look bad.

The door opened and three men dressed in gray uniforms came in. Buck Malneck, Billy Morris, and their big fat friend were apparently home for Christmas. A shiver rose up Socrates' spine.

Buck strutted over to the counter, leaned on an elbow, and tipped his hat backward. "Well! Heard the schoolteacher had kin in town. Look at this pretty Yankee. Don't he look right fine when he's put on a nice velvet dress?" A round of laughter came from his friends, but Socrates and Ben feigned equal amusement. Malneck frowned. "What's the matter, Yank, don't you have anything better to do than dress-makin'? We've got plenty of work killin' Yankees. Maybe you should join us."

Socrates kept smiling. "Haven't you heard? Ben and I've been busy making powder so you boys won't run out. In fact that's what I came over here for, to tell Ben we've got to get back to work." Socrates picked up the wooden keg and started toward the door, then stopped and turned to face Ben, adding, "There's two more canisters over at the supply store. I need you to pick 'em up and bring 'em over to the house right away."

Ben nodded and turned to Mary. "Sorry. If you'd like, I'd be glad to come over after dinner."

"Why, Ben, I'd be pleased if you would."

Hatred shot from Buck's beady eyes like sparks from a blacksmith's hammer.

Socrates quietly put down his canisters, pulled the red velvet fabric off Ben, seized the canisters, and nearly dragged him out the door.

But the icy chill in the street did little to cool Ben. "Hey! What're you doin'? Ya darn near wrecked everything. I paid good money for that stuff."

"We've got a bigger problem than that."

"Yeah?" said Ben. "Like what?"

"Is Mary coming to our house for Christmas dinner?"

"You said it was okay to ask."

Socrates leaned into Ben's face. "*Is* she coming?"

"Yeah."

Socrates shook his head. "This is really going to muck things up."

"Socrates!" Ben yelled, his hazel eyes growing large. "You *told* me it was okay."

Socrates kept shaking his head. "Maybe. Before I knew Buck was sweet on her."

Ben put his hands on his hips and rolled his eyes. "It's a free world, Socrates."

"Yeah? Well, that won't mean a thing if we're *both* dead."

Ben threw out his hands, rolled his eyes again. "They can't do nothin' to me for askin' a girl to dinner. That's what the law's for."

Socrates tightened the muscles in his jaw. "You're wrong, Ben—for two reasons. First, these boys can kill both you and me, and be back fighting in Arkansas tomorrow. No one will touch them there. And even if they could, it wouldn't do *us* any good." Socrates looked away, bit his lower lip, turned and looked Ben in the eyes. "Second, you know what some'd say? They'd say: 'Good! Now there's two less Yankees to kill.'"

Ben stood quiet, his head shaking slightly, face unbelieving.

"Look, Ben. This isn't Illinois. Those men find out you're sweet on Mary, or Mary is sweet on you, the only thing they're going to care about is some Yankee taking their women. Let's get those supplies and get on home. Last thing I need today is a lynch mob."

SEVEN

"Justice is the advantage of the stronger."
—Thrasymachus

March, 1862, Daingerfield, Texas

SOCRATES WATCHED BEN SADDLE THE COAL-BLACK MARE HE HAD CAUGHT earlier that week. Wild and unbroken, the mustang clearly didn't like being tamed. Every day Ben bridled and saddled her, then watched her buck and kick over every piece of dirt in the little corral. When she grew tired, he walked coolly alongside her, giving just enough rein to sense some freedom. And all the time she bucked, he walked, spurs a-jingling, sweet-talking the animal as if she were his girlfriend. Whenever the horse settled down, he reeled her in until she took off again, then repeated the process with composed persistence. This was his second time today, and announcing that she was "plum-tuckered and ready for a whirl," he mounted her, hanging tight on every jump, bouncing free of her when she hit her peak, then walking and smooth-talking her again. Before another hour was up, he rode her around that corral as if he'd owned her all his life. "Incredible," said Socrates. "Like watching an artist—an artist with the patience of Job."

Ben grinned back, two deep cavities dimpling his richly tanned cheeks.

Socrates scratched his thinning brown hair. Ben's rich, thick black hair swayed lightly in the breeze, complementing his black shirt with its double row of buttons. He was always neat and sharply dressed, but that wasn't what dazzled Socrates so. It was the way the boy rode a horse, not bouncing around like most men, but gliding over the saddle as if he were suspended in the atmosphere, back straight, elbows in. Sometimes seemed more like he was a cloud in the sky than a man on horseback. Just the site of him made Socrates want to ride, so he saddled his horse and the two took off together, galloping around the field, then racing for the high ground. It was great fun, feeling the warm spring air whipping across his face, but Socrates' mount was no match for either Ben's riding skills or his young mustang. They'd nearly reached the bluff at the back of his land when Socrates pulled up to catch his wind. Within a couple of minutes, Ben came riding back, the deep-dimpled smile of triumph on his face. "Wanna race to the timbers?"

"No," said Socrates with a frown. "That horse of yours is something."

Ben wrinkled his forehead and raised his reins. "Better than goin' by Longshank's mare. Come on. This girl's just startin' to feel her oats. 'Fraid you'll lose again? Take a head start."

"It's not that. Snakes'll be out there, sunning themselves. Love to warm up outside the woods before they get something to eat. It's a spring ritual for them."

Ben sneered. "I'm not afraid of vipers."

"These aren't like any snakes you've ever seen."

Ben wrinkled up his face. "Don't tell me—even the serpents are bigger in Texas."

Socrates shook his head, smiled a thin-lipped smile. "Must be better than a half-dozen poisonous snakes here. Why, there's even a pygmy rattler."

"Pygmies? I thought pygmies were in Africa!"

"Not these. Home-grown right here in Texas." He leaned forward, pointed his finger at Ben. "And I'll tell you, some of the little snakes'll kill you faster than the big ones. You know that scarlet-colored King Snake?"

Ben nodded. "Red with black and yellow bands. Purty as an Indian bracelet."

"Yeah. We've got one here looks exactly like it, but they call it a Coral Snake. Only way you can tell them apart is the order of the bands. Red bands touch yellow, it's Coral, not King."

Ben shook his head. "Told you I'm not scared of vipers."

Socrates shook his finger hard. "You better be. Coral's can grow to a yard or so, but even a little one's bite can kill you inside of an hour."

Ben's hazel eyes mushroomed. "An hour?"

Socrates nodded.

"Alligators, scorpions, poisonous snakes. Shoot, Socrates. What kind of place you got here?"

"A good one. Look at all the land. Ninety percent of it's unclaimed." Socrates surveyed the stands of tall hickories and shorter oaks. "Where else in America can a man guard a title that was rich before, build refined gold, paint the lily, cast perfume on the violet?" Ben rolled his eyes, but Socrates smiled. "Look," he said, pointing to the trees. "This is a land of plenty. Black hickory.

Water Hickory. Bitter Hickory. There's even Swamp Hickory." He smiled wide. "But you know what my favorite is?"

Ben took a deep breath, sighed. "Peeeecans."

"Mm. Mm. Baked in a sugar pie—that's the best."

Ben perked up in his saddle, laughing. "Sure," he said with a sparkle in his eye. "If some red-yellow baby Coral snake don't bite you before ya eat it. Personally, I'd take a finger full of frost bite and an antler in the butt over a behind full of red venom any day."

"Thought you weren't afraid of vipers," Socrates said with a grin. Then he quietly turned his mount toward home, secretly wondering how his brother-in-law had managed to turn a friendly warning about snakes into another reason for moving back north. The two rode home in silence, and Socrates was just pulling the corral gate closed, when Ellen's voice called frantically from the back of the house. "Socrates! Hurry. Gusty's been bit." She waived her hand and disappeared back into the house.

The first thing Socrates saw inside was Gus sitting on the end of the kitchen table with his pants leg pulled up to his knee. The lower leg was hardly bleeding, though the area around several deep, purple puncture wounds was swelling fast. Ellen washed the wounds with a cool damp cloth, her soft, compassionate eyes glowing like sapphires.

"It was a dog, Pa," Gus said through a torrent of tears. "A big, ugly dog."

"Where at?" snapped Socrates.

"Down by the gully. Jumped right out and bit me."

Socrates eyed him accusingly. Ellen's eyes silently implored. The image sparked a memory, his father yelling, shaking a thick, knobby finger, his mother's tear-filled eyes pleading mercy. And he remembered telling himself he would never be like that. Now he lifted his finger, pointed it at Gus. "What were you doing there?"

"Thought I saw something in the trees, Pa. Just wanted to see what it was." Gus had a strained, tearful look as he stared into his father. "There's a man," he said.

"What man? Doing what?"

"Hanging."

"Hanging what?

"Just hanging!" cried Gus. "Dead."

Socrates felt himself implode. Fifteen minutes later, he and Ben rode up the gully to a place where a black and gray-haired dog came out of the bushes, teeth bared, growling and barking viciously. Socrates pulled his shotgun across the saddle and squeezed the trigger in one smooth motion. The ten gauge buckshot nearly took the dog's head off as it blew the animal straight off its feet and back into the bushes. The blast also sent Ben's mustang bucking again, but in a minute he had it under control. "Damn, Socrates," he shouted "I wish you'd warn me when you're gonna do somethin' like that."

Socrates climbed down and went over to the dead dog. He pulled its mouth open wide. "Doesn't look like rabies."

"I know," said Ben. "Looks like he was guarding his master."

Socrates followed Ben's gaze farther up the trail. A man dangled from a fifty-foot Post Oak in the center of a small clearing on the edge of the gully, barely outside the forest canopy. He was bug-eyed, blue tongue hanging out, feet just above the ground. But even at thirty yards, Socrates recognized the bald-headed Gustaff. "Let's cut him down. Get him into town."

Ben kept staring at the hanging figure, as if the face might tell him something. "This fellah must have tried to hornswoggle the wrong folks."

Socrates rode over to the tree. "Met him once," he said, then grunted as he cut the rope. The stiffened body fell with a thud. "One of the leaders of the Union League I told you about."

Ben dismounted, his hazel eyes quizzical, face unbelieving. "You *know* I don't curry any man's favor, Socrates, but I don't fancy the man who did *this* disliking me."

Socrates lifted his head to look straight into Ben's eyes. "This is no coincidence, him hanging on my land. We may have to leave for a time."

Ben's eyes swelled, as he clenched Socrates' arm. "But what about Mary?"

Socrates turned an angry face. "Forget Mary. Pray this war gets over."

Ben shook his head. "Mary—she's my Helen of Troy."

Socrates' face softened. "I know Ben, but can you hold off for a while, 'til this war is over?"

Ben nodded.

"Good," said Socrates. The two hoisted the corpse over Socrates' saddle. He turned and looked into Ben's eyes again. "See? This is why I don't want to ever kill anyone. Once the killing starts, God only knows when it'll stop." Socrates stared off into the Daingerfield Mountains. "After we take Gustaf to the house, I'll get the sheriff."

April, 1862, Portage, Wisconsin

Swift anxiously checked his pocket watch for the ninth time since leaving Madison. Its dial said five after one, and the train was supposed to arrive at

118

one o'clock sharp. The knot in his stomach pushed acid into his throat, and he wished for some way to make this train go faster. A sudden tremor jolted the car, as it began slowing, pulling into his final destination. He imagined his mother's face contorting with nervousness, his father gently reassuring her. They would be at the first car, and he was at the last, but such things no longer mattered.

By the time the locomotive stopped, he was already on the steps. Thrusting out his crutches, he pulled himself over them and started down the long wooden platform at Portage station. A blast of steam wafted over him, and he found himself at the bottom of a long hill, rifle in hand, wounded and dead men on the ground all around him. His knees shook. The air cleared and he saw his friends and family.

It looked as though every family his father had treated from the area was there. Father and mother walked briskly toward him. His knees stopped shaking. The words of the Psalmist swept through his mind:

"He delivered me from my strong enemy, and from them which hated me: for they were too strong for me."

A small band played *The Star Spangled Banner*. Excitement surged his chest, urging him forward. His left crutch caught between the planks, sending him sprawling onto his chest. The music stopped. Fire shot through his hip. The riders were coming, charging out of the corn field. He must have his rifle. His arms lurched for it, but it was beyond his reach. Strong hands pulled at him, jerking him up and around. A face appeared, like the soft, whiskered image of his father. Swift turned for his rifle, but it was not there, only a crutch, which a lady in a dark-blue bonnet was lifting. As she turned with it, her countenance glowed, though her chestnut-brown eyes filled with tears. "Ma?"

"It's all right," came the sweet soprano voice. "We'll help you."

Swift felt himself pulled erect, crutches appearing beneath his arms. Knees throbbed, stiff and swollen from the scurvy, now freshly bruised. Hands and armpits dripped with sweat. The band stood in tight formation, its silence a haunting specter. Swift tried to smile, remembered the gap where a tooth had recently fallen out. Thought of his gaunt frame, swollen ankles. His father's face was ashen, as if asking, "Is *this* our boy?"

His mother's lips brushed his cheek, planting a firm kiss. "Looks like I've got some cooking to do, if we're going to get some beef back on you. Flap jacks and your uncle's maple syrup. That'll get those cheeks out where they belong. Welcome home, Swift." She hugged him, while his father patted him on the back.

John and Sarah Best slowly approached with the Ramseys, eyes darting between Doc and Emily. The rest of the people remained at a distance, some open-mouthed. Doc's arm slipped under Swift's, pulling him rapidly toward the family carriage. Meanwhile the band stood silent. Folks began wandering off. Others stood around, hands in pockets or on hips, too self-conscious to give the welcome home they'd brought.

Doc and Uncle John helped Swift into the family buggy. Just as it was about to pull away, the soft round face of Bitsy Hyde appeared alongside it. "Welcome home, Swift."

Swift looked at the gentle, smiling face, framed by shiny-brown spools of hair that hung beneath a light-brown sunbonnet. She looked much more a woman than he remembered her. "Thank you, Betsy."

Her face wrinkled. "It's Bitsy!"

Swift glanced at his parents, then back at the girl. "Oh, yeah. Sorry." Bitsy smiled wide, and the carriage rode away.

After the family arrived home, Swift rested several hours before his father awakened him. "Swift, Swift, can you hear me? It's almost time for dinner."

Swift opened his eyes, only to shut them again as Doc threw open the curtains. "I'm awake, Pa," said Swift. He rolled onto his right side, put his lower legs over the edge of the bed. With a great deal of effort, he pushed himself up, then stared at his clothes. "Look at this fine uniform," he said frowning, as he pointed to the coarsely threaded blue trousers. "Army sent it to replace what we'd been wearing since we were captured. Got it right before our exchange. Not good enough for their new soldiers. Just us."

Swift held his arm up toward the window. "These threads can't hold a candle to the ones we wore when we left with the Light Guard. You want to hear a rib tickler? When we got to Washington and were given our back pay, they took out a deduction for these *new* uniforms. Ha! Wouldn't pay anyone for a suit like this, would you, Pa?"

Doc shook his head and looked away. After a few moments he turned back, speaking slowly. "Bull Run, that must have been something."

Swift felt his neck muscles contract. Everything in the room went out of focus. He started to say something, lost his thought, and gave a deep sigh.

Water pooled in Doc's dark eyes. His face muscles contracted, pulling his silver-streaked beard around. "Didn't they feed you? Your letters gave us the impression you were in good spirits. But you look as though they've nearly starved you to death."

Swift shook his head. "Wasn't all *that* bad. After Richmond we were taken to Alabama, where we had this Dutch Sergeant named Wirtz, and though he got angry with us once, and withheld our food for two days, he wasn't bad. One time our salt pork was rotten and filled with maggots, and everyone refused to eat it. When Wirtz found out we weren't eating, he got riled—wanted to know what was the matter with us. When we showed him the meat, I think he was more angry about it than we were. He always called us 'his Yankees.' Like we were his property or something. He said, 'I paid for good meat for *my* Yankees, and by goodness I won't have anything less. Someone is going to pay for this.' Sure enough, he took it out and had good meat brought in."

"If that's true, what brought you to look like this—like death warmed over?"

Swift grunted. "Wasn't much food. Sometimes had to get by with only one or two meals, barely enough to keep us going, and there were seldom any fresh fruits or vegetables. Beans came in stews filled with bugs, but we had to eat everything to stay alive. Kept ourselves busy racing gray-backs, whittling, singing in glee clubs, anything to keep our minds out of our bellies. When the orders came for us to leave, most already had bloody gums—swollen knees and ankles. Then we spent nearly two weeks moving railroad cars around with scarcely a bite to eat. Sometimes while waiting for a train, we'd bury each other in the ground to take the swelling out of our legs."

Doc's eyes widened. "I've never heard such a thing. Did it do any good?"

Swift sighed. "No. Less food we had, more miserable we were. But it did kill some of the lice. Anyway, we only had a few meals in the last couple of weeks, and that's when I lost my strength. Knowing we were going home, we held on. Union doctors in Washington knew what to do when we got there. Fresh vegetables, vinegar, and fruit brought down the swelling in my legs, but I still can't use them much." Something buzzed in the back of Swift's head, and he began to cry. Tears streamed down his cheeks.

Doc's head shook slightly. "Swift, when you first left—I never imagined—how anyone could allow—"

"It's not the Rebs, Pa. It's me. I shamed the family."

Doc shook his head fast. "No. I've read Shanghai's transcripts. He said you were as brave a man as any he's known. How could you say such a thing?"

Swift put his head in his hands, tears falling freely to the floor in little puddles, like spots of blood. "My faith, Pa! I lost my faith. Cursed a man. Cursed him straight to Hell."

Doc's hands took hold of Swift's wrists. "Everyone says things they don't mean, one time or another."

Swift chafed at his father's absolution. "Oh, I meant it all right. Every word of it. I'm not worthy to carry the name of Christ."

Doc's words came softly, just above a whisper. "No man is, Swift. No man is. We just do the best we can."

"Ha!" said Swift. "Men have given their lives rather than disgrace His name."

Doc nodded. "True, but none were perfect. Look at Peter. He walked and talked with Christ, yet failed miserably in many of his early tests. Martyrs, too. You know their stories."

Swift gazed out the window. "I know—but I feel like such a failure. Why didn't we win? How could we lose if God was on our side?"

Doc pulled lightly at his silver-streaked beard. "Often ask myself that, when a patient dies. Especially when it's a good man or a good woman. Certainly find examples of people suffering for what is right throughout the Scriptures. James said not to be surprised at the fiery trials that come upon you, knowing that the testing of your faith brings endurance."

"And endurance—patience," said Swift softly, dropping his gaze to the floor.

Doc stretched out his long arm, placing a hand on Swift's shoulder. It felt large and heavy on him. Swift lifted his head and looked into his father's eyes.

Doc smiled. "Perhaps God isn't so interested in showing his glory as he is in building our character—refining our virtues."

"Then what must I do to be saved?" said Swift.

Doc smiled softly. "You know that. Believe. Be baptized."

"I've done all that," said Swift, a certain harshness in his voice. "There *must* be something more."

Doc took his hand slowly from Swift's shoulder, opened his hands as if reading from a book. "For consider him that endured such contradiction of sinners against himself, lest ye be wearied and faint in your minds. Ye have not yet resisted unto blood, striving against sin."

Swift felt his eyes narrow.

Doc closed his hands. "Don't quit, Swift. He sent the Holy Spirit to help you—to lead and comfort you. You just have to trust. Trust and obey. Follow his example. But you *mustn't* quit. That's the *only* way you can lose."

April 25th, 1862 Paint Rock Bridge, Alabama

Ed Best and twelve Wisconsin volunteers had stood guard at the railroad bridge outside of Woodville, Alabama, for three monotonous days when their supplies ran out. The Union Army controlled the railroad stations and bridges in order to move their men around quickly, and prevent the Rebels from doing the same. This was a long-covered bridge with wood walls and a tin roof that spanned a valley of the Tennessee River near a gap in the Cumberland Mountains. On the east side of the bridge sat a tool shed where the men slept after their shifts, and a fire on the other side of the tracks provided warmth at night in addition to plenty of fresh coffee.

A train rolled by, and Ed and his comrades tried to wave it down, but it didn't even slow. Shoot. Did they think the men were trying to rob an entire train? He sat down in disgust.

Reuben Howard, the only other man from Company D on the detail, approached Sergeant Nelson, rolling his eyes and rubbing his stomach.

"Golly, Sarge! We've got to get something to eat soon or we're gonna starve to death." He put two thumbs into the front of his trousers and pulled, revealing his skinny waist.

Reuben's high forehead, dark black beard, and long narrow face added to the gaunt impression. When he rolled his eyeballs back into his head, Ed laughed.

"Okay," said Sarge. "We'll go see what we can scare up." He turned to one of the privates and said, "Singer, you and Best stay here and watch this side of the bridge. The two on the other side can just stay there. If anything looks suspicious, fire your rifle in the air and we'll come running."

The men gathered their rifles and headed toward a nearby woods. They were out hunting when another train came by. This time the train stopped, and several men in uniform came out and walked down the track.

"Brass," Ed shouted to Singer. "Looks like General Mitchell and his staff."

"What's the division commander want here?" asked Singer.

"Dunno, maybe we better fall in." He fired his rifle into the air, then waved the other guards back across the bridge. They came running and quickly formed a three-man line behind Singer.

Walking over to Singer, the general sneered. "Where are the rest of your guards? I thought you're supposed to have a detachment of fifteen men here?"

"Twelve, sir. We have twelve men."

"Twelve? I only count four."

"Haven't had rations since yesterday, sir. Other men went to forage for food, so we can keep guard as ordered."

The general's jaw jutted forward. He gritted his teeth, and looked wildly about, before turning back toward Singer. "Where is the guard? I want you to call them out immediately. Do you hear me? Immediately!"

Ed felt Singer's frustration in his words." Isn't any guard to call out except us four, sir. Rest are getting food!"

"Listen to me, Private. If you can't call out your detachment, we're not leaving rations. You understand?" But before the private could answer, the general added, "Such a shiftless guard as this is worth nothing. You hear me? Nothing! Why, I and another armed man could take this bridge with little trouble."

Molten anger ran through Ed's veins. Guarding a bridge without sufficient rations was one thing, but deserting one's post was another. No one had done that. No one was going to either, as long as an enemy was around. They guarded bridges with no food, while the other units fought, and this was the thanks they got. What kind of general was this?

Singer's face flushed bright red. "Understand what you're saying, General, and I guess I've got something to say about that."

The officer's forehead wrinkled and his sky-blue eyes bugged.

Singer continued, "General, maybe you could take this post with another man, but I don't think it'd be very healthy for you to try."

"Why, you—" the general started, then stopped and smiled. "You've got guts to talk to me like that, young man. I hope you're as obstinate a fighter."

Sergeant Nelson and his men ran out of the woods with a few scrawny pheasants in their hands.

"Call out the guard, Sergeant!" the general shouted, and the returning men fell into formation.

After asking a few questions regarding their chain of command and general orders, General Mitchell ordered supplies to be unloaded, then boarded the train. Within a few minutes, it crossed the river and passed on down the line. No one talked about it after that, not even Ed. He knew Singer was hot that Sarge hadn't come back sooner, even hotter at the general's words. Guarding railroads was a thankless job. Ed continued to stand watch through the late afternoon, when he glanced across the valley to see a lone figure moving up the tracks in the distance. From his side of the bridge he couldn't be sure, but it looked like a man. On the opposite side of the bridge, the tracks were laid on a ledge cut into a steep hill of the Cumberland Gap. The tracks curved back and around until they disappeared behind that hill, where the figure first appeared.

"Sergeant Nelson," Ed called. "Better get over here and see who's coming." The off duty guards were in a shed about twenty yards from the bridge, where they were either sleeping or playing cards. Ed spoke just loud enough for Nelson to hear, but not loud enough to bother the boys in the shed, then pointed across the gorge to the dark figure walking along the tracks.

"Come on, Best," the sergeant said in a whisper. "We're gonna check this out."

Ed lifted his rifle, and walked into the long, wooden, tin-roofed cave that sheltered the railroad bridge from the weather. The bridge that spanned the Tennessee River, at this point, stood three feet above the trestle timbers below. Through the bridge and alongside of the tracks ran a ten inch wide catwalk. The two hiked rapidly over those wooden planks, and through the dark tunnel to the other side.

Private Francisco Hardiman, or Franz, stood on this end of the bridge. An advance guard was posted about fifty yards out beyond him, and leaned against a tree, unaware of the approaching stranger. Best and his sergeant walked down the tracks past him, and around the curve to where they last saw the figure. They looked around the bushes. No one.

Miffed, the two started back to the bridge when Franz yelled, "Halt! Who goes there?"

Ed sprinted to the bridge. By the time he arrived, Franz was yelling at someone under the sights of his rifle, below the embankment. The embankment here was much wider than it looked from the other side, extending twenty feet down to the river, and covered with thick bushes.

"Don't shoot! It's jus' me, a friend and colored man," came a voice from the bushes below.

"Get out of there where I can see you. Now. Or I'm gonna start shooting," shouted Franz.

The fellow jumped out and scrambled up to the tracks where he raised his hands. It wasn't a Negro, but a white man, dressed in civilian clothes.

"Keep your hands where I can see them," said Franz. "Colored man, huh? Ha! Why, I've got a good mind to shoot you where you stand."

"What's going on, Franz?" said Sergeant Nelson.

Franz kept his eyes on the prowler. "Caught him sneaking up under the bridge, Sarge, and he didn't want us to see him, if you know what I mean."

"I get it. Come on Best, let's see what he was up to."

The two marched the prisoner back across the bridge to the fire. The fellow wasn't interested in talking, but the sergeant grilled him good. He asked question after question, often rewording the same ones, scoffing at the answers and repeating them until he'd caught the Rebel in a lie. Then he really held the Rebel's feet to the fire, alternating accusations and questions, causing the man to drip sweat as if standing in a rain shower.

A whistle sounded in the distance, increasing the intensity of the questions. "What are you doing here? I mean what are you *really* doing here? Don't want to answer, huh? All right. Best, take him to the woods and shoot him."

The man's fear-filled eyes bulged. "What? You can't shoot no prisoner."

"Dead as a Dodo," said Nelson.

"But I'm a prisoner."

"Doesn't look like a Rebel uniform you're wearing. Guess that makes you a spy. Ain't got no rope for hanging, so I guess we'll have to waste a bullet on you."

Ed raked his fingers through his hair, picked up his rifle and grabbed the Rebel by the nape of the neck. He pushed the prisoner so hard that the man nearly fell over. That was all it took. He had come with a company of Confederates who were lying in wait for the next train to come through, and had been sent to set fire to the bridge the minute the next train passed over it. If the train made it through, the Confederates would bushwhack it farther down the tracks.

Sergeant Nelson turned to Ed. "Follow me and bring the prisoner along. Watch him close. Shoot him if he tries anything." He took a piece of burning wood from the fire, and stepped over to the tracks where he waved it back and forth. Several hundred tons of iron strained in high-pitched laments as long metal bars worked to restrain its wheels. Those metal disks slowed until they actually rolled in reverse, sliding along the metal tracks before they'd gathered enough friction to halt the black monster. The engineer's face popped out of a side window, framed by a white cloud of steam as it pulled to a stop before the bridge. The sergeant walked over and talked to the engineer.

"We captured a lone Confederate, and it looks like the Rebs have a company waiting up ahead. Better not go through there. They've got a bunch of rocks and logs on one of those steep cliffs. Plan to drop them when you come along. Could derail you and wreck the whole train. I pressed for their location, but the best I could learn is they're somewhere outside Huntsville."

The engineer eyed the prisoner at the end of Ed's rifle. "Thanks, Sergeant. We'll roll back to Woodville 'til morning—see if we can pick up an escort."

Nelson pointed at the prisoner. "Better take him with you. Colonel will want to question him."

The engineer nodded, and a Union guard stepped down to escort the Confederate saboteur to one of the passenger cars.

Fortified with a company of soldiers, the train rolled through the next day, slowing just enough to salute the guards at the bridge. After the last car crossed, it rolled down around the tracks and out of sight, the guards went back to their monotonous routine. By late afternoon, a couple of Negroes came down the track, stopping near the fire where Sergeant Nelson nursed his ever-present cup of coffee.

"You Yankees gots watuh?" one asked.

His speech was slow, drawled out to the point where Ed could barely understand him. But Sarge had little difficulty. "Sure, coffee good enough?"

"We's jes' needin' watuh—coffee's even bettuh."

The two sat down on a log, the younger one pulling at his friend's sleeve. "Tell 'em. Dey needs ta know."

"Need to know what?" Said Sarge.

"There's men in gray uniforms a comin' ta kill ya."

"How many?"

"Don't know. A bunch."

The other Negro nodded. "Mebbe a hunud. Mebbe two."

Ed's stomach rolled. He'd been itching for action, but those were long odds. For a lingering moment he considered just up and leaving. Nope. He came here to guard this bridge, and that's what he was gonna do. Satisfied with his courage but doubting his sanity, he watched as Sergeant Nelson thanked the black men, and sent them on their way with some hard tack and dried salt pork. "What do we do now, Sarge?" asked Ed.

"You tell the men on the other side. I'll tell those guys in the shack."

Ed hiked across the bridge and was informing Franz of the situation, when another man, this one white, came walking down the tracks. The two stopped talking, and pointed their rifles. He carried a knapsack, and wore civilian clothes. "Who's the officer in charge?" he said.

Ed eyed him warily, saw he had no weapon. "That would be Sergeant Nelson. Come on. I'll take you to him." The two walked through the long covered bridge. Ed kept his rifle trained on the stranger, until they came to the fire where Nelson was sipping coffee with the rest of the detail.

"I've come to warn you," said the stranger. "There's an enemy force at least a company strong, and they're planning to attack you tonight. You must be on guard—get reinforcements if you can. Doubt you can hold them long with these few men."

Nelson showed a poker face. "How do you know?"

"I know it sounds fishy, but I'm on your side. I'm a discharged Union soldier from the Third Ohio—was cooking for my former captain until we were separated. The two of us were going to Stevenson, and while lying on top of a car, my memorandum book fell from my pocket. It contained my discharge papers, and since we were moving real slow, I jumped off to get it. Then the train picked up speed and I couldn't get back on. I followed on foot for several days until I came to a place a few miles down the track. There, a Negro ran out of a field, and told me this bridge would be attacked tonight. Said he'd heard his master talking with Governor Harris about it. Look. Here's my discharge papers. I'm telling you the truth."

The discharge papers were real. Dear God, what had Ed gotten himself into?

"Best and Howard," said Sergeant Nelson, "you take this man into Woodville with you. When you get there, have him tell his story to Lieutenant Harkness. Then make sure to have the lieutenant bring his detachment to the bridge, and be quick about it."

They ran down the road at a double-quick to Woodville, where the story was repeated word for word. But the lieutenant paced back and forth, shaking his head. "How do you know this man's story is true? How do you know that he didn't kill one of our boys and take those papers?"

"Why would he do that?" said Ed. "Besides, there's been more than one warning here. Look. We've only a dozen men to hold the bridge against an entire company."

"I don't know," said the lieutenant, staring down the tracks. "Maybe the Rebs want us to pull out of Woodville so they can attack this station. Already ran to a couple bridges for cock-and-bull stories like yours, and haven't found anything suspicious yet. Last night we ran five miles in the dark for nothing. Sounds like a waste of time and effort to me."

Ed glared at the Lieutenant. "All I know is Sergeant Nelson requested reinforcements before we get attacked. Sounds darned simple to me, sir."

The lieutenant rubbed his scruffy chin as he looked at the man who had brought them the story. "I can't keep running off and leaving this station without a guard, but if Sergeant Makinson chooses, he can take some of the men out there with you."

Makinson was excited at the prospect of seeing some action. He quickly chose twelve volunteers, and Ed led them, double-timing, down the tracks, his mind racing: twenty-five men against a hundred, maybe two hundred. That didn't sound too good. Maybe they'd only send a squad or two. Attack in force. Hot dang. He could be in a heap of trouble. Sol and Nels would never've been dumb enough to get into this hard of a jam. Well, this would be little brother's chance to prove he was a man, *if* he didn't get himself killed.

They arrived shortly before sunset, as the other guards pushed a cart along the tracks. It was covered with a large stack of boards for added flooring in the bridge. Sergeant Nelson grinned at Makinson and his men. "You boys get the rest of our supplies out of the shed, and put them in the bridge. Don't want anyone getting separated once the shooting starts, so no one goes back in there. Then take your men and cover the east side of the bridge. My men will take the west. Station one extra guard ten yards out, on each end of the tracks. Whoever takes those positions stays under cover in case there's an attack. Best, you and Howard get some rest."

Ed went into the bridge. Running ten miles into town and back had worn him out. On top of that, he had pulled two shifts in the past twelve hours, so his eyelids were heavy even before he put his head on his blankets. The world drifted into a dreamy haze.

He had no idea how long he had slept when the voice of little Johnny Camp, whom the boys called "Cat," broke the silence. "Halt! Who comes there?"

Ed sat up. A musket sounded. Cat yelled again, "Ha! You Rebels can't sneak up on me. I see you over there."

A rifle fired at the other end of the bridge, where Makinson and his boys were, followed by a loud volley that catapulted Best up and onto his feet. He stumbled over railroad ties, running toward the sound of the shooting, rifle in hand. When he reached the end of the bridge, he saw Cat approaching in the waning light of dusk as casually as if he were on parade. "They're coming all right."

"Where?" demanded Makinson. "I don't see them anywhere. You sure they're Rebels?"

Ed shook his head. Even his neck muscles felt sleepy. Too many clouds. Had to get out of this haze.

Cat smiled and fielded the questions as casually as he had walked down the tracks. Stepping to one side, he pointed down river. "Right there."

Through the fading light came several companies of Confederate soldiers marching in ranks. They were barely a hundred yards away. "Holy buckets!" shouted Ed. "Must be a hundred and fifty of them. Oh, Mama, what's your boy gotten himself into now?"

The Reb commander issued crisp, clear orders, "File right! March! Halt! Front! Load! Ready—"

Ed felt a sudden dryness in his mouth.

129

"Aim—fire!" Gun powder exploded across the Rebel line that covered the tracks along the bluff. Shot from muskets, pistols, and shotguns ripped through the wood walls of the covered bridge.

"Take cover against the beams," someone yelled, and Ed moved to get the thicker wood between him and the bullets. A second volley ripped through the walls as he hugged the protection of the massive, creosote-covered timber. Splinters and oily chunks of wood flew into his eyes and cheeks, some of them sticking like needles in his skin. His hands shot up to his face, in sympathetic reflex.

No sooner had that hail of bullets slackened than he heard an officer command, "Third line, fire!" and another round of bullets tore through the walls and tin roof, pinging with each strike. Men fell to the floor of the bridge. They shouted and cursed as large balls of lead pounded their bodies. *Stupid* lieutenant. They were all gonna be killed because of one stupid lieutenant.

Someone punched him in the shoulder. The feeling of hot wax spreading across his upper arm followed the sudden pressure. Damn, he'd been shot. Anger followed close behind. "Get them Rebs! Get those stinking Rebs before they kill us all."

Those still standing lifted their rifles, stepped up into the opening of the bridge and fired. It was a curious sight, less than a dozen men firing at over ten times their number, but men fell out there. Metal clanged. Men cried out in pain. Others cursed. "Have a taste of your own medicine, Johnny," shouted Ed. Then the distant command "Fire!" sounded again, and another hail of lead pounded into the bridge. He lifted his rifle to reload, but his arm went numb. The rifle dropped out of his hands. Before he could get it up again, another bullet found its mark in his body, tearing a hole just above the ankle. "Damn!" he shouted, stooping and clutching his ankle. He could hear the voice of his mother admonishing him. Good Christian men don't curse, Ed. "Maybe so, Mama," he said aloud, "but these good Christian men are gonna kill your boy, and what will you say then?"

Small streams of blood poured from his arm and leg. He looked to see who could help. Frank Jokich and Reuben Howard sat on the ground opposite him, working desperately to stop their own bleeding without giving up the shelter of the thick beams. Ed gave up on his musket and switched to his pistol. He worked his way to the opening, taking pot shots alongside Makinson and the other men; but each hail of bullets and splinters sent everyone clambering for cover. Then he heard the sound of cows grazing in a pasture. "Sarge, I hear cows eating grass."

The white of the Sergeant's eyes glowed in the shadows. "There's no cows here. Anything moves, shoot it!"

"But I can't see anything," said Ed.

Just then, the Rebel firing let up, and Makinson and nine other men ran out in front of the bridge. "There they are," shouted Makinson, "coming up the river bank. Get em!" The group fired, reloaded and fired again before scrambling back into the bridge. A hail of bullets followed close behind.

"Sergeant Nelson," Makinson hollered into the darkness of the bridge, "send some of your men down here. I think they're gonna try a frontal assault."

Seconds later, three men marched through the center of the bridge where some moonlight came through. As Sergeant Makinson stood to greet them, a bullet flew through the wall, tearing flesh and muscle from his neck. "Ah!" he shouted. His hands whipped out a handkerchief and he quickly wrapped his wound. Suddenly his head perked up, like a dog's when it hears something no one else does. "They're under the bridge again!" he shouted.

The men at the middle of the bridge stopped and stepped onto the trestle that extended from the side of the bridge. They were out of sight, but their fire sounded loud and clear. Vibrant cheers erupted until another enemy volley ripped through the walls.

After two hours of ducking every conceivable kind of bullet, shot, and debris imaginable, the firing slackened and died. In the quiet respite, splashing sounded on the river below. Were they bringing men across the river in boats? "Sarge. Sarge."

"I know, Best. Can't do anything about it. That's all."

Ed dropped his head. The bridge would be hit from both sides now. There was a certain rest in knowing that. Besides, ever since the last shower of bullets, he doubted anyone was eager to step out into the open again. Wasn't even sure he would if he could.

"Save your ammunition," urged Makinson.

Darkness enveloped the covered bridge. Then a voice sounded on the tracks. "Sirs, I'd like to talk to your commanding officer."

Cat whispered harshly. "Don't go out there, Sarge. Could be a trick."

Makinson shook his head.

"Don't let them get a clean shot at you," said Cat.

"Won't parley with this old boy but a minute," said Makinson, and he stepped into the opening. A well-dressed officer, Confederate battle flag in hand, walked down the tracks under the bright moonlight. Ed moved forward along the wall to get a better view.

"I've come to burn the bridge. If you surrender, you'll be treated as prisoners of war. No one will be hurt. I know what the force in the bridge is, and we outnumber you ten to one. My command is part of Colonel Starnes' Cavalry. You have no choice but surrender, lest you all be killed."

Makinson shouted, "We're here to defend this bridge, and if you've come to burn it, you'll have to take it from us. I'll not surrender while I have a man alive or a round of ammunition, so you can all go to Hell!"

"But you have no chance against us. There are too few of you. Don't condemn your men to death. Be reasonable."

"You may outnumber us, but you made a big mistake by not cutting the telegraph wires. We have an instrument and have sent to Belmont for reinforcements. They'll be here as fast as steam can travel."

"We don't have any telegraph instrument," said a voice in the shadows.

"Shhh! whispered Ed. "They don't know that."

Makinson stepped back into the shelter of the bridge. Behind him the officer continued standing, flag in hand.

The whites of Franz's eyes swelled in the darkness. "Sarge, what should I do?"

Makinson looked back at the Confederate officer. "What's he doing out there?" He smiled wide. "Buying time. That's no flag of truce. Shoot him!"

The soldier took aim and fired, knocking the officer to the ground. He sat still for a moment, blank expression glowing in the moonlight. A second man fired, his bullet kicking up dirt in the officer's face. Ed fired his pistol, but couldn't hit anything at that distance. The Confederate officer suddenly scrambled into the bushes, while a hundred Confederate bullets ripped through the walls of the bridge.

The timber shredded, forcing Ed's head down. The Confederates would probably move in for a frontal attack. The firing increased. Splinters flew everywhere. Ed crawled beneath the cover of a thick beam, while Cat reloaded and fired fast—faster than anyone Ed had ever seen. Some pressed their backs hard against the timbers. Others huddled around the corner beams, firing madly. The firing stopped.

"Fix bayonets!" said Makinson.

Ed's chest constricted and face flushed. He holstered his pistol and reached for his rifle. Fear pounded his heart. What would it be like? Rebels charge in shooting, or would they have their bayonets do their work? He fumbled with his rifle, arm and leg streaming blood.

A man ran from the bushes with a burning torch. Ed pulled his pistol and fired. The Rebel fell in a heap. Another darted from the shadows and lifted the torch. Ed's hammer fell on an empty chamber. The fire glowed brightly in the dark. "I've got a ball stuck," shouted Makinson. "Shoot!"

Ed worked to reload, but his wounded arm shifted into low gear. Another man fired, but the torch kept coming. Makinson's rifle clanged, and he pulled out the rod and fired. The bullet hit the man in one side of the chest, spinning him off the edge of the embankment. The torch dropped among a group of Rebels, sneaking below. Everyone fired. Shadowy figures scrambled for cover. A few made it. Most did not. The torch burned out, and moonlight again covered the land.

"Why don't they charge?" asked Ed.

Makinson shrugged. "Wait for their powder flashes. Take turns firing."

The boys traded off, picking their targets carefully.

Makinson turned to Ed. "Take the wounded to the middle of the bridge."

Ed wanted to argue, wanted to stand and fight, but the sergeant was right. The wounded would only get in the way if the Rebels attacked. He helped the worst wounded to the center of the bridge, the firing again escalating on both ends.

Voices sounded beneath the bridge. A big brass cooking pot sat near the center trestle of the bridge, brought with the other supplies from the guard shack. He kicked it hard, sending it off the tracks and over the side. It banged and clattered until it splashed into the river. Must have sounded like an entire army tramping through the bushes, because the Rebels ran and cussed all the way up the bank.

Satisfied these wounded men would be okay, Ed limped back to Makinson. By the time he arrived, the rifle fire again diminished to an occasional shot. "What are you doing?" said Makinson. "Told you the wounded should be back there."

Ed smiled. "They are, Sarge. All tucked in nice and safe. Don't expect me to miss the fight do you?" He fingered his ammunition pouch. It was empty. "Anyone have revolver caps?" Within the dimly lit entrance, men's heads shook.

Makinson looked around. "Anyone have rifle balls?"

There were only a few "ayes." Ed hung his head. A shrill whistle rent the night air.

Ed plucked out his pocket watch and turned it to catch the moonlight. It was nearly three in the morning.

"Hope that's our boys," said Makinson.

"Me too," said Ed. "But what if the Rebels ambushed the train and are gonna use it against us?"

"Then our goose is cooked," said Makinson. "Best, you and Franz get down to Sergeant Nelson, and find out," he said handing his pistol to Ed. "One shot if it's ours. Two or more and we'll know we're in worse trouble."

Ed and Franz slowly worked their way through the bridge to Sergeant Nelson, the train inching itself toward them in the distance. Franz immediately volunteered to check it out, a move Ed questioned the wisdom of. Nelson agreed, but countered that someone had to go, since his men were nearly out of ammunition, and there was no way to hold the bridge until morning. Franz stepped out and started down the tracks, his rifle across his arms as though he were going hunting.

The train inched toward him, then stopped, it's bright spotlight casting his long black shadow back thirty feet. The voice of Lieutenant Harkness sounded loudly from behind the light, "Don't shoot! He's one of ours," and Harkness suddenly appeared, running along the tracks to meet Franz. Behind him a company of riflemen fanned out to search the darkness, while another marched to relieve the guards at the bridge.

Ed lifted his pistol and fired once, then shouted, "Glory be!"

A relieved smile covered the anxious face of Lieutenant Harkness. "You all right? How many wounded? Damn. Anybody dead? No? Good! Thought I'd gotten everybody killed. Damn. How could I be so stupid? I'm sorry. I mean I'm *really* sorry."

"Forget it," said Nelson. "Just get us off this stinking bridge."

Ed smiled, not mad at the lieutenant anymore. He just wanted to get some sleep. Limping to the train, he watched the members of his detachment board, some walking, some carried. Weary with fatigue, the pain in his arm and ankle seemed sharper than ever. Aboard the train, Makinson grinned. "How many rounds we got?"

"I'm all out," said Ed.

"Me too," said Franz.

Everyone reached in their pouches.

"Got two," said one. "Three here," said another. Others just stared— expressions blank.

"That makes about twelve rounds," said Makinson. "Got more in your rifles?" A few nodded, most just shook their heads. "That's it? One round for every two men? That's calling it too close!"

At dawn, Ed, along with over half the Paint Rock Bridge guards, was brought to the hospital tent near regimental headquarters. He was so tired by then that he paid little attention to anything around him. Doctors poured alcohol over his wounds, while stitching and bandaging; but once that torture was finished, he fell into a deep sleep. When he awoke, it was almost midday. His arm and ankle throbbed. Rolling over, he noticed his brother standing a few beds away.

"Nels, that you?"

Nels head lifted, face lighting up as he wove his way around the beds, cool gray eyes studying Ed's bandages. "Didn't know you were here. Heard you had a rough night, but no one told me you were wounded. Didn't even know you were back."

Ed sat up and shook his head. "Had enough of Paint Rock Bridge to last the rest of my life."

Nels leaned over, still scrutinizing the bandage, "Hurt bad?"

"Nah. Just a couple scratches. Good thing that bridge was thick." Ed gazed across the room. "So, who were you visiting over there?"

"Sol. Been sick since you left. Had some bad salt pork. Was so upset about Elizabeth selling his team of horses and going back to Ohio that he didn't even notice. Me and Sophie spit the stuff out minute we tasted it, but it was too late for him. A couple hours later he came down with the runs and hasn't stopped since. His color is funny, and he's lost a heap of weight. Doc says he's worried about him. I wrote and told Ma and Pa, but I don't dare write Beth."

With John's help, Ed limped over to Sol's bed. Each step on the injured ankle shot pain through the raw muscle and tendon, but when he saw Sol, he completely forgot it. Sol's forehead was dripping wet, sheets soaked with sweat. His cheeks were sucked in. Even more troubling was the golden color of his skin, evidence that something serious was affecting his liver. Together they tried to wake him, but Sol was so weak and exhausted from diarrhea that he seemed incapable of gaining full consciousness. The most he could manage was to open his yellow eyes, acknowledge Ed's presence with a poor attempt at a smile, and go back to sleep.

When Ed returned to his bed, Franz and Singer were there smiling. "Gettin' a unit commendation," said Franz. "Singer heard the word from General Mitchell."

Ed dropped his chin and eyed them.

"It's true," Singer said. "I reported to General Mitchell this morning. When he heard we held off nearly three hundred Rebs, said he wished he had a whole division like us. One of his aides said they only found one man dead, but there were all kinds of weapons left around. Folks in town said the Rebels brought three wagonloads of dead and wounded down the road last night. General even apologized for reading me out like he did. Said, 'Guess I should be glad I didn't try and take that bridge with one other man like I said I could.' Then I said, 'I told ya you could try, General, but I didn't think it would be very healthy for you.' And he said, 'I know a couple hundred Rebs who'd probably agree with you right now.' It was a hoot!"

Ed smiled. The picture of Solon's face came to mind and his smile faded. Would his brother be all right? Sol had always been so vibrant and strong he seemed invulnerable. Should Ed write home, too. Nels had already done the writing—wasn't more Ed could say. Besides, he'd never been any good at writing letters.

EIGHT

"Strike, slight them, spare them not,
for many reasons, but most because
they have blasphemed the gods!"
—Strepsiades

June17th,1862, Big Spring, Wisconsin

SWIFT RODE IN DOC'S CARRIAGE SITTING OPPOSITE HIS MOTHER AND AUNT Sarah. The wagon carrying the remains of Uncle John rolled directly ahead of them, but Swift faced backwards. It was the seat he preferred. John hadn't suffered long. At the first signs of pneumonia, Doc shipped him to Chicago, but to no avail. The Lord took him. But why?

That was the question Swift couldn't answer. He saw no martyrdom in John's death. No just cause. No glory worthy of Jesus' name. As Eusebius once said of the Lord's brother James, Uncle John had "scaled the heights of philosophy and religion." From his youth, he'd refused to see the writings of Plato as a threat to Christianity, but rather as a foundation that prepared men's hearts and minds for the teachings of Christ. The Socratic dialogues were a call to a life of religious discipline and study. The call of Christ. What was it Philo said of the early Christians? They "laid down self-control as a foundation for the soul, building the other virtues on it." There could be no doubt that every sincere Christian fulfilled the Socratic quest. They had found "the One who knows." If that was all God required of John, he had certainly finished his race. But somehow, even with such understanding, the reasoning seemed insufficient. Was there something more? Some insight he was missing?

Behind Doc's carriage came the wagons of cousins Curge and Hub, Uncle Jim and Aunt Sally, Robert, William, Thomas Ramsey and their families. Then the Landts, the Wards, the Stowells, the Woodfords, the Forsythes, the Smiths, and so many others. Neighbors and friends who had cut an agricultural community out of what was once nothing more than wilderness. They pulled together, serving as town supervisors, assessors, treasurers, teachers, justices of the peace, secretaries, or any other office where their talents could benefit the community, and now they gathered together to say goodbye to one of their own. The stream of wagons and people floated down the road for a country mile.

Swift scratched his head and looked at Aunt Sarah. A black cotton-bonnet wrapped her long, gray hair tight around her neck, where it flowed onto the shoulders of her cape. Her soft, pale skin, lightly wrinkled, contrasted with the whites of her soft gray eyes, now bloodshot and filled with tears. She spoke softly to Emily. "They'll never mend that fence now. Stubborn, just too stubborn, both of them."

Emily shook her head. "Wasn't *your* fault. Nothing you could do."

Sarah looked over at Swift, then back to Emily. "I know. It's just *so* hard. Keep thinking about Socrates begging me, 'Mother, talk to him, Ellen isn't married—never was—loved me from the beginning. *Never* would have married that weasel if her father hadn't made her.'"

Emily reached over and put her arm around Sarah. "I know. But divorce and remarriage *is* a difficult subject. John made a stand. Have to respect him for that."

Sarah's hand trembled. She took a white handkerchief from her pocket, and dabbed around the corners of her eyes. "Problem is, I could see both sides. John said it was her cross to bear, but should Ellen be condemned to a life of loneliness for someone else's sin?"

"We *all* have crosses," said Emily.

Sarah's face wrinkled. "Doesn't make sense. Scripture says Christ suffered *once* for all."

Emily forced a smile. "You know what I mean."

Sarah nodded. "Lot of men talk about how women oughta live, while disgracing the name of Christ themselves."

Emily glanced toward Doc, driving the carriage, oblivious to this conversation. Her gaze shifted to Swift. She nudged him with her knee.

"All I know," said Sarah, "is my husband's gone, and Socrates is faraway. What'll become of him and Ellen?"

Emily nudged Swift harder. He turned and looked away. The carriage passed the Landt farm, turned off the road at the town hall, and pulled up to a small hill the community had set aside. Swift grabbed his crutches and stepped down, before turning to help his mother and Aunt onto the grassy field. Men lifted and slid the pine box onto their shoulders. The family followed them up the twenty-foot rise to the top of the knoll where a hole had been dug. The men there lowered the casket into the ground. By the time it was in place, a crowd of people covered the little cemetery.

The new pastor from Portage stood with his Bible in hand at the head of the grave. Dressed entirely in black, with the exception of his white collar, he opened the Bible and began to speak to the people in a soft but clear voice that carried easily down the hill. "We have come here to remember John Best, husband, father, neighbor, and friend, who has departed from us after sixty-two years on this earth. He has played an important part in our—"

Swift stared at the pine box, thought of the deaths of the early martyrs, James, Justin, and Origen. How they went to their graves happily, rejoicing at the heavenly reward before them. He thought about Uncle John, his body in the casket. Were those cool-blue eyes open or closed? Faces flooded his mind. Eyes closed. Eyes open. Green, blue, gray, black, and brown. Staring up. Staring round. Fixed upon the ground. The eyes of men, freshly dead, dressed in blue and gray. Suddenly he stood at the base of a long hill, bloody bodies in blue and gray scattered about the ground. His hands shook, knees trembled at the prospect. He would be the next to charge, but he couldn't find his rifle. Where was it? Of all the times to lose it. Sweat dripped from his fingertips. A hand pulled at his shoulder.

Doc's whiskered face was there, in front of him. "You all right, son?"

Swift nodded.

"Sure?"

Swift turned to hide his tears. The words of Ignatius rolled through his mind:

"I am God's wheat, ground by the teeth of beasts, that I may be found pure bread."

Two local Indians stood over the hole where John's casket was. The Chief, Prettyman, and his son, Jake, wore a mixture of white cotton shirts, buckskin pants, and an assortment of colorful beads and stitching. The French named them Winnebago, the "People of the Long Canoe," though the tribe rejected that name. They were Ho-Chunks, the "People of the First Voice."

Prettyman was solid in build, but with age his back bowed and face wrinkled. Swift remembered Uncle John's many stories, how the Chief brought gifts during their first Winter in '50. It hadn't been much, just sifted corn and venison, but the family's supplies were dangerously low. Prettyman appeared out of nowhere then, just as he did now. "We heard of the passing of our friend, and have brought gifts to help him on his journey to the Spirit World."

He took a colorful pipe with ornamented hand carving, and a leather-laced pouch of tobacco, and rolled them into a colorful cloth. Bending forward, he dropped them gently onto the pine casket.

A few minutes passed before the people walked down the little hill and back to their wagons, horses, and farms. Though this place was no more than twenty or thirty feet above the surrounding pasture, it gave a commanding view of the fields around. Across the hayfields, on the eastern side of the cemetery, Swift saw the long hill where the Winnebago Indians buried their own. It reminded him of a giant loaf of bread sitting on a table, rising up out of nowhere on a flat, open plain, like so many other hills in Wisconsin. Across the top were hundreds of oak and birch. Halfway across the cornfield, Chief Prettyman and Jake strode toward their homes as quietly as they had come.

Emily took Sarah's arm. "Nice of them to come."

Swift grimaced. The left crutch stung his armpit, and he wondered how long they might be here. He shifted his weight and looked at the ground.

"Yes," said Sarah, "John would be pleased. Probably better neighbors to us than we've been, considering all this land was once theirs."

"Maybe so, but the government bought it outright before selling."

"Yes. The government bought it from the Ho-Chunks, but with what— old molding corn worthless to them? Empty promises and outright lies— that's what they bought it with."

Swift jerked his head up. Whites called them Winnebago, never Ho-Chunks.

Emily's chestnut-brown eyes enlarged. She stepped back. "That was a while ago. They get cash money now."

"Yes. Emily, you're right. Some get paid in cash. But I've seen the government's distributions, and every time they pay the Indians, the hawkers are there, giving out whiskey to get them drunk and defraud them of every dollar. Besides, these people came back to claim what they believe is theirs. Say they were never told they were giving up all the land east of the Mississippi, that they were lied to."

"That's not our doing, Sarah. We have no control."

"Maybe so, but it's our government, not theirs. And how many times have you heard that Prettyman or one of his braves helped someone? Yet most of us've never even entered their camp, less to say find something we could do to help them."

Swift adjusted his crutch again. "Pa says you went up there once."

Sarah's eyes stared off for a moment. She took a deep breath. "Yes. John brought me there one spring. Their campgrounds were neat and clean, and the deer skin they use for the walls of their huts kept their dwellings much warmer than I expected."

Emily glanced at the hill, then back at Sarah. "Did you go in one?"

"Yes. Their homes are simple—but comfortable. Don't need a lot of space when most of their time is spent outside, preparing meals, curing hides, stripping deer—not much different than us in some ways. They're just working to survive here."

Swift felt tired. More exhausted than he could remember. His head drooped.

His father reached over and took mother's arm. "Come on, Emily. We need to get back."

Swift started to move his crutch, felt something take hold of it. He turned to see the pretty round face of a young lady, framed by shiny-brown spools of hair. Her bright-green eyes danced and sparkled.

"Here," she said, pulling lightly at the crutch, "let me help you."

Swift snatched the crutch away. "Don't need your help, Betsy Hyde."

Her face stiffened. "Do, too. And its Bitsy!"

Swift shook his head. "Don't need your help. I can walk on my own."

The girl stomped once, turned around, and stormed down the hill.

Early July, 1862, Daingerfield, Texas

"Socrates," Ellen called, "if you're going to get supplies, would you please take Gus? He wants to go with you." Socrates walked into the parlor and over to his wife. She had on a dark black dress with a little white-lace collar that was less than an inch thick. Her hair was tied up behind her head, and between the dark hair and dress, her blue eyes looked almost black. He'd had his mind made up for a while, but decided this would be the time to tell her. "You miss your folks, don't you?"

Ellen nodded, her eyes filled with tenderness. "Of course, but you know how that is now. Don't you?"

"I can hardly believe Pa is dead. Wouldn't have thought it could feel like this, us being so far apart these last years and all." Socrates shook his head and stared at the floor. "Can't ever see him again. Least not in this lifetime. Wish I'd talked to him before he passed on. Wish he'd met my boys." Socrates looked away. Tried to think of something philosophical, something brilliant. The words of Epicurus: "When we are, death is not; when death is, we are not." Stupid play on words! Noah Webster had done better with his dictionary. Socrates' mind searched for something better. Deeper. Aristotle's words:

"Friends and truths are both here, but it is a sacred duty to prefer the truth." But was that it? Had he preferred the truth over his father? Or had his father chosen truth over him? Everything seemed so muddled. The words of Protagoras: "Man is the measure of all things, the existence of what exists, and the non-existence of what does not exist." True. Without existence there was nothing to ponder, but even that seemed stupid. Then came the words of Marcus Aurelius from his *Meditations:* "The mind of the universe is social and each person of the community exists in a "brotherhood of all rational beings." *That's* what he was feeling! A social loss. A vacuum of brotherhood where his father had once been. Didn't matter the distance. Not even the antagonism. It was *his* father. His *father* had died, and no one could fill that void.

Ellen's dark blue eyes stared straight into him. "I wish you could have made up with him."

A knot formed in Socrates' throat. "Can't do anything to change that now. He shouldn't have been so hard on you. Guess he just didn't know how we felt. I was wrong—he was—I don't know! I can't believe how this feels. How could you stand losing both parents in one year?"

Ellen leaned forward and put her thin, little nose on his. "Like you said, there's nothing anyone can do about it."

"I know," he said, peering deeper into her eyes. A gentle warmth radiated there, an abiding comfort that transported him to another time and another place. When he was a little boy and his mother leaned forward like that, pouring her love into him like sweet maple syrup on hot oatcakes. This was the love Ellen had given him, like a sacred gift consecrated solely for the needs of him and his children. In that instant Socrates felt ashamed, sorry he hadn't done more to protect his wife, hadn't taken her away from here. He needed to do that now. The words burst in him, like a hot gas agonizing to escape. But all his emotions were overruled, constrained by some sinister cerebral force with an insane need to explain. "I'm sorry if I seemed—you know—as though I didn't understand. Maybe I didn't. Really."

"I don't think you treated me badly, though it might have seemed that way at the time. I was awful sad. It's hard sometimes, knowing Mama and Papa are gone forever."

"I know now," he said softly. "I know so much more." He pulled her closer to him, wanting to bury himself in her magnificent warmth. Never had he felt such a singular love. He wanted to sound a bell or bang a drum, but all he could do was tell her, offer her what she'd wanted for so very long. "What do you think of leaving here—going north?"

She pushed him away and stiffened, mouth open. Her hands went to her mouth where she put a finger lightly on her lower lip. "Oh! Socrates, you mean sell the farm?"

Socrates smiled, then a sudden fear jolted him. That sinister force was taking over again. "Well. Maybe not *sell* everything, just leave 'til this war is over. Land isn't worth much now, and I don't want to burn our bridges behind us quite yet, but we could live with Ma until this thing is over." Guilt swept through him, tightening his stomach.

Ellen's face was all smile. "But what made you change your mind?"

"Kept thinking I needed to follow the laws of these people—lead them by example. Even if it meant laying down my life for it."

"Sounds like your namesake and 'the laws.' *Crito?*"

Socrates nodded. "I realize now, he was over seventy. He'd lived a full life and had little left. I haven't. Need to see my boys grow up. Pa's death taught me that. It's time to go home for a while."

"Oh, Socrates. That would be wonderful."

"You see? Sometimes even old Homer nods."

Gus came around the corner. "Am I gonna get to see my gramma now?"

Socrates laughed at the little spy. "Yes, son. But right now we need to get some supplies."

"Can I go with you and Uncle Ben?" asked Gus.

Socrates couldn't help but laugh again, this time more warmly. "Ha. Of course you can come with us. I think we can get even some of that sweet, hard rock candy you like so much. Get your Uncle and tell him I'll be out in a minute. He's working in the shed." Little Gus ran out the door so fast that it slammed loudly behind him. Socrates reached over and pulled Ellen close to him again. "Can you feel the baby now?" He asked, in a voice just above a whisper.

"Yes," she said as she guided his hand down to her belly. "I have a feeling it's a girl. I do so want a little girl, Socrates. Can you feel her kicking?"

Socrates touched the stomach stretched out over the baby inside her, hard and firm like a fresh melon. Something bumped his hand. "Yes! I *can*. What does that feel like inside of you? Does it hurt?"

"No, silly. It doesn't hurt at all. Sometimes it wakes me up in the night, but then I just think about what this little one's going to be like when it comes out into the world. I think about all the possibilities. If it's a girl, what she'll be like, what her voice will sound like. Will she like to sing like me or have curly hair? Then I get so excited I can't get back to sleep, even after the baby stops kicking. It's something fearsome, awesome, wonderful—carrying a life inside."

"I suppose. Can't picture it myself, but it does make me a little envious."

Ellen pushed him away, eyes wide again. "You men! You might envy me now, but not when I'm in labor. Then you won't want to be around." They laughed and held one another until the door opened and little Gus stuck his head inside.

"You comin' or ya just gonna stand there all day?" he said.

Socrates laughed. "I'm coming. I'm coming. Just keep your britches on, you little Augustus, you." Then he put both hands on his wife's belly and said, "Take good care of this one. I'll be back soon." He leaned forward, kissed her full and fresh on the mouth until she blushed, then turned, picked up his hat, and walked out the door. Outside, he watched as Ben grabbed Gus from behind, lifted him up over his shoulders and fell in step with Socrates. Gus giggled as he found himself with an adult's eye view of the world.

The three were walking past the hotel, where a number of horses were tethered, when they heard a menacing voice. "Now *there's* a couple of worthless Yankees for ya. Come on out here, boys, and I'll introduce ya."

Recognizing the voice of Buck Malneck, Socrates whispered to Ben, "What's he doing in town again?"

"Forgot to tell you," said Ben. "Mary told me yesterday. Got thrown out of the Titus Rangers. Drunk and disorderly—striking an officer."

Socrates shook his head. Thought of the four companies the county had already produced. Hook's men had left Daingerfield back in March. Malneck's timing couldn't have been worse. How in God's name did he keep showing up?

"Can't have trouble with Gus here." Socrates whispered. He quickened his steps into the supply store across the street. He and Ben barely got in the door before Buck and his friends followed them inside. This time there were four of them, and aside from Billy Morse, he didn't recognize any of the others.

"Where ya goin', school teacher?" Malneck said with a frown. "Didn't ya hear me? Got friends here, and they'd like to meet a damned Yankee. Wouldn't ya boys?"

Hearty "ayes" came from the other men, dressed in dark pants, Spanish boots, and hunting vests, with pockets that bulged and sagged under the weight of extra revolver cylinders. Each wore green shirts with holstered revolvers on each hip and one or two extra in their belts. Just the sight of their scrubby beards and angry faces sent a cold chill down Socrates' spine.

"Ya never met my Missouri friends, Best. These boys are go-rillas. Ride up in Kansas and Missouri. Come down here lookin' for recruits to ride with Quantrill and Anderson, and they don't like no Yankees. Do ya boys?" Once again his friends affirmed their support. "But we don't have to worry about this Yankee, cause he's making powder for us. Right, Best?"

Socrates held his tongue. They stunk of sweat and alcohol. Out of the corner of his eye, he spotted Ben taking Gus down from his shoulders, and whispering something into the boy's ear. Hopefully sending him for the law. But the sheriff was out of town. The boy started out the door, but one of the men caught him around the waist and picked him up. Gus kicked and flailed.

Buck sneered. "Where ya think you're goin', boy?"

Socrates felt his back rise.

Buck grinned as he held Gus out in front of him. "Don't ya know it's bad manners to walk away when introductions are bein' made? Course, I shoulda known! Yankees don't have no manners, do ya?"

Ben stiffened until he was rigid, but Socrates shook his head ever so slightly. Hold on. Don't provoke them. "I just came to get my supplies, Buck, nothing else. Then we'll be about our business." He turned to John Miller, standing behind the counter. The man's face was sweaty and ashen. Now Miller shook his head ever so slightly, but Socrates didn't understand. "If I can get my supplies, John, we'll be out of here in a flash."

Miller trembled. He leaned forward to whisper something into Socrates' ear. Malneck shouted, "There's no secrets here, least not with any Yankees. What you got to tell him, you tell all of us." Malneck placed his hand on his sidearm.

Speaking to Socrates in a quivering voice, Miller said, "Your supplies haven't come in."

Every ear in the place was alert.

"Well, just let me know when they do," said Socrates. "You know where to find us." The storekeeper's face puckered into a pout, and Socrates balked. "What's the matter with that?"

"Can't get more supplies. Army's taken everything they can find, and the ships aren't getting through the Gulf. Don't know if it's the blockade or what, but my supplier says he doesn't know if he can get any more. I'm sorry."

Malneck's face beamed. "Ho! Time you boys joined the cause and fought for the go-rillas. Don't ya think?"

Ben's gaze darted from man to man, then to Socrates.

Socrates shifted his weight from foot to foot. "You can't honestly expect us to carry arms? You know I was hired as a school teacher, not a soldier. If you want, my family and I will leave this place. You won't be bothered by our presence anymore."

"No!" shouted Malneck. "You ain't goin' up north and joining up with the Yankee army so's you can tell 'em everything you know." He glared at Ben, then at Socrates. "You're gonna get what you deserve."

Socrates felt as if he would burst. "If I got what I deserved, it'd be free room and board at public expense—for life!"

"God damn!" shouted Malneck. "That does it. Hang the sons-a-bitches!"

Around the room came loud "yeahs" and "hurrahs". Buck's long arm reached across the counter and commandeered a rope, holding it up for everyone to see.

The group grabbed Socrates and Ben, dragged them out the door and into the street. Little Gus, thrown aside, ran out the door. Other men gathered from around town at the commotion. So many familiar faces, some curious, some looking blank and old beyond their years. Many had already lost their boys. Such pain. Such confusion in their expressions.

Buck yelled, "Kill the Yankees!"

"Hang 'em high!" shouted another.

The guerillas dragged the terrified Yankees to the livery stable, hoisting the rope over a hay pulley, while bringing out two horses. Socrates was lifted onto one at the same time as Ben. A pair of hangman's nooses slid around their necks, then tightened until they could hardly breathe.

Socrates pleaded with the crowd, "I only came here to teach. Let me go home. My wife is pregnant."

But the Missouri men cursed him and called him a traitor. Buck cleared the people away from the front of the horses so he could lead them away, leaving the Yankees to hang.

"Just what do you think you're doing?" demanded a well-dressed man with an ancient looking musket in his hands, his face a stern frown. Behind him a crowd of some twenty people followed. Several had rifles or pistols. The group swiftly blocked the horses' way.

Socrates breathed a sigh of relief at the sight of Sam Pouns, and his squat little partner, John Musgrove.

"Hanging us a Yankee, Mayor," replied Buck. "Like you should've done a long time ago."

"But he's no Yankee," said one of the men with the mayor. "He's our school teacher."

Buck laughed. "Not no more, there's no call for school with a war on."

"Maybe so," said Sam, "but that doesn't give you any authority. I'm the head of the Home Guard, and this is our job, not yours. Besides, he's been making powder just like he promised."

Malneck's face flushed. "Can't do that no more, Mayor. Not with no supplies coming for powder, and these Yankees say they ain't gonna join up—so we're hanging em!"

Sam's brown eyes went wide. "That true, Socrates? No more powder?"

Socrates grimaced, hopelessness twisting his stomach.

"If there isn't anymore powder," said Sam, "then you only have one choice. Aren't going to take hanging over the Army, are you?"

Socrates lifted his head. "I'd prefer working with the sick and wounded."

"Afraid that choice isn't mine. I don't have authority with the military, just with the Home Guard, but if you don't join up, the military *will* have jurisdiction. Either way, we'll have to turn you over to them."

The slight John Musgrove stepped forward. "Socrates, if you and Ben'll fill me and my son's slots, I'll pay you seven hundred fifty dollars and throw in a horse to boot. What do you say?"

Socrates sighed, threw a sideways glance. "We'll join. Won't we, Ben?"

Ben nodded. "Guess it's time to acknowledge the corn."

Turning toward the mayor one last time, Socrates said, "We'll need to get our things."

Buck glared, face crimson, eyes wide. "Oh no, you don't. You ain't gettin' away. You boys go with him, and watch that he don't try nothin'."

Sam stuck his rifle into Buck's chest. "A couple of our folks are gonna go with you. Don't want any accidents, if you know what I mean. Besides, he's not gonna be joining any guerrillas. He'll be going to the Confederate camp. We'll see to that!"

The guerillas nodded, pulled the two off the horses, a group of ten following to Socrates' house. Ellen was standing outside the door with Gus hanging on her skirts when the group arrived. Little Willie straddled her right hip beside the firm, round tummy. Just awakened from a nap, he wasn't fully alert yet. Poor girl, thought Socrates. He walked over to embrace her and their little two-year-old. Unspoken apologies etched themselves deep into the lines of his face. "Ellen," he said, "Ben and I are joining the Army—have to get our stuff."

"But—but—"

"Otherwise we hang."

"But—why can't we just go back home?"

Socrates slowly dropped his head. "Because," he said softly, "they're only giving us two choices, and that isn't one."

August 20th, 1862, Big Spring, Wisconsin

Swift sat across his parent's kitchen table from a bespectacled, brown-haired gentleman, who looked to be forty years old. His name was Mr. Marx, and he had come from some state military office. He shuffled papers around, alternately shuffling, messing, and then stacking them again. "Terrible thing about Mankato," he said without looking Swift in the eyes.

Swift stared. "Don't know what you're talking about."

Marx focused his gray-green eyes more closely on his papers. "The Sioux. That's who I'm talking about! Massacred settlers at New Ulm. Hundreds, I hear."

"New Ulm?"

The man nodded without looking up. "German settlement on the Minnesota River, somewhere near Mankato. What was its founder's name? Something trite. Herman the German, I think they call him. Anyway, Wisconsin folks are loading up their wagons and coming into Portage from all over. Scared to death."

"Why? That's hundreds of miles from here."

Marx glanced at Swift, then back at his papers. "Word is, runners have been sent to every tribe and nation, calling for a general uprising."

Swift ran his fingers through his dark hair, and thought of his sister at Lake Erie Seminary. "I'm going to be a missionary," she'd said. "Lord called me when I was a child, and I can't deny it. Indians. He's calling me to minister to the Indians of Minnesota. Isn't it exciting, Swift?" Maybe, but not right now. He silently thanked God that she was safe in Chicago. He followed Marx's eyes, which continued to avoid his. "How bad is it?"

"Gov'nor says it's a farce. Can't be more than ten thousand Indians in the whole state, and most of those are pretty poor. Most have a gun for hunting, but no stockpile of ammunition. Compare that to over two hundred thousand whites, and you'll understand why most of those poor red men are hiding out in their reservations—more afraid of us than we are of them."

Swift shook his head. "But *that's* not what you're here for, is it?"

Marx jerked a piece of paper from his pile, while keeping the rest in perfect order. "No." He pushed it across the table, toward Swift, never lifting his eyes. These are military orders. You must report next month at Benton Barracks in Missouri. There you'll be given a physical and rated for incapacity. Your pension."

Swift looked at the paper, scratched his head. "Since when does the government send an agent out to give military orders? Postage is a lot cheaper."

Marx shuffled the papers again. "Your father is well-known in Madison. His friends in the department felt you could be of some assistance to us before mustering out. Word is your wounds are healing well."

"Maybe so," said Swift pointing to his crutches, "but I won't be fighting any more battles. And college starts in September."

The man's gray-green eyes went wide. "Oh, no!" he said, looking quickly at the crutches, and then away again. "Not for soldiering. We need someone to help us with an investigation. Someone who's been in and knows the ropes. Someone who can keep their findings confidential."

"But school—"

"Won't interfere. You'll be through in time to be at Benton Barracks for your physical. Besides, the complaints you will be investigating are probably unfounded."

"Where at?"

"Camp Randal in Milwaukee."

"Training base?"

Marx stared out the window. "Used to be. Now it's a prison camp. Anyway, gov'nor's been getting complaints from the Confederacy. Seems they think we aren't treating their boys well. The State has certainly provided ample supplies, but the question is whether or not the prisoners are getting them. Of course, I don't think any of this is true, but the gov'nor wants someone to investigate. Someone who's been on the other side of those walls. Someone who knows how it feels to be far away from home and totally at another's mercy."

Swift stared ahead. The words of Micah gently stirred him:

"He hath shown thee, oh man, what is good, and what doth the Lord require of thee, to seek justice and to love mercy, and to walk humbly with thy God."

He felt an urge to go, a desire for justice, but it was all so confusing. "I don't know."

Marx finally let his gaze fall upon Swift. "But you're *perfect* for it."

Swift pointed at his crutches. "You've *got* to be kidding, With those?"

"Yes, perfect. War Department's been putting paroled prisoners— especially wounded ones that still believe in the cause—into all kinds of desk and guard jobs. If you want to, you can even stay in until your enlistment is up.

Anger flashed in Swift. "*That* isn't right. We signed papers. Gave our words. Promised we wouldn't fight anymore—conditions of the parole."

Marx's forehead folded into long flat lines. "Tight conscience?"

"I'm a Christian."

"Me, too, but I wouldn't worry about it. Both sides are doing it, from what I hear."

Swift grunted. "Doesn't make it right."

Marx shrugged as he pointed to the paper in Swift's hand. "I know, but it's not in my hands. Not in yours, either. Look. You'll still have to go to Missouri to get your rating and final discharge. Won't you at least reconsider?"

Swift felt as hard and cold as iron as he muttered, "No. Not a chance."

After Marx left, Swift explained to his parents that he would be gone for several weeks, pursuing his separation from the military, but said nothing of Marx's strange request. Before leaving for Missouri, he would stop and see his Aunt Sarah, then catch the train out of Kilbourne.

Though he retired early, it did little good. He spent a sleepless night, thoughts of doubt working to capture his imagination. Should he have gone? Confederate prisoners deserved to be treated well, but was that what he had received from them? And what about his *word*? Was nothing sacred anymore?

The long, torturous night drove Swift out of bed at first light. Not a soul stirred in the house as he buttoned up his uniform, grabbed some corn muffins, and then saddled a sorrel mare. The road to Big Spring was hot and dry, wheat fields and cornfields lush with growth. An orange half-circle bobbed up on the horizon, illuminating a spectacular sky, irradiated in reds and orange-reds. Amidst those hues, lay lofty cirrus streaked with gray, silver, and violet ribbons.

Along the road, there were no human sounds other than the mare's hooves thumping on the hard dirt; yet the concert of nature was in constant crescendo. Crickets and cicadas buzzed. Bullfrogs along the ponds and the creeks seemed to compete as they briveted their calls across the waters. Yes. There was peace here. Here in the daylight, where God's glory glowed for all to see. The only men who loved the darkness, were those whose deeds were evil.

He stopped at a small bridge running over a creek, and watched dragonflies hover and cruise along the shore. An old water wheel slowly dipped and scooped up the black liquid, squealing loudly at certain points of its circumferential journey, while gently returning it on the other side. About half way to Big Spring he met his cousin, big Bob Ramsey, who stopped to say hello. He drove a huge wagon pulled by ten burly oxen, that few other men could manage. The lead oxen was an enormous beast named Jake. Bob reached him with a long, thick, leather whip. From him Swift learned that Big Spring was in a tither over the Indian uprising, but not Bob. He was more concerned with the reports of highway robbers lying in wait along this stretch of road, stealing people's money after they exchanged their grain in Portage.

"Pa wants me to carry a shotgun," said Bob with a frown. "Promised him I'd be careful, but I'm not shooting anybody! I don't care—"

Swift's mind rolled back to Bull Run, to bodies all over the ground. The hail of bullets. Men crying. It was all so vivid—as if he were there now. Men on black horses charged out of the cornfields."

"Well!" said Robert with a grunt. "I'm burning sunshine with all this talking. Better get rolling." With a flip of the reins he rolled past Swift, who merely nodded.

Twenty minutes later, Swift rode up to Big Spring Town Hall, which was simply a square, white building with a wood platform porch at the top of several wood steps. At the base of the steps, his uncle Jim Ramsey and cousin Hub stood talking to Fred Landt. "Howdy, Swift," said Hub with a wide smile. "What's with the uniform?"

"I'm leaving to get my separation papers in a couple days. Wanted to stop and see Aunt Sarah first. How is she?"

Hub shrugged his thick shoulders. "Best as could be expected, with Pa gone."

Swift stared down the street, where a dozen old men and young boys were gathered. They carried old muskets and shotguns at their shoulders, while a gimpy-legged veteran hollered a stream of steady instructions. "Left - left—left, right, left." The cadence sounded in perfect time, but the men were all over the place, their feet completely off beat. A boy of about thirteen sounded a steady rat tat tat on a drum that looked as if it were left over from the War of 1812. Beside him, a tall old gentlemen played a lively fife. Those two were the only ones marching consistently in time with the music. "What's going on?"

"Everybody's spooked about the Indian trouble," replied Hub.

Swift shook his head. "Heard there's nothing in that. Least not around here."

Hub stretched out his arms and gave a big yawn. "Probably true, but a few members of the town council went up to powwow with the old chief. Some of the community thought they should let him know we mean business by forming a drill company."

Jim shook his head hard, and muttered, "Hope to Heaven Prettyman doesn't see this. If he does, he'll know he can take us for sure."

Swift laughed hard. "Might even tempt Jeff Davis."

Everyone laughed.

"Well," said Swift, placing his Union cap back on his head, "about time I check out Sarah's corn muffins. Good luck."

When Swift arrived at Aunt Sarah's, a sweet aroma tickled his olfactory, causing his stomach to rumble. Inside, Sarah busily shuffled pie tins about the kitchen table. Her silver hair was tied up in a bun, and the white apron she wore over her blue cotton summer dress was covered with flour. To one side was a large pot of red sugared cherries. "Swift," she said, flashing a half-smile. "Wasn't expecting you."

Swift nodded. "I'm headed to Missouri for final muster. Thought I'd stop in and say hello. See how you're getting along."

"How nice of you. Tom Ramsey dropped in this morning."

"How is cousin Tom?"

"Pretty good. He and Adey are expecting a baby."

"That's great!"

"May be, but Tom just can't get enlistment out of his head."

Swift shrugged. "Maybe I should talk to him."

Sarah shook her head. "Don't think it would do much good. Jim and Sally have done their best to discourage him. Adey, too."

Swift thought back to an earlier day, when he had been so eager to fight, so fearful of missing out on the action. The thought shamed him. "So what else is going on?"

"As you can see, I'm baking."

Swift took a deep breath. "Smells great, but why did you make so many."

Sarah frowned, glancing in the direction of the table. "Look at those. Not a good crust amongst them. Not a one."

On the table sat four pie crusts. One was obviously burnt while the others looked normal. Swift felt compassion rise within him. "Are you all right?"

"Fine. Fine. Curge and Hub are wonderful. Stop by all the time to help. Even hired some men to work the fields and feed the livestock for me. Could hardly tell there wasn't a man around this house."

Swift nodded. "Everything's looking good. But how are *you*?"

"Fine. Fine," she said, opening the iron door of the wood stove and peaking inside.

"How's it look?" said Swift, leaning forward to peak over her shoulder.

"This one's ready," said Sarah.

"Can I help you?"

"I'm fine. Just fine." Sarah took two hot pads from the table and pulled out a nicely tanned pie crust. As she set it on the table, she stared closely at the crust. "Darn it! Just *look* at that. What is wrong with me? Can't bake anything right today."

Swift leaned forward and examined the golden-brown crust, though he could find nothing wrong with it. "You *sure* you're alright?"

"Fine. Fine. All I need is a good pie crust."

Swift waved his hand over the crust. "What's wrong with this?"

Her pointer finger shot like an arrow. "Look at that! It's cracked."

Swift leaned forward, found two hairline fractures in the crust. "Looks good to me."

Sarah straightened until she was rigid. "I'll *not* have people laughing at me, saying I can't make a decent crust."

"No one will even notice."

"I will!"

Swift stepped in front of her, saw her gray eyes clouding. He placed his hand gently on her shoulder and looked deep into her. "It's all right to cry, Aunt Sarah."

"Over pies?"

Swift nodded. "Over pies. John. Anything."

Her eyes welled over with tears and she began to sob.

Swift put his arms around her, felt her little body shaking.

After crying for a few minutes, she dabbed her eyes with the corner of her apron. "How did you know?"

"Just did."

"I miss him so much."

"I know."

"What's going to happen to my boys?"

Swift shook his head. "Don't know."

"You *feel* my pain?"

Swift nodded.

"Why? What have you lost that you loved so much?"

Swift looked into her swollen, red-rimmed eyes, felt like a wall of water was aching to break loose inside of him, too. He looked around the room and shrugged. "I don't know."

August 1862, Tennessee

The candlelight in the tent drew a horde of mosquitoes, which in turn drove Ed to distraction. He dropped his copy of Harpers Weekly and turned to see his brother Nels faring no better in his effort to write home. "Infernal mosquitoes," said Ed. A buzzing droned on until he swatted the side of his face. A candle stood in the rifle attachment of his bayonet two feet away, the sharp blade's point buried well into the ground. By lying flat he was able to read by the little light it offered. He swatted at another bug near the side of his face, then slowly lifted his hand away. "Good." Then he looked at the swarm hovering around the candle.

"Little good that'll do," said Nels. "Just look at them. Must be two dozen blood suckers swarming that candle."

"Oh, well, said Ed. At least we can fight Tennessee mosquitoes. Those Rebs just keep runnin'." He tossed his paper aside, and went to the tent, where he grabbed their instruments. He tossed Nels the banjo, then sat on a log and put his guitar across his knee. "Remember the one those Kentucky boys taught us?" His fingers bounced across the strings, as he sang in a tight rhythm.

Where did you come from?
Where did you go?
Where did you come from Cotton-eyed Joe?

Soldiers gathered round, hand-clapping and knee-slapping. Some brought guitars, harmonicas, or mouth harps. Others danced around the fire. A jug of corn whiskey appeared out of nowhere. As they finished, Sergeant Dowd walked up, face glowing in the firelight. "Seen Solon?"

"Last time was the day before yesterday," said Ed, "and he was still under the surgeon's care. Wasn't feeling like himself yet. Said Doc is sending him home. Should find him in the hospital tent."

"Afraid not. I talked with the steward who said he okayed Solon to return to duty yesterday, but he didn't show up for roll."

Ed looked around in confusion. "Nels, you seen Sol?"

Nels looked up from his banjo and shook his head. "Not since two days ago."

The sergeant took a deep breath and sighed. "Look. Let me know if he shows up. Captain Twogood listed him AWOL. If you see him, tell him to report to me immediately."

"You bet we will," said Ed. "But that steward doesn't make any sense. If the doctor was sending him home, why would he okay him for duty? Sol never missed muster long as I've been here. Certainly wouldn't without good reason."

"I appreciate you being straight with me."

A string of cursing burst out from one of the nearby campfires, causing Ed to jerk around. "What's the matter with that guy, Sarge? Cusses like a sailor at every little thing. About drives me crazy."

Dowd smiled. Can't let it get your goat, Ed. Some of these boys are just a little light on the finer Christian virtues. Doesn't mean they won't be good fighters when the time comes."

"I know. I know. Wish it didn't bother me, but it does. Pulling details with him is a pain. Always complains about everything, blows up over nothing, but it's the cursing that gets me the most. Never talked that way around our place. Can't understand why anyone would. Can't help but wonder what his ma would say either, if she ever heard that talk coming out of his mouth."

"If it bothers you that much, I'll try to keep you apart, but remember that you two may have to rely on each other to stay alive so be careful what you say."

Ed nodded, and Dowd walked away from the fire toward another group of men sitting a short distance away. After he had spoken with them and moved on, Sophie Landt came walking between the tents and sat down between the Best brothers.

"You seen Sol?" asked Ed. "Dowd is looking for him—says he's AWOL."

Sophie's big head shook slow and even, but his mouth turned up at the corners.

Ed tightened his jaw. "What's goin' on? You holding out on us?"

"Okay! Okay! I do know more. But it doesn't make sense to me neither. The surgeon told him to pack up and head home last night, so Sol came by the tent and took his things this morning, then headed toward the railroad. The hospital steward doesn't like Sol—said he was gonna fight it, and ordered Sol to stay until evening. With a medical release in his hand, he wasn't about to wait around for that fellah to mess it up. He figured it was best to leave while he had the strength. Said, 'Too many men are dying in that hospital, and I'm *not* goin' *that* way.'"

Sophie leaned forward and whispered to the boys, "Surgeon who gave him the release said Solon's liver is bad. Only way to nurse it would be to get away from here. When he gave Sol those papers, Doc was leaving for another unit himself. The steward knew—wouldn't honor those orders—told Sol he had to wait until he'd spoken with the new doctor. Knowing the guy has it in for him, Sol decided to get while the getting was good."

"Said if anyone started asking questions, not to tell you until after the sergeant had grilled you. If you didn't know anything, couldn't be blamed for withholding information. He said to tell you he's tired of being sick all the time. Said he was tired of not knowing if and when he would get paid. Said he was tired of trying to explain to his wife how that could be. Said, if the government won't hold up their end of the bargain, he won't be obliged to stay here neither. His medical release got him on the train, so he's gone to Ohio to find Elizabeth at Bowling Green. Feels bad for your mother, even worse for Elizabeth. Said, a man's no better than a heathen if he can't take care of his own family."

Ed stared at Sophie. "Doesn't he know that if the steward didn't post his release they could list him as a deserter? Hope that doctor filed his papers with headquarters before he left. If he didn't, Solon could be brought back and shot! I can't believe he'd do something like this. He's supposed to be the smart one—being First Sergeant and all."

Sophie shook his head. "I know. Told him the same things you're telling me, but he's so disgusted with hearing nothing but bad news from home, and from being sick on account of the lousy salt pork, he couldn't be swayed. Says he's going to Canada with his family where he'll start over. Personally, I don't think he's right in the head yet. That heat stroke, on top of the dysentery, hit him bad. He'd better not lose that medical release, or they could bring him back as a deserter, just like you said. Being a first sergeant, they'd make an example out of him. Let's wait and see—keep our mouths shut."

The brothers nodded and looked around to make sure no one else had heard. Satisfied, Ed went back to picking his guitar, but he couldn't shake the troubled feeling that haunted him. Should he write his mother and tell her what was happening? No, Nels would take care of that. What he wanted most was to talk with his father, who had always made sense of difficult situations.

NINE

"Many bear the emblem,
but the devotees are few."
—Greek Proverb

October 8th, 1862, Perryville, Tennessee

THE SUN ROSE RED OVER THE EASTERN HILLS, AND THE MEN BREAKFASTED early on tin plates around a warm campfire. Ed watched his friends eat, dreading the thought of another day of marching. It had become an exhaustive routine, beginning with breakfast, followed by the taking down of tents, then packing everything onto regimental wagons before forming into columns. After that, it was just dust and marching; endless marching. Hundreds of miles across Kentucky's hills he'd marched, though he couldn't remember half of it. It seemed as though his mind went off somewhere while his body kept its place in line, something like the way a train stays on its tracks, the boxcars not thinking but faithfully following the engine.

But if those miles didn't register with his mind, they did with his feet, especially the ones burned into his soles on long downhill roads that wanted to pull him along faster and faster. That was the one thing he couldn't do, allow his marching to get out of time, and so he'd leaned back and braked, skin on socks and socks on leather, building up this incredible heat that burned all the way up to his knees until he wanted to scream. But through all of that he never stopped—just went on singing songs and marching in time. Oh, God. Not another day of marching. Where was the war he came to fight?

The breakfast fire was laid out within a circle of rocks. Around it Ed's friends sat on various lengths of rough cut logs. It was the usual bunch, Corporals Bill Day, Ole Gilbert, Sophie Landt, Jackson Webster, and Privates Nels Best and Rufus Cowles. Those men had become a close-knit group of friends since leaving home. Their tents ran in long rows parallel to the road, with fires every six tents and rifles stacked in neat tepee fashion halfway between the fires. A larger tent was pitched toward the center of the regiment, barely thirty yards from where Ed sat. From there flowed a continuous stream of orders, that, up until now, had only meant more marching.

"What's this?" asked Bill Day, pointing at a piece of hard tack. He bit hard and pulled it out, then bounced it off a big rock near the campfire. Then repeated the trick several times.

The two-striped Swede Ole Gilbert laughed. "Dat's not even makin' a dent,"

"How's yours, Rufus?" asked Ed.

The mild-mannered private smiled. "Mine's bobbing in my coffee like a cork on a fishing line. Won't soak up or soften up."

Everyone nodded except Jack Webster. He was watching the camp, paying little attention to his friends.

"I got news dat hired help's been goin' fer fifteen dollars a month," said Ole.

"Makes it hard for our folks at home," said Day.

"That's nothin'," said Ed. "Bandits came along with the railroad crews. They've been jumpin' the farmers between Kilbourne and Portage. Caught them on the way back from selling their grain in Portage. Got away with some folks' entire year's wages—everything they'd gotten for their crops."

"What kind of a rodent would do that?" demanded Jack.

"A dead one," said Nels.

"That's right," added Ed. "My cousin Bob Ramsey saw two of them lyin' in the weeds and put his whip to one. Killed him dead on the spot."

Jack scoffed. "What are you smoking in that pipe of yours? Loco weed? Nobody gets killed with a whip if he can defend himself."

"It's no joke." said Nels.

Ed put on his serious face. "Guess you've never seen Big Bob on his wagon. It's a huge rig pulled by ten oxen. His lead oxen is called Jake."

"Yeah," added Nels. "And he's got a whip a mile long to hit him with."

Ed nodded. "Two big ball bearings, give it enough weight to reach the entire team. Ma's letter said one of those balls hit the thief right between the eyes. Killed him on the spot, just like David and Goliath. The other ran off—scared, I guess."

Jack shook his head. "Can't hardly believe that."

All eyes were on Ed. "Wouldn't of believed it myself if I hadn't heard it from Ma. Would've figured it a tall tale."

"What's wrong, Yackson?" asked Ole.

"Nothing," said Jack. "Looks like we better get our gear though. Time to move out again."

Ed followed Jack's gaze to the headquarters tent where several officers and sergeants were leaving. John Gaffney stood with the other sergeants. Every time Ed saw Gaffney, it brought to mind the incident outside Pettibone Hall over one year prior. He ran the thought off, eternally embarrassed by actions he still couldn't understand. Fortunately, Gaffney had turned out to be a good sergeant, one who didn't give the men a hard time unless they deserved it. He was tough but fair, and had never asked what really happened on that crazy night. Instead, he seemed content to lead the other sergeants on, spinning stories around the campfires about his first, second, and third wives. Ed secretly laughed, knowing they had never existed.

A lieutenant walked directly toward Ed and hollered over the long line of company fires, "Break camp and fall in." Sergeants echoed his words down the line as Ed doused the fire by turning over the leftover coffee. The process of repacking knapsacks and folding tents was completed in about an hour.

The bugler sounded assembly, and Ed headed into formation where he heard a familiar voice calling. Rifle in hand, he sprinted to Captain Twogood, whose long, lanky figure floated surreally beneath the early morning sky. A golden aura, a halo of sunlight glowed around the captain, playing off the coarse edges of his long hair and beard. He appeared taller than life, like some giant cherub, and the sight made Best feel as if he should bow, but the angel smiled a pleasant approving smile. Beside the captain stood First Sergeant Dowd, casting a pale shadow.

"Corporal Edward Best reporting as ordered, sir."

"Corporal Best," said Dowd, "there won't be a full-color guard today, but Major Johnson wants you to carry the colors with Corporal Landt, Corporal Webster, and your brother as guard. Give your rifle to Sergeant Major Darrow, procure the Stars and Stripes, and fall in."

Ed took off running, this time toward the Sergeant Major who was overseeing the loading of regimental supplies onto various wagons. As he ran, he wondered at Dowd's words. Normally the guard accompanying the colors only included corporals, so the fact that Nels was included was a curiosity. Was he about to be promoted, or was Major Johnson just allowing him to share the honors? Ed realized the answers to those questions would have to wait, as he came upon Sergeant Major Darrow, who quickly showed him where to pack his rifle. Then Darrow handed him the Stars and Stripes, saying, "Guard this with your life."

"Yes, Sergeant Major," Ed said proudly. Then he marched the regimental flag to the road and to a position at left center of his regiment, where Landt, Jackson, and Nels were already standing at attention, waiting. Ed turned and faced forward. Major Johnson stood out in front of them, talking about the importance of having adequate water.

Water. They'd need plenty on a day like today. At least it wasn't sultry. That'd be a killer. He stood at attention, facing straight ahead. The major rambled on. Ed wasn't one for excess talk. Straight to the point and no fiddling around. That's the way he liked it. But none of that seemed to matter anymore. He was color bearer. He felt his brother's presence beside him, as if he too could hardly contain himself.

"You carrying the colors," whispered Nels. "What an honor!"

"Yeah," Ed whispered back. "But what if I get shot or somethin'? I don't want to be the one to drop the flag. Promise me you'll stick close, take the colors if anything happens."

"Bet your life on it, brother. We're in this thing together. I'm not leaving no matter what happens."

Johnson stepped down and Colonel Chapin took his place. Chapin didn't mince words. "I know you men are tired of marching, tired of eating dust, but you mustn't lose heart. We'll keep pressing the enemy for as long as it takes. We're not afraid to march on, not afraid to press forward, not afraid to *fight*." These were good words, strong words, the words of a confident man. Just the words Ed wanted to hear with the colors in his hands.

"You've done us proud," whispered Nels.

"Shhhh," replied Ed.

"Don't you wish the whole regiment could march through Big Spring right now—you carrying the colors and all?"

"Shhh. You're gonna get us in trouble."

"Hero. That's what you are—a certified hero."

Sergeant Gaffney stepped up between the two. "Knock it off and listen up."

The colonel's words carried through the cool morning air like a swallow on a breeze. "Bragg can't run forever. We're going to pursue him 'til he either stops and fights, or dies of exhaustion."

Ed grinned. Maybe this *would* be the day. Within a matter of minutes the company turned to march in four columns, and Ed moved to the front of the regiment. The cool morning air offered invigorating freshness, and he marched strong for four miles before hearing cannon fire in the distance. The sound sent a rush through his blood, compelling him toward the beckoning thunder.

He marched hard over the first incline, which separated him from the sounds of battle. Below him were low, lush, hills that rolled gently one into another. Off to one side lay a sleepy town whose high church steeples and square buildings reminded him of home.

Somewhere behind him the voice of Sergeant Dowd barked, "Double-quick, march!" and the entire column began to run. They kept a steady pace for two miles, passing pleasant houses and running over long green hills covered with shady oak groves, before coming over the top of a second rise. It was that lofty perch which offered the first glimpse of the battlefield ahead, but the smoke was so thick, Ed couldn't make out what was happening. He wished for a hawk's eye view of this thing. Then a line coursed through his head, "Tis but a base ignoble mind that mounts no higher than a bird can soar," and he remembered his brother Socrates proudly reciting Shakespeare. Where might he be, out there? Somewhere amidst the enemy? No. He wouldn't be, couldn't be.

Rifle fire sounded—like so many wine corks liberated at once. Yet it was distant, unlike the close, threatening volume he remembered from Paint Rock bridge. The faraway rifle fire was intermittently drowned out by the heavier sounds of artillery explosions that sounded like the pounding of a big bass drum.

Dowd yelled above the cannon fire, "Form skirmishes!"

Ed scrambled into place. Everyone was dead silent.

"Load rifles!" commanded Dowd.

By this time artillery guns had been placed ahead of the regiment and were returning the Rebel fire, steadily pounding the battlefield, shaking the ground with every blast. Wind carried the smoke backward, blinding the Wisconsin soldiers even more. They stood fast, unable to see anything for thirty minutes—an eternity of waiting for men with hearts racing, mouths dry, hands sweating.

Colonel Chapin appeared on foot in the smoky fog where he gathered his officers. He looked the part of a warrior in every sense. Tall and well-muscled. Hair black as coal. Dark complexion baked richly brown from endless days riding under the torrid southern sun. One might readily have feared him at first meeting, had it not been for those intriguing green eyes—eyes that studied and questioned everything before him. His presence instilled confidence. Ed watched the man speak to his officers. A few minutes later, Chapin mounted his horse and rode off into the cloud of smoke, an image of composure. No sooner had he left than the captains divided the skirmishers into two groups, one in advance, and one to be held in reserve. Ed and Nels were in the forward group with some three hundred and fifty men.

Dowd's voice broke through the cannon fire. "Forward, march!"

Ed stepped with the flag held high, blinded to the field ahead by the cannon's smoky fog. The skirmish lines moved alongside the road for fifty yards.

"Company, halt!"

The firing stopped, with the exception of a nearby cannon. Ed was ready to jump out of his skin in anxious frustration. Had Bragg pulled back? Had this regiment missed all the action again? Memories of Paint Rock Bridge flashed through his mind like lightning across a night sky. He could feel the splinters ripping through the beams, could feel the bullet strike his arm, could hear the shotgun pellets rattling through the tin roof again. Men fought in the smoke out there, somewhere, someplace. He could hear and feel it, but couldn't see a thing.

A squad of horsemen rode up alongside him, appearing like specters in the unearthly fog. Then the cannon fire stopped altogether, and the cloud dissipated like a curtain rising on the next act of an ongoing play. For the first time, Ed saw the beautiful green pastures below him. They were littered with countless corpses of men in blue and gray, whose horses were either lying dead, trying desperately to get up, or crazed and running wild. Men were strewn about in every conceivable fashion, in clumps of blue, clumps of gray, or mixed. Some lay alone. Some were whole and covered with blood, while others were horribly mutilated. Bodies were missing limbs and cut in half. This was the battlefield's harvest, and the site burrowed deep into Ed's mind, like a badger tears earth, rock, and root to make its shelter.

He stood perfectly still, open-mouthed, mutely surveying the destruction before him. His hands clenched the flagpole so tightly that his fingers and knuckles turned white. He tarried for only a minute, though it seemed like an hour. Then the enemy artillery opened fire, and cannon balls exploded in the field around him. The cavalrymen struggled—only half successful in keeping their horses from rearing and bucking, but Ed didn't see any fall. They were expert horsemen. Had to be in order to stay on their mounts under these conditions. Dirt rained from the sky as shells blew earth into air. Someone shouted orders in the distance, and the cavalry pulled back. A battery of Simmons' artillery flashed past, the cannons and crews riding wildly in front of Ed's company. When they got twenty-five yards beyond him, they halted, dismounted, and brought their cannons to bear on the enemy.

Captain Twogood waved his sword. "Sergeants!" he said. "Move your men to support the artillery!"

"Forward!" shouted Dowd.

The Union cannons struck hard. A Rebel battery exploded in the distance, its men thrown like so many rag dolls into the air. Other shells landed amidst soldiers in long gray lines. Human beings were shredded, body parts blown in every direction. And all that time, the Rebel artillery shells exploded in the smoke around Ed. Unhindered, the line double-quicked to a position directly behind the artillery. They were told to halt and lie down. With cannon shells flying overhead, the order didn't have to be repeated. Just ahead and slightly below him, Ed watched Simmons' artillerymen loading and firing their guns as fast as humanly possible.

An explosion dropped more dirt on Ed. "Gall dang!" he cried. "They're gonna get us one of these times."

Then a shell landed in their midst, sending Ed flying a few feet into the air, spinning full around before sprawling to the ground face down. The sound was terrifying and the force even worse—like the end of the world. He pushed his head hard against the ground, imploring its shelter. It yielded none. Men screamed. Others cried like school children. How many had been hit? He wished he knew something about medicine, something to help those poor men. Then he remembered the flag, his duty, and groped amidst the smoke to find it. His hands touched something cold and clammy. He drew it nigh. A man's hand. He threw it away, turned the other direction, and groped some more. Then he found the flag. Rising to his knees, he raised the colors. It seemed lifeless on the mast, a wrinkled mass of stars and stripes hanging straight down the pole. Then Nels was there beside him. Where he'd come from or how he'd found him, Ed had no idea.

Nels gaped at Ed—terror in his cool gray eyes. "Did you see that? Somebody's hand landed on me over there. Ed, we've gotta get out of here before we get killed."

But Ed kept knelt in a crouch, shaking his head hard. Fear could spread like an epidemic in this atmosphere. The flag above him was a sure target for the distant gunners, visible even amidst all this smoke. He wanted desperately to get closer to the ground. "There isn't any place to run. Gotta wait or we'll end up runnin' straight into the Rebs."

The dirt on his hands from the explosions caused him to wipe mud across his forehead as he tried to keep the salty drops of sweat from stinging his eyes. He noticed his hands shaking and looked away.

Nels squinted through the smoky fog. "Right. Better stay here. Gotta keep an eye on that flag in case you drop it."

Ed grinned at his brother and dropped lower on his knees, until his heels dug deep into his butt. Through the smoke he saw Colonel Chapin seated high upon his horse near the gunners, talking to Captain Simmons, and pointing off toward the left side of the battery. Within seconds, Chapin rode over and shouted something at the company commanders.

Captain Twogood turned and yelled at his lieutenants, "Form up!"

"On your feet!" shouted the sergeant. "To the left, march. Double-quick, march."

Ed ran at the head of the column, around the front of the battery, and some one hundred twenty-five yards further to where the regiment formed into two firing lines. He had clear vision from here. On the other side of the valley, an entire Confederate regiment formed into battle lines, their cannons firing beside them. Large puffs of smoke shot out of the barrels, and a second or two later, the sound of their discharge reached his ears. Then came a short whirring sound just before the shell erupted and the ground shook. The Union's artillery explosions landed in and around the Rebel regiment as their commander led them into a small woods. It looked as though he would use that cover to gain a flanking position without letting the artillery pound his men to pieces.

Colonel Harris, the acting brigadier, rode up on a white horse.

"There they are, men—going into the woods. Don't worry. They won't get far before they bump into one of my regiments. Then they'll come out running. Don't fire 'til you've got a sure shot."

Just as he'd said, less than five minutes passed before the woods erupted with rifle fire. Shoot! thought Ed. The enemy was about to run out of the woods and directly at him. Rifles rose in a long line beside him as he anxiously waited, mouth and throat dry, heart beating as though it would explode out of his chest. Then came a sudden bladder urge. Instead of giving in to it, he gripped the flagstaff tighter in his sweating hands. A line of gray charged out of the woods screaming like nothing he'd ever heard. The hair on his arms stood up. His scalp tightened.

Captain Twogood shouted, "First line, kneel! Ready—" The first line dropped to their knees, while the second line stepped up behind them, forming Johnson's wall of fire. Major Johnson had never liked the single battle lines in the book, since it gave neither side any advantage. To remedy this, he'd adopted the British method, where the front line knelt, firing at once. Immediately afterward, the first stagger of the second line fired. The third then fired in turn, making a fast and furious wall of lead for the enemy to come through.

The rifles beside Ed lowered, leaving him feeling naked and exposed. Instinctively he knelt beside his brother, wishing himself closer to the ground.

The screaming enemy was within sixty yards when someone shouted, "Fire!" A volley of muskets fired. An entire line of men dressed in gray fell.

But others hurdled their fallen comrades and kept advancing. The second line of Yankees fired, shredding the second line of attacking Rebels like the first. The remnant of the Confederate infantry continued within fifteen yards of the skirmishers, until the third line, still standing, opened up.

The Union men fired, reloaded, and fired again. The anguished faces of the Rebels buckled beneath multiple hailstorms of Yankee lead. Why would anyone charge into sure death like this, Ed wondered. He suddenly found himself feeling sorry for them—for this slaughter—for the men and boys crumbling on the field before him, and wished he could make it stop. The enemy's momentum broke. The survivors turned and fled. Shouts of victory filled the air as Union men threw their hats in triumph. Ed stood numb, unable to savor the victory.

Nels stood up and pounded him on the back. "Glory be! We drove them off like a pack of dogs with their tails tucked 'tween their legs."

"Maybe so," said Ed, "but holdin' this flag and standing like an open target gives me the willies."

While the men in blue congratulated themselves, the Rebels gathered another regiment at the brow of the nearest hill. Bullets filled the air. Sergeant Dowd shouted, "Skirmishes! First line kneel and return their fire!"

The enemy charged up the hill in long lines, screaming their awful noise as they jumped over the dead. The Union men in the first line remained mostly uninjured, firing, reloading, then firing again. But the men in the second line were falling here and there. Some dropping straight to the ground, others staggering backwards. Ed felt disconnected, merely an observer of the forces battling around him. He stood in the open field, holding his flag and watching men fire and fall, pushed along by a tempest of its own fury. What role did he play here?

The rifles fired in volleys on one side of him as Simmons' men wheeled a cannon up on the other. A long, black, iron barrel mounted on wagon wheels, shined and clean on the outside, as if ready for inspection. But when they filled it with powder and bombs the size of small boulders, it could wreak havoc at a distance. Now the artillerymen prepared it for use at close range, stuffing the barrel with a bucket load of nails and lead the size of big fat grapes. It fired. Flames belched, smoke shooting ten feet from the end of the barrel. Like a giant shotgun it tore a bloody hole through the oncoming line, shredding men's bodies as if they were paper.

The air was black with a hail of rocks, dirt, flying debris, and lead coming from all directions, from huge explosions in the air and on the ground, and from carefully measured charges that propelled little balls from long pipes. Musket fire flew in showers back and forth across the rolling hills. Bullets whizzed and buzzed around the heads of the defenders. Arms and heads jerked in reflex spasms as bodies splayed themselves grotesquely across the field. And somehow amidst all the rifle's fire and cannon's explosions, Ed heard the sounds of the wounded wailing and crying for help, clawing at his heart with every moan.

Sergeant Dowd stepped to the front line and shouted orders. A shell struck him with such force that his feet left the ground. He fell backward. Whether unconscious or dead, Ed couldn't know. Bullets ripped through the flag in his hands, threatening to pull it out of his grip. One passed through the mast, driving splinters into his face. It stung so badly that he rubbed the side of his cheek, only to return with a handful of blood.

The Rebels continued advancing before him. So many, and they just kept coming. He turned to his friends. Sixty or seventy lay dead or badly wounded. No one helped the wounded away, either. They were too busy digging madly through the belts of their fallen friends to find more ammunition.

Major Johnson lay in the middle of them, his golden shoulder straps covered with blood. Sergeant Forsythe's body lay just a few feet away, his head painted red. Colonel, captain, sergeant, or corporal—rank made no difference. Men of every social status were dying, men who had been his friends for months or years. It seemed a miracle that anyone was alive, yet nearly a third still stood. Nels pulled a cap from the belt of Jim Dickinson and stuck it on the nipple of his rifle. Dickenson, dead too?

Soldiers stopped ransacking their fallen comrades' pouches, as the enemy pressed in. Those who were able stood up, drawing pistols and knives, fumbling with bayonets, determined to defend their ground or die.

Ed pulled out his pistol and fired fast into the patchwork of gray cloth. It felt good, bridging the chasm that had made him a spectator. The battle swallowed him into its fury. He holstered his pistol and marched forward with the colors flying overhead. A bullet struck him in the hip and tripped him hard. The flag slipped from his grip. He reached to regain it. He could not. He watched in horror. He'd let his regiment down, failed in his charge. At the last possible moment, a pair of hands snatched it before it hit the ground.

A cheer leapt from Ed's mouth as Nels lifted the colors high. Then the back of his brother's head exploded into pieces of bone and blood. "Neeels!" he screamed, as the limp form crumpled before him. Someone rescued the flag, again catching it before it hit the ground. Ed looked around as though suddenly lost. The man who'd caught the colors turned around just in time to catch a bullet in the chest, but before the flag could touch the ground, another caught and raised it. The sight sent a fury through Ed he'd never known, and he pulled out his pistol, reloaded, and started shooting every Rebel he could see. "Dogs," he shouted, "burn in Hell!"

He fired until the gun was empty, then picked up another from the ground and fired it, shooting wildly, blindly amidst the melee of struggling men about him. The battlefield was reduced by this time to a chaotic mass of bodies—wrestling, kicking, biting, stabbing and choking—men doing everything possible to stay alive. A few feet away, Sophie Landt grappled over a knife against a huge man with a long beard. A wounded Rebel, sitting on the ground, reached over and took a bayonet from his rifle, raising it to drive into Sophie's leg. Ed picked up another pistol and casually shot the man in the side of the head. Blood poured out from the place the bullet entered, and the man fell forward over the body of a dead Yankee.

"Bastards," hollered Ed. "Die." And he laughed at the corpse, laughed at the sickly figure of death. "You killed my brother," he shouted, as he fired again and again at the men around him. His pistol wasted, he plucked another from a fallen Rebel and fast resumed firing. Sophie was above him, swinging his rifle in a wide arc, batting down Rebels as they tried to come at him with bayonets. A loud cracking noise signaled the breaking of his weapon, but he instantly picked up another and swung it in the same way.

Reinforcements charged into the fray. Ed spotted the yellow Indiana patches on theirs shoulders, and silently thanked God for Indiana. A lanky one with long gold braids discarded his rifle and pulled out a revolver. Darting wildly through the chaotic tangle of bodies, he seemed to drop a Confederate with every step. He looked so good, so fresh, so strong. The Tenth Regiment was in shambles, an army of rag-suited men on a field covered with dead and wounded. And when the Indianans had finished the Confederates at short range, they turned their rifles on the other advancing gray lines. Their fire turned the tide, and the remaining Rebels scrambled back down the field.

The firing stopped. The enemy was out of sight. The newly arrived soldiers turned and tended the wounded. Ed gave thanks for a rest from the carnival of death this madness had spawned, but it was a respite short-lived. Before anyone could get to him, another line of gray—incredible, irrevocable—surged up the bloody hill. "They're coming!" he shouted.

The Union soldiers formed ranks and fired in unison. Two Rebel lines fell, but more took their place. Lines formed, clashed, broke, and more lines formed, relentless blue and gray. Ed emptied his revolver, filled it with shells from a fallen comrade, and emptied it again.

Someone behind him shouted, "Fall back and form skirmishes!" The order instantly eroded the men's confidence. Some turned their backs and ran. Others fired and reloaded before running back a few steps. There they turned and fired again. Ed felt the sudden terror of being abandoned.

A pair of arms reached beneath his shoulders and jerked hard, pulling him to a standing position. "Can you hobble on your good leg?" It was Sophie—pistol in hand.

"Sure," said Ed." Then he remembered his brother. "What about Nels? Can't leave him."

"Nothing we can do for Nels, but if we don't get out of here, we'll join him real soon."

Ed relented, scared and confused. Somehow the two hobbled back to the new Union skirmish lines without being hit. Fresh ammunition was distributed, and everyone continued firing—unwilling to retreat further. The Confederates had lost so many, that they pulled back to trade volleys. This continued for another hour before it was reduced to only occasional rifle fire.

Ed turned his foot inward. The bullet ripped away the outer part of his hamstring. The muscle jumped, jerked his leg in spasm, and bolted hot pain to his brain. A curious thing. He gently turned it again. This time it didn't jump, though it burned with every movement. He could see the open sore, hardly deep enough to call a wound. He straightened the game leg, began to roll onto his knees, but the minute his knee bent, the pain jolted him again. He decided to wait for the doctor.

By evening, the foes set up camp on opposite sides of the valley. Ed sat beside a campfire, staring into the glowing flames, mesmerized by their dance. He looked at his hands and saw them shaking. Felt like his whole body was trembling.

"You okay?" asked Sophie.

Ed started to cry, looked away. "No. I'm *not* okay. Hell. I'll never be okay."

Sophie nodded. "It was tough out there. Sorry about Nels."

"Damn," said Ed. "I'm sorry about Nels, too. Sorry those Rebels killed him. I was shooting everybody, just shooting and shooting. I don't even know who I was aiming at half the time. Can't remember their faces. Can't remember who I shot. Maybe I shot some of our own. Can't remember. Can't remember a single goddamned face." He started to cry again. So sorry for killing. Sorry for not aiming. Sorry for shooting at all. Hell. He was even sorry about all this goddamned swearing. Mother wouldn't like it. Wouldn't like it one bit. None of it. Well. He'd wanted to be a man—and look at him now. A man all right—

a *murdering* man. He hated himself. Hated everything and everyone, everyone except mother. But mother wasn't here, couldn't make it better.

"Listen," said Sophie. "That was no picnic for me neither. Shoot. I was swinging my musket everywhere, and didn't care if I caught a bullet. I just didn't want to catch one of those pig-stickers in my gut. Couldn't think of anything except lying on the field with my belly slit open and my innards hanging out. Damn. Ed, I nearly hit one of those Indiana boys who came in to help us. Would've cracked his head open, but the poor guy took a bullet in the face right before I was gonna hit him. Look. I've been thinking. Maybe it was predetermined. You know—his time to go, one way or the other, and it didn't matter one lick what we did out there because it was just gonna be that way no matter what."

Ed didn't say anything. He was looking for those faces, the ones he couldn't see. They *were* there, somewhere. He knew it, but he couldn't call them up, couldn't recall a single one. When would he see them? When he closed his eyes? When he was asleep? Damn! What had he done? God damn. Yes. God damn everything. Would God damn him? Who in Hell was he anyway, and what was he doing here? Killing people? Killing *Americans*?

The questions went on and on, over and over, with no answers to quell his burden. Throughout most of the night he lay awake, afraid to go to sleep. Every shadow harbored familiar images, the pointed dragon-wings of the long-forgotten cockatrice, the face of some familiar friend, or some unknown specter. Then came the night sounds, the cries of the wounded and dying men still out there, still lying on the battle field. He cried on and off before finally falling asleep, but then the faces came, one by one, and he was killing them all over again. They were Confederates and Yankees, soldiers and civilians, even horses, and they were all coming after him, and he just kept shooting, killing them all. He awoke and thought, What have I become, Mama? Oh, God. What have I become? Then he fell asleep, only to awaken again and again, terrorized by the sounds of the wounded and dying.

October 10th, 1862, Perryville, Kentucky

Sophie Landt walked over to the fire where Ed Best sat, coffee cup in hand. "How's that leg?" said Sophie.

"All right. I guess. Anyway, better than the ones we loaded on ambulances yesterday."

"That bandage help any?"

"Yeah. If I keep it tight, it's almost as though there were no wound." No sooner had he finished speaking than his eyes wandered off—staring into space. A depressive gloom clouded everything. The stench of death was everywhere, and the bright colored leaves blowing gently in the autumn wind rippled like miniature yellow, red, and orange flags over the mangled mass of humanity strewn over the hillside as far as the eye could see. Horses lay about the field, like toppled statues—legs stiff—frozen in rigor mortis; while ravens flew everywhere, picking at the flesh of the fallen warriors and animals alike. No one bothered to chase them away any more. None had the strength.

"Captain says we'll be pulling out by noon," said Sophie. "You want to go and say a few words over Nels before we leave?"

"No. Couldn't stand to see his body all swollen up. At least we got the wounded out. What do you think they'll do with all those bodies? They won't just leave them to be picked at by the buzzards, will they?"

Sophie shook his head. "Captain Twogood says the general made arrangements for some of the slaves from the city to start burying the bodies this afternoon. They're his boys, too. He's just as concerned as you. Come on. Let's get our things together."

They rolled up the blankets they had slept on under the cool, clear autumn sky. The first night it was nearly impossible to sleep with the images of battle so fresh in the mind, the adrenaline coursing through Ed's veins, and the terrible cries of the wounded filling the night air. In fact, it was a relief to go and help those poor fellows when the sun finally rose on the second day.

Sophie had recruited him then, to help load ambulances with wounded, probably to take his mind off Nels. But it hadn't helped much, seeing men he had known to be strong and healthy with portions of their limbs blown off. Some were left with arms dangling by a few strands of muscle and tendon, their bones shattered by musket balls. Others lay dead, their abdomens puffing up like balloons in the hot autumn sun. Others could not be found at all, their bodies blown into little pieces that now littered the field.

And amidst this countryside of carnage there was the most peculiar sight — the sight of men in gray and blue, working side by side, ministering to their fallen brethren, oblivious to the malice they had known for each other only hours before. Ed had seen them, even observed them, but couldn't look them in the eyes, couldn't hate them as he had before, couldn't forgive them, either. So he just worked around them, almost ignoring them, but not quite. They were all working for the same cause now, trying to put the pieces back together again. It was impossible, and it was all their faults, all the work of their hands. They were brothers again, whether blue or gray, brothers in devastation and death. But like brothers after a mean fight, they weren't talking to one another, maybe never would.

Strangely, the scene had brought some kind of closure to the battle, allowing Ed to sleep on the second night. In fact, he slept so soundly that the next day he forgot the nightmares the carnage had spawned. Instead, he awakened with a certain numbness, something like a cheap-whiskey hangover, only worse, for he wasn't merely trying to forget having made himself a fool, but for having tasted the lust for blood—for having struggled with his fellow man for the *right* to survive. Behind it lay the terrible guilt that where others had failed, fallen, and given up the ghost, he had survived and *earned* the right to live another day. Somehow it marred the future, made everything drab. He had seen a different side of human nature borne out in the person of his enemy, his friends, and worst of all, himself.

Ed assembled his belongings and entered formation once again. The sergeants called roll, Ed taking careful note that nearly half of those who had gone into battle were no longer present. Nels Best, Major Johnson, Sergeant Forsythe, Corporal Dickinson, Bill Whicker, Sergeant Dowd, Lewis Shelby, Charlie Donaldson, Jim Cummings, Hiram Luther, Lyman Burlison, and so many others—all familiar faces—all wounded or dead. When roll call was completed, Colonel Chapin addressed the men, commending them for their "bravery and steadfastness under the most savage fighting in this battle." Ed could barely relate to the things being said. Then General Rosecrans, or "Old Rosie" as the men called him, addressed the regiment.

"You and your color bearers have set a standard here," he said. "One which will not be forgotten. When a color bearer went down, another took his place. Every time your flag fell, it was lifted. It was your sixth man who left the field with it—a flag so battered, it bore forty-one holes through the cloth and two through the staff. You have fought gallantly, and I commend you all."

Ed listened in numbed silence as Captain Ely was promoted to major in place of the deceased Major Johnson. Tears pooled in the corners of his eyes as he remembered his brother pledging not to let the flag fall, snatching the colors, his head exploding.

When the accolades finished, he faced left with the rest of his column, marching out of camp past the field of swollen dead bodies, where the ambulances and grave diggers were fast at work. The stench was so terrible in the heat that the workers wore bandanas over their noses. Ed wondered why the smell didn't bother him. Because this was the work of his own hands? He thought about the story he had heard as a child—of the Garden of Eden, and Adam's and Eve's boy Cain slaying their good son, Abel. Then he remembered God's words, "The blood of thy brother cries out from the ground to me." His thoughts digressed to: "Thou shalt not kill." The shame weighed like a millstone yoked about his neck.

For the first time since September of 1861, Ed didn't feel like a conquering hero. He was a murderer—a participant in the death of his own brother. His thoughts fled home to when he was a boy and his little brother Rosewood died. Such sadness in their house, so many tears, such unbearable grief. What would it be like for his mother now? She had just lost her husband and now another son. They were all supporters of Lincoln and his policies, supporters of the war. The Union must be preserved, slavery abolished. But at this price? All these dead and wounded men? Were they committing murder to prevent a few miserable slave whippings, or was there something greater at stake here? The thoughts ran helter-skelter through his mind. Everything was nonsense. What had once seemed so clear evaded him now. Why had Nels died? He couldn't bear to think about it. Instead he turned his attention to the marching men who sang *The Red White and Blue*, for a lively cadence to take their minds off of the fields they left behind, and Ed lifted his voice to join them.

As the column marched past the fallen men along the road, Negro workers lifted lifeless bodies by their arms and legs, placing them onto wagons and carts. They too sang a song while they labored, the song of Moses: *Let My People Go*.

A huge, muscular slave, able to lift these bodies by himself, unlike the others who worked in pairs, reached down to lift another fallen Yankee, when the corpse suddenly groaned and moved.

The slave stepped back, eyes white and wide, his heart pounding like a bass drum.

Another groan came, followed by some incoherent mumbling.

"Co—pral," he shouted, "dis one's alive. Come quick."

A short, thin, Yankee corporal walked over to the place where the troubled black man stood. Looking down, he understood the fellow's surprise. It appeared as though part of the skull had been chipped out on the back of this soldier's head. White tissue shone through bloody brown strands of hair.

"Poor fellow, doesn't look as though he has much chance. Does it?"

"No, sir. Is a miracle."

"Let's get that wagon over here, and take him to the hospital. If he's stayed alive this long, maybe he'll survive the ride." The black man went to get the wagon, and the corporal leaned closer to feel for a pulse. "Well, Private," he whispered softly. "I don't know what we can do for you, but if you've made it this far, God must have given his angels charge over you."

TEN

"The last of those qualities which make
a state virtuous must be justice,
if we only knew what that was."
—Socrates

Early November, 1862 Portage, Wisconsin

SWIFT WALKED INTO THE COLUMBIANA COUNTY COURTHOUSE AT PORTAGE WITH a distinct limp, but his leg and back muscles had recovered to the point where he walked erect with the help of a handsome black cane. His brown hair was neatly combed with a part straight down the center of his head. He wore a brand new suit, new brown leather shoes, and a bright gold watch with a shiny gold chain that hung from his pocket. He looked every bit as agile as before, with the exception of the left leg, which still refused to carry his weight. His arm leaned heavily on the hand-crafted cane. A silver lion's face stared from its head. It was the first thing he bought after returning from Missouri. Before discharge, the army awarded him a fifty percent disability pension, as if proclaiming him to be only half a man. He was determined to prove them wrong.

A precursory glance about the room revealed a diversity of folks. Normally he enjoyed meeting and talking with people from different ethnic origins, but the faces in this crowd shot hard and calloused glances toward Robert Ramsey. Their demeanor made Swift grateful for his own family and friends gathered to support Robert. It reminded him of how alone he'd felt at Libby Prison, even amongst his comrades. Living in the midst of overt hostility could do that.

There could be no more doubting the words of Jeremiah: "The heart is deceitful above all things, and desperately wicked: who can know it?" He had seen it on the battlefield and in the Rebel prisons. But worst of all, the Chicago papers were now claiming that a small ring of corrupt Union soldiers had been uncovered at the Camp Randall Prisoner Facility. The group had been shorting the prisoners while selling their allotted food and blankets for profit, and Swift felt guilty that he hadn't been willing to help.

Behind the desk sat a fat little gray-haired man in a judge's robe, sifting through a pile of legal documents. Swift had never seen him before. Uh, oh. He turned to his father, who gave him a reassuring look before pointing toward cousin Robert. The big fellow followed Swift like a lost puppy looking for a home. Swift spotted Robert's forehead furrowing over arched eyebrows. His troubled eyes studied those hateful faces around him. Swift took him by the arm and ushered him into a seat beside his own.

"Don't pay them any mind, Robert. Just concentrate on me and the judge." Was he really good enough for this? Pa said so. Uncle Jim, too. But Swift was only a legal assistant, wasn't finished with his studies. What if Robert went to jail? He shouldn't have to—not for what he did.

This case gave Swift a sense of purpose. He felt strong again, almost confident. Before pulling out a chair for himself, he looked back over the seats to the rear of the room. Fred Landt and his wife were there, as were Doc, Emily, Curge, Hub, and Sarah Best. The Wards and a few more families stood near the door. The place was packed. On the other side of the room sat several large families.

"Where'd all these people come from?" whispered Robert.

"Seen some of 'em around Portage," said Swift, "but I don't know any of them."

"Me, neither. Just wish there weren't so dog gone many."

"More people coming every day, Robert, especially with so many men off to war. There's plenty of harvesting, railroading, and logging work to be done." Turning his attention toward the table, he pulled his heavy wooden chair along the floor, which made a loud wailing sound as its legs vibrated on the hard wood. "Darn," he mumbled. "Why don't I just drop my drawers and shout so everybody'll look our way at once?" As he spoke, he sensed the crowd's eyes focus on him and his cousin. He turned and flashed a reassuring grin at Robert.

Robert returned the smile, but his forehead wrinkled again over his arched eyebrows.

"Relax, cousin. I know you're nervous, but don't worry. The district attorney will summarize what he's found and then present his witness. After they've had their say, we'll have ours. Don't say anything while those people are talking. Understood?" Robert nodded, and Swift went on, "Good! Just remember: this is an informal hearing. The judge is simply going to decide if there's enough evidence for a trial. From what you've told me, I don't think you'll have anything to worry about."

A gavel snapped crisply on hard oak. "Order in the court," said the judge, and he peered through round, turquoise eyes, until the talking stopped. "The purpose of this informal hearing is to determine if there's enough evidence in the state versus Robert Ramsey, for the wrongful death of Ryan Radigan, to warrant a formal trial. The district attorney will go first."

A tall, thin, eagle-eyed, blond-haired man in a gray, three-piece suit, stood up from the table on the right side of the room, and took two steps toward the judge. Swift knew him. Dan Brown, a young, up-and-coming lawyer with obvious political aspirations, a true intellectual in the matter of book learning, but a little short in the common-sense department. Even so, he'd demonstrated an unusual amount of savvy lately in that, while so many good community leaders were off fighting the war, he'd managed to land a job that exempted him from such service.

"Your Honor," he said, rising from his chair and standing in place. "Ryan Radigan, a worker on the local railroad, who was staying in our town while conducting business for his employer, was found dead at roughly four o'clock in the afternoon on the first day of this month, about five miles this side of Kilbourne, along the road to Portage." He stopped and surveyed the room, then looked straight at Robert.

"It is known that the accused, Robert Ramsey, was in Portage earlier that day, selling produce from his farm at Big Springs, in the Township of New Haven, and that he left for home shortly after noon. Furthermore, Sean Radigan, who was walking along the road with his brother, Ryan, will testify that he watched as Robert Ramsey willfully struck Ryan with a deadly force. As mute testimony of Robert Ramsey's malicious intention, Sean will also testify that the accused made no attempt to help Ryan, even after he had seen the poor fellow fall under the power of his blow. Instead, he rode on to Kilbourne, while Ryan Radigan lay helpless beside the road."

A smirk worked its way across District Attorney Brown's face. His head turned slowly, and he scanned the room before sitting back down.

"Thank you for stating the case of the state so succinctly," said the judge. "Now, would the counsel for Mr. Ramsey please stand and state the particulars of his defense?"

Swift pulled himself over the table, and manipulated the cane beneath his left hand.

"Your Honor," he began. "I believe the defense can show that Robert Ramsey has never intentionally injured any man, and that the death of Ryan

Radigan was accidental. In the course of this short hearing, the state will come to the realization that to prosecute my client would be a travesty of justice. Thank you."

Swift sat down, expressionless. Robert turned and stared him in the eye. "Why didn't you tell them everything? They need to know—"

"Don't worry. I know what I'm doing. We'll have plenty of time to tell our story." Worries of losing scratched at his mind, but Swift wouldn't let them take over. In order to win he must show no fear. Then came the words of the Psalmist:

"The LORD is my rock, my fortress, and my deliverer; my God, my strength, in whom I will trust."

The judge turned to Brown. "You may call your first witness, Counselor."

"The state calls Sean Radigan to the stand," said Brown.

A small man with thin red hair and beard arose from his seat, stepped into the middle of the aisle, and walked to the front of the room, where he was sworn in before sitting down. "Mr. Radigan," Brown continued, "please tell the judge, in your own words, how your brother was killed on the first of this month."

Radigan sat for a moment scratching his red beard. A straight part coursed down the middle of his red head, brown eyes blinking repeatedly, as he looked about the room. "Well. It's like I told the man here. Me and me brother was walking down the side of the road when Bob Ramsey comes toward us, his big wagon and oxen taking up nearly the whole thing. I told me brother, Ryan, God rest his soul, that he'd better step aside b'fore the idiot runs him over. We'd just stepped into the grass when that big fellah lifts his long whip and smacks me brother right in the face. I run to Sean's side, but couldn't bring him round. He died in me arms. I cried for Ramsey to send help, but he just rode away and left me poor brother to die."

A short, portly woman at the back of the room stood and yelled at the top of her lungs, "Murrrderer! You should be ashamed of yerself, ridin' off and leavin' me poor boy to die like that." The room buzzed.

The judge pounded his gavel until the place was quiet, then looked straight at the fat lady. "There'll be no more outbursts like that, or you'll be removed from this courtroom. The purpose of this meeting is to determine the facts, and that will be accomplished in an orderly manner." He turned to Brown. "Now, is there any other evidence the state desires to present?"

Brown nodded. "Your Honor, I would like to present the death certificate of Ryan Radigan, signed by Dr. Seaman, which shows the cause of death as being struck in the forehead by a blunt instrument. Also, we have the murder weapon, the whip, with its large steel balls sewn into its ends." Brown stepped forward and offered these items for the judge to examine, which he did for several minutes, rolling the big ball bearing ends in his hands and slapping them against his wrist.

"Very well," said the judge. "We will now hear from the defense. Mr. Best, what evidence do you have to refute the claims of the state that your client willingly took the life of Ryan Radigan, on the road between Portage and Kilbourne, on the first day of October, 1862?"

Swift remained seated as he addressed the bench. "First, I would like to ask a few questions of Mr. Radigan, your Honor." The judge nodded, and Swift turned to face the red-head. "Mr. Radigan, you say you were walking on the road from Kilbourne to Portage. What was your business in Kilbourne that brought you down the highway on that day?"

Radigan shifted his feet, looked nervously around the room, eyes blinking. "I don't rightly remember. Maybe it was business."

Careful, thought Swift. Lead him gently. Can't tip my hand yet. "So, you don't rightly remember what brought you down the road that led to the death of your brother. Well. Let me ask you another question. Can you tell me the *exact* place where your brother died?"

This time the Irishman smiled, eager to answer. "Sure. About five miles out of the Kilbourne turn off, where the woods rise above the road. Everyone knows that place."

Swift smiled. Got you now, you little weasel. His jaw slid forward. "And is it true that your brother was carrying a rifle with him at the time?"

The witness's gaze darted nervously around the room. "Sure. We had our guns fer hunting. That's right! We'd just been out hunting. That's what we were doin' out by Kilbourne."

Go ahead, squirm, Radigan. "Isn't it true that you had a .58 caliber rifle, and your brother had a .44 caliber pistol?" as Radigan nodded. Swift stood up. "Since when do you hunt with a .44 caliber pistol?"

Radigan's brown eyes blinked without ceasing. "Me brother just had his pistol. We shared the rifle and took turns shooting at deer. Say, what is this? I'm not the one what *killed* me brother. He is!" He pointed a shaky finger at Robert as a chorus of voices chattered around the room.

"Hang the murrrderer!" a man shouted.

The judge's head jerked up as his gavel pounded the table. "Sheriff," he demanded, "remove that man from the back of this room, and anyone else who speaks up."

Swift looked to the back of the room and spotted the burly, blond-haired figure of the local sheriff. He hadn't noticed him standing there, but was expecting him to testify on Robert's behalf. The sheriff took two long strides and jerked a skinny young man up from his seat and out the door. The image caused Swift to whisper a quick prayer that Robert wouldn't leave this place in the same manner. The burden of responsibility pressed on him.

Satisfied that the crowd was in order again, the judge turned his attention to Swift. "Do you have any more questions of Mr. Radigan, Counselor?"

Swift smiled at the judge. "No. I don't, your honor. But I would like to call Mr. Ramsey to tell his side of the story."

Robert arose and walked quietly to the waiting chair. After swearing to the truth, he looked nervously about the room so clearly divided between friend and foe. Swift knew how he must feel, like going up that hill above Bull Run—lips dry, tongue stuck to the roof of your mouth, knees wanting to give way, kidneys making water. Robert hated speaking publicly, too, but that didn't matter. He was fighting for his life.

Swift walked closer, pacing back and forth to block Robert's view of the district attorney. Robert started with a slight stammer, but once he got rolling, everything poured out. He told the story of the two highwaymen on the road—how he was riding home from the market, pocket full of money from the sale of his crops, when two gunmen jumped out from the bushes. He cast his whip out, trying to jerk the rifle out of one man's hands. But it hit that gunman in the forehead and he went down. The other simply ran away, and Robert headed for town as fast as his oxen could move. He never looked back, never thought he might have killed someone. His story finished, he looked around, blue eyes wide.

"Thank you, Robert," said Swift. He smiled, placed a reassuring hand on Robert's shoulder and said, "Your witness counselor," but Brown declined, and Swift turned to the judge again. "Your Honor, I would like to call the sheriff to tell the court what's been happening along the road between Kilbourne and Portage."

Murmurs started, but one knock of the gavel silenced the crowd as the hefty sheriff stepped to the front of the room, swore in and sat down. The silver-haired judge shuffled some papers, picked up a pencil, lowered his head, and started writing. "Is it true, Sheriff," asked Swift, "there have been numerous robberies on the road between Kilbourne and Portage this fall?"

The sheriff put his hand to his chin and replied, "Why, yes. That's true."

"Have you obtained any descriptions of these highway robbers from their victims? If you have, please tell the court about them."

The sheriff smiled wide, flipping his hands and gesturing as he spoke. "Why, yes. I've had numerous descriptions of these villains, and from what I've heard, I believe the same two men have conducted all these robberies. From the descriptions I have, they're two short, red-headed men. They generally lie in wait along the edge of the woods where the hill comes just over the road from Portage to Kilbourne. Most everyone says they speak with an accent, but their faces have always been covered by bandanas. One man uses a pistol and the other a rifle."

"I see," said Swift, pausing for effect. "And just how far out is this area in relation to the spot where Ryan Radigan's body was found?"

"Why, it's about five miles outside of Kilbourne, the same general area where Ryan Radigan died."

Swift turned to Brown, who was flexing his chin muscles and staring at the ceiling. Come on, come on, thought Swift. Surely *you* can see it now. "Your Honor," said Swift, "the defense moves that all charges against Robert Ramsey be dismissed, and the death of Ryan Radigan be listed as accidental."

Brown's pointy eyes closed to narrow slits. "Objection, your Honor, the evidence Mr. Best presented is strictly circumstantial and *not* hard evidence."

The judge took a deep breath and sighed, picked up a pencil and started scribbling on a piece of paper. Without raising his head he said, "Objection sustained. Mr. Best, you have any more questions for this witness?"

Swift had been hoping the circumstantial evidence would be sufficient, that he could just lay down enough cards to show he was holding a flush, and the game would be over. But just in case, he'd held his best cards for last. "I have one more question of the sheriff, before he steps down. Sheriff, what size bullets do the Radigans use?"

"Irrelevant, your Honor," said Brown. "The charges against Mr. Ramsey here have nothing to do with anyone being shot."

The judge didn't look up. He shuffled his papers around, continued scribbling, and said, "Maybe so, but somebody's sure been busy on that road. I'll allow the question. You may answer the question if you can, Sheriff."

"There are two types of bullets—.58 caliber used in a rifle, and 44 caliber, in a pistol."

Swift turned back toward Brown. "Your witness, Counselor," he said, and returned to his seat.

Brown didn't bother to stand up. "Sheriff, did you find any ball bearings or other blunt instruments on Sean Radigan, which might have been used to kill his brother?"

"No, I didn't."

"And did you ever suspect Sean Radigan of having killed his brother?"

"No I haven't."

"And about how many rifles and pistols in the county fire .58 and .44 caliber bullets."

The sheriff rubbed his chin and smiled. "Most, I suppose—but people round here don't usually carry those, just shotguns. If Robert did, I reckon Ryan would've had his head blown off!"

The Ramsey half of the crowd rocked with laughter until the judge pounded his desk top.

"I move to strike that last statement as unresponsive," said Brown.

"You can move to strike," said the judge, peaking up with one eye, "which I'll do, but I'm not likely to forget what he said, now am I?"

Brown's gaze turned toward the floor. "No, sir."

The judge continued staring through that one eye. "Do you have any more questions of this witness?"

Brown's shook his head. "No further questions, your Honor."

The judge turned back to his scribbling and shuffling papers.

"Your Honor," said Swift from his seat, "the defense would like to call Dr. Seaman."

Brown jumped to his feet. "Objection. Your Honor, everyone knows that Dr. Seaman works with Mr. Best's father, and cannot be considered an impartial witness."

The judge lifted his head.

"That may be so, your Honor," replied Swift, "but Dr. Seaman's report was introduced by the district attorney, and it has already been accepted as evidence. Therefore, he's already opened the door for Dr. Seaman to be cross-examined at the very least."

"The report was introduced," shouted Brown. "I didn't call him as a witness."

"But the witness has testified," countered Swift. "Whether through a sworn affidavit or in person, should make no difference.

"I'll allow your witness." Said the judge. He turned to the sheriff and added, "Thank you. You may step down."

A small, skinny man with a head so bald it shined came forward, took the oath, and sat down. Swift began, "Dr. Seaman, you've been a physician and surgeon in Portage for how many years now?"

Seaman looked straight at Swift with an air of detachment. "About five years."

"And as a practicing physician, did you examine the body of Ryan Radigan following his death in October."

"I did."

"And what were your findings as to the cause of death?"

"He was hit by a blunt instrument that struck him between the eyes, thus causing an effusion of blood to the brain."

Swift nodded, looked at Radigan, then back to Seaman "I see. And were there any other signs of injury?"

Dr. Seaman rubbed his chin. "No. There were none."

"Have you or any of your associates, over the past year, examined other individuals who were found dead along the road from Kilbourne?"

"Objection," cried Brown, turning in his chair. "There is only one murder on trial here."

"Sustained," said the judge, still intent on his writing.

"I'll reword the question, your Honor," said Swift smiling happily. "Have you, over the past year, and in the course of your duties, examined other individuals shot along the road from Kilbourne?"

"Yes."

"How many?"

"Two."

"And how did they meet their demise?"

The district attorney jumped from his chair. "Objection! Your Honor, the question is irrelevant. This trial is for the death of Sean Radigan, and not for any other deaths."

"Your Honor," countered Swift, "this question is very relevant. The reason for the Radigans being at the said location is not clear. If they were there to rob Robert Ramsey of his hard-earned money, then at the very least, my client has acted in self defense."

The judge looked at Swift, then Brown, turned back to his papers. "Objection overruled. Go ahead and answer the question, Dr. Seaman."

"They'd been shot, apparently by highwaymen."

"And did you remove the bullets from any of these victims?"

"Yes, I did."

"What caliber were they?"

"There were two types of bullets in those people, .44 and .58 caliber."

"Thank you, doctor." Swift walked back to his chair and sat down.

Brown arose and stood in place. "Doctor, is there any way you can tell that the bullets which killed these unfortunate people were shot from the Radigan's guns?"

Swift pushed his jaw forward, said, "Your Honor, the question is irrelevant and misleading."

"Your Honor, it is not! I'm trying to establish—"

The judge lifted his head and pounded his gavel. "Order in the court! Counselors, approach the bench."

Swift approached on the heels of his antagonist.

"I thought I made it clear from the beginning that this was to be an informal hearing. All this grandstanding is completely unnecessary." The judge stopped, glowered at the two. "I'm willing, in the interest of finding out the facts here, to allow considerable latitude in the questions being asked. However, before we go any further in wasting everyone's time, I'd like to know how many more witnesses you have, Mr. Best, and what you hope to achieve here."

"I have several witnesses who will attest to my client's character and long-standing within this community, sir."

The judge shook his head. "Won't be necessary."

Swift pivoted. "But, your Honor, it's important to show—"

"Yes, yes. I'm sure you can show him to be a pillar of the community, and all that sort of thing, but I said it isn't necessary! I'm tired of this. Prosecutor, do you have any evidence to show cause as to why Mr. Ramsey would have wanted to kill Mr. Radigan, previous arguments, fights, or anything of the sort?"

"Well. No, sir."

"And you drag all these people in here to waste my time, and besmirch a good man's reputation, based on the word of a probable thief and killer? It seems to me the only case you might have would be that of aggravated assault, but with only one witness, even that is a tenuous case."

Brown stood aghast, his mouth hanging dumbly open.

"Next time you want to further your career," said the judge, "don't waste my valuable time. Get hard evidence. Is that understood? Good! Mr. Best, I think you should make another motion."

"What was wrong with the one I made earlier?"

The judge sighed. "Your previous motion called for a judgment of accidental death. No evidence has been offered to support such a premise, therefore I couldn't accept it. Any lawyer with even a smidgen of experience should know that. Perhaps you need to rephrase your motion in a manner in keeping with the evidence, or lack of evidence presented heretofore."

Swift stepped backwards, feeling like an ass, and unsure of what he

182

should say now. He desperately wished the judge would do it for him, but figured that might be some kind of grounds for a mistrial. Could one even have a mistrial in a pretrial? And shouldn't the witness step down first? How much he had yet to learn.

"Well, Mr. Best, are you going to make the motion, or will I have to do it for you?"

"I—I make a motion that all charges against my client be dropped, for reason of—" his mind went suddenly blank.

"Failure to show *cause*?" suggested the judge.

"Yes! Failure to show cause."

Brown waved his hand in a display of resignation. "Your Honor, in light of the evidence brought forth at this inquiry, the state agrees to the motion of Mr. Best."

The judge frowned. "The case against Robert Ramsey is hereby dismissed. Bailiff, you can bring in the next case."

The room once again filled with talk. Robert embraced his wife and mother, while his father patted him heartily on the back. Swift exhaled, relieved to see everyone so happy, despite his own inept efforts on his cousin's behalf.

Sean Radigan stepped up and spit in Robert's face. "Murderer! Don't ever let me find you on a dark street, me boy, or I'll be showin' ya what we do to killers where I come from."

The scene looked almost comical to Swift. Sean threatening an innocent man. Why, Robert could crush him with his bare hands. Then came a sudden awareness that it wouldn't matter how strong Robert was, if faced with guns and knives. Guess he'd better not come to Portage again without a shotgun.

Hub stepped out and pushed his round body between Ramsey and Radigan, his fair face flushed, chest sticking out like a barnyard cock picking a fight. "Listen, Radigan. Your brother's dead because of *your* thieving ways. As far as I'm concerned, the sheriff oughta put you in jail and throw away the key. If I hear of you giving my cousin any grief, I'll come after you and break every bone in your body. Do you hear me?"

Hub was shaking, a thick blue vein bulging at his forehead. Swift had never seen Hub so angry. He turned toward his Aunt Sarah to see her pale gray eyes softly pleading with her son. Hub was so outraged, he didn't even notice her. Swift's heart filled with compassion for his aunt—the loss of her husband, Nels' barely clinging to life in a Louisville Hospital, and now this. He wished he could help her, wished he could take away her pain. Jesus' words came to mind:

"Blessed are they that mourn: for they shall be comforted."

Curge stepped in front of his brother and placed his hands on the big fellow's barrel-chest. "It's okay, Hub. Everyone here knows what happened, and just what kind of person Sean *really* is. It wasn't Robert that abandoned his brother to die. It was *him*. Let him live with *that* for the rest of his life. He's not only a thief, but a coward, the kind who hides behind bushes, and uses a gun to take other people's hard-earned money."

Swift's concern for Sarah turned to amusement. It was a curious scene, the slight Curge standing in front of the staunch, angry Hub, calming him with simple logic.

As if suddenly aware of his mother's presence, Hub turned to her. "Sorry, Ma. Just irks me something terrible when trash like that can bring charges against someone like Robert. Guess I lost my temper."

The atmosphere returned to one of joyous celebration as the Bests and Ramseys laughingly embraced. Everything seemed to be at peace. Swift caught a glimpse of Sean Radigan staring at Hub. The man's brown eyes shot fire, and he wasn't blinking.

December 18th, 1862, Confederate Camp in southwest Arkansas.

Socrates looked across the hospital where he had been assigned to work, which was simply one long row of tents, sewn together.

At break time, he stepped outside to a small fire, where the smell of fresh coffee greeted him.

"Want a cup?" asked a friendly voice.

Socrates turned to see Ned Crawford, a young, dark-haired hospital steward who looked to be about twenty. "Don't mind if I do. Smells good."

"It is."

The two sat content, warmed by the sugary coffee and gently glowing embers.

"How did you get to work here?" asked Socrates.

"My pa is a doctor. Spent most of my time growing up helping him. Now he's a surgeon with the army. Asked me to come and work with him here, but by the time I arrived, his regiment was gone, so they put me to work in the tents 'til he returns. You?"

Socrates scratched his head. "I didn't want anything to do with killing. Only joined to keep from hanging. When I got here, first thing I did was ask questions about the officers—heard of a colonel from West Point whose family

184

is fighting for the North. I went and spoke with him—explained my situation—practically begged him to let me and my brother-in-law work here."

"And he said yes?"

"Not at first. Said he'd look like he was favoring Yankees."

"I'll bet," said Crawford with a frown. "Most of our boys'd rather shoot one than look at one. How'd you get him to go along with you?"

Socrates smiled, nodded. "Put it to him this way. Sir, if you were going into battle, and facing a whole line of Union guns. Where would you rather have me, a Yankee, right behind you with gun in hand—or miles away tending your wounded?"

Crawford's indigo eyes lit up. "That did it?"

"Yep," said Socrates with a wide grin. "It was just the ticket. Put me to work in the hospital, and Ben to work as a cook for the cavalry."

"Pretty smart."

"Got the idea from the Bible. Second Samuel."

The boy's eyes narrowed, then lit up. "David and Achish?"

"You know your Bible."

"Father read it to me since I was a child. You some kind of minister?"

Socrates shook his head. "Little too modern thinking for that. Can't say I believe in miracles. Devil neither—least not literally."

Crawford's dark eyes narrowed again. "Why?"

"I think God doesn't interfere much. Leaves it to us. That's the only way this world could have gotten to be such a mess."

"Not me, I believe every jot and tittle. But listen, I don't wanna shoot nobody neither. Even the sicknesses bothers me, men dyin' in their beds every day. Seems like the hand of God done reached down and struck the camp—like we were the Israelites in the desert or something."

Socrates nodded. "I know what you mean. Doesn't seem like we're helping much. Does it? Fever, dysentery, bloody flux, measles, consumption—God knows what else. Sometimes I think the medicine does more harm than good."

A group of fifty or sixty cavalrymen rode down the road on the other side of the hospital tent. The leader was long and thin, had flowing dark brown hair, thick beard, and thin mustache. He was clad in a black felt hat, black coat, black pants, and black velvet shirt. The brim of his hat was folded up in front, revealing a golden star pinned on the center of its crescent. His eyes were beady, glancing everywhere at once, and long ropes of hair streamed from his bridle. The other men wore loose-fitting hunting shirts with large pockets, neatly embroidered across the front and around the cuffs with red and blue flowers, and green garlands. Each wore black leather boots that reached to the knees of their black trousers, and at their sides were holstered revolvers. Many had extra pistols stuck diagonally in their belts. Each hat was pinned up in the same fashion as the leader's, with a plume of squirrel tail attached to the pin, and various colored ribbons as well.

"That's Bill Anderson," said the boy, "but people around Missouri are calling him Bloody Bill. Two behind him are his brother, Jim, and Archie Clemens. Archie's always playing with that ugly knife of his, and the whole lot are a bunch of murdering drunks. Some say Bill rode with Quantrill through Kansas and Missouri. Others say Quantrill and his men won't have anything to do with him or his brother. Just showed up out of the blue about a week ago with a good lot of horses for the cavalry. Doc told me General McCullough was glad to see them at first, but after a few days he couldn't hardly stand the sight of them."

Socrates stared in disbelief.

Crawford nodded. "Been a few farms plundered and people killed not far from here, and everyone's wondering if it was their work. Anderson says he's gonna kill every Jayhawker in the country, but Doc says he's every bit as bad as they are, and some worse. Thinks Anderson's men would kill anybody that got in their way. Those are real scalps hanging from his bridal. Some say women's and children's too. General probably paid him for the horses just to get rid of him."

Socrates shook his head. "Why doesn't the general arrest him?"

"Whoever's doing the killing doesn't leave anyone alive. McCullough's only district commander, and Anderson claims he's under the command of General Sterling Price. Besides, isn't anyone gonna arrest those boys without getting a whole bunch of people killed. Better to send them back to Missouri where Price and the Yankees can worry about them."

As the last of the group rode by, Socrates spotted the long lean frame of Buck Malneck. Scalps? Good God. A wave of nausea swept through him. Now he understood who those boys back in Daingerfield had been. The only kind of fighters who would welcome someone like Malneck. What were the chances of running into him here? It was like a curse. Seemed wherever Socrates went, Malneck kept showing up. Only good thing was, he was leaving camp without spotting Socrates.

An ambulance wagon pulled up in front of the hospital tent. Tossing his remaining coffee into the fire, Socrates nodded to his new friend, and they walked together to see the latest arrivals. "More sick. I'll have to check the beds and see who's expired before we'll have room for them."

"Can't leave them out here for long," said Crawford.

"I know," said Socrates.

The hospital tent wasn't very warm, but at least it had wood stoves. It offered a bit of shelter from the wind, too. Inside he found two open cots and several corpses before returning. "Someone get those litters and bring them in here," he ordered. "That man over there is deceased, and so is the one next to him. Remove them, and bring some of those boys over here, closer to the fire."

They never questioned his orders, though he was just a private. Perhaps it was because he was older than most, or maybe because no one here had much time to think about that sort of thing, being so busy. He walked toward the tent as two of the younger boys brought a litter over, and laid it down on the ground beside a dead man's bed. One lifted the sick fellow under his arms while the other lifted the feet. A third man rolled the dead body off the bed, where the lifeless form fell onto the empty litter. Socrates walked toward them. It was crude, handling dead men like that. But there was too much death here. They were getting calloused about it. He hoped he never would, or was he already and didn't even know it? As the men laid the sick fellow on the bed, Socrates stopped beside it. The face was so flushed that he didn't know him at first, but on second glance he recognized Ben. Socrates stood over him for a moment, whispering his name, but Ben couldn't hear him, just mumbled something about crazy Charlie. Socrates gentle hand touched the sweating forehead. He was burning with fever. Probably had been for days.

At a barrel, Socrates took a cloth and soaked it. Returning, he unbuttoned Ben's shirt and tenderly washed the sweat from neck and face. "Ben. Ben," he whispered. "Can you hear me, Ben?" But the words went unanswered. "Why him, God? He's never hurt anybody." Socrates tended to the other patients, but returned repeatedly to see his wife's beloved brother. Socrates bowed his head. "What is happening here? So much sickness. So many deaths. He raised himself up and pushed the thoughts from his mind. "I have to pull myself together," he told himself. "Have to help these men. Have to do my job."

ELEVEN

"... not possessing any real knowledge
of what awaits us in Hades, I am also
conscious that I do not possess it."
—Socrates

December 23, 1862, Confederate Camp in Arkansas

SOCRATES' SHIFT IN THE HOSPITAL TENT ENDED HOURS EARLIER, BUT HE WOULD not leave Ben alone. Too many young men died in isolation. And Socrates couldn't bear the thought of leaving his brother-in-law for a moment. The sun was going down outside, its long shadows crowding out the light, bathing the tents in darkness. Lamps and candles gave out little golden auras of warmth through the long corridor of tents, where so many young men desperately clung to life.

He dipped a pad of cotton cloth into a fresh bucket of water, lifted it, squeezed enough out so it wouldn't drip, then walked to Ben's side. It had been nearly a week since the hospital orderlies brought him in, and like so many others, he lost ground daily. For the last three days he had eaten nothing, reducing his body to a pale, flesh-draped skeleton, and with every movement, he coughed blood. Socrates had seen such cases before. They all ended the same. The fire of hope was extinguished. The cold dread of despair filled its place.

Sitting on the bedside stool, he dabbed the cool cloth across Ben's forehead, so heavily beaded with sweat. Now awake, Ben's hazel eyes stared across the tent. As Socrates wiped the brow, Ben turned and looked directly into Socrates' eyes. Then, with a soft voice that strained against a wheezing sound from deep within, Ben said, "I think the world of Ellen. With the folks gone, it's bad for her. Sell my horse. Buy a dress. Nice one. Tell her, think of me—"

Socrates wanted to say that Ben shouldn't talk that way, that he was going to be all right, but Socrates was filled with dread. He wanted to curse this terrible illness and command it away, but every man he had seen like this

188

had died. Not one had survived this degree of illness, and that knowledge added its own ache. He could barely speak through the lump in his throat. He choked as he asked, "How do you feel, Ben?"

"Oh—just tired. Hold my hand."

Socrates wrapped his arms around the wasted form. Holding one hand in his, he gently kissed him on the forehead. Ben let out a brief rush of air, and then there was silence. Taking the lifeless hand in his own, Socrates placed it across Ben's heart, then reached up and pulled the two eyelids closed with his thumbs. His lips gently formed the question, "Why can't I do more? Why can't I save anyone? Help me. God, help me. He's just an innocent young man." But no answers came. Was God merely an unreachable entity—someone who sat for eons meditating on the deeper philosophies of life? Had he no intimacy with his creation? If that were true, how could he have sent his own son to suffer here in this miserable existence?

Socrates' hands clasped his head, squeezing, as though he could equalize the pressure building up inside. He remembered this pain, how he'd prayed hour after hour for his little brother Rosewood to live, but to no avail. "I keep praying for faith," he told his father. "Faith and patience. But all I see is more and more trouble. If God is good, why doesn't he answer my prayers? And why couldn't we raise Rosewood up, like the apostles did?"

His father's face shown vividly in his mind. A face tortured with its own unspeakable pain, though Socrates could only now see it. Blue eyes, not cold and steely, but soft and sorrowful. Then the words came: "I know your hurt son. Your mother and I, too. But you can't dictate to God what your circumstances will be. This life is a crucible. That's all. Just a proving ground for a longer and better life. James probably said it best. 'Blessed is the man that endureth temptation: for when he is tried, he shall receive the crown of life, which the Lord hath promised to them that love him.' That's our hope—our only anchor in this angry sea of life."

Socrates felt suddenly ashamed. How selfish he'd been. Never thinking of his parents' pain, only his own. Without another thought, he uttered the words he had once forsaken. "Our Father, who art in Heaven, hallowed be thy name . . ."

After arranging for the care of Ben's body, Socrates went to his bed, exhausted, yet sleep wouldn't come. He couldn't stay here any longer. It was too much, watching these young men die for nothing. He thought again of his namesake's argument with the laws. It seemed like nonsense now. Was something greater at stake here than some hypothetical moral idealism? This was his life. He could no longer sit aside like a detached spectator in an audience, criticizing and analyzing the players. It was time he played an active role. But how? Could he escape and go north, where he belonged? What would happen to Ellen and their children then?

Socrates struggled with those question for hours, knowing the army would never allow him a furlough. On the other hand, staying here wasn't helping his family any either. What would the town folk do to them if he deserted? He'd heard some strange stories about home guard activities around Texas, Louisiana and Arkansas. Still, the folks in Daingerfield had always been good to him and Ellen. He meditated deeply. His namesake's words flowed through his mind:

"You are mistaken, my friend, if you think that a man who is worth anything ought to spend his time weighing up the prospects of life and death. He has only one thing to consider in performing any action; whether he is acting justly or unjustly, like a good man or a bad one."

He decided to quit the hospital, seek other duty, and run away at the first opportunity. The week sped by, and he was transferred from hospital duty to the infantry on the twenty-sixth of December. No one seemed suspicious. Even he was impressed at his cool exterior, as he collected extra hard tack and salt pork in his haversack. Mostly he stuck to himself, only participating in casual conversations, fearful of unwittingly tipping his hand.

The evening of December twenty-seventh, nervous and excited, almost lightheaded, he marched in step with the sergeant of the guard to his evening post. The sound of water sloshing around in his canteen made him wonder if anyone suspected his intentions. Along the rail fence that spread across the long rolling field, a repetitious procedure was conducted. First, the sergeant was challenged by each sentry. Then each sentry, given the proper password, was relieved by another guard.

So it went along the line until Socrates and a young fellow were the only guards left to be posted. Arriving at the final post, the sergeant relieved the guard and turned to his last two men. "Since Best is new at this, Josiah, you'll have to share duty with him. Don't want nobody falling asleep and lettin' any Yankees through here. Anything moves out there, shoot it. Don't ask no questions. Anyone coming along the back of the fence, challenge 'em for a password. Understood?"

The two guards bobbed their heads in the moonlight and the sergeant nodded. "Josiah, come with me. Wanna talk to you in private for a minute."

When the two had walked twenty paces down the trail, the sergeant lowered his voice. Socrates couldn't make out anything said. Didn't matter. He figured the guy was telling Josiah that Socrates was as much a Yankee as anyone else he would see out here tonight. Probably didn't want the boy to let Socrates out of his sight for even a minute.

After the sergeant left, the two leaned over the fence line with their muskets pointed down field. If Socrates were ever going to get away, it had to be now, before he was forced to fight against his own. Funny, he'd rather be dead than a slave to these men, and that made him think about the Negroes and all the outspoken abolitionists who'd argued against slavery. People couldn't be property, no matter what race.

The sergeant left, and the two quietly stood together for several hours before Josiah said, "Gotta relieve myself, Best. You'll have to keep an eye out for both of us. I'll be right over there if you need me." He pointed to a downwind clump of bushes about fifteen steps away. Socrates nodded. As the boy walked away, he looked back every few steps. Socrates' heart pounded, waiting for the right moment. Once Josiah dropped his drawers, squatting half in and half out of the bushes, he balanced the rifle across his knees. Socrates lifted his canteen and took a long swig. Nothing was working as he had hoped, but he continued watching, calculating his chances. If he could get over the fence in one piece, chances were he'd be half way across the field before Josiah got to the fence, but Texans were sure shots. Socrates would have to get further before the boy took aim, or he'd be dead for sure. Nearly forty and slow, he wished for the speed and agility of youth. Didn't matter. This might be his *only* chance. He *had* to take it. His heart pounded as a relentless drum, while winds of fear and hope swept through his anxious mind.

Josiah reached to pull a broadleaf, but leaned so far forward that his rifle fell out of his lap, and into the weeds. Socrates dropped his rifle, planted his foot on the first fence rail, put his two hands on the top one, and launched himself over. Adrenaline imparted a burst of strength he hadn't experienced since youth, and he hit the field with his legs pumping hard.

Josiah yelled something about "damned Yankees" from the bush, but Socrates was beyond turning back. His feet pounded the ground nearly as fast as his heart was beating. Josiah shouted again. Socrates knew the boy was abandoning his toiletries and waddling over to the fence. He pictured Josiah with one hand on his rifle and the other pulling at his trousers as he waddled to the fence. Socrates frantically prayed to go faster as he realized he was only halfway across the field. Worse yet, the field was bathed in moonlight.

He darted madly through the brush, zigzagging, exhilarated by the night air, the hope of freedom, and the fear of being shot. He guessed that Josiah would be sighting on him about now, and the trees instantly seemed too far away. The ground dipped suddenly, and he nearly lost his footing. Panic rushed through his bones. He struggled to keep on his feet. His right toe hit something hard. Josiah's rifle exploded as its projectile ripped the quiet night air. Something hit the back of Socrates' head as he fell, slamming him hard to the ground. Pain wrapped his skull, squeezed with all its might, but he lay flat, motionless within the field of dried-out, chest-high weeds. The top of his head burned fire where the bullet had torn a path through the crest of his scalp. Blood flowed freely across his face, washing him with its warm liquid. He was bleeding like a stuck pig, but couldn't move or Josiah would know he wasn't dead. He waited silently, wondering how badly he was wounded. Mind worked good. Neck didn't hurt either. Couldn't be all that bad. Then came the sound of Josiah, hallooing and shouting to the sergeant of the guard. His voice sounded excited, very excited, and it was getting farther away.

Fate had given him a second chance. Socrates wasted no time in crawling on his hands and knees until he reached the woods, where a mixture of scrub pines and firs provided more cover. Unfortunately, the oaks and dogwoods had lost their leaves long before, so he kept away from them. Amidst the evergreens, he stood and listened while his dirty fingers inspected the wound in his crown. It wasn't deep, but it was nearly four inches in length and traversed several minor arteries that were pumping out a considerable amount of blood. He moved through the trees and down a small ravine to where a shallow creek softly babbled. He washed his bloody hands in the cool water, thinking it too cool not to be spring fed. His fingers brought refreshment to his lips before pouring several scoops of the water over his wound. The effect was immediate, and the fire upon his head gradually subsided. Over the sound of the brook came the noise of excited voices coming toward him in the distance.

He moved as quickly as he could, the shale offering a good flat surface to step on, but sometimes wobbling, threatening to turn his ankles and do him in. He slowed slightly, taking the time he needed. Within a few hundred yards, the ravine, which was bounded on each side by three-foot banks and tall dry grass, cut across a flat plain. He climbed the south bank and parted the weeds to spy backward. The voices were farther away now, almost too far to be heard, but there were several torches moving around in the field he'd passed over. He stepped back down the embankment, carefully brushing away the marks of his shoes, before rushing down the creek.

By sunrise he'd covered several miles but kept under cover every step, increasing his pace as the sunlight illuminated his path. About mid morning he found a stand of pines with a large oak in the center, which he decided would be his best shelter. He climbed high into the fork of an old oak, and promptly went to sleep.

He had no idea how long he'd been sleeping when the sound of horses awakened him. The steady clop-clop-clop came closer, stopping just outside his stand of trees. It felt as though his heart would burst through his rib cage. A loud baritone voice broke the silence "Casey, you take two men around the other side of these trees, and send one through the middle to see if he's in there. The rest of us will fan out and wait for you to flush him."

"But what if he's got a gun?"

"You heard sarge. He left his rifle and skedaddled. Can't have gotten too far on foot. If he's in there, he'll flush—easy as shootin' quail."

Socrates waited for the longest time, before he heard a horse pushing through the brush on the other side. After a few minutes, the gray uniform and cap of a Confederate cavalryman appeared. The man had a pistol drawn, and worked back and forth across the dead brush, staring intently from side to side, as if expecting someone to jump out at him at any moment. He rode in a semicircle, working one side, then the other, always coming back to center where he moved forward another five yards before repeating the pattern.

Socrates watched the rider's every move, knowing that if the fellow looked up it would mean sure death, but the man appeared to be so certain his prey was somewhere on the ground, amidst the pines, that he never looked up. When the fellow reached the big oak, his head passed less than five feet below Socrates' boots. By the time he'd worked his way through the brush to the other side, Socrates stopped holding his breath and relaxed.

"There's nobody in there."

"Damn. Sarge is gonna have our butts if'n we come back without that deserter."

"Why don't we just tell him he's dead, Corporal?"

"Cause he probably ain't!"

"But you saw all that blood. Who could live after being shot up and bleeding that much?"

"Yeah. Maybe you're right. I'll tell Sarge *you* found him dead—that *you* said his corpse was all messed up from some old bobcat. That way if this deserter shows up later, *you* can be the one to explain how a dead man walks."

"He ain't gonna show. He's dead."

"Better not—for your sake. Anyway, enough's been said. Let's move out."

The patrol headed back the way it had come, and Socrates waited until dusk before moving again. He finished off his water and hard tack, as the temperature dropped and the sky darkened. Then he headed northeast, all night and into the daylight hours. By late afternoon, he encountered a large river where he found a log to float across. The water was cool, but very muddy. He wished he could drink some, but didn't dare without boiling it.

Not a soul appeared the entire time he swam, and once he'd reached the other side, he rested in another tree and slowly dried in the sun. The sunset was a sure marker of west, and it was easy to make good time across the fields in the waning daylight. As the landscape darkened around him, the temperature dropped all too quickly, forcing him to keep walking in order to stay warm. A vast expanse of stars provided simple points by which to navigate, but without a torch, Socrates tripped over so many rocks and logs that within four hours he was sitting on the ground rubbing his sore ankles and knees. He had to find some high ground. Someplace where he wouldn't see any Rebels.

He knew that a broken leg would be his end, but so could the cold night air if he sat too long. He scanned the fields. Beneath the silver moonlight, he spotted a narrow ridgeline with no signs of a campfire anywhere. Took a good half hour to make it there without hurting himself, but following the high ground, he found the going much easier. At first light he found another stand of trees in which to hide. There he finished his salt pork, wishing he had saved some water to wash it down. So far the weather had been in concert with his actions, a secret partner in his effort to gain freedom. He prayed it would remain so. A freezing rain could be as bad as getting caught. Within a short time, he nodded off to sleep. And after several hours, a gray squirrel took offense at his camping in this tree, and woke him repeatedly by dropping twigs and pieces of old acorns on him, chatting a fierce scolding.

"All right. All right," said Socrates. "Can't get any sleep around here anyway." He rolled over onto his side, and climbed down from the tree. The minute his feet hit the ground, his stomach rolled. He was ravenous, but the first and more pressing business was to get water, which he knew could not be found along a high ridge. By dusk he had worked his way back down through the trees and into the forest below. He liked walking through the woods. It was peaceful: almost mystical in the way it unfolded its secrets with each passing moment. Even as the forest slowly darkened, his senses switched to a keen night vision, allowing him to follow an old, worn, deer path. It was certain to lead to water, and in a little while he found a small brook barely two inches deep.

The water was cool and stunk of sulfur, but he forced himself to drink. Dehydration was a real threat after he'd lost so much blood, and the salt pork had given him a bad cotton mouth. As he drank, his fingers ran over the wound, its blood well crusted and caked into a large scab. "Socrates, my boy," he said, "this is one scar you'll look upon with gladness, *if* you get home alive."

After drinking his fill, he worked his way farther down the hill. The plain below would house many farms, and Socrates made up his mind to avoid them all. Folks around here were likely to be more Confederate-minded than otherwise, and he couldn't chance an encounter after coming this far.

He walked two more hours before making it out onto the plain, where he found a wagon road. It was a good one, free of the rocks and roots on which he'd stubbed and twisted his toes through field and forest. Exhausted, he followed the road northward for several hours until it dropped off sharply into a long, narrow valley. Three hundred yards below, the road curved around a hollow where a campfire glowed. Just on the other side of the fire were two covered wagons, their white canvas covers painted orange by the cavorting flames. Guitar music and singing carried clearly through the night air, spurring memories of his father's house in Wisconsin. Mother playing the piano, father guitar, Solon and young Nels on banjos.

Socrates paused and swallowed. Were these campers Rebels? He was starving. Couldn't go on without food or water. He thought of his namesake's words when facing death:

"No evil can harm a good man in this world or the next."

He stepped off the road and worked his way into the hollow, its pines and firs standing in a near perfect circle around the wagons. He spotted four Negroes, two men and two women, sitting around a fire, then heard the distinct click of a pistol hammer locking into place. "Don't move, Rebel," came a deep-throated command.

Socrates froze. "I'm not a Rebel."

"Yeah. And I'm Jeff Davis." The man moved forward, his raven eyes bright in their reflection of the firelight, his facial muscles outlined in dark contours that made him look incredibly strong, fearsome in stature. He wore an expensive white shirt, with a ruffled collar and ruffled sleeves that stuck out around his wool coat—the kind typical of gentleman card players on river boats. The man's expression was hard, like something carved out of black marble.

"I know I'm wearing a Confederate uniform," said Socrates, "but I'm from the North. I'm a school teacher, not a soldier."

"Go on," said the man with the pistol, and Socrates proceeded to tell him everything; how he had been forced to serve, how he had escaped, and how he'd stayed alive up until now. When he was finished, the man's face remained expressionless. "Maybe I believe you, and maybe I don't. You sound like a Northerner."

"So do you," remarked Socrates.

"Name is Enoch Markson. Came from New England to settle in Kansas—back in '55. Land was plenty. Abolitionists there seemed to think we could make a difference, being educated and black. Then the whole territory turned ugly, people killing each other—now the war. We've had enough. Heading for St. Louis, then home."

Socrates scratched his head with one hand, saw Enoch's face harden, put the hand back up with the other. "And you came from Kansas?"

Enoch nodded.

Socrates smiled. "Well you must have taken a wrong turn or two along the way on account of—"

"On account of what?" The black stone-face wrinkled with curiosity.

Socrates chuckled. "On account of the fact you're standing in Arkansas."

The whites of Enoch's eyes widened until they looked huge. "Certain?"

"Been a little lost myself, but I know the river I swam yesterday was the Arkansas."

"Damn. I told Jacob to go the other way—this way was wrong—had to be. Now where in Hell's kitchen has he gotten us to?"

"Don't know, but I'll help you folks get north if you give me a little water and food. By the way, my name is Socrates Best."

Enoch eyed Socrates warily. "All right, but you walk ahead of me nice and slow, with your hands up."

Socrates did as he was told. He could see the people more clearly now. The two men were of smaller stature and looked as if they might be brothers. One was playing a guitar, the other a fiddle. Both sang in high tenor fashion, and the two women danced, their dresses coning out as they twirled about the fire. One woman had silver hair, which somehow looked strange above her black face, and Socrates guessed her to be in her late fifties. The other woman had long black hair and long limbs that floated like clouds through the air, as she danced about the fire. Her eyes were little black dots that danced around with every word she sang. She was the most ravishing woman he had ever seen.

"Beautiful, isn't she."

Socrates blushed at his obviousness. "Yes. She is."

"That is my wife. Bought her freedom myself. Fell in love with her the moment I saw her."

"I can see why," said Socrates.

The people around the fire spotted them now, and the music stopped, as did the dancing. The man without the guitar lifted a shotgun from behind him and walked out to meet the two. He leveled both barrels at Socrates' abdomen, smiled a big white smile that showed a wide gap in his front teeth. "What you got there, Enoch, a Rebel?"

"Maybe, Jacob. Says he's not, but he's wearing grays."

"Oooh Eeeh! Looks like somebody done split his head open—all that blood in his hair and beard. What you fixin' to do with him?"

"Haven't made up my mind yet. Might put a bullet in him and hide the body. Might just feed him and take him along so he can show us the way to Missouri."

"What? We are in Missouri."

"Maybe so, maybe not. According to him, we're in Arkansas."

"Oooh Eeeh! You can't trust him, Enoch. Can't trust any grays. One mistake out here and we're all dead. You, of all people, know that."

Enoch eyed his friend warily. "Can you guarantee me we're in Missouri, Jacob?"

Jacob looked at the ground, then away.

"All right then. We might be needing this fellow after all."

Jacob stepped aside and the three started toward the fire. They hadn't covered more than five yards when a gunshot sounded from somewhere near the road. Several horsemen rode out of the bushes and into the campfire light. Jacob lifted his shotgun and blew the first man sideways off his horse. The second rider fired a pistol, whose bullet struck Jacob in the shoulder and knocked him backwards. Enoch turned his pistol on one of the Confederates just as quick. A series of shots flew back and forth while Socrates dove to the ground, hoping desperately to become one with it. Horses neighed, women screamed, and guns went off in every direction.

Socrates had never seen men shoot each other and had no wish to now. He pushed his head to the ground. Then the shooting stopped. He slowly lifted his head. A tall, bony man in a black hunting shirt came running toward Socrates, and pulled him to his feet. The man's hat was pulled up in a half-moon, pinned with a star, and had several feathers and two long yellow ribbons hanging from it. "You okay?" he asked.

"Yeah. I'm all right," said Socrates, as he brushed himself off and looked around the ground. The bony fellow had two pistols stuck into his belt, in addition to the side arms in each holster. Long strands of matted hair hung from beneath his hat. Socrates realized he was staring and turned away, focusing upon the scene around him.

Enoch sat a few feet away, trying to stop the blood gushing from his leg. Both arms were wounded, and he was obviously having trouble using his hands. His face was covered with sweat that dripped off his chin and onto his bloody white shirt and jacket. A few feet away sat Jacob, holding his bloody right shoulder. A man with high black Mexican boots and bulging pockets stood between them, a pistol in each hand pointing toward the wounded black men's heads. A horse lay dead near the fire, along with four men in gray, their bodies spread in the haphazard manner they had fallen. Another man in black helped a wounded comrade toward the fire. That poor fellow was bleeding from chest and stomach, wounds which experience told Socrates would soon result in death. The Negro who had been playing the guitar sat with his back to a rock, as if resting, but a bullet had taken off the right side of his face. The two women stood against the first wagon, the elderly one crying hysterically, the other trying to comfort her.

"I'm Corporal Denton," said the bony fellow. "What in hell happened to you? And how'd these niggers get ya?"

"Actually, I found them," said Socrates. "Was out on patrol and got wounded, separated from my unit. Been wandering around trying to find my way home ever since." Socrates winced at his own lies. He *was* trying to get home. He only hoped these men hadn't heard about his desertion.

The corporal turned back toward his charge. "Sheeeit. Lost five good men for five run'way niggers. Sergeant Malneck ain't gonna be too pleased."

"Sergeant Malneck?"

"Yeah. Know him?"

Something inside of Socrates squirmed. Malneck! These were some of Anderson's guerillas. If they found out who Socrates was, he'd be worse than dead. And this Corporal thought he had trouble? Socrates casually threw his hands up, shook his head. "Nah. Just heard of him, I guess. When you expect to hitch up with him?"

"Should be back any time now. Rode over to the far side of the ridge to see if there were any Yankee fires in the west. We just came over this here rise and saw fire in the hollow—thought we'd check it out before he got back. Sheeit. He's gonna be all over my ass when he gets here." Denton shook his head, then gathered the four remaining Negroes toward the front of the wagon.

One of the men climbed into the back of the wagon and started throwing out trunks of clothes. "Hey! Corporal, look what these here slaves done stole,

198

fine clothes, even a case of Burgundy. Looks like we might have something for the sergeant so he won't get so mad after all."

"*None* of that is stolen," shouted Enoch. "It was rightly paid for. And we aren't runaway slaves. We're *free* men!"

Denton walked over and kicked Enoch in the face, sending him sprawling backwards. The old woman screamed again. "Shut your mouth, nigger. If I say you're runaway slaves, then you are. Now don't be givin' me no lip. Got enough trouble already."

After awhile, Corporal Denton came over to Socrates and handed him a pistol. "Know how to use this?" Socrates nodded. "Good. Watch these niggers while me and the other men see to our dead. If they give you any trouble, shoot 'em."

Socrates watched the prisoners as the man walked away. Denton took a rope and tied it around the neck of the dead horse, then tied the other end to the horn of his horse's saddle. Using the bridle, he led the horse as it dragged the dead animal far back into the brush. Then he did the same with the guitar player's corpse. Once this work was completed, the bushwhackers set about the business of digging graves for their friends. They had just begun when Enoch managed to sit up again.

"Should have *known* you were one of them," he said. His mouth bled profusely, spreading a bright red sheen all around his lips. It looked gross, brighter and thicker than any blood Socrates had ever seen before.

"I'm not," whispered Socrates. "Everything I said is *true*."

"Then you've *got* to help us."

"How? If I try, they'll kill us for sure."

"They'll kill us anyway! Besides, if what you say *is* true, what do you think is gonna happen when they find out you're a deserter? You won't be any better off."

Socrates thought hard. Things wouldn't be good for him when Malneck got here. That was certain. Enoch's face glowered at him. Socrates had never killed anyone. How could he now?

At that moment a lone rider appeared some fifty feet away through the bushes. Even at that distance, Socrates recognized the long, tall frame of Buck Malneck. Socrates leaned into the wagon's shadow, where the campfire light was blocked from his face. His arm and gun remained in the light so everyone would know he was there. Panic rushed through him like an untamed animal. He had to control himself. If he ran they'd track him down for sure. Probably knew every inch of this country. But what could he do?

Malneck dismounted and glared at Denton. "What kind of shit hole've you dug for yourself this time, Denton?"

"Found these run'way niggers with a gun on one of our own, Sergeant. Couldn't help it. One thing just led to another."

"Always does with you. I oughta take those yellow ribbons off your hat and stick 'em to your ass. That's where they belong. Where's Billy?"

The Corporal's face went pale. "Over by the fire. Got himself gut shot. Don't look like he's gonna make it."

The eyebrows rose above Malneck's menacing eyes, and his hand went to his holster. Socrates thought Buck would shoot this Denton dead on the spot, but then the hand paused, fell back at Buck's side, and he turned and walked toward the wounded soldier.

Billy—Morse? Was he the wounded man? Socrates watched intently as Malneck walked to the wounded guerilla. "Billy," he said. "You okay?"

It was Morse all right. He'd lost some weight and didn't look so chubby anymore, but Socrates could see the familiar, bright red hair the minute the Sergeant pulled him up, and the hat fell from his head. Gurgling sounds came from Billy's mouth, but no words, just a bubbling of blood with each breath. Malneck put his nephew back down, and cursed loudly before walking over to Socrates. "Who you with?" he asked.

"Texas Rangers," said Socrates, but he stretched out the word Rangers so it sounded: Raaaynjus, and kept his face in the shadows.

"Voice reminds me of someone I know. We ever met?"

Socrates strained to shrink his five foot eleven inch frame. "Nope. Not as I recall."

"Well, you better be one hell of a soldier to replace these five men! Billy and I've been fightin' a lota years together. Ain't no replacin' him."

"Don't imagine I could."

"Damned right." Malneck turned and walked toward Denton who had liberated some burgundy. "Give me that wine." He grabbed the bottle and swigged it in a stream of long lusty gulps.

"You want us to shoot the niggers?" asked Denton.

"Nah. Not yet. Let 'em bleed. If they're not dead by morning, we'll string 'em up by their short hairs. For now we'll take them women and see what good they be."

Socrates watched as the men sat around the fire, telling lewd jokes and getting drunk. After two hours, Malneck and a short blonde fellow yanked Enoch's wife, and started her toward the second wagon. Her face was defiant, but she lifted her head high and turned boldly, knowing full well what was to come. The other two tugged at the older woman and started her toward the other wagon, but she cried and protested vehemently. Denton hit her so hard that her face went blank, and she looked around as if suddenly lost. He then walked her to the back of the wagon, and shoved her hard up into the back of it.

Socrates was alone with the prisoners now.

Enoch glared, terrible in his conviction. Though growing weaker, his anger showed he wasn't giving up.

"I can't do anything," whispered Socrates.

"Have to," whispered Enoch. "We're helpless."

"But I've never killed anyone. How could you expect me—?"

"Slip up behind that man by this wagon and slit his throat. Then climb in from the back and get the other one inside. Just like that—one wagon at a time."

Socrates remembered butchering cows, slitting their throats, seeing their huge eyes roll back into their heads, watching them fall as their life's blood poured onto the ground. The thought of it made his knees week. Do *that* to another human being? No. He shook his head.

"You've *got* to," Enoch whispered harshly. "Those are *bad* men—bad as they get. You'll make your stand here and now, in front of these men, or tomorrow before your maker, because sure as flies eat shit, I'm gonna tell them what you're doing here."

Socrates face flushed. "I could shoot you and say you were giving me trouble."

"Yeah. Guess you could. So the question is: Who you going to kill—them bushwhackers who kill for no reason—or me, an innocent man?"

The older woman screamed and cried in the wagon, unsettling Socrates. The black man was the easiest target, so simple, but also helpless and without guilt. The cries of the old woman were drawing him, begging his help. "But I don't have a knife," said Socrates.

Enoch's gaze didn't waiver. His large black hands dripping with blood and shaking from pain, inched into the top of his boot. Thick fingers worked clumsily for a minute before gliding back out with a big, thick Bowie knife that glistened in the light of the fire.

"Like this," said Enoch, as he motioned his head back to expose a long, muscular neck. "Can't let them yell."

Socrates swallowed hard, took the knife and walked slowly, quietly around to the back of the wagon. The man standing there was so intent on watching the older woman being raped that he never turned around. Socrates took one fast swipe, felt the razor-sharp blade cut through the man's throat, as if it were cutting nothing more than grass. The throat gargled blood through the slit, but the two arteries spewed forth a red stream that poured down the man's shirt and pants. Socrates caught him as he fell, then laid him beside the wagon. The world was spinning and Socrates' knees weak. He refused to give in to it. Before he could make another move, he heard Denton climbing down. "There ya go, Henry. She's a fightin' black bitch, but she'll clean your pipe if you knock her hard a couple times."

Socrates met Denton stepping onto the ground. He took him the same way he had the other fellow. It was easier this time, and he felt a certain numbness come over him as he killed. Everything seemed far away, as if he were watching from a distance, and it wasn't really him. This time he wiped the blade clean on the dead man's shirt as he pushed the second corpse over the first. Inside the woman was crying, and he thought he should go to her, say something comforting; but then he looked at his bloody hands, realized he couldn't comfort anyone. On the heels of that perception came an awareness that if he didn't get the last two guerillas, everyone else was going to die. He walked over to the other wagon, rocking with the movement of the people inside. Enoch's wife hadn't cried out even once, as if she wouldn't give these animals the satisfaction. Malneck was inside, probably for his second visit, the blond fellow was outside, buttoning his pants.

Socrates stepped stealthily behind the guerilla. The fellow suddenly turned. It was the first time Socrates had seen the man up close, and his first glimpse momentarily paralyzed him. The soldier was more a kid than a man, probably no more than sixteen years old, his sandy hair reminding Socrates of one of his young students. The boy's face popped a couple of dimples as he grinned with recognition, but then he saw the knife and instinctively recoiled. Socrates slashed sideways. The kid was too limber and easily dodged it. Within seconds the boy pulled a knife from his belt. The two stood face to face, parrying with their blades. The boy raised his blade and charged, slashing at Socrates' chest. Socrates caught the plunging arm, and twisted it away from him as it came down. The boy's face plunged headlong into the corner of the wagon, making a loud, cracking noise. Whether he was alive or dead, Socrates didn't know. One thing he was sure of, was that Buck had probably heard the noise and would be popping out to investigate. The boy had to die. He'd just pulled his bloody knife through the kid when he heard a commotion in the wagon.

"Aagh," shouted Malneck. "Bitch. Where'd you get that? Stick me, will you?" A loud slap sounded, then Enoch's wife flew out of the wagon and onto the ground. She landed on her arm and shoulder with a shriek of pain.

"Nigger whore!" shouted Malneck. "I'm gonna kill you *real* slow for that." He jumped to the ground with a deep-throated groan.

Socrates stepped up behind him. Malneck spun around. A bloody knitting needle was in his left hand, and a thin red stream flowed from a round spot over his abdomen. "What?" he demanded.

Socrates felt Malneck's beady eyes probing, saw the look of recognition in the man's face as something registered within that evil mind. "You? Goddamned Yankee! How did *you* get here?" Then his eyes darted over the camp, scrutinizing the situation in a glance. Three more rebels were dead. Billy would soon join them, and Buck was the only guerilla left. But none of that mattered now. He palmed his belt and out came a knife. "*This* is gonna feel good, school teacher. This is gonna feel *real* good."

Socrates dove forward with his knife, but Buck merely stepped aside to avoid the blade. As Socrates body came even with his own, Buck tripped him with one foot, and punched him over the back of the head with the handle of his knife. Socrates hit the ground like a rock, losing control of his senses. Before he could get up, Buck kicked him in the stomach, causing him to buckle at the waist. A series of kicks came rapidly thereafter, pummeling his ribs and shoulder, and turning him onto his back.

He watched Buck's face come down over his own, felt the man's fingers moving in his hair; then the world became a blur as Buck lifted him by his mane, and slammed his head against the ground over and over again. Socrates felt the world slip away as he drifted off into a dark, far away place. As he was losing consciousness, a loud gunshot sounded, as if very close by. Then nothing.

TWELVE

"So it is from the dead, Cebes, that
living things and people come?"
—Socrates

December 30th, 1862, Murfreesboro, Tennessee

ED BEST WRAPPED HIMSELF IN A THICK WOOL BLANKET, AND COILED HIS
rubber one around it to block the wetness from above and below. Large,
cold drops fell from above as water condensed on the leaves above him.
The cold December air, combined with the previous day of marching, should
have made falling asleep effortless, but the blankets weren't thick enough to
restrain the moist, chilly air, so he tossed fitfully until exhaustion finally
overtook him. Before long, the frigid morning air bit him awake again. This
time the thoughts of his brothers rolled through his mind. Word had come
that Sol picked up Elizabeth and their boys in Ohio, before making a quick
trip to Ontario, where he'd decided to wait out the war. Then came a report
that Nels was alive in a hospital at Louisville. That brought more backslapping
and hooting than any war news ever had amongst the men of Company D,
but after the celebration was over and the nights closed in, Ed hated himself
for not having had the guts to check on Nels following that battle at Perryville.
Worse yet, Nels was now suffering from some kind of delusions, and was
missing from the hospital. Ed couldn't shake the feeling that it was somehow
all his fault.

His shame sent him to the refuge of the fire, where Sophie Landt and a
few other men sat, staring dope-like through thin-slitted eyelids. Ed pulled
his wool blanket around him, poured a cup of coffee, and dipped some hard
tack in it. "Mmmm. If that don't beat all," he said. "Here's some hard tack
that don't bite back. Now if Old Rosie gets some decent salt pork, we'll have a
real meal."

Sophie's head perked up as he offered a hunk of meat on a stick. "Try some of this. Best I've tasted for a while. Maybe Old Rosie's already talked to Suttler."

Ed was taking a big, mouth-watering bite, when Sergeant Gaffney walked up. "Colonel Chapin says to form up—and hurry. Rosie's moving some divisions across the river over on the left flank. Wants to catch the Rebs with their pants down. We're to form skirmishes."

"Looks like today's gonna bring fire," said Ed. He spoke casually, as he would about the weather or some other routine event, without fear or worry. In fact, he was glad to face the enemy again. Marching back and forth across Kentucky and Tennessee to fight an enemy who showed no desire for a rematch had become boring and tiresome. He'd come to peace with himself over all that killing at Chaplain Hills, as much as one soul could. Now he just wanted to end it, whatever it took.

Sophie stretched his long frame, clutched his rifle, and said, "Come on, let's give Johnny what for!"

The men formed into skirmish lines as the sun came over a distant hill. Colonel Chapin and the redheaded Major Ely sat nearby on their horses, talking excitedly to the company commanders. Ed smiled at the sight of Captain Twogood's beard, a frizzy, brown tangle in the cold, wet air. A few feet behind those officers, the woods ended at the base of a railroad track, covered with small, white rocks. On the other side stretched a long field covered with dry, brown grass that sloped down and away for several hundred yards, before disappearing into the valley below.

When the company commanders dispersed, they walked back and spoke to their sergeants and lieutenants, who, in turn, walked down the line informing them they would move out as light infantry, meaning the Tenth Regiment would march off to find the enemy, make contact, and hold them until the rest of the division arrived. A minute later, the regiment marched forward, every odd man staggered one half step behind the even numbered ones. From the front they looked like one solid wall, but the stagger would provide two alternate and continuous lines of fire when they found the enemy.

Ed, near the center of the first line, stepped over the railroad tracks and into the open field. The air was biting, piercing to the bones, but the brisk walk soon warmed his legs. Down the railroad embankment and into the brown grass he plodded. Long, dry grass stems crunched beneath his feet. Within minutes he crossed the first field, only to find another set of railroad tracks, followed by a larger field, this one covered with old cotton plants. The line disintegrated as it jumped a two-rail fence, and started into the aisles that ran between the long parallel rows of lifeless vegetation. The bushes were nearly waist high, and their dry, brown leaves scratched and pulled at his trousers with every step. On the other side of this field came a second stand of cedars, and to its left, a rocky bluff, covered with large boulders and sparse cedars.

From the crest of a long, tall hill that flanked them on the right, came a dull clamor like the sound of men shouting—a sound so faint, it was nearly lost in the gentle breeze.

"What's going on, Sergeant?" asked Ed, his words muffling the noise of distant rifle fire and cannons blasting.

"Can't be Rosie making his move," said Sophie. "Wrong direction."

Ed stared around the field. "Gives me the willies."

"Whatever it is," said Gaffney, "it's a ways off."

Ed marched across the last cotton field and entered the woods, maintaining his position abreast of the first line. The ground was strewn with rocks, forcing him to watch every step as he stumbled his way forward for thirty yards. Halfway down the heavily wooded hill, he spotted numerous gray lines advancing through the cedars before him. He didn't need to be here—had already proved he was a man. The sight of his brother's head coming apart burst into his mind. "God help me," he whispered.

Captain Twogood shouted, "Company, halt! Don't fire 'til I give the command. First line—load—ready—"

Ed loaded his rifle, picked up his hat, ran his fingers through his thick brown hair, then took careful aim. Rifles protruding from the rebel lines popped in the woods below, little puffs of smoke rising from their barrels. As the smoke arose, it formed a thin white cloud within the woods, while the first volley passed by, harmlessly snapping branches and twigs overhead. Excitement surged through his limbs like the roar of a wild animal, but still no command came. The smoke cleared, unveiling the long lines of gray that continued advancing through the woods below. Someone in the regiment fired down the line. Jackass. Wait for orders. The Rebels were getting closer now, close enough to see the colors of their beards.

"Fire!" shouted his captain.

Rifles leapt up and down the line. Tiny explosions and clouds of smoke ensued. Ed picked a target and squeezed, then reloaded. He could feel the staggered presence of the rifles on each side of his head as he took a paper charge and stuffed it into his barrel.

"Second line. Ready—aim—fire!"

His ears went momentarily deaf as the rifle barrels beside him let loose. Then came the incessant ringing as a hollow sort of hearing returned. His anxious fingers jammed a bullet after the charge, and pushed the ramrod home. As he did, he stole a glance at the Rebels in the first line. Most of them went down, but those in the next line simply stepped over their falling friends and kept on coming. He reached for a cap at his belt and pinched it into place.

"First line. Ready—aim—fire!"

The commands were cool, calculated, giving little indication of the deaths they meted out below. But the enemy came dangerously close.

"Fall back!" shouted Captain Twogood. Lieutenants and sergeants echoed his command down the line.

Why weren't they standing their ground? And why hadn't the division moved up at first contact? Ed was certain they could hold the Rebels if reinforcements arrived in time. They had the high ground. Instinctively, he turned and looked back. No reinforcements there, no support. His comrades turned to flee. To stay here was to invite death or capture. He ran through the wooded thicket, back across the cotton fields to the fence line he'd vaulted earlier. His officers and sergeants were already there, waiting, Colonel Chapin riding up and down the rear of the fence line, hollering, "Form skirmishes!"

The officers and sergeants echoed his command, and waved the men into place behind the long wooden fence. Ed stopped, leaned over the top rail, and laid his rifle across it. Two long lines of blue, staggered only eighteen inches apart—hundreds of Wisconsin men tending their rifles, waited against the fence. Ed was loaded and ready to fire, but the Rebels hadn't yet come out of the woods. When they did, they marched in near perfect formation.

"Ready—" hollered the colonel.

Ed took careful aim as the long, gray lines paraded onto the open field. My God, look at them all. How many regiments did they have in there?

"Fire!"

Lead tore into the Confederate lines with deadly force, making little difference. Instead, the men in gray raised their rifles as they marched, and unleashed a counter fire several times greater than what they'd received. Ed thought his enemy would stop and reload as they had at Chaplin Hills. They didn't. Just kept on marching, reloading and firing as they swept across the cotton field. He had never seen anything like it. The sight made his flesh crawl.

Bullets whizzed and whirred past his ears as he reloaded and fired again. The enemy kept coming—like a spring flood pouring over a broken dam. Goose bumps rose on his neck. The hair stood up on the back of his head. A bullet ricochet tinged off his canteen, sending a surge of raw energy through his body. Line after long, gray line extended as far as he could see. His regiment broke and ran, leaving him. His knees wobbled. We have to hold our ground, he thought, but they're too many. Way too many. A wildfire swept through his stomach, into his chest, and finally to his head. He turned and fled across the grassy, brown field.

Amidst the chaos, he heard the voice of Colonel Chapin speaking clearly above him. "Steady men. We must maintain order." Ed was sure the colonel was gonna get his butt shot off that horse.

By the time he arrived at the railroad tracks where they had started the day, he was shocked to see thousands of Union men formed into the longest set of skirmishes he'd ever seen. The lines extended three deep for as far as he could see within the cover of the forest, with the exception of a regiment-sized hole directly ahead of him. He wasted no time in filing into the position, leaning forward with his left hand on his knee, and his right hand on his rifle. Panting heavily, he said, "Damn! Sophie, we've been had."

"Bait for the trap," said Sophie, standing straight and tall, neck straining to see the lengths of the Union lines. "Least they waited for us."

Colonel Chapin's voice sounded hard in the cold morning air. "Good job, men. Now, don't fire 'til they see you. Then beat them to the punch."

Over the lower lip of the hill came countless thousands in gray, their flags and colors streaming in the cool December air, their ranks marching in perfect order. They crossed the railroad tracks, approached the woods, and were within sixty yards when the division let loose.

This time the Union fire was magnified by a line that went as far as the eye could see. Grape canister—bucket loads of miniature cannon balls dumped into the short, dark cannon barrels—exploded into the Rebel lines, splintered human beings, painted gray uniforms red. Artillery pieces posted on a ridge above and behind the Union, pounded the Rebel ranks with shrapnel that pierced them like spear-shaped bullets. The enemy was caught in a trap, but instead of retreating, they returned the fire with savage ferocity, turning the air black with bullets.

How could anyone survive this? More men fell. More bullets flew. Yet Ed remained unharmed. He was indestructible. "Come on Johnny," he shouted. "Come on."

One of the officers hollered behind him "Fix bayonets! Forward, double-quick!"

Ed secured his bayonet and stepped forward to meet the enemy. The two lines clashed in a fury of hatred. He struck the first Rebel to step forward, driving his bayonet into the man's stomach. He felt the blade drive through the gut wall and internal organs with little resistance. It came out even easier. The man buckled and fell. A second Rebel charged Ed before he could raise his bloodied rifle. He dropped the useless weapon and grabbed the man's wrist, just in time to stop a ten inch knife from striking his chest. A bullet struck the Rebel hard in the temple, splattering Ed's face and chest with blood. The Rebel's body went limp, and his hand opened, presenting the knife.

The Confederates fought with handguns, bayonets, knives, even bare hands in an all-out effort to take the woods. But they'd been badly battered and thinned by the first rounds of rifle fire and grape shot. Blue uniforms outnumbered the grays by nearly two-to-one by this time. Finally the attackers buckled, turned, and ran for their lives.

Ed picked up his rifle and charged forward, his entire regiment moving as one, chasing the enemy from the woods and out into the field below. He crossed three quarters of the grassy field, and was approaching the previously abandoned fence line, when more gray reinforcements appeared in the cotton field before him. The Rebels unleashed a heavy counter fire that buzzed, hummed, and beat the air around him. But he was invincible.

Chapin's horse whinnied as he shouted, "Form skirmishes at the fence!"

Ed reacted without thought. The regiment now in a long line, fired and drove the enemy out of the cotton field and back into the cedars. Then the unthinkable happened. Cannon fire came from the right and rear of the regiment, followed by a volley of rifles. Ed turned, confused, not knowing which way to aim his weapon. Rebels near the trees and in the cotton field below stopped retreating and started firing again, catching him in a deadly crossfire.

Down the long, high hill, which covered the right flank behind the colonel, Ed spotted Union soldiers scattered and running in his direction. A swarm of Confederates chased them. The Rebs had two of the Union cannons firing from the highest point on that hill, and the woods which Ed's division had just left behind was filling with more men in gray, who added a torrent of fire from the rear. The entire right side of General Thomas's long, blue line was being butchered.

"Left flank, double-quick!" hollered the colonel.

Ed ran for all he was worth. A hundred yards away he spied the cover of the cedar scrub brush and large boulders that skirted the high ridge. He stole a glance back to see how close the enemy was. Rufus Cowles fell to the ground just a few steps behind him, and someone stopped to help. Doctor Marks. What the heck was the Doc doing out here? Dear God, the Confederates had overrun their camp from behind, sending the doctors, cooks, and stewards fleeing for their lives.

Terrified, he glanced toward the cotton field. Rebels hustled to get into position for better shots. Onward he ran, amidst a hellfire of rifle and cannon. Fifty more yards to go. The back, right side of Irwin Clark's head came apart. Ed hurdled the body as it fell. Twenty yards—ten yards—George Downing went down with a bullet in the leg. Ed glanced sideways, saw Sophie Landt grab the wounded man's right arm.

"Here, give me a hand!" shouted Sophie.

Stop? They'd all get killed. Still, something within overruled logic. He grabbed the wounded man under his left arm, and the two dragged the soldier toward the shelter of rocks. Swarms of bullets flapped the air around them. He was dead for sure. No way he could make it through this. Couldn't just leave a wounded man, or was it that he couldn't abandon Sophie? What did it matter? Thirty yards of hell and he was asking himself stupid questions. Five more and he'd be there.

The ground rose steeply. His strength faltered. Somehow he reached the cover of the rocks alive. Sophie ripped George's pant leg, and formed a bandage. Ed turned to face the enemy he'd left in the cotton fields. They were now out in the open and less than a hundred yards away, charging in long broken rows of gray. Ed grinned wickedly. "They're sitting ducks out there," he shouted. "Vengeance is mine." He raised his rifle and fired, then reloaded and fired again. Everyone around him did the same. Men in gray fell to the ground in agony, while their bullets bounced harmlessly off the rocks and trees where the Union men had taken cover. The defensive fire broke the charge, and the Rebels faltered nearly fifty yards away, before withdrawing to the safety of the cotton field and its fences.

Those Rebels had barely made it to cover, when the routed Yankees Ed saw earlier came running across the brown, grass field. They were headed straight into the Rebels and must have realized it about then, because they immediately turned in mass toward the rocks where Ed and his regiment were. The sight appeared to catch the Rebels so off guard that few had enough presence of mind to shoot. But over the hill, behind the fleeing Union men, came another swarm of Confederates, loading and shooting as they ran, cutting the Union soldiers down like so much wheat on the open field. Perhaps a third made it to cover, the others falling dead or wounded along the way. Two Union privates sprinted wildly, diving headlong into the rocks near Ed and Sophie. Both were badly winded. One didn't even have his rifle.

Ed glared. "Where in blazes did you come from? Had Johnny on the run 'til you folded."

"What happened?" asked Sophie, finishing the bandage he'd applied to George Downing's leg by tying it into a knot.

The man with no rifle wheezed, trying to catch his breath. His face was white with red blotches on his cheeks. He'd obviously run far. "We're with General Johnson's division," he gasped. "Were sitting down to breakfast when the Rebs came on us. Most of us didn't even have our rifles."

"Yeah," added the skinny one. "Got shot up so fast everyone started running."

"Didn't get fifty yards before they turned our artillery on us. Chopped us up with our own grape shot. Bragg's whole damned army was in our camp— chased us down like hounds on a coon's trail."

Bitterness crowded Ed's angry mind. He shook his head and looked at Sophie. "While we were baiting and setting General Thomas's trap, Johnson was eating breakfast. Must've turned the entire right flank."

"Yeah," added Sophie. "Probably the commotion we heard when we moved out this morning. Well, at least we've got good ground and cover here."

Ed nodded. From this place, they could defend themselves against the enemy on three sides. But no one knew about the other divisions. General Thomas's boys had held their ground, but with the collapse of the right flank, they'd lost communication with their commander. Worse yet, they were completely cut off from all supplies. No more ammunition or food would come until this contest was settled.

For two hours the Wisconsin men shot every target that appeared within range, being careful to preserve their limited ammunition. Even the Confederates seemed satisfied with trading shots at a distance. When the firing finally died, white flags were tied to the ends of rifle barrels, and raised by several Union officers so they could collect the wounded. Hundreds lay over the field, moaning and crying for help.

Union men moved out. Ed and Sophie retrieved a man lying ten yards away, bandaged his bleeding leg, and set him in the shelter of the rocks. Others worked toward the center of the field until the Rebel artillery opened up on them. Ed watched in horror as his friends scrambled for cover again. It was against the European Rules of War and an incredulous act. He'd never heard of anyone firing upon a flag of truce. He sat in the rocks and listened to the cannons' explosions interspersed between the pitiful cries of the wounded men abandoned on the field. A nearby explosion picked up one man and threw his limp body through the air, like a leaf in the wind.

"Damn you!" Ed shouted, standing and shaking his fist. "Damn you, all." Sophie grabbed him by the collar and pulled him back behind the rocks.

When the cannons stopped firing for twenty minutes, some of the men raised white flags again and started out a second time. The wounded were desperate for help, and might not survive long without care. The temperature dropped. Large, dark, gray cloud swells rolled in low over the hills. His breath turned to smoke in the cold, winter air, and his ankle ached, warning of the icy rain those clouds must carry. Sophie was directly behind the boulders tending the wounded they'd brought back from their first rescue attempt. Ed was to the left of the rock, with a clear animal path to the field below. The white flags were carried out into the open field a second time, but no sooner did Ed stand to his feet than another barrage of artillery and rifle fire sent him scrambling for cover.

"Idiots!" he shouted. "What's the matter with you Johnnies? Them's wounded men out there, blue and gray, and they'll die." What kind of officer would order fire on a white flag? He turned his questioning face toward Sophie, who read it and merely shrugged before turning back to the injured man he tended. In angry frustration Ed watched his friend hold up a canteen from which the injured man gulped in small, grateful swallows.

A light rain fell, its pitter-patter the only sound besides the cries of the wounded men on the field. Then it grew colder, and the rain changed to sleet and snow. Hour after hour it fell—dripping from his hair and cap—pouring down the back of his neck. His aching fingertips grew so cold and numb that his white-knuckled hands clenched his rifle in a grip of their own. Let them come, he reasoned. Let them come. He'd settle this right here and now. But the Johnnies didn't come no matter how he wished it. By nightfall his clothes were soaked, and every inch of his skin was void of feeling. All night long he huddled beneath his rubber blanket, but it provided no relief from the icy air. Yet the worst suffering he endured that night was not the rain and the cold, but the sounds of his wounded friends lying in the muddy fields, crying for help, begging for mercy. Their voices haunted every night shadow. But no help came to them. Edward Best cursed the darkness.

When daylight found its way through the dark gray clouds, the Rebel cannons resumed their odious work—explosions dumping dirt, rock, splinters, and tree limbs everywhere. Amidst the bombardment, Ed huddled beneath his poncho, clinging to his miserable shelter in the cold, wet rocks. There he watched the dirt land on his head and hands, only to be washed away as mud beneath the continuing rain and sleet. About mid-morning the firing stopped.

"Sophie, maybe we can put our ponchos together, make a lean-to and start a fire. What do you think?"

Sophie shook his head. "Waste of time. Even if we could get sticks for a lean-to without getting our heads shot off, there's no dry wood. Then, there's this little matter of making a better target for the cannons."

Ed nodded, sending a watery mud dripping off the bill of his cap. "Guess we'll have to dig into the rocks."

Sophie offered a half smile. "Good thing we're Badgers."

"You what?" asked one of the wounded men.

Sophie turned and gawked at the man, obviously surprised to see him conscious again. Sophie moved to reinspect the private's wound. The bleeding had stopped, but the leg was swelling badly—turning black.

"Why they call you that?" asked the man.

"It's nothing," said Sophie, "just that some of the first settlers in Wisconsin were lead miners—dug dwellings in the soft dirt along the Mississippi bluffs. Reminded folks of rock badgers, I guess, so they called us the badger state. This here situation might be tolerable—if you were a real badger, wouldn't you say, Ed?"

Ed frowned. "I don't know no rock badger would care much for getting cannon balls throwed at him, Sophie."

"I know, Ed. Can't be serious all the time."

"Sorry," said Ed. "But this here shit is driving me crazy—those boys bleeding and freezing to death out there, when we can't do nothing for them. Damn that Rebel artillery. It's their boys dying out there, too. They nuts?"

"Don't know," said Sophie. "Doesn't make any sense."

Ed sat quiet for a time, then said, "Wish I had some food."

"Me, too," said Sophie, peaking over the rocks, "but it looks like Johnny got it all."

Nearly evening on the second day of battle, the Rebel artillery started in again, forcing Ed to hug the big rock in front of him for shelter. The rock was cold, draining what little body warmth he had left, and for the first time he started thinking it would be better to surrender than to die from the elements. Even the cries from the field were now few and far between.

December 30th, 1862, Arkansas wilderness

Socrates Best's first realization that he was alive came as he felt something sharp dig into the back of his hand. He willed himself up, but something weighed on him, holding him down, and then his head pounded with pain.

The moment his eyes opened, he found difficulty focusing, but realized something heavy was on him. With a surge of strength, he rolled onto his side and pushed the bulky mass aside. A flash of light made him instantly aware that it was now day. Something moved over his hands and feet. Feathers rustled and birds squawked around him as he lifted his head to investigate the world he had awakened to. The form lying next to him was Buck Malneck's body. He had been shot from behind, the bullet blowing straight through the top of his breast bone, causing him to fall on, and then bleed all over Socrates, whose jacket and shirt were thoroughly soaked. Several turkey vultures lurked about. A few picked at the bodies of the men Socrates had killed. The hollow was empty except for dead men and vultures.

"You don't get any more of this hide," said Socrates to the birds. His eyes focused on the place at the back of his hand, where one of the birds had bit through his skin. "I'm not feeding a one of you" he shouted hoarsely. "Not a one."

He groaned and pushed to a standing position. His head pounded. The scenery moved in several directions at once. He took a deep breath and steadied himself before trying to walk. His legs were weak, but the fresh air helped clear his head. The air was cool, but not cold enough for a frost. It all came back to him as he walked. What had become of Enoch and his family? Why had they left him? With blood all over him, must have thought he was dead. The picture of that blond kid's face was suddenly there again, just as he'd looked the minute he died. The memory nauseated Socrates, but his stomach was too empty to throw up.

Wandering down the road in search of water, his feet slapped in time on the hard, dry ground. The sun brought a welcome warmth in the cloudless sky, and he soon found himself singing to keep his mind off his misery. He sang over and over until his mouth was dry as cotton, and his mind a tangle of confusion. Pictures of the boy popped into his mind, interspersed with other images of death and destruction in the night, destruction he'd authored. Delirium took hold as uncontrolled thoughts scrambled for some nonexistent stage. "I've killed little Telemachus" he cried. "Poor Odysseus. Poor, poor Odysseus. He's lost his golden boy—and why not? The cowards never started and the weak died on the way. What else could befall those who stayed behind?"

He stopped and scanned the scenery. Everything around him seemed familiar—as if he'd been here once before, in another life. "All roads lead to Rome," he whispered, "but Rome is not my quest." His feet turned to the left, taking him off the road and over a long hill. Images shifted in and out of focus. The fine horses he'd left in Texas flashed through his mind. "Ah!" he shouted through his graveled throat. "A horse! A horse! My kingdom for a horse—but alas—friend—I have no horse—and why not—I am Amicus curiae—am I not?" He stopped beside a large boulder, looked around for something, but lost track of what he wanted. The image of the boy appeared before him again. "Ah," he said, "the horn of my dilemma. My madness has made me a murderer, and I can find no cure. Oh, for a cup of alyssum." He walked on.

After a time he stopped talking, thoughtlessly wandering in circles. By evening he'd collapsed on a big rock, where he slept the entire night, but early the next morning he awoke and wandered off again, oblivious to direction. Two blue riders appeared some thirty yards ahead and moving in his direction. Farther behind them was an entire column of blue. The sight jerked him back to reality, and he started in their direction.

A spark of hope hurried him. They're here, he reasoned, men of the North, and I'm saved. "Take me to Rome," he shouted through a fiery throat, delirious and unaware of what he was saying. He stepped hard, causing his weak knees to buckle, sending him sprawling onto the rocky ground. He started to get up, but his legs refused.

Horse hooves appeared a few feet away, but he couldn't lift his head enough to see the riders. One pair of boots appeared alongside the hooves, then stepped briskly toward him. Strong hands turned him over until all he could see was the midday sun scorching his eyes. He spoke rapidly, babbling whatever came into his head. Someone lifted his head. Cool water streamed into his mouth. He gulped lustfully, choked, then gulped again. The man asked him something, but the words seemed distant, as if Socrates were at the bottom of a well. More water flowed into his mouth, just a small stream this time, and his tongue parted, greeting it in open welcome. The man was asking his name.

"Soc—Soc—ra—tes," he said.

"Socrates?" asked the man.

A brown-whiskered face came into focus, head covered by a short, blue, cavalry cap. The man looked to be in his late twenties, though he was darkly tanned and weathered. His left cheek was distended, as though he had a rock in it. He turned and spat a large wad of dark juice on the ground.

"Uh huh," said Socrates

The soldier stood and turned toward a broad-shouldered officer, riding up to him. "Cap'n Crawford," he said through a wide grin, "we got us a Reb."

Socrates tried to lift his head and talk. I'm no Reb, I'm a citizen of

Rome, he thought, but his tongue lodged in the roof of his mouth, and the words wouldn't come out.

The captain returned the salute. "What rank? Anyone with him?"

"Shoot, no. And he's just a private. Looks pretty rough too—had a bullet part in his scalp. Hair and jacket drenched with blood, like he's been through a heap of fightin'. Thought he had red hair and jacket 'til I got up close. Seemed crazy too. Shouted, 'Hallelujah, I'm saved!' like he just came from a tent meetin' or somethin'. Keeps talkin' about bein' "Socrates.""

"The Greek?" asked Crawford.

"That what he was? Anyway, this here fellah's half-starved. Nearly spent."

"Any sign of bushwhackers?"

The scout turned and looked around, spat some tobacco juice on a big weed. Turning back to the captain he shook his head.

"Thanks, Silas. You and Delbert did good. We'll make camp here tonight and see what we can find out from this fellah. Where there's one Reb, there's bound to be more."

While the scout turned and headed back to Socrates, a young officer pulled alongside the captain. "Sir, you aren't camping the entire column up here on his word, are you?"

"What's the matter, Lieutenant? Scared?"

"How do you know there aren't Rebels off in those trees just waiting to hit us tonight? Maybe we should send out more scouts."

"And weaken the column? No, Lieutenant, we can trust those two."

Socrates knew exactly where the Rebel camp was, but couldn't seem to get his mouth to coordinate with his brain. Every word came out garbled. He gave up and just listened.

"How do you know?" the Lieutenant hissed. "They're just a couple of hicks who don't know anything about military discipline."

Socrates saw the scouts' heads turn at that remark, saw pure hatred flexing their jaw muscles, anger crowding out every smooth line. He turned to see the two officers facing each other, the heads of their horses overlapping.

The captain frowned. "Some things you can't learn from a book, Lieutenant. Those two spend weeks out here without any column to back them, yet they stay alive. If something's wrong a mile away, they know it. Not because of some book, but because of instincts—raw instincts. They sense what's going on without seeing or hearing it. Don't ask me how it is. It just is. I'll put my life in their hands before I'll follow some book. Now, get out of my way and tell these men to set up camp."

"Yes, sir."

Socrates drifted off into a dream world. How long he slept, he had no idea, but when he awoke, he realized that the man sitting nearby had a rifle trained on him. Why would they be afraid of me? he wondered. No answer came to mind, so he slowly sat up and finished the canteen the scout had left him. Somewhere behind, he heard a sergeant dispatching men to different duties and guessed he'd been asleep for an hour or two. A soldier came and handed him a plate of pork and beans, which he hastily devoured. After eating, he brightened to see the Union officer walk over and crouch beside him. Socrates moved his tongue around in his mouth, determined to stop talking gibberish.

The captain's broad face was expressionless, shoulders back, thick neck held straight and stiff. "I'm Captain Crawford of the Second Kansas Cavalry. You're my prisoner."

Socrates shook his head. "Prisoner? What do you mean—prisoner?"

The captain pointed in the direction of Socrates' jacket. "Well, if I'm not mistaken, that's a Confederate uniform."

Socrates looked at his bloody clothes, nodded, then stopped and shook his head. "I'm a Northern man, not a Rebel." He pointed to a second canteen setting near the fire. The Captain handed it over, and Socrates took another swig, this time rolling it around in his mouth. "I came from Wisconsin with my wife to start a school in Texas. When we heard the war was starting, we wanted to go north, but the people wouldn't let us. Had to make powder to keep from being drafted." He stopped, slugged another drink, then took a long deep breath before continuing. "When our supplies ran out, my brother-in-law and I were forced into service—to keep from getting hanged. He died of fever before the new year. That's when I decided I'd had enough. Ran away the first chance I had. Just kept heading north—even left my wife and children behind."

Crawford studied Socrates. "Then you won't mind telling us what you know about the Rebel camp."

"No, sir, I don't mind a bit." He told Crawford everything he knew regarding the enemy's deployment and strength, even giving the names of various officers. He relived the events of the past six months with all its frustration and pain. Everything from the hanging party to the raping of the Negro women, the three men he'd killed, and his final fight with Buck Malneck."

"Must be a hard way to kill a man," said Crawford, "seeing his face up close and all. I've never used a knife up close like that."

Socrates nodded. He had only wanted to teach their children the wonders of the written word. To make philosopher kings. Make Texas great. Now he wasn't just eager to help the Union, he was angry, get-even angry.

Crawford leaned forward and grinned. "Ready to trade that gray cloth in for some blue?"

"You bet!"

January 1st, 1863, Stones River, Tennessee

A sudden movement behind him caught Ed's attention. At first he could see nothing, then he spotted them in the rocks near the top of the bluff. Two men worked their way toward him. They wore the dark rubber ponchos of the Union, but that was all he could make out from where he sat. Every once in a while the figures moved from rock to rock, but only after a battery of explosions completed their rounds. Then the men made their moves, dodging around, barely making it to cover before the next round of explosions started. By the time they were within ten yards, Ed saw that one was a lieutenant. Two more salvos and the officer crouched for cover between Ed and Sophie.

Ed leaned back against the big boulder, his poncho bunched around him, water pouring off. "Where'd you come from?" he shouted over the cannon fire.

"Ohio," replied the lanky lieutenant.

Ed laughed, shook his head. "I mean what command?"

The officer didn't crack a smile. "General Thomas."

"So are we. At least what's left of the Wisconsin Tenth."

The lieutenant glanced around. "General Thomas wants to know how many are left down here."

Ed pushed himself into a half standing position, looked around the rocks, then down by the trees. "Dunno."

"Me, neither," added Sophie. "Got shot up bad yesterday. Been dodging artillery since. Can't put our heads out for long, or we'll get 'em blown off."

"You look like a couple of drowned rats," said the lieutenant.

Ed looked at the water running down the man's red hair and beard. "You don't look no better." They all laughed.

The lieutenant stiffened. "General Thomas says you've gotta fall back before you're completely cut off. Says McCook's entire right flank was caught out of position yesterday. The line's been pushed so far back, Thomas is afraid we'll be cut off from Nashville—wants you to withdraw and provide support for some artillery about a quarter mile from here. "Where's your captain? Still alive?"

218

Ed squinted through the cold rain, pointing to a clump of trees twenty yards away. "Last I saw, he was down there, helping the wounded. Didn't look like he'd been hurt. I suppose we didn't lose as many as we should have, given what happened."

"At least you got here before you were overrun."

"Johnson's boys didn't," said Sophie, pointing to the field.

"Yeah," added Ed. "Got cut up real bad. Some of 'em are here. Most are out there."

Ed stopped talking loud—realized the artillery barrage had ceased. The desperate cries of a few wounded men out there—alive, but rain soaked, exposed and helpless—sounded so much weaker—fewer. It was maddening. He leaned forward and looked into the deep-blue eyes of the lieutenant who squinted with every cry. "Come on," said Ed, "I'll take you to Captain Twogood."

He led the Ohio officer to the captain, who was with Colonel Chapin and some other officers. Water, sleet, and rain ran from their beards in little streams that flowed down onto their jackets. The colonel looked sickly, his face pale and gray. He coughed repeatedly, but after hearing General Thomas's orders, gave instructions for an immediate withdrawal, sending Ed through the rocks and brush to pass the word. All the time he dodged from rock to rock, he expected the shelling to resume, but it didn't, as if the Rebels knew of the command and were letting them go. They spent nearly two hours gathering the wounded from the rocks, and working their way back over the bluff behind them. At the top of the bluff they found another stand of cedars, which they worked their way through for another hour before coming out on a long ridge, where a Union artillery unit was firing. The Wisconsin regiment was ordered to dig in and support them.

Ed and his comrades ignored the cannon fire, and dug trenches until nightfall. The snowy rain kept falling amidst the ugly gray sky, making it impossible to make a fire for warmth. By midnight, the water in Ed's trench formed a miserable pool of mud. He slipped and sloshed around in it all night long, trying to get comfortable, but it was impossible. He laid his rubber blanket down with the woolen one inside it, but within minutes the muddy water soaked into everything. At least he was farther away from the pathetic cries of the wounded they'd left behind. Even so, when the wind shifted, he thought he could hear them, ever so faintly. Was it really them, or just his memory playing tricks? He couldn't be sure. Relief came when exposure and exhaustion finally drove him to sleep.

A dim morning light worked its way through the cold gray sky, and with it the enemy resumed its barrage of the area. Ed popped his head above the trench, enough to see a volley of explosions strike along the ridge. No one was out there except the Union artillerymen, preparing to respond in like form. Realizing he might be stuck all day with several inches of icy water and mud in this boggy trench, he reached down, picked up his rubber blanket, shook it off as best he could, then laid it against the side wall of the trench, where he pressed his body against it.

The cannons didn't stop firing until after sunset, and by that time, his skin was swelling from the cold dampness. No matter how he detested it, he could do nothing. Even the ghostly cries he'd heard the day earlier no longer came on the gusts of wind.

With the fall of night the firing ceased, but the snow and sleet resumed. Weak with hunger and exhaustion, he somehow kept alive, kept on going despite the impossible conditions. Another night passed, then another day with more rain and sleet. Cannon balls continued crashing into the hill, but the huge boulders around it provided ample protection from those explosions. He no longer wished for the rain to stop or the air to warm up. Ed was beyond that, beyond hope, simply waiting for death to come, or the army to surrender. He looked at Sophie. The two had withdrawn within themselves, saying nothing the entire day. "Looks like we're about done in."

Sophie shook his head, sad bronze eyes set within two dark caves. "Can't take more of this."

"Three days without food and working on four. Starvation's got an ugly face. Don't it?"

Sophie nodded. "Hunger doesn't bother me half as much as the cold."

Ed closed his eyes. "I'd just as soon surrender as spend another night in this mud hole."

"I know. The water is over my ankles on this end. One way or the other, we're through. If we don't catch our deaths of cold, we'll starve to death for sure." He looked around. "Hey. Look at that! Rain stopped."

The nearby cannons started firing again, but this time their thunder was magnified by the echoes of thunder all around the valley walls. Ed dragged his listless body out of the trench with Sophie, and forced his frozen feet to bring him to where he could see what was going on. He'd thought moving around would feel good, but his muscles were cold and cramped, aching with every motion, resisting every stretch. The two were half way to the cannons, when several new artillery detachments arrived, their horses pulling hard in the soft mud, their men scrambling to move the new pieces into place on the other side of the camp. Within minutes they aimed their barrels and stuffed them with balls and charges. One by one, they lit their fuses. The now longer row of cannons rained incessant fire on the valley below, sounding like a horrific thunderstorm that shook each rock and mud puddle with every blast.

Ed walked to the edge of the bluff. A division of Bragg's men swarmed across the rain-soaked fields on the open plain below, forcing the Union right flank back, but the artillery shells rained all over them. They were taking huge losses.

"Trying to finish us," shouted Sophie.

Ed shouted with glee, "Cannons to the left of them, cannons to the right of them volleyed and thundered. Suckers didn't figure on Thomas getting all this artillery up here."

Sophie pointed down below. "Look at those poor Johnnies."

"We're cutting them to pieces," said Ed, "and they deserve it. Die, Johnny, die. Just like the Light Brigade." He watched the scene, as if held in a trance by this picture of human beings thrown like twigs under the force of so many explosions.

After the first attempt, the Confederates fell back, rallied, and charged again, only to be pounded mercilessly by the artillery above and the rifles ahead. As they died below him, he cheered, venting his pain, releasing his anger for all those wounded left to die in the cold rain. Finally the Rebels staggered, like a boxer who'd taken a hard punch. Ed could see it as they faltered, could see their resolve wither amidst a fire so great no army in the world could have endured it. With no other options available, the Confederates relented, retreating and leaving their dead and wounded all over the field. He cheered even louder as the Union forces counterattacked with a vengeance. And through it all, the artillery poured down fire from the heavens against the fleeing Rebels, who fell back and attempted to re-form in their trenches. But they were too weak. The Yankees pressed in force until the Rebels turned on their heels and ran.

By afternoon, Bragg's army had completely withdrawn. Ed and Sophie devoured a little meal of dried jerky and hard tack, then gathered a group of men and formed two detachments to help the wounded.

Nothing, not even Perryville could have prepared them for what they found. Some of the soldiers lying in these fields were the victims of shrapnel or rifle fire and could be rescued, but so many were ripped apart by cannon shells, it made a grisly portrait. Bloody bodies were everywhere, some headless, some torn in half, their blue intestines scattered over the ground, others missing any number of limbs. And everywhere around the field, grown men wept openly.

Ambulance wagons carried the wounded away until there were no more. Then Ed led his men to the field beneath the rocks, where so many of his friends had been left to die. They gathered the bodies and organized them by units. It was a sickening sight. Those who stood in formation only a few days before, now lay in lifeless lines, waiting to be buried, their hands and faces an eerie blue, bodies hardened into twisted statues, eyes open, as if questioning or accusing. How many of these could have been saved? How many would be alive if those damned Rebels would have honored the white flag?

Such thoughts stalked him, triggering memories of helpless screams in the night. Some had whimpered like puppies, while others cried like babies, reducing him and his friends to tears. Yet, amidst such woeful desperation lay other men, the kind who cried and screamed for help until their voices failed from strain. Then, with every last ounce of strength they could muster, they'd turned their graveled voices, hurling curses at their enemies, their generals, their countries, and finally, against the comrades who'd left them there to die. Ed's weary shoulders felt as if they carried boulders on each side. He searched everywhere to find someone alive, through the cotton bushes, over the grassy fields, and back into the woods. There were only a few, and they didn't hold much promise of survival, but extracting them from certain death saved his troubled conscience.

After that, he walked away and left his detail behind, moving up and down the railroad tracks where they'd first set out to do battle. Four days had passed, though time stopped long before now. Farther up the track he found other Union detachments finishing their duties, laying out the stiff bodies of fallen warriors in uneven rows that alternated in color. Long lines of gray uniformed dead lay on the ground here, at least three for every line of blue. The Union was whipping them good up until then, but everything changed so quickly. How could that be? And who was to blame? Johnson? Us? He couldn't think about that anymore. Had to help the wounded. He walked through the woods and back into the field, where the artillery had pounded the enemy so brutally. An ambulance, which was nothing more than a horse-pulled box on wheels, passed him, and he fell into step behind it, blindly following.

He'd joined the army to prove he was a man. What good would that do if he were dead? No good. No good at all. He looked at his filthy uniform, the long thin sleeves covering his arms. They didn't look anything like the massive arms the recruiter at Big Spring had displayed so proudly. That man was a big, burly sergeant with three stripes. Ed had earned two stripes himself, but that was as far as the likeness could go. He was now emaciated. What a joke. The army hadn't done anything to make him a man, nothing he wasn't already. It had only taught him how to hate—how to kill.

He passed several houses where wagonloads of wounded were being unloaded and taken inside. The ambulance he followed stopped at the fourth house, where Ed helped unload the injured. Weak from fatigue, exposure, and starvation, he couldn't rest until the last ones were in the hands of the doctors. Picking up a skinny old Rebel who looked to be sixty years old, he carried the old man like a mother carries an infant. Even though the old fellow was weak and bleeding, he seemed genuinely grateful and whispered, "Thanks, Yank."

Ed wasn't prepared for what he found inside. The owners had left the place when the Yankees approached, and someone had broken the door down to get in. All the furniture on the first floor had been thrown outside, and the beds from upstairs moved down to the first floor, where some of the wounded men now lay. The table, once used for fine dining, supported a man having his arm sawed off. Amputated limbs were stacked in the corner of the room and blood pooled everywhere. Medical corpsmen ripped sheets to use for bandages, while the wounded groaned and cried. It was the most horrible thing he had ever seen—more terrible than the battlefield itself.

He could be of no more help here and turned to walk out. Dr. Marks stood wrapping a bandage around a man's head. Ed walked up beside him, pulled lightly on his sleeve. "Dr. Marks, I thought you were taken captive."

Marks turned, but kept on wrapping the bandage. "Oh, it's you, Best. Yes. The Rebels came upon our camp from behind, and chased us right into the fields. I was taken captive when I stopped to treat Rufus Cowles. Poor fellow, he was already dead. Rebels put me to work taking care of the wounded in a house down by the river. I was still tending them when our boys routed them this morning. Ran away and left me with the wounded. General Thomas found me, had me brought here by the cavalry. Promised the ambulances would bring the ones I left."

Ed looked around, eyes fogging over. "Looks like we took it bad."

The doctor turned around and put a hand on Ed's shoulder. "This is nothing compared to what I was treating this morning! The Rebels were so torn up by our artillery that most of the time I didn't have to amputate. Their limbs were blown clean off—a horrible mess it was. Anyway, I'm glad to see you're okay."

Ed shook his head, stared at the floor. "I don't know, Doc. I've never seen anything like this—hope I never do again."

The doctor's hand tightened on his shoulder. "You'll feel better after some rest."

Ed lifted his head, looked out the window, and stared into the distance as he spoke, as if to focus on some far away place. "Right now I'd rather be dead."

The doctor stepped between Ed and the window and stared into his eyes. "I know. I know. Now go and get some rest." The doctor turned him, took him by the arm, and ushered him to the door. Ed wove his way back down the road to where his company's fires burned, and meals were being prepared. A fire never felt warmer, nor the taste of food better. It had been the worst New Year's experience imaginable. Sergeants Gaffney and Gilbert huddled close to the fire, while Corporals Bill Day and Jack Webster sat with their shoes off, feet close to the fire. Everyone's shoes sat on rocks near the fire. Sophie stood nearby, staring into the flames, spellbound by the cavorting colors.

Exhausted, Ed gazed across the fire at Sophie and spoke in a slow, tired monotone. "Give me the cold, dry snow of Wisconsin. I'm about done in by this milder stuff."

THIRTEEN

"The way up and the way down is the same."
—Heraclitus

January 1st, 1863, Arkansas wilderness

A FTER A PEACEFUL NIGHT'S REST AND ANOTHER GOOD MEAL, SOCRATES RODE with Crawford's column to Emerald Spring, where he met the Adjutant, Lieutenant French. Like a master storyteller, that officer related the unit's history of fighting around the borders of Missouri, Arkansas, Kansas, and Oklahoma. They'd whipped Marmaduke's Confederates at Maysville, Boonesboro, and Cove Creek—taking on forces many times their size— capturing pickets, supply trains, and an entire artillery battery. Those stories only strengthened Socrates' resolve to fight. He signed his enlistment papers that day, and later a horse and saddle were provided on loan from the local livery stable, pending the Army's reimbursement, which would arrive with his first paycheck.

A few days after receiving those supplies, Captain Crawford met him on the street. "Saddle up, Socrates, bushwhackers hit Springfield, and we're gonna get 'em before they make it to their lines."

A nervous charge shot through Socrates. Bushwhackers meant the likes of Quantrill's and Andersons' murdering crews. Would he have to kill again? He saluted and turned toward the stables, but his thoughts wandered back to the boy he'd knifed in that little knoll. "Stupid questions to ask now," he mumbled. "Should have thought about that before signing those papers."

The group covered more than forty miles the first day. Yet the column stopped often, waiting while Delbert and Silas rode ahead to look for signs of ambush. During those times, he drew into the shelter of a warm bearskin he'd purchased for protection from the elements. Most every man wore one, and although they weren't army issue, the Colonel was liberal when it came to keeping his men healthy. The temperature dropped rapidly. If it had been like this when he'd run away from the Rebel camp, he could never have survived

225

the experience. He found riding to his liking, but the steady bobbing on the horse's back wore his inner thighs and buttocks raw. After two days in the saddle, he found blisters in places he hadn't thought they could grow. He was hoping they would stop soon, when he spotted the upraised hand of Captain Crawford, halting the column. White clouds of frost formed about the men's bearded mouths. Horses snorted, white puffs of steam billowing from their nostrils.

"My feet are freezing," whispered Socrates.

"Mine too," replied Vince Osborne, the private who rode beside him. He was brown-haired, under twenty-five years of age, and angular, like most of the privates in the column. Their bony bodies and gaunt faces made them look as if they might all be brothers. "Glad I'm not walking on that frozen ground."

Socrates liked Vince. His family had come from New England to promote abolition, like most of these Kansans, and he was diligent and precise in everything he did, never complaining about anything. "Feels as cold out here as Wisconsin," said Socrates, surveying the brown, dead fields around him. "If you hadn't warned me to get this bearskin, I'd have pneumonia by now."

Vince smiled. "Missouri, Arkansas, Kansas, Indian Territory—you can ride a fifty mile preacher's circuit and touch every one. Makes a mighty hot spot when they're split and warring at each other. That's why the colonel is fired up to get these raiders. If they get past us and into Indian Territory, it'll be impossible to chase them down." He clutched his elbows and pulled his arms together. "Brrr. Don't ever remember it being this cold. Reckon we're getting near Hartsville now. Should catch the bushwhackers somewhere around there. Delbert says there's plenty of sign on the trail ahead."

Socrates winced at the words, but at the thought of killing again, his heart quickened. "Think we'll be in the thick of it?"

Vince nodded. "If we catch 'em."

Socrates bit his lower lip. "How'd I get myself into this?"

"Dunno," said Vince with a laugh. "Thought you'd go to Wisconsin rather than stick around here."

Socrates turned in his saddle and looked directly at Vince. "Would have, but home is in Texas. Can't go back there now, 'less I want to die real quick."

"Even so," said Vince, tilting his curly head, "you didn't have to join. Sorry now?"

Socrates thought for a minute. "No. Guess it's the only thing to do. Can't even write my wife until the war is over. Seems right working to end it.

Who knows what they'd do to her if they knew where I was? One thing's for sure, if the Confederates get me now, I'm finished."

The captain's hand fell forward, and the column started moving again. By mid afternoon, the temperature dropped further, and the weary column stopped to camp for the night. Socrates gathered wood, and quickly lit a fire. The cold air on his back and the blistering heat of the flames at his front, left him feeling as though he were trapped between Heaven and Hell. The dichotomy sent his thoughts back to Daingerfield, to his warm little house, the feeling of his wife's soft, warm flesh against his, and then it turned to the cold, bitter hatred of Buck Malneck and his friends. Socrates drove the thoughts away. There could be no room for either nostalgic or bitter meditations. No place for unobjective emotions.

Morning was slow in coming, and the men warmed their frigid bodies at the cooking fires one last time before mounting up and moving out. By the middle of the next day, the scouts returned with blank expressions, shaking their heads at Captain Crawford's many questions. After riding out in different directions, they returned the same way. Some of the men began to grumble, complaining of how their feet were freezing.

Another cold night was spent outdoors before the enemy trail was relocated, but too much time had expired. The cavalrymen's spirits plunged throughout the day. Socrates turned in his saddle and asked, "Anyone know how cold it is?"

Men shrugged, looking about as if to show there was no thermometer handy. Then he answered, "It's so cold my pee froze in mid air!"

The men laughed.

Vince said. "That's nothing! My feet are so froze—every time I step on 'em, a different toe breaks off!"

Another added, "It's so cold, my mustache is one big icicle!"

By this time, everyone was giddy, laughing at the most ridiculous jokes, but the humor lifted their mood, giving them something to think about besides their misery. By the next morning, a dozen men had serious signs of frostbite, and the column turned toward home. But even as the troops rode into town, they continued to laugh and joke.

"Waste of time," said one.

"At least we found the tracks of the enemy," said another.

"Sure," replied the first, "but the tracks were so cold, over twenty men froze their feet just walking in 'em!"

Said Socrates, "Them tracks weren't just cold, they were cold and old. So old, the oldest man around couldn't remember when they were made!"

That one set them laughing hard. But he couldn't resist another. "Well! Now that we're getting home, we can just sit back and reflect on our maneuvers—and the genius who planned it all!"

The riders bent over in their saddles, laughing at the idiotic notion of their winter campaign. But amidst the laughter, some were gripped in fits of coughing. Socrates himself could feel a scratching sensation in the back of his throat, but resisted the urge to cough.

The following weeks saw one man after another fall sick, as they settled into the monotony of winter picket duties. It was a record cold winter, and the frigid mud around his boots was ankle deep as Socrates kicked two footholds into the side of the ditch. Using them, he could step up out of the mud and gain momentary relief for his frozen feet, but the ground was soft, maintaining his weight for only minutes before he slid back into the muck again. The trench was three feet deep, built up at the front by the dirt from below, and by wooden pickets that provided protection from a frontal assault, should the Rebels decide to make one. In three weeks of continuous guard duty, the Second Kansas Regiment had seen no enemy activity. Now all that could be heard among the pickets was the sound of men coughing, hacking hard in the cold winter air—trying to stop their lungs from filling up with fluid.

Socrates' chest squeezed his heart. Sweat ran from his brow. He coughed several times before realizing he was thirsty. It was a cool February day. Too cool to feel so warm. The fields on the other side of the picket-logs blurred under his tired gaze. Another fit of coughing struck. Chest muscles spasmed as his ribs contracted in quick powerful motions. A blood vessel in his throat ruptured, peppering the logs with blood as he coughed. The sky went suddenly black as he found himself in darkness, riding a runaway horse, galloping wildly through the fields and down a steep ravine. He leaned back in the saddle to balance his mount, then everything around him began to swirl. He was falling, and he thought he felt his left foot come out of the stirrup. Cold water slapped his body as he fell into the muddy pool beneath him. Excited voices shouted frantically for the lieutenant, and Socrates slipped into a dark abyss.

For the next three weeks, he floated in and out of consciousness, racked by coughing spells that left him without strength. Midway through the fourth week, he opened his eyes to see a large warehouse-like room with high ceilings. He lifted himself onto one elbow in confusion, then collapsed back onto his side. Black-hooded figures moved about the room. Where could he be? The vision was strangely familiar, but he couldn't make a connection. One of them moved directly in front of him, blocking the image of a man lying in bed three feet away. The creature bent and turned, as if sensing his presence. He could see the face of a woman framed by white strips of cloth, her head covered with a long black veil that melted into the loose black dress below it.

"You're awake, Mr. Best? I'm afraid we'd about given up hope for you. Excuse me while I get the doctor."

Socrates reached out and grabbed the pleat of her dress, the fabric slipping through his weakened fingers, and she turned. Socrates asked, "Am I in Heaven?"

The nun gave a high-pitched giggle. "I'm afraid not. Besides, I hope God has something better in mind for us than what we have here. You're in a hospital at Springfield. You've had a bad case of pneumonia, and we thought you were as good as gone. Just goes to show the Lord has everyone in his hands. If you'll excuse me, I'll get Dr. Root. He told us if you awoke, we were to get him immediately." She started to turn and walk away, then stopped and looked at Socrates again. "Oh! I almost forgot. So did the lieutenant who came by to check on you. Said he'd signed you up, and didn't want you dying on him. Stopped by to check on you nearly every day. Seemed very concerned. You're lucky. Most of these boys cough their lungs out and die without a single soul ever visiting them."

Socrates watched her black gown and veil float across the room, then fell back asleep. He awoke to a thudding sound as a fist rapped him on the back. The nun stood before him, a string of wooden beads dangling beneath her veil. At its lowest point, hung an intricately carved crucifix.

The doctor pounded again, starting a bout of hacking that ripped at Socrates' lungs. When it was finished, the tickle remained, enticing another cough, but he resisted. His throat ached, and his head resonated with every pulse. The last thing he wanted to do was start coughing again. He wished he could go back to sleep.

"Excellent, excellent," said the doctor. "Not many patients come back from where you've been. We might have given up on you if sister hadn't insisted on tending you. You're a fortunate man, Best, but you must stay in bed until you regain your strength. This cold damp air could exacerbate your condition. That is, make it worse. There hasn't been much fighting since December, so we've more beds than usual. You take all the time you need to get your strength."

Socrates stared long and hard at the doctor who looked strong and vibrant, face bright and rich with color. The words of Socrates' namesake came to mind:

"The best physicians are those who both know their art and have had the greatest experience of disease. They would better not be themselves too robust in health."

He laid back on the bed, thanked the doctor, and fell into a deep sleep, a dream world where he found himself with his beloved Ellen and children again. The image was strong—inviting. He felt someone shaking his shoulder, but resisted, clinging to his family.

"Come on, Socrates. Haven't got all day. Doc said you should get up for a while."

He opened his eyes to see Lieutenant French standing beside him, hat in hand. "Hey," Socrates replied from a hoarse, dry throat.

French let out a loud sigh and smiled. "Thought you were finished. Even felt bad about signing you up after everything you've been through. If you'd died and your widow ever came looking for me, I'd be cut to the quick. Sure glad you're getting better. Here, have some water." The lieutenant sat him up and poured water from a tin cup, slaking his thirst. Socrates gulped it, but French lowered the cup. "Take it easy or you'll start coughing again. Just a little at a time. There'll be plenty of time for more later."

"Thanks," Socrates whispered. "What's happening with the regiment? Doc said it's been quiet."

French shook his dark mop of hair, then turned to the bunk beside him. "Should I tell him or should you, Captain?" Socrates recognized the long lean face and thick brown moustache of Captain Lines as he sat up and smiled.

"Are you supposed to be in here?" asked Socrates softly.

Lines smile widened.

"Wouldn't go in the officer's Ward," said French. "Wanted to be in here with his men."

Lines waved him away. "Go on. Just said that to sound benevolent. Real reason was I wanted to be in here with Root. Only decent surgeon around."

Socrates remembered the first time he'd seen Captain Edward Lines. The man's demeanor had struck Socrates so, that he couldn't help but comment to Vince about the similarities between Ben and Lines. He handled a horse just like Ben had, and dressed every bit as sharp. Vince said that after the battle at Elk Horn Tavern, Lines had been taken from the Second Kansas Regiment by General Mitchell, to serve as his adjutant in the Army of the Cumberland. But Lines couldn't stand being away from his Kansans for long. He returned as a Lieutenant, but was quickly made Captain of a company, by unanimous vote.

French took a deep breath and sighed. "You going to tell him or am I?"

"Go ahead," said Lines. "I'd like to hear you explain that one, myself."

French leered at the captain before turning to Socrates. "Same old stuff. When the officers don't have anyone else to fight, they go at each other."

Socrates' felt his face form a question.

French blushed, smiled, and stared across the room. "Guess I left that out when I told you about the mighty Second." He paused, looked at the officer's hat in his hands. "When the regiment was formed and dubbed the Second Kansas Volunteers, Captain Welborne tried to take control of the regiment. Claimed he was the ranking officer, since he'd been promised the rank of colonel." French stopped and looked at Socrates, olive-green eyes wide. "Can you believe that? He was a surgeon, had no business commanding cavalry, and everyone knew that except him. Well. Headquarters set him straight—restricted him to medicine—but he still made full colonel."

"Threw him a bone, I suppose. Anyway, he left and was replaced by Dr. Root, a good man with little military ambition. After the companies were formed, the army changed our name to the Ninth Kansas because we had nine companies. But Captain Crawford, being the ranking captain, thought his company should be Company A instead of H to designate it as such." French stopped again, shaking his head. "You know what? Sometimes you just can't win for losing. The companies were reorganized under Colonel Mitchell to satisfy Crawford, but now Crawford wants to arrest Colonel Bassett and take command of the regiment. This stuff drives me crazy."

A smiling steward, with the round, pink face of a cherub, came over and put his hand on French's shoulder. "Hey! Captain Lines, Lieutenant French, heard your friend was awake so I came over to see for myself. It's good to see him coming around, just don't tire him out. Remember, he's been close to the edge."

Socrates recognized the words, a phrase used himself when dealing with the sick in the Confederate hospital. Words like: "he nearly gave up the ghost," "nearly left us," "passed away," or "he's no longer with us." Anything but to say another man had died or was near death, when it seemed like the whole world was dying, dying in a world gone mad with sickness, hatred, and killing.

"I understand," said French. "I'll leave in a minute." The hospital steward turned and walked away before French added, "That's Friendly Reuben, one of the stewards who's been caring for you. Dr. Root speaks highly of him. If you need any help, just give him a holler."

The lieutenant smiled amiably and stood to face his recruit.

Weak and tired, Socrates lay back on his bed. The room was slowly moving counterclockwise.

"Better leave you to rest now," said French. "I'll be back tomorrow. You just rest and get better."

Madison, Wisconsin, March 2, 1863

Swift squirmed in his chair. Sitting long hours on the hard wood seats made his butt-bones ache. Even with a healthy diet, he hadn't regained much of the weight he'd lost in prison. Doc told him that other returned prisoners were having similar problems. Some suffered a chronic diarrhea that killed them within one year of coming home. Others seemed to have just given up on life.

Dr. Milton, dressed in a light-gray suit, came into the front of the room and laid papers on a yellow oak podium, before slipping wire-rimmed glasses over his brown eyes. His long muscular frame stretched over six feet, and his face held a manly firmness that bordered on arrogance whenever he glanced sideways at a student.

"Last week we completed the study of summary arguments in estate planning. Each student represented a plaintiff and presented his case quite well. But today I turn the tables. Over the weekend I want you each to prepare the opposition's closing arguments. You should have a thorough knowledge of the defendant's case, based upon your study and presentation of the evidence on the other side. Furthermore, you must present every bit as convincing a case on the behalf of your new client as you did for his or her opponent."

Swift raised his hand and Dr. Milton nodded. "Sir, I don't understand. What if we don't believe in the defendant's case?"

Dr. Milton grinned. "Remember Gorgias of Leontini?"

Swift nodded. "One of the Greeks. Teacher of rhetoric. Developed some of the formal logic we use for debate."

"Very good. But he also founded the prose of rhythm and literation, and a topical outline that have been the tools of oratory since his day. His effect on the Greeks was mystical, almost magical."

Dr. Milton stopped and looked around the room, commanding every ounce of attention. "In the Defense of Helen of Troy, Gorgias came to Helen's side against a society that had been embroiled in a war for years because of her apparent infidelity. Surely she had been the cause of the death of their fathers, sons, and cousins. And if ever a court was stacked against someone, Helen was that one. But Gorgias made a brilliant defense, arguing that Helen deserted her husband to go with the King of Troy because of fate or passion, or overpowering persuasion. Fate, he said, allows us no choice. Surely she could not be held responsible for fate's choice. Yet, if it weren't fate but simply passion, passion, too, was overpowering. So powerful, he argued, that it exceeded the human will."

"But what about persuasion?" asked Swift.

"Ah!" said Dr. Milton, brown eyes wide and shining. "That was his greatest argument, for it was *the* purpose he had carved out for himself. Persuasion left one with no human choice whatsoever, because words have the power to master both mind and will."

Swift shook his head. "I still don't understand. He may have believed in Helen of Troy."

"True, but from Gorgias' school came Protagoras, who trained his students to argue both sides of a legal case. He had an innate ability to propound either side and gain total sympathy of the jury. Athenians were shocked at the idea, believing a case could have only one just side."

A creepy feeling swept up Swift's spine. "Doesn't it?"

"That's *precisely* what we should learn from Gorgias and Protagoras. We are not judges, only legal counsel. Counsel that is paid to represent an individual within our democratic court system. It is our responsibility to know the law and present the best possible case for our client, without bias or prejudice, and for that we are well paid."

"But Protagoras also said, 'Man is the measure of all things.' Don't those words fly in the face of Scripture and allow man to pervert justice?"

Dr. Milton grinned with amusement. "And what makes you think we have the ability or responsibility to determine justice?"

"It is written, 'Learn to do well; seek judgment, relieve the oppressed, judge the fatherless, plead for the widow.'"

"Ah! now you bring in religion."

"Okay, how about Plato? He wrote that injustice could never be more profitable than justice."

"True, but it is not the position of legal counsel to determine justice or injustice. That is the sole responsibility of the judges and justices of our land. It has little to do with you as an attorney."

Swift ran his fingers through his wavy hair. "I understand that, but I'd never represent someone I thought was guilty or wrong in their actions."

"You will always be free to choose your clients. But what if they hold to another faith? Is it not a constitutional right for everyone to have legal representation? Isn't that something our forefathers fought for?"

"Only if I didn't believe in the innocence or the rightness of their cause."

Dr. Milton slid his hands into his gray suit pants. "That's admirable of you, but your righteous standards may do you little good if you are no longer in business. I suggest, young man, you take this exercise seriously and place your ideals on the shelf."

July 1863, somewhere in Tennessee

A languid pallor hung over the Union camp when Ed Best returned from picket duty. He was looking forward to getting some rest, when he saw Sophie Landt and a number of other men detached near the provost marshal's office. Sophie sported three stripes on his sleeve, and he looked as robust as ever, but the lines of his face were drawn. "Sophie, where've you been? Too bad you missed guard duty. We could've used a fresh sergeant of the guard."

"You take care of the Rebs," said Sophie. "I only collect AWOLs and drunks."

"How'd you get one stripe up on me again?"

"Captain Brum. When he found out I'd been to college, he slapped a third stripe on me and put me to his paper work. You wouldn't believe all the forms he has to fill out for every drunken derelict we arrest. I wouldn't have a captain's job if they gave it to me."

"Never liked filling out forms myself, but don't worry. Just because he's dumb enough to make you a sergeant, doesn't mean he's crazy enough to make you an officer."

Sophie glared at him.

Ed glanced around "What gives anyway? Everybody's on edge or something, not singing and laughing like usual."

Sophie stared past Ed and pointed. "Over there. That's what's going on."

Ed followed Sophie's gaze to a field that separated their regiment from another. As he watched, two regiments marched into it in double columns. No drums played and the men moved almost silently. "Someone gonna get a medal or something?"

Sophie shook his head, rugged face somber, bronze eyes half-moons. "Captured one of the Indiana AWOLs in a Confederate uniform. Was riding with their cavalry. Been condemned to die for desertion and treason."

Ed's mouth dropped. "You mean they're gonna shoot him? Never seen anything like that before."

"Well, looks like you're going to now."

Sergeant Dowd walked through the camp hollering, "Form up on the field. Form up."

It was good to see Dowd had recovered enough from his injuries at Perryville to return to duty, but Ed had a sinking feeling as he followed those commands. Most of the men caught violating rules were given detestable details like all-night picket duty, or burying the cavalry's dead horses. In the frozen ground of winter that could prove quite a chore. Some were even hung by their thumbs, or locked in a stockade. The severity of punishment varied from unit to unit, according to the preferences of individual commanders. Although there was talk of hangings and firing squads, the morale and dedication of the average soldier had made such things seem impossible until now.

The three regiments formed ranks with the Indiana and Ohio boys on one side, and the Wisconsin boys on the other. A space of about thirty yards stood between them as the formations faced inward. A division colonel standing at the center of the field shouted, "Regiment—" Which was followed by the captains relaying, "Company—attention!"

The heels of nearly two thousand men snapped together in unison. A drum began beating, and a group of men dressed in their best uniforms marched forward carrying an empty casket. Behind them came the turncoat, a lanky figure dressed in Union blue, with two long gold braids of hair. Directly behind him marched a detail of seven men, their rifles at right shoulder arms. Time inched along with agonizing slowness and Ed began to sweat. The men with the casket stopped, set the long pine box on the ground, removed the top and set it alongside. One of the men walked back to the prisoner, and moved him to a place directly in front of the casket, facing the line of riflemen.

The drum stopped. An officer stepped forward with a piece of paper. He read the date of the prisoner's enlistment and desertion, followed by the date of his capture, and the fact that he had been apprehended while in the service of the Confederacy. He was guilty of treason, and therefore condemned to die. Cold harsh words. To each man came a warning—deep and penetrating. Ed's mind flashed back to Perryville, those long golden braids of hair dancing amidst the struggling forms. Rebels dropping at his every step. This was a hero, not a traitor!

The officer turned right, marched to a position directly behind the firing line and stopped. Another officer walked over to the condemned man and offered him a blindfold, which he took, but his hands shook so bad he couldn't tie it. The officer stepped forward and helped tie the blindfold. Once he had moved away, the senior officer spoke again.

"Detail, load—ready—aim—fire!"

Ed jumped at the sound. He watched the bullets tear into the man's torso, saw the blond headed body fall backwards onto one side of the pine box. There it rolled into the opening—feet sticking up and out of the narrowest end. The casket bearers moved the body farther into the box until no limbs were visible. Two men placed the top on, while two others nailed it shut. Then four riflemen did an about face. The drummer drummed again, and the line marched out the way it had come.

FOURTEEN

"Know thyself."
—Socrates

September 1st, 1863, on the Poteau River in Arkansas

SOCRATES STARED INTO THE FIRE, WHERE A POT OF COFFEE WARMED IN THE early morning hours. He'd just finished guard duty, and figured it would be a waste of time to try dozing off, when the entire regiment would be awake in a few minutes. The solitude of the sleeping camp matched his melancholy mood. Every available soldier was needed to oppose a massive Confederate campaign that could decide the fate of this entire region.

Socrates' regiment had joined the 3rd Wisconsin Cavalry, Kaufman's Howitzers, and the 3rd Indian Home Guards in chasing the Rebels from Honey Springs to the Red River. But while the regiment was out defending the Indian Territory, word arrived that another force of Confederates was working its way through Emerald Spring from Darnedalle.

He poured a cup of coffee and wondered what would happen to the Union folks at Darnedalle. Visions of Anderson's murdering bunch paraded through his mind—men who had become so infected with killing that their infestation threatened every Union sympathizer in Missouri. What kind of men wore human scalps on their belt? His stomach went queasy. Maybe nothing would happen. The Union had lost Springfield in '61, but they had gotten it back just as fast, without endangering civilians. He breathed deep, but anxious thoughts kept popping up, like weeds in a garden.

Whatever was happening in Emerald Spring and Darnedalle, the regiment had exacted its pound of flesh. Still staring into the fire, he recalled how angry he had been, and what he'd done. With the Confederate army moving in force throughout the Indian territory, his officers decided that only the destruction of the Rebel supply lines could slow their progress. The Kansas cavalry then rode behind enemy lines to Perryville, Arkansas, where they destroyed countless supplies and captured a supply train. After taking all of

237

the clothing they could use, they burned the rest. At North Fork Town, they captured a Confederate paymaster and his entire outfit of wagons, with little resistance, then moved to meet General Blunt, only to find the Rebels retreating. The Union army followed in vicious pursuit, catching them on the open road to Perryville.

The picture was so vivid, as if it were happening now. Like Achilles who had sought to avenge the death of his warrior friend, Mannedoitios, Socrates had charged into the Confederate skirmishers. Storms of lead filled the air as he rode like a man possessed. Explosions ruptured the earth around him. He sucked in the musky odors of black dirt and gunpowder, then exhumed their insipid fury in shouted curses. And like the Achaians of long ago, the Confederates stood their ground for only a short time before fleeing. In a stampede of terror, he and his comrades split and chased them like wild animals over the broad, flat land.

Not a morsel of mercy was in him as he rode through the enemy's position, French Le Mat pistol in one hand, knotted leather reins in the other. The Rebels who had done their best to kill him only scarce seconds before, paid dearly for their insolence. Bodies fell in lifeless heaps across the plain as he and his comrades trampled them. He rode fast, faster than he ever had before, firing his pistol at nearly point-blank range, and watching his victim dive headlong into the lush, green sod, dead. A moment later he caught another runner, a man who dropped his rifle, darting wildly about the field. His head turned, childish face filled with terror. Socrates squeezed the trigger, then jumped his horse over the crumbling corpse. More men fell beneath him until the pistol was emptied, then out came the cavalry saber. With the words, "Recipe foram!" he cut into a fleeing rebel's shoulder, heard an ungodly cry as the fellow's arm dropped several inches. A severed upper arm bone shone milk-white, the bloody lower arm hanging by a few tendons. The man fell to the ground in agony, eyes bulging. The next Rebel was less fortunate, his head flopping to the ground beside his lifeless body. But the site of such misery brought no remorse. Socrates had gladly cut his enemies to pieces as they scurried over the field before him.

The sights and sounds replayed in his mind over and over again. In the little knoll where he'd sought refuge barely eight months prior, he'd been cornered by Buck Malneck and forced to fight, but even then he'd been hard pressed to take up a knife, revulsed by the idea of killing. But this, this was fun. Feeling his enemies crumble beneath his strength. Watching them flee in terror. He'd never known such exhilaration, such power. "I laugh at a sword," he whispered, "for I could wish them no better death."

As he stood alone by the fire, he fingered the envelope Captain Lines had given him as he came off duty. "If I don't make it back this time," he'd said, "mail this for me." Those words had caught Socrates off guard, but not as much as the ashen look on the Captain's face. Socrates worked the wax seal until it broke, then gently pulled two pieces of paper out and unfolded them in the golden glow of the fire.

Dear Father,

We have just stopped here for a few moments; we are on a forced march to join General Blount, at Gibson. We have had a hard trip since we left Cassville, but of this hereafter. I will only say that I have had the advance, and we have done some good work. We expect some hard fighting, and if I should be killed, I want you to settle up my business. I have pay due me from July 1st, and Kittie will be entitled to a pension. I would like to have it attended to at once. I fear not to die, but tremble to think of the effect it would have upon my dear wife and little one; but God rules and I trust all to him. You will know, as soon as the battle is over, of me, and, either dead or alive, it shall be a good account; I have brave men, and we will do good work. I can't write more, I have so much to do, If I fall, my papers will be sent to you. My love to all.

In much haste, your affectionate son, Ed.

The hair on the back of his hands stood up as Socrates slowly pushed the paper back into its envelope. The two had enjoyed some good talks in the hospital, but nothing to prepare him for this. The captain was candid and outspoken about his love for his wife and daughter. But that was only half of it. Lines repeated again and again that he hoped God, in his goodness, would spare him and his wife for each other. Over and over he gave thanks to God for giving him such treasures, while often interjecting, "Could I ever really thank him as I should?" But no one had ever known the Captain's deepest thoughts and fears.

Socrates silently vowed to never open another person's mail.

"You up already?" asked Vince Osborne.

Socrates pushed the paper back into the envelope before turning to see his friend strap on a sidearm.

"Looks like a good day for chasing Johnny," said Osborne.

Socrates stepped over to the fire, pulled off the coffee pot, and held it out. Osborne pushed a tin cup under the flow, dragging in the sweet aroma as he watched his cup fill with black liquid. "Man, I miss my family. Haven't gotten a letter in a week. Long as we're on the road, probably won't be getting any more mail either." He tilted his head and stared at Socrates. "How come you never talk about your wife and kids?"

Socrates shrugged and looked away.

"Come on, man. You've got to miss them."

"What if I do?" said Socrates, turning to look him in the eyes. "Thinking won't make it better. Talking neither."

Osborne took a drink, then swirled the coffee around in his cup. "It's the only pleasure we have, thinking and talking about our families."

"Maybe so, but this sensation we call pleasure. It's remarkable how close it is to it's apparent opposite, pain." Socrates turned and looked away again. "Left my family in Texas, where I brought them. They could all be dead now. And why? Because God wants to try us—wants to refine us through this hell we call life?"

Osborne took another sip of coffee. "Not gonna argue the Bible with you. But you keep riding into fire the way you did at Perryville, and you won't ever have to worry about feeling pain. You'll be dead."

Socrates scratched his head. His namesake's words:

"If this is so, will a true lover of wisdom who has firmly grasped this same conviction—that he will never attain to wisdom worthy of the name elsewhere than in the next world—will he be grieved at dying? Will he not be glad to make that journey?"

A bugle sounded assembly. Both men threw their coffee in the fire and headed for their bed rolls. Within a short time, the entire regiment was up and fed, then the men fell into formation, where they stood at the head of their horses.

Captain Crawford, sharply dressed and crisp as a new paper dollar, rode up and addressed the regiment. "The Rebels," he said, "have deserted Fort Smith. Captain Mentzer's men have raised the Stars and Stripes over it."

The news sent a chill down Socrates' spine, and he cheered hard with the other men. That city hadn't seen the Union flag over it since the beginning of this war. If the Rebels had left Fort Smith, they had probably left Darnedalle too.

The Captain raised his hand for silence. "Now we face the task of driving the Rebels out of here for good."

"We'll give 'em hell, Cap'n!" someone yelled.

Everyone started cheering again. Crawford waited for the noise to subside, a broad grin on his rough, square face. "In a minute," he said smiling, "we'll mount up and find some Rebels to give that to." The men laughed. "General Cabell and his men are retreating into the Backbone Mountains. Looks like they're regrouping until they can be reinforced and resupplied. It is Colonel Cloud's intention to press them hard, before they can accomplish either. He'll join us along the way with Rabb's Battery and the Sixth Missouri. Captain Lines, take Company C in the lead, companies A and B to follow. Remember, that's rough country up there, and we don't want them to get the jump on us. Now, mount up."

The men moved with practiced precision. The long winding road to Backbone Mountain was open until it approached the higher ground, where they met up with the rest of Colonel Cloud's command. This was a desolate, rocky area, with high rises that were thick with gravel, a terrain impassable for the artillery had it not been for the roads. The trees were mostly scrub pine and spruce, too poor for useful lumber. The road itself was rougher than any they had traveled before, and was being made even more difficult by Cabell's men, felling trees to impede the army's progress.

Socrates could tell Crawford was getting nervous when he sent more and more scouts up the road looking for sign. Just before noon two came riding in at a full gallop. Crawford went out ahead to meet them, and was soon joined by Colonel Cloud, his long black hair curling over his shoulders.

Smiling faces and rapid hand motions showed something was up, but they were too far away for Socrates to make out what was being said. After a minute or two, the officers dispersed, and the column continued forward. Captain Crawford rode beside the column, stopping to talk to his lieutenants along the way.

The Rebels were in the valley ahead, near the little settlement of Jenny Lind. Captain Lines would take his company, along with Companies A and B, around the left side of this hill, while the artillery and the Sixth Missouri followed. The remainder of the division was to move through the gap on the right, and come in on them from the side. "If we catch them unaware," said Crawford, broad face gleaming "we'll have 'em for sure." He turned and rode back along the column, leading the other companies off toward the narrow gap between the two rocky hills.

They had a good head start before Socrates' detachment moved forward. He spurred his horse into a canter for several hundred yards, then into a controlled gallop. By this time, the late morning sun cast small shadows through the hills. The rocky ground and loose gravel around the hillside made hard going for the horses, so the detachment eventually slowed to a trot. Ahead lay nothing more than a well-worn animal path that coursed along a narrow ridge around the steep hillside. Small farmhouses appeared here and there amidst the hills. He followed in single file until he made it to the opposite side of the hill, where he sighted the other portion of the division moving toward him in the distance. The first three companies flowed forward in a steady stream, their flags, rifles, and hats becoming clearer with every step of their horses. A cloud of dust rose all around them, causing it to look as if they were riding straight out of a mist on the mountainside. The two columns would meet at the road. Not a single Rebel in sight.

The coarse rocks and gravely slides, interspersed with small scrub-pines and anemic-looking Cedars, made Socrates think of the lush green pines of Wisconsin. He loved the look and smell of fresh pines, the sticky resin oozing from its knots, the supple moisture of its soft yellow wood. How easily it was cut and molded into any form of furniture. The image of his father and mother came to mind. A sudden heart pain. He turned his attention to the trail ahead.

Colonel Cloud's column was only a quarter mile away, when rifle fire sounded from the wood line on the opposite hill. Captain Lines shouted to dismount. Socrates climbed down and secured his horse before taking cover behind a large boulder. He peeked across the dip separating the two hills. Two or three hundred yards away, little puffs of smoke appeared amidst a stand of scrub pines where ten or twelve Rebel rifles fired, but the distance was such that neither side did any damage. Socrates aimed his brass-plated Sharps rifle and fired at the little puffs, but doubted he hit anything. The skirmishing continued for a short time until the Rebels mounted and rode away.

Colonel Cloud re-formed his division on the road. Socrates and part of Crawford's company fell in about half-way back of Captain Lines's detachment, which was sent out as an advance guard. Everyone seemed eager, determined to catch the fleeing enemy. Spying the stern look on the captain's face made Socrates ever so conscious of the letter in his pocket. The rest of the army followed a safe distance behind. An hour later, the column passed through a thin gap, where the road narrowed between a rise of rocks that fell into a gully on its left and a small fenced pasture on its right. As soon as Lines's men came alongside the fence, gunfire exploded, trapping the advance riders against the steep gully.

Socrates' horse whinnied and reared. Blue uniformed men ahead of him fell to the ground, some thrown by their bucking horses, some shot. His first reaction was to ride ahead and help, but his sergeants shouted to find cover. He leapt from his mount. Forcing the animal backwards, he melted into a sumac thicket beneath a large tree, firing at the puffs of smoke emanating from the fence line ahead. A corporal's horse reared, throwing him. Before he could regain his feet, he was shot twice and fell motionless. Horses fell everywhere. Some pinned their riders, others crushed the wounded. A few ran about in confusion. The only survivors of the men who'd been caught along the fence, lay behind their horses, using them as shields.

Socrates fired into the fence. Unable to discern any real target, his Sharps carbine joined with the rapid fire of his comrades. A hail of fire ripped the crude wooden rails into a shower of splinters. As quickly as the firing had begun, it stopped. An eerie silence descended over a road littered with bloody men and horses. Figuring that the bushwhackers had retreated, Socrates mounted and rode into the skirmish area. Most of his friends were beyond help. The lucky ones died outright, while the less fortunate, like Captain Lines, lay on the ground with mortal gut and chest wounds. The sight gave Socrates goose bumps all over again. A sudden yearning for his wife and children poured through his spirit and into his mind. He felt like running away. A group of men and officers gathered around their captain, while Socrates went around offering water to the others. A sergeant walked around shooting the wounded horses.

The first man Socrates tended had been struck by a rifle ball which exited the arm, shattering the bone, and leaving the lower half hanging lifeless at his side. That would be another amputation for the surgeons. Socrates took off his shirt and formed a sling. The man's skin turned cold and pale, and he started shaking, prompting Socrates to grab a bed blanket from a downed horse. It was partially covered with blood, but he shook it and wrapped it around the sitting fellow. Putting his hands on the man's head, he gently laid him back, then placed a sack beneath his feet. "That should help for a while," he whispered. He turned and started toward the body of another, shot through the head. Taking a blanket from another dead horse, he covered the corpse.

Captain Crawford rode up, eyes darting. "You seen Captain Lines?"

Socrates pointed to the crowd of men gathered around their fallen captain. "Over there, sir. Gut wound. Looks mortal."

"Damnation!" shouted Crawford. "He's as good an officer as we've got. He shouldn't go this way. Bushwhackers must've fired off a few rounds and run like hell." Crawford looked toward Lines again. "Should've known they'd pull something like this. The place is named right. It's the Devil's Backbone for sure." The captain grew quiet, surveyed the bloody road, then turned toward Socrates, who'd found another survivor and was ripping up the man's shirt to make a compress. "Looks like you're good at that, Best."

"It's what I did in the Rebel camp, sir. Worked as hospital steward, taking care of the sick and wounded. It's what I wanted to do here too, but the colonel said he was short of men. I'm just a school teacher, never wanted this killing."

Crawford slowly nodded. "None of us did, Best. Just happened that way. You know? If I were wounded, I'd want a caring man, someone experienced like you to take care of me." He took off his hat and scratched his thick brown hair. "You did your share at Perryville. Not a coward or shirker. I'll see what I can do."

Socrates half smiled, then wandered around feeling helpless. One of the wounded men he tended earlier was gasping for air. Socrates watched the chest rise and fall, straining for oxygen while the lungs filled with blood that flowed in a little stream from his mouth. Finally the chest collapsed. A few feet beyond, Captain Lines' men huddled around him, listening carefully. Socrates stood and watched them, marveling at their dedication. After awhile, the huddle broke, and the men dispersed in different directions, some crying openly, others hiding their tears. The First Arkansas arrived then, carried in fifty ox-pulled wagons. Soon as they climbed out, Captain Lines's cold body was laid in the back of a wagon alongside six other corpses, while the four worst wounded were placed in another. The two wagons headed home.

Socrates watched the scout Silas reporting back. He had a natural way of riding that prompted the memory of Ben, but his clothes were seedy, beard mangy and dripping with tobacco spit. "Colonel," he said through a cheek packed with brown plug, "ambush was to slow us down while they dig in up Backbone Mountain." He turned in his saddle, spit, pointed toward a nearby peak. "Whole division is throwing dirt up there, burrowing their artillery in too."

Colonel Cloud paused, staring off toward the horizon. His shoulder-length, coal-black hair glistened in the midday sun. "Good! We'll show him how brave men fight." He turned to the officers. "Captain Crawford, take two companies of your cavalry and cover our left flank. Rabb's Battery will set up in a central position behind you. The rest of the Second dismounts and advances in one skirmish line up the left center. Two companies of the Sixth, dismount and cover the right flank, while the rest advance right center." The First Arkansas will form a second line and follow up the center, filling in as needed.

Socrates sensed in the men an aching to fight, an eagerness to exact revenge for Captain Lines, as the column moved to the base of Backbone Mountain. "I had forgotten the taste of fears," he said softly, as he dismounted and moved into position.

He was standing at the right side of the skirmish line near Rabb's artillery when the skirmish line started through the thick timber and up the steep hill. Rocks and gravel gave way as he pressed hard to plow himself upward. The line had only gained thirty yards when the artillery began dueling, its horrendous thunder roaring overhead. A few feet to his right, Vince Osborne drove his boots through the loose stones, gaining three feet before losing two. Enemy cannonballs and bullets passed harmlessly overhead, the uneven grade affording unexpected cover until the dismounted cavalry was within close range.

Socrates took a position behind some large rocks and commenced firing. The Rebels were straight ahead, but had shallow breastworks made of dirt, logs, officers' trunks, and camp kettles, which provided effective cover. A bullet clanged off an iron kettle, about the same time as one zinged off a rock, within inches of his face. Rabb must have realized his artillery was having no greater effect on the enemy than the Rebels' fire was on him, due to the slope and close range, because he suddenly switched to canister. The moment he did, the air filled with the sound of grapeshot and canister ripping into the Rebels' breastworks.

"Listen," Socrates shouted to Vince, "sounds like hail on a tin roof."

Vince, holding his hat down with one hand and rifle in the other, crouched behind a bolder and winced. "Wouldn't wanna be on the other side of that."

The contest continued for nearly two hours, with neither side gaining advantage. Reloading his carbine, Socrates spotted Captain Crawford leading two companies of men and horses around the left side of the hill, and up a narrow goat path. "Looks like Crawford's going to flank them," Socrates shouted. "Cover him." The Union men along the ridge turned and laid down a blanket of fire. Socrates emptied half his ammo pouch by the time Crawford's men made it to the top. There, Crawford's detachment mounted up and charged the Rebel's left flank, causing it to fall back around the center. Within minutes, the Missouri Sixth charged the enemy's right flank, driving it back in like manner.

Cabell's entire army mingled in chaos, like wild horses suddenly corralled, then they turned and ran. Socrates charged the pickets, cheering loudly, raising his rifle overhead in a sign of triumph. They were all together now, the Kansas and Missouri men, laughing, shooting and shouting at the fleeing Rebels. By evening, they made camp at Fort Smith.

Two days later, the cavalry rode to Darnedalle, where they routed more Confederates, captured two hundred cows, and set up camp. Hundreds of Unionists were coming to join with Colonel Cloud's forces, many still wearing Confederate uniforms. Socrates dismounted, tied his horse, and brushed the dirt from his uniform. A cloud of dust appeared around him. His throat was dry, parched by the sun and caked with dust, but he was anxious for the townspeople. All seemed peaceful, and none of the buildings had been burned. In the distance a sizable storm approached, its huge black thunderclouds riding above a thin, gray veil that looked to be several miles across. On the plains, he could see them coming at a distance, never sure where they would end up. Sometimes they came straight at you, other times, they changed directions and went another way altogether. The Rebel storm had obviously blown by like that, leaving everyone safe.

After bathing in the river and changing uniforms, he mounted up and headed into town. Socrates had a letter to mail. Halfway across town he pulled his horse back sharply. A woman approached on horseback. She wore a dark blue dress, and though she was pale, sapphire eyes framed by dark circles, his heart raced at the sight. It was Ellen.

He rode up to her in his clean blue uniform and flashed his biggest smile, but her face wrinkled in fury as she scowled, "Sir, get out of my way."

Socrates felt his eyes go wide. "Ellen, don't you know me?"

She stopped and leaned back in her saddle, eyes peering sharply, as if seeing but not seeing. Her pale face formed a question. "Socrates?" Her body went suddenly limp.

That she didn't recognize him caught him by surprise, but the dark circles amidst her pale complexion brought immense concern. "Help!" he shouted, as he grabbed her by the arms to keep her from falling. Vince Osborne and another nearby cavalrymen rode over and helped him to steady her, while he dismounted. They lowered her gently, and he took her into the closest boarding house. A plump little lady stood behind a small desk with her mouth agape. "I need a room," urged Socrates.

"That's Mrs. Best, isn't it?"

"You know her?"

"Yes. Her room is right this way." The lady rushed out from behind the desk, petticoats bristling up the stairs to a modest room with one large bed. Socrates was just putting Ellen down, when Vince appeared at the door. "Anything more I can do, Socrates?"

Socrates shook his head and looked down at Ellen. The plump woman's short pink hands shot up to her mouth, and her gray-green eyes grew large and round. "You're her husband? But—but Ellen said you're dead!"

Socrates squirmed. "Not quite. I couldn't send word to her. But how did she get here?"

"Rode over four hundred miles in a buggy. Said she was going home to Wisconsin. Poor gal buried her baby girl just thirty miles from here."

Socrates shook his head again, felt a burning conviction in his gut. "She wanted a girl so bad. God, what have I done?"

The woman reached out and took his hands, shaking her golden hair. "Don't blame yourself. Couldn't help leaving her from what she told me—them wanting to hang you and her brother. Confederates told her you were both dead, so even if you'd risked going back, you mightn't have found her. Poor gal dressed up in black and grieved like a proper widow."

The room was in a cloud. If Socrates *had* risked. But he hadn't. Hadn't bothered. He turned to the woman. "And you are?"

"Mrs. Fillmore. This is me and my husband's boarding house. He rides with a Missouri regiment."

Socrates forced a weak smile. "Thank you, Mrs. Fillmore."

The woman offered a warm pleasant one in return. "What should I do with your boys?"

"My boys! You mean they're here too?"

"Hate to say this, but they were driving me crazy. Kept running around the house so much I finally sent them to the barn. Said they could help the stable master. He got some of the livestock out before the Rebels came, and returned a few days ago. Go ahead and see them. I'll stay here with Ellen."

Socrates looked at Ellen, still unconscious, and knew he should see his boys. He kissed her gently on the cheek and headed for the barn. Out on the street a cold metallic taste filled the air, the kind common before a rain. He untied his horse and led it to the stable, where he gave it fresh hay and water. In the next stall he found Gus feeding a baby lamb with a bottle, while little Willie sat on some straw watching Gus run his fingers through its curly wool.

"Hey, Gus! Willie!" shouted Socrates. "Look who's here." The boys ran into his arms, and he knelt and hugged them with all his might. "Oh. I've missed you boys so. Can hardly believe we're all together again."

Gus stared at his father with a one-sided smile. "Rebels said you were dead, Pa, but I never believed 'em. They're a bunch of liars."

Socrates smiled. "Nearly did get me," he said. "Look at this." He took off his cap, showed the scar where the sentry's bullet made its long groove.

Willie eyes went wide. "Gosh! They did that?"

"Yep. Bled like a stuck pig too. Wonder if they really thought I was dead." He thought of the trackers who hadn't found him in that big oak tree, then of Malneck and all that killing.

"Don't matter, Pa," said Gus. "Ain't a Rebel alive can stop you."

Socrates laughed. He hugged the boys again, looking at the baby lamb Gus tended. "Where's this little one's mama?" he asked. "She should be feeding that lamb herself."

"Can't, Pa," said Gus. "Coyotes got her. This one would've died, but Mrs. Fillmore gave us a bottle to try on her. Took it right fast. Now she thinks I'm her mama."

"Well! Doesn't that beat all?" Socrates laughed. "My son—mama to a baby lamb." He paused and scratched his scalp. "Seriously, Gus, you've taken responsibility. I expect you to see it through."

Gus nodded.

"Yeah!" added Willie. "We'll take good care-a-her."

Socrates watched them for a while. Would they kill men someday as he had? Should he teach them, prepare them for the hell men make of this earth? The memory of Captain Lines flashed into his mind. The image of that bloody body on the ground, gut-shot and slowly dying was depressing, driving him back to the shelter of the boarding house, away from his children's boyish innocence.

Mrs. Fillmore sat beside Ellen, knitting.

"Rebs give you any trouble?" whispered Socrates.

Mrs. Fillmore shook her head. "When they first came, I thought we were in for trouble, but when they heard there were sick here, didn't even look around. Thank God they were regular soldiers, not those wild bushwhackers who kill every Union sympathizer they see. After a few days, the army just up and left. Took every wagon, horse, and supply they could steal. When Colonel Cloud rode in with the Union cavalry, you'd have thought it was the return of the Lord the way everyone was cheering. Listen, as long as you're here, I've got to get some wash done."

Socrates nodded, watched her gently close the door on her way out.

He waited at Ellen's bedside through the night and the next day, taking only a few minutes here and there for himself. Even Gus and Willie couldn't lure him away. Nodding off from time to time was his only means of rest. In late afternoon, he went to the post office and mailed Captain Lines' letter, then found a bath and a quick change of uniforms before reporting to duty. Standing guard made for a long difficult night, and when it ended he jogged straight back to the boarding house. Inside he was greeted by Mrs. Fillmore's pleasant smile.

Socrates felt a grin work across his face. "Ellen is awake?"

Mrs. Fillmore nodded. "Fever broke right after you left. She's weak, but took some broth and honey last night. This morning she had a respectable breakfast—eggs and corn muffins. Heart's still broke over her little girl, but I'm sure that seeing you'll help her get over it. Said when she first saw you, thought you were a ghost." The woman smiled again. "Enough of my chatter, go see your wife."

Socrates grinned. He hurried up the wide wooden staircase, and opened the door to his wife's room. She was sitting up reading, her blue eyes sunken, face drawn, but to him she was beautiful. He stopped at the door, not knowing what to say, but her face lit up and eyes sparkled so when she saw him, that he rushed to her side and embraced her. "Ellen, I'm so sorry I left you in Texas."

The lines around her eyes tightened. "I thought you were dead!"

He gently pushed her away. "I wanted to write, but was afraid what some fool might do to you and the children if they knew where I was. I wrote your sister Eliza, but she said she didn't think any of her mail could get through to you either. I joined the cavalry thinking the sooner the war was over, the sooner we could be together again."

Ellen's lines softened, then hardened again. "But I thought you were dead!"

Muscles tightened at the base of Socrates skull. "I know. I know. But what else could I have done?"

Ellen turned her gaze inward. "Nothing, I suppose. It's just that—I can't believe you'd leave us down there all alone—us thinking you were dead."

Socrates' frustration grew. He couldn't bear the guilt, needed to change subjects. "How—how did you get here?"

"I sold the ranch, but the banker wouldn't give me its worth."

"How much did you get?" he asked too quickly, an itching feeling creeping up the back of his neck.

"Only a few hundred dollars in gold."

Socrates felt his eyebrows raise. "Sheesh! All is lost save honor."

Ellen shook her head, squeezed Socrates' hand. "There was nothing else I could do. They talk big about how they're going to win the war, but they're holding on to their gold and silver in case their scrip isn't worth anything later."

Socrates nodded. "Northerners are doing the same, Ellen. I guess it's natural to doubt." He paused, reflecting on their situation, what they had left. "Forget the money and everything else. We'll start over."

Ellen's eyes filled with tears and she began to quiver. "Socrates, our baby girl died."

Socrates took her into his arms, as a torrent of sobbing released. When she finished crying, Socrates pushed her back a few inches, placed his thumb and finger on her chin, pulled it upward, and looked directly into her red, swollen blue eyes. "It's Divine Providence, Ellen. That's what brought us together again, and that's what took our baby. If you'd been with me in the Confederate hospital, you'd have seen men and boys dying everywhere, not from battle, but from illness. It's a miracle to me that you and the boys are even alive."

"But—but—"

Socrates shook his head. "Ellen, you mean the world to me. If I lost you, I don't know what I'd do or what I might become. I'm sorry we lost our baby, but grateful we're together."

Ellen wiped her tears. "Does that mean you'll go to church? Take the boys?"

Socrates rolled his eyes. "Why is that so important to you?"

"I think God has been punishing us, testing us." She started crying again.

He laid his hands upon her, gently stroking. The words of his namesake came to mind:

"God, if he be good, is not the author of all things, as the many assert, but he is the cause of a few things only, and not of most things that occur to man. For few are the goods of human life, and many are the evils, and the good is to be attributed to God alone; of the evils the causes are to be sought elsewhere, and not in him."

"I don't believe that," he said shaking his head and staring into her face. "If there is a God, he must be good—not the angry hater of all mankind some say he is."

"But look at everything that's happened to us."

Socrates shook his head. "It's not just us, Ellen. The whole country."

Her tears stopped as she eyed him warily. "Will you or won't you?"

Socrates felt himself nod, saw her relax and curl up in his arms as though content just to be close to his heart. "I know I've never told you," he said, "but wherever I've been, teaching school, working in the field, riding with the cavalry, I've always thought of you. Even when I didn't want to. Even when I pushed your name from my mind a hundred times a day. My namesake said that emotions are our enemies. But I can't live that way anymore, using all my strength to hide the very core of my being. There's no way to tell you what it means to me having you and the boys here."

Ellen rested her head on his shoulder, causing him to feel suddenly self-conscious, aware of his smells from guard duty, the campfire smoke, body musk, horse and dust odors. "I must smell something terrible," he said.

"Maybe so. You're here, and we're together. Like you said, that's all that matters. I wish you never had to ride out, that you could be here with me all of the time, like it used to be."

Socrates brightened, "That reminds me. When I reported for guard duty, I asked Colonel Cloud if I could tend the sick and wounded. He was so glad to hear of your deliverance, he gave me special orders. Grinning wide, he reached into his pocket and pulled out a folded piece of paper. "Let me see now, where was it on here? Oh, yes. 'By Special Order No.196, Socrates Best assigned Ward Master, shall continue in that capacity until further notice.'"

Ellen's face beamed. "We'll be together?"

Socrates watched tears of joy fill her eyes. "Yes," he said, and she began to laugh.

The Arkansas-Texas-Indian Territory Border Area

Fayetteville

Texas Road

Fort Gibson

Fort Smith

Arkansas River

Devil's Backbone

Little Rock

Perryville

Overland Road

Indian Territory

Arkansas

Texas

N

Daingerfield

Louisiana

FIFTEEN

Wealth does not bring goodness, but goodness
brings wealth and every other blessing,
both to the individual and to the state.
—Socrates

Portage, Wisconsin, September, 1863

SWIFT STOOD WITH HIS REGIMENT AT THE BACK OF TWO COLUMNS, BEFORE A long deep valley with lofty green hills that shot sharply upward, forming distinct natural boundaries that shaped a mile-long grassy oval. Each man held a huge bouquet of purple wildflowers at his belt, and at the far end of the valley sat the cream-colored main street of Portage. Over the eastern hills stretched a wine-colored sky with long cirrus stripes streaked in red, blue, and purple, but the western sky was pitch-black, save for a thin crescent moon and the flash-points of a million stars. "Foreword—March!" came the command, and the regiment moved ahead.

They tramped nearly a hundred yards before kettle drums sounded from above, echoing back and forth across the valley. A line of blue Union troops appeared above the eastern valley walls. Cannon tubes, rifle barrels, and sabers shone blood-red under the rising crimson sun. Dark black cannons appeared at the same time along the western ledge, followed by a line of men dressed in gray. Their sabers and rifle barrels sparkled silver in the moonlight. A trumpet sounded "charge" and the valley walls exploded with the thunder of rifle and cannon fire.

Men buckled and fell, rolling down the sharp grassy incline and onto the valley floor. Some lay crying, some cursing. Others looked around at their fallen brethren, trying to help them, as huge crystal tears filled their eyes. There were hundreds now, scattered all over the valley, and Swift stepped out of formation to an old Confederate with a long gray beard. The man was bleeding from a chest wound and his eyes were red and swollen from crying. Swift set the flowers down, pulled a glass vile from his pocket, uncorked it, and collected the man's tears before returning the bottle to his pocket. Taking up the flowers, he handed one to the old Confederate, who stopped crying and smiled. A few yards away sat a Union officer, blood squirting from his arm like a fountain. Swift collected the officer's tears and handed him a flower. Instantly the flow of blood and tears ceased. When those who cursed their enemies saw what Swift's regiment did, they shouted the most vile condemnations.

Midway through the valley, he spotted the people of Portage standing on the sidewalks, cheering, and waving handkerchiefs. President Lincoln stood in the middle of the street with Vice President Hamlin, and they too waved handkerchiefs. When Swift straightened and waved back, the cursing men shouted to their friends on the valley walls, who turned their rifles and cannons downward. Even some of the men on the city streets aimed rifles and shot into the valley. Friends and flowers flew through the air and fell to the ground as cannon fire and bullets pounded the volunteers. But Swift and his comrades continued collecting tears and dispensing flowers. And all the time the people of Portage cheered.

More men fell around him, while more and more bodies rolled down the hill. He could no longer see Portage, and doubted if the president and the people had any idea what was happening here. Someone had to tell Lincoln about the traitors in the camp. Handing out his last flower, Swift started toward Portage, but the way was now blocked by a huge wall of bloody bodies. Powder smoke filled the valley like an early morning fog. He pulled out a pencil and notepad from his pocket and wrote down everything he saw. A raven landed on his arm. He quickly tied the note around the bird's leg before pushing it into the air and watching it fly over the wall of corpses. *Now* he could fight.

Smoke stung his eyes as he groped about the bodies that filled the valley. There had to be a rifle here. Should be hundreds of them. But he couldn't find one. They'd be coming for him soon—those who cursed so vilely—those haters of Christ and everything good. And God only knew what they would do to him when they found him. His hands groped frantically, touching the stone-cold bodies of the dead, and he cried, "Unclean! Unclean!"

Strong hands clasped his arms, pulling him upward. They'd found him. He wrestled to get free, still blinded by the smoke.

A deep baritone voice called, "Swift, Swift, wake up."

Swift's father was over him, hands clamped hard on his biceps. "Ouch. What are you doing to me, Pa?"

Doc's eyes widened. "What am I doing? *You* were yelling in your sleep! Woke everyone up, even the boys."

Swift ran moist fingers through his wet hair. "What time is it?"

Moonlight glowed through the window, making the gray streaks in Doc's beard look like inlaid silver. "Too early to get up and too late for going to bed."

"Sorry. It was just a dream. You can go back to sleep."

Doc shook his head. "Not 'til we've talked."

Swift looked away, fumbling with his sheets. They were sopping wet, as was his night shirt. "You said it's the middle of the night. Was only a dream."

"How many of these you had?"

Swift shrugged. "I don't know. Not many."

Doc's eyes looked dark, hard as iron. "More like every night."

"How'd you know *that*?"

"Swift, we *hear* you. You're either crying or shouting. One night I came in and you were just hitting your head on the wall. Wouldn't stop until I took you away and put you back into bed. Didn't even remember it the next day. The whole family's walking on eggshells."

Swift felt blood rush into his face. He gripped his hair and pulled, as though such a pain could equal what he felt inside.

"Swift, *talk* to me."

"What you want me to say?"

Doc threw his hands out. "What's bothering you? What's so bad you can't talk about it with me or your mother?"

Swift's stared into his father's eyes. "Death."

"That all? *Just* death?"

"No, Pa. Not just death. Men mangled, decapitated, covered with worms. Eyes open—staring at me—accusing me. Why'd they die and I live? I wasn't a better man than any of them. Not a better soldier either. But they died and I lived. Why?"

Doc placed his large hands on Swift's. "We can't question Providence. But we must go on. Always."

Swift pulled his hands away and pointed out the window. "Why? So we can make more money? So we can have a better life? What's the value of a better life when my friends are buried at Bull Run?"

"Vestigia nulla retrorsum. No one can retrace their steps, Swift, but we press on. Have to. We're responsible for everything God's given us. Why has he given us more and them less? I don't know. Only know he loves us, comforts us, and salves our pain." Doc placed his hands on Swift's again. "You've got a wonderful life ahead. And now that you've passed the bar, there's so much *good* you can do. Think about it. Philosopher kings and princes, educated in the spirit and power of philosophy, washed by the cleansing power of God's Word, and endowed with the gifts of wisdom and knowledge."

Swift pulled his hands away and crossed his arms. "That's *not* what I see, Pa. I see selfishness and greed—senior partners who won't take on a veteran-widow's claim because she has no money. What happened to the one thousand dollars promised to every family who sent a man off to war?"

"County can't cover a thousand thousands, Swift. Federal Government has to." Doc looked out the window and folded his hands. "Just too big a drain for small towns and counties."

Swift felt his stomach twist. "But what about the widows who lost all their men folk and are now losing their farms? *That's* not right. Some lose their cases on mere legal technicalities. Law has become a stumbling block for justice."

Doc turned and stared at Swift. "Our government isn't perfect. But it does have the foundations of greatness. You're practicing law is everything my brother and I ever hoped for our children, and you stand on the edge of it. Political wisdom and greatness have met in one. Christ has shown us the way, but Lincoln has brought it home." Doc held his hand out, palm up, and clinched it into a fist. "Don't quit when you're right on the edge of grasping the prize."

Swift's stomach twisted tighter. "I can't suffer it, Pa. Can't sit and watch the unrighteous triumph in the courts."

"That's because your life has been almost entirely dedicated to studies. You're unbalanced. Perhaps if you spent more time at social functions you'd meet others who share your beliefs. People of your generation who *will* change the world. Might even meet the right woman."

Swift unfolded his arms. "What woman would be interested in a near cripple?"

"*That* how *you* see yourself? Others don't. Some think you're a hero."

Swift looked out the window where the first light of dawn pushed back the curtain of darkness, and laughed.

Doc took out his reading glasses and rubbed them on his sleeve. "I mean it. Mr. Hyde's daughter is always asking about you. And she's blossomed into a fine young lady. Never misses Sunday church, and grows prettier by the day."

"Betsy Hyde?"

"They call her Bitsy."

"What kind of name is that?"

Doc smiled. "What kind of name is Swift?"

"I get it. But she was kind of a pain when we were kids, following me around in school and stuff."

"Nothing wrong in spending time with a girl who *likes* you. Chasing after someone who doesn't, well, you might catch her and ruin your whole life."

Swift laughed. "Never *thought* of it *that* way."

"When I met my first wife, I couldn't think of anything else. Weren't even married a year when she died." Doc reached out and took Swift's hands. "It shook me so, I thought my life was over. Never realized her cousin nursed a crush on me 'til after that."

"Ma?"

Doc nodded, silvery streaks glistening. "Don't think anybody could've loved me and my children more than her. Her faith's been rock-solid. Lost three children without ever wavering in her love for God. Not to say we didn't shed any tears, plenty of those, but *even that* strengthened our bond."

"So you think I should call on Bitsy?"

"Why not? You need someone to love. Someone who'll love you back with the same measure of commitment."

"Will that stop the dreams?"

Doc took Swift's hands and squeezed them. "You have such a giving heart, such strong ideals. The good in you will eventually drive out the guilt and pain. Until then you must live your life well, with a spirit of gratitude. Only then can you let the dead bury the dead."

Swift nodded. "You know what I could use right now?"

Doc shrugged.

Swift stood and rubbed his tummy. "Something to eat."

Doc gave a hearty belly-laugh. "So could I!"

After breakfast, Swift went to work. He was flipping through a law book, when Mr. Alan Horde's smiling face appeared in the doorway. Senior partner of the law firm, he was a large man who had a deep bass voice with a musical ring to it. His balding red head glistened eternally, as if sun burnt. "Eusebius, you must come to dinner at seven tonight."

"Sir, I prefer Swift."

"Don't be ridiculous, Eusebius is a name of honor. My wife is preparing a pork roast, the likes of which can't be found any place else."

"Thank you, sir. I'll be there. About that widow's case I talked to you about—"

"Sorry, Swift, don't have time to talk about that. Seven tonight. Don't forget. Oh, and by the way, wear something appropriate, my daughter Marianne is keenly interested in meeting you."

Mr. Horde disappeared as fast as he'd appeared, and Swift went back to researching his law book. Before long he was completely immersed in the case studies. The law itself held some allure, but it was the stories of the people that captivated his imagination. These weren't simply arguments of law, but stories of folks' lives and the issues that deeply affected them. When he looked up at the clock, he was surprised to see it was nearly six o'clock. Slamming down the book, he walked through the empty corridor, and locked the door. After changing into a fresh black suit at home, he apologized to his mother, waved his cane on the way out, and headed down the street. By the time he entered the tall iron gates and rapped at the carved oak door, he was fifteen minutes late.

Mr. Horde opened the door wide and smiled big, his bulky frame taking up most of the doorway. "Swift, I was starting to worry about you. You know you're never supposed to keep a lady waiting."

"Sorry, sir. Time got away from me."

"Always does when you're young, son. Always does. But don't worry, you'll mature in good time. Come in and meet my family."

Swift felt an itch work its way up his spine as he followed Horde into the parlor. The house was rich with waist-high, hand-carved, oak woodwork that filled the next room.

Elegant lamps with polished brass that shone bright as gold sparkled around the room. White lamp-bowls with intricate rose maling lit the room up with a pleasant brightness. One entire wall was filled with books that climbed the oak shelves to the second floor ceiling.

Horde put his hand forward. "Adrian, my dear, here is the young man we've been waiting for. May I present to you the son of Dr. Thomas Best, Eusebius."

A middle-aged woman with long, flowing black hair and elegant cheek bones stepped forward and nodded. A mother of pearl cameo and a cream-colored ruffled blouse topped a long brown skirt. "So you're Swift. So glad to make your acquaintance, dear."

Swift nodded. "Thank you, ma'am."

"And this," said Horde, pulling his wife aside, "is our daughter, Marianne."

A young woman with long crimson hair tied with a red ribbon, stepped up and curtsied. Her blouse was white and her skirt red, otherwise she was nearly the mirror image of her mother in dress and appearance. Blue eyes sparkled as she said, "Pleased to meet you, Eusebius."

"My friends call me Swift."

"Why? I much prefer Eusebius. It's so unique, so honorable."

Swift shrugged. "Nobody calls me Eusebius."

Marianne looked at her father and mother, and the three smiled wide. "We'll fix *that*," said Marianne, and her parents nodded.

"Let's not waste time talking," said Mr. Horde. "Food's getting cold."

Mr. Horde sat across from his wife and beside Swift, who couldn't help admiring the beauty of Marianne. A white servant moved about the table, seeing that everyone's wine glass remained full. Marianne's complexion was milk white, with colorful red cheeks that brought out the brilliance of her hair. Sparkling blue eyes danced with a life all their own as she talked, and Swift found it difficult not to stare.

Finished eating, Adrian dabbed around her mouth with a bright white napkin that had a silver H embroidered on it. Placing the napkin beside her plate, she sipped at her wine goblet. "My husband tells me you graduated top of your class, Eusebius."

Swift nodded before swallowing the last bit of pork. "This roast is excellent. I've never tasted a sauce like this."

Adrian dipped her head. "Thank you. It's a port sauce. You know, a young man like you could go *far* in this county. Maybe even at the state level. What are your career plans?"

"My father expects me to follow a career in politics, but I'm not sure that's what I want."

"Of course," said Adrian. "Young men seldom know what they want. That's why God gives them wives. Isn't that right, Alan?"

Mr. Horde grinned. "Yes, my dear," he said in that musical bass voice. "Makes for a wonderful team. One fighting in the field, so to speak, and the other commanding from the heights. Wonderful to work as a team."

As Horde spoke, Swift felt something brush against his leg and moved it back reflexively, but the brushing followed, moving up his leg and to his thigh. Fire swept through him, and he quickly downed his wine.

"Charles," said Mr. Horde, "we have a thirsty man here." The servant refilled Swift's glass.

He felt his face flush. "Sir, I have a lot of work to do tomorrow, perhaps I should be going."

"Nonsense," said Adrian. "The night is young and we're just getting to know you. I absolutely forbid you to leave, or I'll hold my husband accountable."

Horde threw his hands up. "Can't leave now, Swift. Wouldn't want me to be in trouble, would you?"

Swift shook his head, felt the brushing at his thigh fan the flames in his chest. His mouth was dry, throat tight.

"Let's go into the parlor where we'll be more comfortable," said Adrian.

Swift arose and followed them, his napkin hanging before him. He barely managed to sit before Mr. Horde said, "My goodness, what are you doing with that, Eusebius? Charles, take that napkin out of here immediately."

Swift pulled up his left knee and crossed it over his right, holding it with both hands. Adrian talked about how she and Mr. Horde had first met, what a brilliant student he was, how they'd planned his law career together. But Swift heard little of it. Blue eyes sparkled beneath long red hair like a lighthouse in the night, and he couldn't take his eyes off Marianne.

September 18th, 1863, Chickamauga Creek

The day's march had been a long dusty one. Ed Best and the boys of his Wisconsin Infantry Regiment were exhausted. For weeks they had marched across Tennessee, engaging in small skirmishes with the enemy, who made certain they could not travel through Rebel territory unimpeded. Felled trees, burnt bridges, and harassing fire slowed everyone down, but tramping behind the Army of the Cumberland, the Tenth had eaten dust for over a hundred miles.

Darkness was falling. Good. The regiment would soon camp, and he could finally rest. As he marched over the top of a long, high hill, tents and campfires glowed in the early evening darkness as far as his eyes could see. The sight was serene and beautiful. He forgot his parched throat and fatigued body as he marched past the Union fires. The regimental band began to play, and he found himself on parade, watched by every eye in camp. His tired back stiffened, stomach sucked inward.

"We're the mighty," he said. "Members of Scribner's First Brigade, First Division of the Fourteenth Corps. Our commander is General Thomas, the greatest general in the Army of the Cumberland. How can you Rebels stand against us? We're sixty thousand strong and growing every day. Sixty thousand! Look at those fires, Johnny, and surrender."

The next morning, the sun rose red over the valley walls in a fiery ball that seemed to take up the whole sky. His company was camped on a plateau overlooking the Chickamauga Valley, where only a series of fields, thick woods, and the river divided them from the Rebels. Above and on the other side of that valley, sheer cliffs and rugged inclines thrust upward along one side of the valley and into Lookout Mountain, like gates to an unseen world above the billowing vapors. And even though the mountain's high ground was invisible, buried in a cushion-soft ceiling of low lying cumulus, its high walls conjured up visions of Zeus on Mt. Olympus, huge Titans warring in the heavens, and the now forbidden Garden of Eden. The sun's bright red sphere appeared above the landscape for only a few minutes, before hiding itself in the higher stratus clouds. From there it sent out golden rays that shot straight through the heavenly mist, like an archer's arrows cut through straw. Farther below him, where the ground met the river, a thick fog obliterated everything, as if declaring those lower places subject to the enchanted one above. Wandering over to a small cooking fire where his friend Sophie sat on a fallen log, Ed inhaled the sweet inviting aroma of freshly boiled coffee.

"Hey! Hope you're saving some of that for me, Sophie. After all that marching yesterday, I think it'll take a gallon or more to wake these tired little doggies." Ed pointed to his feet and walked stiffly on his heels.

"Shoot!" replied Sophie with a wry smile, "Better get over here and drink some of this quick, before you fall over, roll down the hill, land in that creek, and drown. Then I'll get stuck putting a detail together to drag your sorry butt up here, chop down some perfectly good trees just to make a pine box, and waste an entire day digging a hole to bury you. Come to think of it, captain'd probably make me write a letter to your folks, telling 'em how the whole thing happened just because I didn't get you your coffee!" The men around the fire laughed.

Ed's eyes went wide. "Take it easy, Sophie. Comin' as fast as I can." He shortened his steps and swung his arms backward, as though walking on stilts and losing his balance. "Oh! Sarge, I'm falling, falliiing. Oh! Heeelp! I'm faaalling." Sophie stepped over and handed him a cup of black coffee. Ed smiled. "Thanks, Sarge. You saved my life."

The two walked over to the fire, where Ed picked up a sharpened stick left over from his cooking the night before. A tin plate nearby was stacked with salt pork. He stabbed a piece and hoisted it over the fire. "Heard from Ma yesterday."

"Any news?" asked Sophie.

"Nels took off from the hospital."

"Again?"

Ed nodded. His pork spit grease, cackling and popping as he turned it over the fire.

"Did they find him?"

"Nope," Ed sighed. "Walked from Louisville clear to Toledo looking for Sol and Elizabeth. Letter said he stopped at her folks' home at Bowling Green, found out they were in Canada, and kept walking all the way to Detroit, where he crossed over to Ontario. He's living with Sol at Kent Bridge now."

"He okay?"

"Better than the Army doctors expected. Sol told Ma he's fine as long as he doesn't get any sun on his head. Guess that makes him crazy." Ed remembered the bullet hitting Nels' head, wondered how the Army could have put a steel plate over that. He shook his head, wondering what it looked like. Was the steel on the outside where you could see it, or did his hair cover it normal like? Whatever it might look like, he was glad his brother was alive. "Wish Captain Twogood was still with us," he said.

Sophie took a drink of coffee, cleared his throat and spit in the fire. "I know. But he can't. Same as Colonel McMynn and Colonel Chapin. Stones River nearly killed 'em."

Ed pulled the pork away from the fire, eyed it closely, turning it to see that it was well cooked. Finding a large pink area, he stuck it back over the fire. "Nearly killed us too. You think Captain Collins'll do all right?"

Sophie nodded, took another drink of coffee, and stared into the fire. "He'll do. Was a sergeant, then a lieutenant. Anyway, his men say he's done his share. Don't doubt a man before you've fought beside him."

Ed's stomach rumbled as the scintillating pork grease vaporized, wafting into his nostrils. Saliva flooded his tongue. He surveyed the hillside, spotted the tents where the regimental officers were gathered. "What about Colonel Ely?" You reckon he's ready to lead an entire regiment?"

Sophie looked at Ed and scowled. "He did all right with Company E. No reason he won't do the same by the regiment."

"I know, but he's not much older than us."

Sophie nodded. "Twenty-eight, but age doesn't mean much. Some say he loses his temper too easy, typical of any redhead I've ever known. When the fighting starts, I'd rather skirmish with someone who's mad, hopping mad. You know—with fire in his bones—someone who'll stand his ground."

Ed's face tightened. "Like we did at Chaplain Hills?"

"Exactly."

Ed looked to the tent where the officers were.

Sophie followed his gaze. "Better eat up," he said. "No telling when we'll eat again if the fighting starts today."

Ed shivered. "Like Stones River?"

"Yeah. Like Stones River."

After eating, the regiment formed and took its place in the brigade. Roll was called, and preliminary matters dealt with. Then the division marched ten miles to the left of a huge battle line Old Rosie's army was forming. Tens of thousands moved precisely as ordered, each brigade falling into place exactly as directed. By ten o'clock, the Tenth had moved off the road, and onto a wide field, where it formed two long battle lines. "Forward, march!" hollered Colonel Ely.

Ed wished he could unload his blankets and guitar as they marched a half mile through alternating stretches of thick woods and open fields. He'd just come through a thicket that smelled of fresh bacon, when he saw the enemy's camp ahead. They were perched on a field of grass overlooking the woods surrounding Chickamauga Creek, and hadn't posted sentries. Ed spotted them cooking and eating, at the same time as he heard the order to open fire. At the Union's first volley, gray uniformed figures fell about the camp. Those still standing grabbed for muskets and pistols.

The blue tide swept over them. Ed pulled out his pistol, firing at close quarters. Others fought hand to hand with knives or bare hands, their bodies mired in a tangle. Ed picked a target and fired. Then again. He shot a third man. The Rebels broke and ran. A fourth he shot in the leg. A good number managed to scramble away, but the few remaining grays stopped fighting, threw down their weapons, and surrendered.

Ed dropped his pack, blanket, and guitar, and was checking for weapons and getting prisoners into formation when Captain Collins called, "Sergeant Landt, report!" Sophie moved toward the officer, rifle in hand, where he was given the Rebel prisoners to march back to division headquarters. The prisoners filed through the trees, as several officers on horseback rode up and stopped in front of Colonel Ely. "Second and Fourth brigades are missing," one said. "The right flank is bare, and the Rebel lines are advancing. Scribner is moving up the artillery to cover you. Have your men lie flat until the shelling is finished."

Behind the officers was a long grassy field, where Union artillery crews rolled their cannons forward. Before his officers could issue a command, Ed dropped his pack and guitar on the ground, then threw himself down. He was about to get much closer to those fire-spitters than he'd ever wanted. The cannons rolled into place within inches of his feet. There the crews loaded and fired with mechanical precision. Thunderous explosions ruptured the air above and quaked the earth below, as the long black barrels discharged in concise sequence. And every time the piece above him fired, it seemed as if some invisible hands lifted him from the earth, and slammed him to the ground again.

He hugged the earth, dug his nails into the dirt, and clawed the sod beside him. Even so, his legs sucked upward with every blast, bending his back like a mighty bow. Then the grass started to rip, and his torso lifted again. The displaced air sucked him up off the ground, then let him go, slamming him to the ground again and again. His hands searched for more grass. Hugging the ground for all he was worth, he saw the Rebels scrambling up the hill below. "Damn!" he shouted. "Everything's flying over their heads! Cannons are no good!" But his words were devoured by the sound of the cannon fire.

The artillery officers must have realized that too. They suddenly quit firing and rolled back. Ed stood with the other men of his regiment, ears ringing, back aching, head pounding. Commands would do no good. He could hear nothing. Charging up the hill came a Rebel with stripes on his sleeve. Ed took careful aim and fired, but before he could see the result, bullets flew from every direction. Union men fell all around him.

Confused, he looked to see the source of the fire. Rebels flanked him on the ridge and filed toward his rear. The artillerymen must have seen them coming, for they had their pieces turned, and were fast pouring buckets of grapeshot into those barrels. Bill Day, thirty yards ahead of the rebels, ran in panic, charging into the mouth of a cannon. The ringing stopped in Ed's ears. Sound returned, as if in a hollow shell. He held his breath, expecting to see his friends blown to bits, but the cannons held their fire long enough for Bill to get by before they let loose. When they did, grape shot exploded from each cannon, tearing the Rebels to shreds, blowing human remains backwards for thirty yards. The first wave of Rebels floundered, but others fast overran the battery, whose survivors fled for their lives. Officers shouted, but their voices sounded far away, "Fall back! Fall back!"

As the Rebels turned the cannons, Ed took off running, all the time remembering what the grapeshot did to the Rebels barely minutes before. A man fell to the ground ahead of him, holding his knee. Without thinking, Ed reached down and pulled the fellow up with his free arm. "You can make it," he said. "Lean on me." He had barely spoken those words, when the boy was thrust forward, out of his grip, three red holes in his back. The sight drove Ed's legs wild, pounding them across the field and into the woods. He sprinted for nearly a half mile before coming to a place, where his officers and sergeants stood.

"Form skirmishes!" Colonel Ely shouted. He had lost his hat, and was waving his sword wildly above his fiery red hair.

Ed had scarcely entered ranks, turned, and loaded, when the Rebels burst through the woods some fifty yards away.

"Wait!" shouted Ely. "Ready—aim—fire!"

The command set off a volley that the screaming Rebels had not expected. They ran full force into the bullets, the first line of men dropping every which way. "Take that!" said Ed. He reloaded fast as he could, and took careful aim. The rifle jumped as the trigger again reached its firing point. A gray uniformed figure in his sight dropped face down. The Union skirmishers fired at will. It wasn't a textbook skirmish, but the force was enough to send the Rebels fleeing back into the woods.

Guessing they wouldn't return soon, Ed turned to the wounded. He spotted a boy with an Ohio patch on his shoulder, sitting in the open field with a blank stare on his face. Poor fellow couldn't be more than seventeen. Probably hadn't been with the division but a few weeks. Ed surveyed the damage. A bullet had pierced the forearm, which was so badly fractured that pieces of bone stuck out every which way. Ed took off his rucksack and pulled out a shirt, which he tore and bound around the wound, then formed a rough sling.

Once the arm was secure, Ed took him by the good hand and led him back to the road, where the wounded were being loaded into ambulances. All that time, Ed kept talking, asking questions about where he was from, if he had family, but the kid never said a word. He just stared off into the distance. By the time they'd reached the ambulance, the boy's face was pale, almost blue. Ed sat him on the ground, watched each breath come harder and faster until it completely stopped. A medical corpsman came and covered the corpse with a blanket.

Ed shook his head. "He wasn't hurt bad—didn't look mortal."

The corpsman nodded. "I know. Seen it before."

"How?"

"Don't know. Just does."

Ed squinted. "He didn't bleed that much."

The corpsman looked away. "Maybe the wound that killed him wasn't the one in his arm."

Ed thought hard. What this must have been like for such a young one. He couldn't imagine it, couldn't remember what his first battle felt like. Maybe his heart was nothing more than a hard callous, one having no room for gentle memories, no place for sadness and grief, emotions that could lead to cowardice. Shaken, he picked up his rifle and marched back to his regiment, which now consisted of only a few hundred men. After forming skirmishes, they moved back through the woods and fields given up only two hours before. When they arrived at where they'd been routed, they found the enemy had left the camp and taken the captured artillery battery with them. His pack and guitar were still there.

"Corporal Best," said Sergeant Dowd, "get some men together and dig a long trench here. Corporal Webster, get some men and drag all the dead wood you can find in those woods over to the trenches. Form one long trench diagonal to the corner of this field. It must be continuous from company to company, regiment to regiment, for the entire brigade. We'll meet with the Fourth at front center. Colonel Ely doesn't want us caught without proper cover again."

The camp was located on the edge of a corn field, surrounded in the front and on the right by two separate woods. The one in front led sharply downhill toward the creek. Directly behind them lay a stretch of field that led into the woods they'd advanced through twice before. Throughout the remainder of the evening and well into the night, Ed worked relentlessly, digging dirt from his part of the ditch, and piling it in front. Satisfied with the mound he'd formed, he piled fallen tree limbs and dead wood in a manner that would give him various slits to shoot through, while stopping most bullets. He had no idea what had happened to the Union brigade beside him, but he understood what their absence meant. The enemy could flank them unless the Fourth built good breastworks there. Two hours of hard work and the ditches joined diagonally, forming a wide V. The only means of retreat would be straight back across the field. When he could no longer push his burnt-out body, he lay down and fell into a deep sleep.

The next day, he finished breakfast shortly after sunrise, the men eating in shifts, not to be caught unaware by a sudden attack. Ed sat by himself, tuning his guitar and thinking about Sophie. Had he been caught by the Rebels? Was he dead, or worse? Nels was left for dead. Sophie could be wounded somewhere in those woods. Why else wouldn't he have come back?

Bill Day sat with his back against a large log. "Stinking war's been going on so long, can't even remember what we're fighting about."

Ed nodded. "Pa said it's about philosopher kings. Says you can't have two kings with opposite philosophies in one country. Davis has one idea about

Union and slaves—Lincoln another. And each has his philosopher helpers. When we've killed enough of theirs, this thing'll be over"

He picked up his guitar and started playing. There was something powerful in strumming cords and rolling fingers over the hollow body as though it were a little drum. He backed off and let his fingers dance upon the strings, finger picking a melodic bridge. A new rhythm came to mind as he strummed softly, then harder, and harder still. Rhythm begat rhythm and cord begat cord, as the guitar gathered an energy all its own. The player had become the puppet of the instrument. Harder he strummed, then softly, then harder again. Lyrics flowed, word upon word and line upon line.

Wasn't worth a dollar,
and that isn't worth anything now.
Just buy you some memories,
that cannot be found.

You pawn your soul,
that you walk on.

Men quickly gathered around, one playing spoons, another sticks, and others harmonicas. The music was now the center of the universe, drawing everyone into it. As it built into a final crescendo, the words grew forceful, more and more desperate.

You pa-a-a-a-awn
your so-o-oul.

The men clapped and cheered as he finished.

"Yeeeeheee!" came a concert of high-pitched screams.

"Stupid Rebel shout," said Ed, "scares the crap out of me every time. Okay, Johnny, we're comin'." He set the guitar against a log, lifted his rifle, and hurried to the breastworks. There he took his place in the second line of the right trench skirmishers. The jagged wall of gray trudged up the hill below. Nearly bent over, they leaned forward to keep their balance on the incline.

The first line of Union skirmishers fired on command. Powder smoke blew back over Ed, burning his eyes. A second later the air cleared. Rebels fell all over the hill. More took their place and kept coming. He raised his rifle between the two reloading on each side of him. Aiming at a gray uniform, he squeezed the trigger in time with the second command. The smoke burnt his eyes again as it wafted past his face. He wiped away the forming tears with the back of his hand and reloaded.

"This is gonna be a dogfight," he cried, "a bad-assed dogfight! Come on Johnny. Let's dance."

Volley after volley rained down the hill. Wounded and dead Confederates fell in every direction, their bodies obstacles to those who followed. They no longer ran up the hill, but stopped halfway, as if hoping to get a better shot, but showers of lead rained down until the few who remained pulled back into the woods and out of sight. "We're licking you, Johnny!" he shouted, then shook a fist in defiance.

Rifle fire was hot on his left flank. The Fourth left their diggings and fell back into his own. "Damned Fourth!" he railed. "Don't you ever hold your ground?" Raising his rifle, he shot a Rebel less than thirty yards away, then reloaded. "Candy asses. Getting flanked—doing nothing to stand." Officers and sergeants of the Tenth clamored for Ed's line to support their besieged neighbors. The routed men stopped at the Wisconsin firing line, turned, and fired. The combined fire drove the Rebels back down the hill.

"Well, I'll be," said Ed. "That's what Mama calls Divine Providence. Thank you, Lord!" He pulled the trigger again, watched another Confederate fall on the brow of the hill. "Doggies," he shouted. "We'll bleed white before we give up."

The few remaining Rebels darted back over the Fourth's diggings, disappearing over the edge of the hill. From the field Ed helped a wounded Union man to a trench. The fellow's left calf muscle streamed red. It wasn't a deep wound, just bad enough that he couldn't walk. Must have gotten hit when he was running, thought Ed. Next time he won't have any choice but to stay put. "Thanks," said the man," as Ed put him down. "Thought we were done for sure."

Ed glanced in the direction the rebels had come. "We're holding our own." He ripped the man's pants leg around the wound, then ripped the cloth into long strips that he used to bandage the leg. "We've lost a lot of men. But what I don't understand is why General Thomas hasn't sent relief. Haven't seen any division officers since yesterday."

The man tugged Ed's sleeve. "Haven't you heard? Whole division was cut off yesterday. Thomas could have pulled back but wouldn't. We're holding, hoping Rosie rallies the troops."

Ed sat down, staring across the field of twisted bodies. "So that's it. Wonder why Ely didn't tell us. Shoot. Rosie better get his show on this road, or we're sunk. Can't fight forever without supplies."

A hand touched him on the shoulder, and he turned to see Sergeant Dowd standing behind him. Dowd's beady eyes drilled straight into Ed. "Ely thinks it best only the officers and cadre know what a tight spot we're in. I'll trust you to keep what you heard under your hat."

Ed smiled, threw his hands up. "Keep *what* under my hat?"

Dowd nodded. "Listen, it's time to rotate. Take your rifle and move into the first line."

Ed carried his rifle to the breastworks where he leaned forward, closed his eyes, and drifted away. He waited, half awake and half asleep, until the sound of shrieking Rebels jolted him awake. This time, the colonel allowed the enemy up the hill to within thirty yards before dispatching his hailstorm of death. Rifles popped. Gray uniforms turned red. And by the time the second line fired, the enemy ran. Men cheered all around him. "Owoooo!" howled Ed. "They run faster than greased lightning. We're still top dogs—kings of this here hill."

Just before noon Sergeant Dowd came by and ordered them to eat. Ed was ravenous. "Don't that beat all?" asked Bill Day. "We're plum out of coffee."

Ed shook his head. "Coffee? Who cares about coffee? I need some water." He took his canteen and rapped on it.

"Here," said Bill, stretching out his arm. "I have plenty." The warm liquid went down easy. The two were finishing eating when the lieutenant came by. "We need more breastworks to your rear. Best, get your men digging, throw dirt on the back side of your ditch, then get every piece of lumber you can find and pile it on. Day, get some others to help."

"More digging?" cried Ed. "Didn't we do enough last night?"

"Depends on how you look at it. You want more cover if the Fourth folds again, or don't you mind getting shot in the back?"

Ed put together a detail to bolster the defenses. Digging and piling, then stacking what little wood was left for cover. It was late, afternoon when he ordered the men to rest.

"Look at this place," said Bill Day, pointing across the lush valley. "You couldn't find a better place for a picnic."

Ed looked at the flourishing trees with autumn hues breaking through here and there. Sumac bushes stood in bunches, scattered along the hilltop, their leaves painted bright orange and fiery red. Those were always the first to change. A few maple trees sported an equal complement of colors, one split directly in half, its right side bright yellow and colorful with splashes of orange-red, its left side green and unchanged. Poplars added bright yellow to the picture, but most of the trees were green. Then he looked at the hillside before him, littered with bodies, both blue and gray, some so bloody he couldn't tell which uniform they'd worn. Others were mangled, faceless. The ground was covered with them, sometimes in stacks several men deep, their rifles protruding in confusion from the piles.

He turned from the ugliness of the battlefield. "What time you got? I'm guessin' around five."

Bill reached into his pants and pulled out a silver pocket watch. "Not quite, but close," he said. "Half past four." He closed the watch cover and put it back into his pocket.

The Rebel cry sounded. Ed snatched his rifle and jumped to the breastworks. The enemy charged straight up the hill again. Volley after Union volley sounded, cutting the Rebels below to ribbons. Ed felt strangely sorry for those boys. What kind of officer would send them up a hill like this to be slaughtered time and again? They must have families, brothers, sisters, wives, and children. The attackers below slowly pulled back to the cover of the trees, but the firing on the flank persisted. He turned to see the Fourth Brigade routed and running toward him. This time he simply stepped around to the cover he'd piled behind him, and resumed firing. When the routed Union men saw they were supported, they turned and fired on the advancing Rebels. Once again the combined fire sent the enemy scurrying down the left side of the hill.

Satisfied, Ed returned to his position on the front line.

"How much ammunition you have?" asked Dowd.

Ed searched his pouches. "Three balls and six caps. But I've got plenty of powder."

Dowd shook his head, pointing toward a corpse. "Search the dead and find what you can. From now on we make every shot count."

Ed rifled through several fallen comrades' ammo pouches and found more caps, but only four more rounds. He passed the caps off to the other men, then turned to watch the woods below. The sun was setting as the Rebel charge came. He fired, reloaded, and fired again. With each shot his enemy fell, but it wasn't long before he found himself fingering an empty pouch at his waist. The sound of firing along the Union line died, replaced by the cries of men calling for ammunition. Turning toward Dowd, Ed saw men jump out of their diggings, and run across the field toward the woods behind them. His stomach shrunk into a hard knot. No more rallies, no more turning back to fight. He took up his rifle and ran.

Captain Collins called for Company D to fall back, but they were way ahead of him. Bill Day ran across the field in a different direction. What was he doing? Ed sprinted into the woods ahead. Made it this far, he told himself, have to get to division headquarters before we're cut off. The regiment was in total disorder. Everyone ran. He came out of the woods and across the next field. Just over this rise they'd be at General Thomas's headquarters. Reserves would be waiting with more ammunition. Then he topped the rise. A wall of gray uniforms charged in his direction. Turning toward the opposite flank, he saw even more.

"Ain't no place in Heaven, ain't no place in Hell," he shouted.

"Form skirmishes!" bellowed Major McKircher, and Ed rushed to join his comrades.

"Who's got ammunition?" he cried, but his voice was echoed by the others. Everyone looked at each other, baffled and completely flustered. He turned to the regimental color bearer, Billy Wheeler, holding the colors in the midst of the officers. The poor fellow looked more confused than anyone, and the sight reminded Ed of how it felt at Chaplain Hills to carry the colors and not be able to fight. But no one could fight now, except with their bare hands, and the Rebels weren't about to come that close. They could turn this into a turkey shoot. His spirits dived. Couldn't fight and couldn't run. They were finished. His gaze wandered to Major McKircher and his captains as one of the lieutenants lifted a hastily made white flag. The Confederate lines closed in.

"Drop your arms!" shouted a Rebel officer.

"Do as he says," replied the major.

Rifles and pistols clattered to the ground, and Ed threw his down hard, hoping it would break. He started counting heads. Couldn't be more than a dozen officers left in the whole regiment. Maybe a hundred enlisted men stared at Colonel Ely, lying on the ground beneath the flag. He had been carried several hundred yards, but now lay dead, his red hair looking even darker beneath a veil of thick crimson blood. Captain Collins stood beside Lieutenant Patchin and George Hand, both wounded. Sergeant Dowd's normally immaculate uniform was torn and dirty. Sergeants Ole Gilbert and John Gaffney shifted their weight from foot to foot, looking puzzled and uncertain for the first time today.

Ed counted his friends from Company D, his fellow corporals John Doughty, Jack Webster, George Hand, John Burke; and privates George Rouse, Harley Wittum, Willard Ellis, and Peter Montier. All stood in silence. Had Bill Day gotten away? Montier was wounded and Webster tended him; otherwise no one moved. The survivors of the other companies clustered around close friends. Every face wrinkled in hopeless resignation. They were exhausted and defeated; conquered on the ground they had so bitterly contested. Major McKircher stood directly beside the color bearer as a Confederate officer rode up on a white horse with several of his aides. "I am General Clayton, of Alabama."

The Major nodded. "Major McKircher, Tenth Wisconsin. Wish I could say it was good to make your acquaintance."

The general looked over the Union men as if trying to figure out what to do with them. "Sir, you know that you and your men are my prisoners."

Major McKircher nodded again, pointing to Billy Wheeler. "I surrender our colors. May we tend our wounded?" His voice sounded deep and dignified, though the faces of the men around him filled with tears. Wheeler stepped forward and offered the colors.

General Clayton took the pole and gave it to one of his aides, who carried it away on horseback. He watched the flag unfurl as the rider moved across the field, then turned to the major. "Where were your men on the line, sir?"

The major pointed toward the trees. "Over there, sir."

Clayton's gaze followed McKircher's finger. He nodded and smiled. "Why, you and your men have been thrashing my troops for two days. They fought bravely. You should be proud of them."

The major's tired eyes went wide and face blank. "I am, sir. Fact is, if we'd gotten to General Thomas, we'd still be giving your boys what for."

The Confederate officer smiled politely. "Why, sir, I'm afraid that would've been impossible. You see, the force behind you pulled out a couple hours ago. You've been holding us off by yourselves, and quite valiantly at that." Turning to another of his aides he said, "Y'all see these men are treated kindly. They were brave soldiers today."

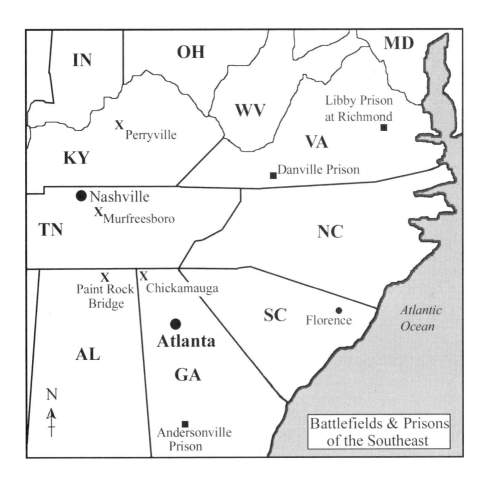

Battlefields & Prisons of the Southeast

SIXTEEN

"The virtues are one."
—Socrates

September, 1863, Fort Smith, Arkansas

SOCRATES STEPPED SLOWLY, QUIETLY ACROSS THE PARLOR FLOOR OF HIS NEWLY rented house, and peaked into the kitchen. The back door swung open and slammed closed. Willie darted through the kitchen laughing, followed by his older brother, Gus, who shouted something about how he was going to kill him. Ellen turned from her cooking at the stove, and yelled, "Willie! Gus! How many times I told you not to run in the house?" But the two giddy boys only laughed and dodged around the kitchen table, ignoring her. "Willie! Gusty!" The two stopped in their tracks. "I said there'll be no horsing around in our home. You two want to play like a couple of wild men, go outside, before you wreck my kitchen."

The boys answered in unison, "Yes, Mother," and filed back out the door.

Socrates quietly retraced his steps through the parlor and back out the front door. Within minutes, he re-entered and snuck through the room a second time. Ellen was cooking, singing *Nearer My God to Thee*, while stirring a pot of stew.

Socrates slipped behind, lightly grabbing her around the waist. He now came home every day for lunch, a privilege deeply and mutually appreciated. Both knew how close they had come to losing each other, and had vowed to never again take each other for granted. Her dark hair was tied up in a bun, and he began nibbling softly at the white skin of her neck.

"Socrates, you're giving me goose pimples!"

He kept kissing, moving up and around her ears. She turned her slender body to face his. Her sapphire-blue eyes flamed with passion. Then her forehead wrinkled, as she whispered, "What about Gus and Willie?"

Socrates smiled. "Don't worry. I gave each a penny for candy, told them

274

to feed, water, and brush down the horses before lunch. That gives us a good hour."

His mouth went back to work, steered its way up her neck. He pressed his body against hers. Her mouth melted as he forced his lips over hers. A rush of heat swept through him. He ached for her. She knew it. He could sense it. And he wanted to love her, wanted to give her another child. He pulled away. His heart filled with love, passion, lust, as he led her into the bedroom.

"First in the train of gods, he fashioned Love."

Afterward, they lay together, side by side, her right pointer finger twirling the hairs of his chest, his arm cradling her head. "Ellen," he said softly, "I've been thinking—even talked to Colonel Cloud about this. So far, he's been good to me, letting me work at the hospital and all, but I'm supposed to be with the cavalry. That's what I signed for, and there's no telling when there'll be more fighting. Bushwhackers are getting more bold, too, murdering Unionists all across the Missouri River Valley. And they're not satisfied with murder, their burning barns and houses, stealing everything they can get their hands on that's worth a dollar. Quantrill, Yeager, Todd, the Andersons - seems like we hear of more groups of them all the time, yet the Missouri militia can't seem to find a single one of them. I'm worried for you and the boys. There's talk of the regiment going east. Cloud says he'll honor your pass to St. Louis, and I have enough money to get you and the boys home from there."

Ellen rolled back, propped her head on her hand and smiled. "My dear Socrates, you know what it was like when I thought I'd lost you? My life was in ruins. I'll never leave you. Like Ruth said, 'Whither thou goest, there will I go also, and where the dwellest, there will I dwell.' Only death can part us."

Socrates felt suddenly ashamed that he'd asked her to leave, though it had only been for her safety. He didn't want to lose her again. But he didn't want to be away from her either. "That settles it," he said. "You and the children stay. We'll live everyday like it was our last."

He felt a passion, an unquenchable fire within, realized he'd never loved her as much as he did at this moment. A spark shot from her eyes, and he instantly understood that she felt that way too. There's nothing that can separate us, he thought, not ever again.

September 24th, 1863, Chickamauga Creek

The crisp night air sent a chill into Ed Best that penetrated deep into his bones. Working his hands beneath the blanket, he managed to shift it into a position covering his shoulders. As night crept into morning, the cooler air nipped his nape, then his spine, making sleep impossible. Over two hundred Yankee prisoners shared this small field, most of whom were from the Wisconsin Tenth and Ohio Thirty-eighth, and everyone lay flat on the ground, huddling together for warmth.

The stone-faces of his dead friends rolled through his mind, their bloated bodies covered with black crows. Royce Hawkins, Elijah Hunt, Henry More, John Rosabaugh, each left unburied on the fields of Chickamauga. His friends—friends who might never get a proper burial. Damned buzzards eating their flesh. How could the Union have lost? He pictured the campfires in the valley the night they'd first arrived, the invincible army. Rolling quietly onto his side, he shifted the blankets, but it was impossible to fall asleep. After a stretch of time during which he fell in and out of sleep, someone sat up. The fellow moved without making a sound, Ed sensed his motion, and as always, the man's movement attracted the attention of a guard.

"What ya doing, Yank? Ya know you can't get up to pee, or I'll have to shoot. Y'all best lie down and get back to sleep."

The sitting fellow grunted, and lay back on the ground.

After sunrise, Ed walked over to the fire with his friends, hoping for food. His stomach growled to beat the band with no food in sight. Only one meal in three days. There were too many prisoners to feed. He watched as a covered wagon rolled down the road and pulled off nearly twenty rods away. Captured Union artillery pieces followed, then wagons loaded with rifles collected from the battlefield, stacked in piles as high as Ed was tall. And he begrudged them all that booty. To the victor goes the spoils, but *damn* the victors.

A wagon load of wounded prisoners rolled by, followed by two columns of Union men who had volunteered to tend them. Bill Day offered a half smile toward Ed and his friends as he marched by, but no one said anything. No one dared rile the guards. Ed remembered Bill running off in the wrong direction, losing sight of him when the regiment hit the woods. It looked for a time as though he was the only one to get away. But after the major surrendered and the regiment was put under guard in the woods, Bill came tearing through the brush, running straight into them. He'd followed a course that changed every time he saw Rebels, and ended up doing a complete circle. "Shoot," he'd said panting. "Thought I was getting away for sure." Ed chuckled at the memory as his friend passed out of sight. It was the only light-hearted thought he would have all day.

How had the Rebs beaten them? What happened to their flank? Anger quaked within. Someone had messed up. Some dammed fool—or fools. What had they done, run at the first sight of Johnny? Damn. Damn the whole lot of them. Miserable excuse for soldiers. That's what they were. But what about General Thomas? Why had he left them? They fought hard for him. Damn hard. Would've gone to the wall for him, and he just up and left. No warning. Nothing.

"Okay, you Yankees," said a tall, thin Rebel, "we've got some food for you on that there wagon, so police your area, do your toiletries, and form into a single line."

Ed rolled up his blankets and secured his pack, while several guards kept close watch. Food was passed out, which amounted to less than a half ration. Stale hard tack, some old, dry salt pork, and a few swallows of water was all. When one of the Ohio boys complained that it wasn't enough, the Rebels laughed. "What's the matter, Yank, ain't our vittles good enough for you? With your damned blockade, we've been on half ration for months. What we get is what you get, and that's all there is." Were his enemies short of supplies? Fighting the way they had, he'd never suspected they were hungry. Within an hour, the men formed up and marched down the road. One of the men said they were in Georgia, but Ed was unsure. They marched all day, stopping twice for rest and water, before arriving at a small town railroad station where they climbed aboard open boxcars. Guards sat atop the cars, rifles in hand. Ed was famished. The train pulled out and traveled for an hour or two before entering a large city. "That's Atlanta," said a prisoner with an Ohio patch on his shoulder. "Used to go there on business."

Ed stared at the city, its massive railroad yards framed by large brick warehouses, and overshadowed by numerous church steeples. It was the fairest looking place he had seen since entering the South. "Looks like a nice place."

"It is," replied the man. "Was one of my favorite places to go before the war. I'd guess as many trains go through here in a day as through Chicago or Louisville."

Resentment soured Ed's belly. These were his enemies and he begrudged them every good thing. When the train stopped, the prisoners were taken to a large pen and kept under guard for the night without food. The next morning they were transferred to another train, and traveled north for the entire day, slowing for many towns and villages, stopping only to replenish water and firewood. Nothing was said as the trip dragged into the evening, then into the night and another day. Some couldn't sleep, with the hunger gnawing within and the noise of the trains all around, but the mundane regularity of the sounds worked together to put Ed to sleep. He awoke occasionally, when the train slowed or sped up, but then nodded off within a minute or two. He was growing weaker by the hour with no food and little water. It was early dawn when the train came to a complete stop. Guards appeared at the doors, their rifles ready, but the Yankees had no fight left.

Ed stepped down, peering up and down the tracks. His first opportunity to behold all the Union men the train carried revealed several hundred. Tables were set up, and he was given his third meal since being captured. Though meager, he snatched up some water, bacon, and hard tack, and sat down to eat with his friends, Jack Webster and Ole Gilbert.

"Bacon's all right," said Jack, "but the hard tack'll break your teeth."

"Yeah," said Ole. "Better soak it."

Ed dipped his into the tin cup he cradled in his hands, then looked around. "Where you suppose we are?"

"Sign says Richmond," said Jack, pointing toward a broad wooden plaque near the river. "The heart of the Confederacy."

"My cousin was held prisoner here," said Ed.

"Yeah?" said Jack. "What did he say about it?"

Ed shrugged. "Just heard it through letters from home. Said he didn't look too good when he got back."

Ole's sad blue eyes went wide. "Yumpin' yimminy, dey keep feeding us like dis, we won't live long enough to get home."

Ed reflected on Ole's words. What kind of care would he and his friends receive here? For several hours, the wounded were gathered up and marched away, accompanied by men with medical experience. Bill Day left with the second of many such groups, while Ed and the others waited. That night he slept in a boxcar, without any more food, then marched in the morning down a street that ran parallel to the nearby river. People walked about the city in all manner of dress. Others rode in carriages or on wagons. If it weren't for the men in uniform here and there, and his fellow prisoners being marched through the town, it looked as if this land were at peace. Eventually he passed a tall brick building, from which men in Confederate uniforms shouted curses. "Don't pay them no mind," said one guard. "That there's Castle Thunder, where we keep traitors and ketched spies. Yonder is Castle Lightning. We keep the rest of 'em there."

"Glad we're not going there," said Ed. "Looks like something from the middle ages."

"Guards too," added Ole.

The group continued on to a complex of large brick warehouses, where they were halted. Beneath the azure blue sky, a short but stocky Confederate officer watched them. His uniform was more blue than gray, and Ed would later learn he had left Maryland to join the Rebel cause.

"Good morning, gentlemen. My name is Major Turner," he said.

Ed chuckled at what sounded like "Majuh Tunah."

"You are my prisoners, and will be assigned to the building in front of you. This place is known as Libby Prison. Normally we hold officers here, but we took so many of you at Chattanooga that we'll have to house you here until some kind of exchange can be worked out. Do not attempt to leave the building without an escort. Do not stand too near the windows. If you do, you will be shot. You may write letters to home if you have stamps, and you will have opportunity to pay for postage and paper. I suspect your families are eager to learn how you are doing, so I encourage you to write as soon as you're settled. That is all."

The officer walked away and the men marched into a large warehouse. On each end of the warehouse was a sign that said, "Thomas Libby and Sons, Ship Chandlers and Grocers." Ed was standing in the middle of the room, when a board was lifted from the floor above and someone hollered down, "Psst, anyone down there from the Wisconsin Tenth Infantry?" Ed scrambled up the staircase, which was boarded up to separate the two floors. Jack Webster crouched ahead of him, but Ed could see a face looking through the boards.

"Captain Collins," said Jack. "How long you been here?"

"Got here yesterday. Who all is with you?"

"Gilbert, Best, Hand, Rouse, Gaffney," said Jack. "Rest must be in another building."

"Everyone all right?" asked Collins.

Jack nodded. "Everyone's all right."

"Bill Day came through here yesterday," said Collins. "Had Peter with him. Must have moved them out before you came in. Gosh, it's good to see you men. Anyone know what became of Major McKircher?"

Jack looked behind him to see expressionless faces. "Guess not," he replied.

"Listen," said the captain. "Don't let them take your money or your valuables."

"Turner's coming back," someone said, and the men hustled down the steps, while the board was quickly replaced in the floor.

Major Turner entered with a couple of guards. "We must check you for contraband and the like," he said. "Line up in ranks and empty your pockets for inspection."

Ed, being in the back row, quickly pulled out his stamps, paper money, and a pocket knife. Being careful not to be seen, he bent forward and slid them into his socks, then straightened up. The inspection went fast, and in a few minutes, one of Major Turner's tall lanky guards stood in front of him. "What you got?" he asked.

Ed held out an empty hand.

The lanky guard looked at Ed's hands, then at his out-turned pockets. "That's it? Nothing?"

Ed kept a straight face. "Yep."

The guard leaned his skinny frame forward, getting into Ed's face. "How come?"

"Guards in Atlanta," said Ed, throwing out his hands, "took everything I had."

The guard shook his curly head. "Shucks. They oughtn't have done that." He moved on, collecting knives, money, stamps, and anything else of value. The guards then brought food in and passed it out on plates. The meat was bad, filled with maggots, but everyone was desperate to stay alive, so they picked through it, devouring whatever looked edible. After the meal, they were marched to another building that reeked of tobacco, and still had several large iron machines for treating it. Mattresses stuffed with straw lay about the room, but only half as many as they needed. Ed was one of the first in, and secured a sleeping area away from any windows, expecting Winter to bring plenty of cold air through them. A second group came in, and Sergeant Dowd was one of the last to enter.

"Hey, Sarge, how you doing?" asked Ed.

Dowd's beady eyes glanced around the room. "Guess I got here too late. Can't find a mattress."

Ed placed his hand on Dowd's back. "Don't worry, Sarge. I've got one. Tell you what. I'll trade off with you every other night."

Dowd stiffened. "That's your bed, Corporal. Won't take it from you. Appreciate the offer, but I'll get by."

Ed's shook his head hard. "Shoot! I'd rather you have it than me, Sarge. I'm comfortable on the ground. Besides, I've got both my blankets with me and you don't have but one."

Dowd rubbed his stubby chin and nodded. "All right, Best. Better not think this means I'll be going easier on you than the others. I've got responsibility. Have to maintain discipline as long as we're in the army."

Sheesh. Prisoners of the Confederacy and Sarge still thought they were in the army. He grinned at Dowd. "Don't want anything, Sarge. Like I said,

I'll sleep better without it. Besides, we'll probably be home in a month or two. Union won't let us down. We've fought hard for her."

October 1863, Portage, Wisconsin

Swift sat atop a wooden keg outside the local exchange, staring down the road to Kilgore and Big Spring. One hundred yards distant, Hub's horse-pulled wagon drew steadily toward him, followed closely by that of Curge's. A bumper year for crops had everyone making multiple trips to unload their grain, and Swift enjoyed meeting with his cousins on such occasions. The Ramseys marketed their grain's earlier in the week, collecting a better price per bushel than they had seen in many years. The government was buying large quantities of farm produce to keep its armies fed; and that, coupled with the needs of regular families, served to push the price of grain ever upward. That was the only good news worth celebrating for what seemed like an eternity.

The autumn colors in the trees flashed in fiery splashes of orange and yellow maple leaves, bright red sumac bushes, red-brown oaks, yellow birch and poplars, all of which contrasted deeply with the evergreen pines and occasional black maples. In a short time the two wagons pulled up, pleasant smiles breaking from Curge's gaunt face and Hub's round cheeks.

"Glad to see you, Swift," said Hub. "Been waiting long?"

Swift shook his head. "Don't have any cases today. Besides, it's nice to get outside and enjoy the fresh air on a day like today."

"It is beautiful," said Curge. "But we have to get this grain in while the prices are good."

Swift nodded and watched the brothers unload and sell their produce in short order. Within the half-hour both brothers stood smiling, money in hand.

"Why don't you stick around town for a while?" asked Swift.

"Been awhile since I've been to Portage," said Hub. "Would like to see Doc and Aunt Emily before heading back."

Curge climbed up into his wagon and leaned forward with a playful grin. "Nothing for your thirst?"

Hub blushed, smiled sheepishly. "Thought I might get something. It's a looooong ride home, you know. Join me?"

Curge looked at the ground for a moment, then back at Hub before shaking his head. "Got too many things to get done—more grain to get to market before the road gets muddy or the snow falls."

Hub shrugged. "Suit yourself. Just watch out for highwaymen. They'd like to get their hands on your money."

Curge smiled, put one hand on the rifle beside him, the other on a pistol at his belt. "No one is getting what's mine without getting some of this."

Swift nodded. Who'd want to get shot by Curge? Never missed anything, and now he even had a pistol.

Hub smiled wide, showing his second chin. "Got an Army Colt, eh? Me, too. Keep mine under my wagon seat."

Curge's eyes narrowed. "Can't be too careful."

Swift nodded again, then watched Curge pull his team down the street. Before the wagon was out of sight, he felt Hub's hand on his shoulder.

"Aunt Emily have any of that apple pie I like so much?"

"Sorry," said Swift, "but she's in Madison. I'd be pleased to have a couple drinks with you though."

Hub stared. "Since when?"

Swift shrugged. "Nothing wrong with a drink once in a while. Besides, everybody does it."

"Not *your* Ma."

Swift held up the silver lion's head on his cane and said, "So? Like I said, she's in Madison. Besides, I'm a big boy now." He snapped the cane to his side, turned and started down the street. Hub caught up and the two walked a short distance to the closest tavern.

Stepping from the sunshine into the relative darkness made Swift stop while his eyes adjusted. Satisfied that he could see the floor, he walked over to the bar where Hub smiled and said, "Two beers." His words were soft, not demanding, and he placed a silver coin on the counter.

"How you doing, Hub?" asked the bartender, Ricky Phillips. He was a short, round fellow with thin blond hair and a patented laugh that was highly contagious, and wore a dark, red flannel shirt, mostly covered by a large white bib. He stared wide-eyed at Swift. "*Never* thought I'd see *you* here, your Ma being pro-temperance and all."

Swift shrugged.

"I'm all right, Ricky," said Hub. "Curge and I just hauled our grain to market. Fetched a good price too. How about those drinks?"

Ricky held two glasses under the tap, stopping each draft as the foam rose to the top. He set them on the counter, leaned forward, dark eyes questioning. "Heard anything on the boys of the Tenth? Everyone's dying for news, one way or the other."

Swift took a long drink, as Hub shook his head. "Ma's getting testy as blazes. She's good at putting on a smile and acting cheerful, but her temper's short. Looks tired, too. Waiting for word is wearing her down."

The back door opened, sending light cascading inward. Swift turned in time to see the back of a small man going out the door. "Who was that?" he asked.

Ricky shrugged his round shoulders. "Couple-a-immigrant railroad workers."

"Didn't notice them when I came in." said Hub.

"Don't say much," said Ricky. "Mostly stick to themselves, which is fine with me. Not exactly the type I want my daughter to marry."

Ricky stared at Swift. "You were with the Second at Bull Run. I hear that was Hell."

Swift drained the glass, looked toward the little window covered with cobwebs and back at Ricky. The forced-march to the battlefield, the rolling hills, the beckoning thunder of cannon fire all came back to him. "Green fields and forest," he started, then forgot what he was going to say.

Hub tossed another silver coin on the bar. "How about a couple more?"

Swift drank the second beer in long lusty gulps. His hands felt hot and wet, face cold and sweaty. Somehow his throat was parched, and even the cool moisture of the bitter-sweet brew couldn't seem to quench this thirst.

Hub and Ricky talked for better than an hour, while Swift finished his third and fourth beers. He thought about law school and its standard of justice, the truth of reality in the courts today. Fire swept up his spine and his stomach rolled into a knot. He walked toward the cobwebs at the window as the room grew silent. Outside wagons rolled and people scurried about their business. "Men of Portage," he bellowed, "you are citizens of this city, which is the greatest in the county—a city most noted for its wisdom in money and how to increase it, and about your reputation and your honor, instead of caring and worrying about the knowledge of good and truth and how to improve your soul."

He lifted his glass in a toast, beer splashing onto the sawdust floor. He felt a tear roll down his cheek as he said, "What does it profit a man to gain the whole world if he loses his soul?"

Hub stepped in front of him, moist round eyes glowing in the light of the window. "Come on. It's time to go."

Swift reached into his pocket and checked his watch. "Yeah. Almost forgot the time. Need to hit the outhouse first, though." As he went out the door, he heard Ricky asking Hub, "Sure you don't want one for the road?"

Relieving his bladder, Swift heard someone talking in a harsh whisper outside the outhouse. Who would be out here this time of day? As he fumbled with his buttons, he peered through a knothole in the wall. Outside, long September shadows stretched across the alley, eerily interspersed beside the alternating patches of golden sunlight that worked their way between buildings. Someone stood there, though he couldn't see who it was. He turned and looked through a crack on the opposite side. Another? Who were they, and what were they doing here? Must be no good, or they wouldn't be so quiet. He spotted a third figure through a chink in the door, the man's slight build, fair hair, and complexion all too familiar. The hair stood up on the back of Swift's head, and his heart raced. Radigan. Should have known. What was he gonna do now?

Swift pushed the door wide revealing Sean Radigan's sneering face and tight-fisted hands. He stood alone nearly six feet away. A light rubbing sound on the left wall reminded Swift that others were hiding in the shadows. His mind sped. His opponent snarled. "So ya thought yer folks could get away with killing me brother without having to pay for it, did ya? Well! I got ya where I want ya now, and there's gonna be Hell to pay. Do ya hear me, Best? I said Hell to pay, 'cause that's where you're gonna be tonight."

Swift flexed his jaw and raised the cane in his hand. His throat was dry, heart beating so heavily that he couldn't speak. He swung the door hard, and jumped as fast as he could across the space that separated him from his nemesis. He hit Radigan hard across the head with his cane, before dropping his shoulder and knocking Radigan flat on his back. But the blow stopped Swift's momentum, pushing him farther from the door of the tavern. He turned to face the others. Three short men slowly advanced, and each had a club. He thought of bolting for the door, but knew they'd hammer his head before he could open it.

As his opponents came shoulder to shoulder, Swift circled to the right. A searing pain flamed from his scarred hip, he ignored it. Had to think fast. Keep them in line, fight them one at a time. Keep circling, get away from Radigan. He'd be getting his wind in a minute. The first man swung his club from side to side, as if trying to bat Swift's head off, but he ducked the club and swung his cane hard into the man's groin. The fellow crumbled into a pile on the ground, where he lay groaning, desperately clutching his privates. A second man swung his club in a short arc, which Swift easily ducked. As the assailant's arm went by, he caught a solid punch in the stomach that dropped him beside the other attacker. Before Swift could turn, the last man's club struck him square across the shoulder, knocking the wind out of him, and reducing him to his knees. A volcano of pain exploded in his hip.

Out of the corner of his eye, he spotted Hub's thick frame barreling out of the tavern. Hub hit the man standing over Swift with a punch that knocked him straight to the ground. Swift tried to stand up, but the pain in his back and hip took his breath away.

Hub stood above him, throwing one man aside while fending off another's club. His eyes went big and wide as he blocked a second blow that struck his left forearm with such force that the bone cracked loudly beneath it. Hub wrenched the assailant's throat with his right hand, as though he would rip the man's larynx from its body. A hoarse choking sound came from the fellow as his eyes bulged from their sockets.

Sean Radigan regained his feet, picked up the other man's club, and wielded it like an ax. The blow hit Hub so hard he dropped his grip on the bug-eyed fellow's throat, and fell to his knees.

Swift managed to lift his cane and swing for Radigan's shins, but he was out of reach. A second and third blow followed in rapid succession as Radigan pummeled Hub. But like a wounded animal suddenly cornered, Hub pulled erect, swatting the blows away with his good arm, and charging Radigan. With a powerful right arm, he punched the little Irishman so hard it swept his feet from the ground, and landed him hard on the back of his head.

A shotgun blast sounded less than twenty feet away. Swift turned to see the white bib covering the short, round figure of the bartender, Ricky Phillips, who stood with a glower, double-barreled shotgun in hand. The three remaining thugs dropped their clubs and ran. Swift turned to Ricky to say thanks, but the movement fired pain through his hip and back again. A few feet away, Hub cradled his broken left arm, grimacing.

"What have they done to you boys?" said Ricky. "Let me look at that arm." He unbuttoned Hub's cuff, rolled back the sleeve to reveal a bulge on the outside bone of his massive forearm. The fracture had nearly broken through the skin. "Better get you to Doc's," said Ricky.

Hub turned, looked toward Swift.

Swift waved him away. "I'll be fine. Nothing more than a bruise here." He glanced in the direction of the blue-faced Radigan laying flat on the ground. "What about him? Doesn't look too good."

Ricky bent forward, bib bulging over his large stomach. His fingers searched for a pulse at the neck, moved around to several other places. He shook his head. "This fellow is dead."

Hub's eyes widened. "Didn't hit him *that* hard."

"Doesn't matter," said Ricky, shrugging. "Had it coming. And if those other boys hadn't left when they did, I'd have filled 'em with buckshot." A considerable crowd gathered at the end of the alley. The bartender waved to one of them. "Bobby, come help Swift. Henry, tell the undertaker he's got some business here. Come to think of it, better get the sheriff too. I'm taking Hub to Doc Best's. He can find us there."

Swift felt sick to his stomach, but Hub was quickly turning pale.

"Come on," said Ricky. "Let's get these boys to the doctor."

SEVENTEEN

"A man's wisdom maketh his face to shine,
and the hardness of his face is changed."
—Eccl 8:1 (ASV)

Mid-March 1864, Danville, Virginia

ED BEST SAT UP AND LOOKED ACROSS THE CROWDED ROOM TO THE DOORWAY. He had no idea how long he had been sleeping. He focused on the large room where he slept. This was another tobacco warehouse, similar to the one he had been in at Richmond. The prisoners were moved west to this place at Danville, in late January, and although this new prison seemed large at first, it was fast overcrowded with new arrivals. Sergeant Dowd sat only a few feet across from him. Ed squinted, focusing. "What time is it?"

Dowd wrinkled his face and looked toward a window. "Late morning, I guess. Longer than you usually sleep."

Ed nodded. "With all the snoring and snorting in this place, takes me hours to get asleep. When I finally do, I'm conked out."

Dowd shook his head. "Pretty soon you'll have your nights mixed up with your days. Don't want that to happen, do you?"

"Doesn't matter. Nothing to do except play cards, sing with the choir, or whittle." He scratched his head and smiled at Dowd. "Never had any luck with cards, don't have guitar or banjo, and I'm sick and tired of whittling."

Dowd nodded. "Me, too. By the by, they found a couple more cases of typhoid this morning. Smallpox too."

Ed groaned. "More smallpox? Shoot! We're dying here. Why haven't we been paroled? Damned Rebels too afraid we're gonna fight again?"

"It's nothing like that. Guards tell me the South is trying hard to work out exchanges. They say the North is dragging its feet."

"Hogwash!" said Ed. He ran his fingers back through his hair, felt blood rush to his face. "The Union would never let us down. There wouldn't even be a Union if we weren't fighting to keep it together. No *way* they'd leave us here. Damned Rebels are starving us just to keep us from being any good. That's all there is to it."

Dowd's face showed no emotion as he pointed to the guards. "Even these Rebs don't get more than half rations. They're not equipped to take care of their own with the blockade and all. How can they feed tens of thousands of prisoners?"

Ed shook his head fast and hard. "You're making me sore, talking like that, Sarge. Why you defending them? *They're* the reason we're here, and I don't see any of *them* starving to death. Do you?"

Dowd looked straight into Ed's eyes. "No. I don't, but I sure see a lot of skinny Rebs. Talk to the guards. You'll see. They've got a heap of complaints with their own government, especially since Jeff Davis exempted people with four slaves or more from serving."

Ed glared back at the sergeant. "You *believe* that?"

Dowd glared back. "Yeah, I do." He paused and pointed toward the doors. "That guard over there says it's just a rich man's war; and that one over there says Bragg's men hate him and shout curses when he rides by—that he keeps one tenth of the army back to shoot anyone who turns away from the fighting."

Ed shook his head again. "Would you quit taking their side? Sound like treason or heresy or something."

Dowd looked as though he were going to smile, but couldn't quite manage it. "Call it what you will, Ed, but I think it's the truth. Like I said, there's a lot of skinny Rebs around. The South can't feed us if they can't feed their own."

Ed looked away. Damned sergeant. Gums swollen, teeth loose and joints aching. Men dying here, and Sarge wanted him to believe their own government was at fault? Never. No way. He'd never believe that. It was times like this he wished Sophie hadn't been dispatched to headquarters with those prisoners—hadn't gotten away. Not that Ed wished Sophie were a prisoner, just that he missed his company so.

Across the room, three men dragged another dead soldier over to the door. Was it right not to cry? Men were dying all around and he couldn't cry. Just hard and cold, waiting to see who went next. If he didn't get some vegetables to keep the scurvy down, he'd go out the door the same way. He scanned the room for a familiar face. Bill Day was playing cards with Ole Gilbert and George Rouse. Just beyond them stood a young, dark-haired guard. Good, thought Ed, just who I need to talk to.

He stood up and stretched, stepped across sleeping bodies. Should he ask about the exchanges? Sometimes the truth was better unknown. "Darnell," he whispered. The guard at the door turned. Ed reached into his pocket and pulled out two hand carvings he had recently completed. One was the figure of a Union officer from mid chest up, and the other was a Confederate soldier. Each better than anything he had made to date. "Want to buy some more bone carvings? Need onions and a stamp." He tried not to sound desperate, but this Rebel had bartered onions, berries, and stamps for a handful of Ed's other carvings.

"Sorry," replied the skinny boy. "Can't even get stamps for myself. Tell you what I'll do though. I got a friend, a cook who liked what you made before. Maybe he'd trade you a couple potatoes."

Ed ran his fingers back through his hair. "Potatoes! I could go for that. When will you know?"

Darnell rubbed his chin. "Can talk to him tonight, but I'm not sure it'll do you any good." Ed felt the question forming in his face, saw Darnell's soft blue eyes recognize it. "Wasn't supposed to let prisoners know, but I think you'll keep this under your hat. Last month, the people of Danville wrote to Richmond complaining about the conditions here, smallpox and the like. With the prison and hospital in the middle of town, they're afraid an epidemic will wipe 'em out. Last I heard, sounded like they're fixin' to move y'all again."

Ed felt a shiver go through him. "What about parole or exchange? If they exchange us, they won't have to waste the men and supplies to guard and feed us. That'd be better—right?"

The guard shook his blond head. "Not up to me. From what I heard, they tried to get you exchanged more than once. Union keeps turning it down. Don't ask me why, 'cause I don't know. Word is you'll be moved to a better place soon. In the meantime, I'll try to get you those potatoes."

Ed nodded and handed the bone carvings to the guard, unable to hide his anger. They were *all* liars. He couldn't trust them to tell the truth. Saying the North wouldn't exchange them—turning him against his own. A wave of discouragement swept over him and he suddenly felt nauseated. Head down and feet dragging, he slowly made his way back along the wall to where Sergeant Dowd whittled at a piece of bone. "What's the matter, Ed? Look like you just saw a ghost."

Ed dropped his head and spoke slowly, devoid of feeling. "We're not gonna be exchanged. They're moving us again."

Dowd nodded. "The officers have known for a few days. Colonel Smith informed them when he first heard the news, and they told the sergeants, but we weren't allowed to tell anyone. We all agreed the bad news would cause more men to give up hope." He stood and put his arm around Ed's shoulders. "Look, Ed, everyone's barely hanging on—hoping they'll go home again. Doesn't matter why we're not getting exchanged now, or whose fault it is. Got to believe you'll make it, otherwise they'll bury you here. Keep hoping and believing. Understand? Doughty's already nearly too sick to travel, and I don't want to leave anyone else behind in this place. Hang on to your hope. Don't let it go for anyone or anything. Understand?"

Ed nodded, but couldn't raise his head completely. He didn't want anyone to see the tears forming in the corners of his eyes, didn't know how long he could keep the dam from breaking inside him.

The commandant came into the room with several guards. "Attention, prisoners!" he shouted, but Ed still didn't raise his head. "The War Department in Richmond has decided that the conditions here are overcrowded and unhealthy. We are moving you to a new camp in Georgia." Ed wiped his eyes and turned to see Colonel Smith pacing as he spoke. "It will have more room, and will be further south, where the temperatures are more mild. I'm even told you'll have fresh air." He stopped pacing, looked around the floor, at the sick men who couldn't stand. "I sincerely hope your sick get better." He lifted his head and looked at the men standing. "The guards will march you to railroad cars after morning rations. I wish you well."

He smiled, turned, and started to exit the room, when someone shouted after him, "Hey, Colonel, what about our exchange? Should be going home by now." But the commandant just walked out the doorway and disappeared.

After Smith left, food was brought in, and every able man formed a line. Ed stepped up to a large kettle, where he watched as a thick, soupy stew was spooned onto his tin plate by a big Rebel. The man's pants seemed barely able to stay up beneath his burgeoning belly, and he carelessly picked his nose and wiped it on the edge of the kettle. Boogers, bread, and mush. Worse than the bugs and beans yesterday. The fat man turned to pick up something from the floor, revealing a milky white skin, covered with black hair and an enormous butt crack. Ed bent forward and scooped some of the hot stew into the gaping aperture.

"Aaahh!" the man screamed as the hot liquid followed gravity's sure path. His head whipped up and back, and he took off running around the room, and out the door. The prisoners roared. One of the guards asked what had happened, but no one said a word, and the matter was quickly dropped.

An hour later, Ed and the other prisoners marched to the railroad station.

The streets were empty, the people obviously afraid of sickness. At the station he quietly boarded a boxcar teeming with men. Cold air wailed through the wallboard crevices, biting into Ed's uncovered skin, causing him to huddle with the others for warmth, but it did little good. Sergeant Dowd's and Corporal Jack Webster's faces were cold and expressionless. The ride was more monotonous than the previous ones. They rolled from town to town, slowing, stopping, then moving again, only to repeat the cycle every half hour or so. The train traveled day and night, stopping to feed the prisoners only once per day. By the third day the temperature rose to a bearable level. But with no means of bathing or washing one's clothes, the lice multiplied immeasurably, and everyone became sick, constantly scratching and moving, burning up what little energy they had.

After nearly a week, the train pulled to a stop at midday, and the doors on the boxcars opened. A loud voice with the thickest Southern drawl he had heard since Chickamauga broke the silence. "Okay! Yankees, time to get off and form up. You's arriiiived at your new home."

Ed stepped down from the car, ankles and knees rebelling at the sudden change in load. He turned to help ones with more difficulty walking, or those who couldn't withstand the jolt of jumping. Dowd directed while Hull and Weber handed down Ole Gilbert, too weak to stand on his own. The prisoners gathered on a crude platform, from where Ed spied the edge of a woods made up of long pine trees, nearly sixty feet high. Most of their green branches appeared at the top third of the long thin trunk. Along the outside of the woods, lay a thick, lush forest, almost impossible to penetrate. But where the tracks crossed the woodlands, a swath had been cut that laid its center bare. Patches of silver-gray bark gleamed in the Georgia sunlight, like long silver poles holding up a green leafy tent above.

Ed formed with his fellow Wisconsin Volunteers into four lines on the wooden dock. Scattered around the platform were various crudely built cabins. Below them rose the rust-red Georgia clay. Most of the stones and larger rocks looked white in contrast. The men were counted, gathered into groups of ninety, and marched along a well-worn trail. A half mile farther, they came upon a place where teams of Negro slaves felled trees and dragged them toward log buildings. Other teams wielded broadaxes and other tools to square and notch the lumber. A few older buildings were complete, but the new ones were all in various stages of completion.

Behind this setting was the largest log wall Ed had ever seen. Twenty foot logs slipped straight into the ground, side by side, forming a huge picket fence that surrounded over fifteen acres of land. Platforms stood outside those walls, their floors set nearly three feet below the top. At every station stood a Rebel guard, musket in hand, surveying the grounds within the walls. Outside the prison, some prisoners labored to complete the buildings. Alongside the twenty foot high walls was a dry ditch nearly five feet deep, and beyond that, two openings on each side of a stream that ran into the west wall. As he entered the first, Ed found a small stockade surrounded the inner gate, and since the outer gate doors had not yet been hung in place, a dozen soldiers stood guard there.

Ed was at the front of his line, and was directed toward a wagon where a very young Rebel handed him a ration of coarse corn meal, sweet potatoes, beans, and pork. With the food in hand, Ed wandered away, followed by Sergeant Dowd and the other men of the Tenth. Ed was already finished with his sweet potato and pork, when Dowd hit him on the shoulder. "Don't eat that stuff," he scowled. "Doesn't look like that corn's been sifted. Wait 'til we get inside. Bill Day and some others have mess utensils. We'll sift and cook before we eat."

Hungry men around Ed devoured their meals. Damn, he was hungry. But he'd better do as sarge said. Bill came up with his rations and smiled. "Looky here," he said, holding up a small tin bucket. "Looks like we'll get water inside."

Dowd nodded. "They're handing out buckets to every fifth man. You'll be our mess sergeant, Bill, since you have the bucket. Webster, make sure everyone uses their mess kits and keeps them clean."

Ed turned his attention to the wagon, where the last of the food was being dispersed. Atop the wagon stood a fortyish, tall, thin, and slightly stooped man. The top of his head was covered with a Rebel army cap, but nothing about him looked military. His face held a full beard, with streaks of gray here and there. His shirt was of white linen, and the trousers were also white. He moved about anxiously, hazel eyes darting every which way. At his left side was a revolver, but his right hand was wrapped in a towel. This strange figure of a man pulled himself erect, then spoke with an accent that sounded something like the Milwaukee Germans Ed had met.

"I am Captain Wirz, the commander of this prison. Twice each day, you will be provided a ration of food, distributed inside the prison. I am a fair man, but I will not be made a fool. If you try to escape, you will be shot. If you get too close to the walls, you will be shot. If any of you are carpenters or shoe makers, you will be allowed to work outside, but you will be paroled to do so on your honor, and must return to the prison. Those who want to help build your cook house can do so in the morning." He looked around with an air of satisfaction, then said something to the wagon driver, who lifted the reins, and urged the mules past the wall of guards at the unfinished gate. The inner gates opened and Ed entered with his friends.

The compound was spacious, fifteen acres, but thousands of small tents poked their canvas up in random fashion as far as the eye could see. Along the north wall was a much larger tent, and a few crude log houses sat within the grounds. Ed wrinkled up his face. "Ooh! What is that?"

"Good God," said Dowd. "Smells worse than a pig sty."

"Can't breathe," said Webster. "Air is putrid."

Ed Best walked in a daze, every sense screaming mutiny at the sight of this place. Sergeant Dowd walked ahead, and was greeted by a number of boys from Libby Prison.

"Dowd!" said a stocky man, with broad shoulders and a yellow Ohio patch on his arm. "Haven't seen you since we got to Danville."

Dowd reached out his hand, beady eyes wide with shock. "Sergeant Major Lowry, what in the name of God is this place? And where are we, anyway?"

Lowry shook Dowd's hand with a foreboding grin. "We're near Anderson, Georgia. Those few houses you passed near the station are all there is of it. Anyway, the men call this place Andersonville. Wasn't bad two weeks ago. Seemed like plenty of room to move around in; but hundreds arrive every day, and some days there haven't been enough rations." He turned and pointed across the grounds with a sweeping motion and a frown. "If they keep bringing men here, we'll be in deep trouble. Only water to wash and drink with is the creek." He pointed to the place where the creek ran through the far wall. "Don't drink from the swamp downstream. It's what everyone uses as a latrine. The middle is where we bathe, and the farthest point upstream is our drinking water. But don't go near the dead line, or the guards will shoot you. It's marked by stakes inside the walls." He turned and pointed to the big canvas tent. "That's the hospital, but it's already full, and there's no medicine anyway." He leaned forward and whispered, "There's smallpox in the camp. Keep your boys together and don't mix around. There's tents for you over there."

Ed followed Dowd toward the pile of canvas. It was as though he were in a dream, swept along by some unseen river to a place he didn't want to go.

April 1864, Fort Smith, Arkansas

Socrates stepped in long strides toward his house, where Ellen stood outside the front door waiting. Since becoming pregnant again, she seemed

293

to sense his coming and was always waiting there when he came home. Gus pushed his barrel ring down the street, as Willie rode on Socrates' shoulders. Willie lifted his father's soldier cap and switched it with his own. The diminutive brown hat barely balanced on Socrates' large head, and he could imagine little Willie's head swallowed up in the Union cap. Ellen's hands went to her mouth, and Socrates could almost hear her giggling. She waved a hand and he waved back. Little Willie shook Socrates' head as he imitated his father. Ellen's hands went up to her mouth again, and this time he heard her laugh. Gus lost control of his barrel ring and sprinted by the house to catch it.

With Ellen nearly six months pregnant, the promise of new life was gradually crowding out the painful losses of the past. Socrates stuck his hands beneath Willie's armpits, lifted and set him on the ground, then turned toward Ellen and kissed her squarely on the mouth.

"Socrates! What do you think you're doing?" She pushed him away, but he pulled her closer to him. "Socrates! Someone might see." He kissed her again, this time on the cheek, but she craned her neck away. "What's gotten into you? Want everyone on the post talking about us?"

Socrates stopped and looked at her very seriously. "I don't care what people think. I've got the best wife of the whole lot, and I don't care who knows." Then, putting the flat of his hand on her stomach, he said, "Hope this is a girl. If she's half as beautiful as you, she'll have every boy around calling on her."

Ellen blushed and pushed him away, but his right hand caught her left, and he walked alongside her to the door. "I hope you've got something good to eat. I'm starved."

"Me, too," said Willie. "What's to eat?"

Behind her, Gus came running—ring over shoulder and stick in hand. He was puffing and his cheeks were flushed.

"Horse stew," said Ellen.

Willie's face wrinkled like a prune. "Oooh! Who'd eat a horse?"

"Me!" said Socrates. "I'm so hungry I could eat a horse. In fact, I'm so hungry I could eat a kid." Grabbing little Willie by the back of his jacket and drawers, Socrates lifted him face up, and pretended to chew on the boy's belly. The motion of jaw and whiskers on Willie's skin started him laughing, squirming, and kicking wildly.

Socrates' chest swelled as though every molecule of air was one of these, his family members, and the passion of his love had super-heated them, expanding to the point of explosion. So much love. So much happiness.

April, 1864, Andersonville Prison

Ed Best awoke with heavy pressure in his bladder, pushed himself up onto one elbow. He breathed hard, his strength slowly being siphoned. A shortage of firewood meant that the only prepared meals now came from the cook house. Unfortunately, it could only produce enough to feed half the prisoners on any given day. Though he did his best to prepare it, the poorly sifted, uncooked corn meal was irritating his bowels, causing gas, stomach pain, and diarrhea. Meanwhile, the cooked rations on the alternate days were not enough to restore his energy, since the cycle was constantly repeated. After crawling out of his tent, he walked to the swamp to relieve himself. A few feet from the tent, he stepped around the stiffened corpse of Wallace Darrow, who was removed from the tent until he could be brought to the gate for burial. His face looked blue-gray in the predawn light, prompting Ed to turn away and make his way to the slough.

He rambled slowly along the creek for ten or fifteen minutes. At the far end he worked his way to the deadline, where wooden stakes marked the invisible boundaries of death. Without a sound, he waded into the water, watching the guards out of the corners of his eyes. This stuff was for drinking, but it always tasted brackish. Guards probably cleaned their cooking wares upstream. He hoped they didn't use it for toiletries. The thought sickened him. The two nearest guards appeared to be asleep until one swatted a troublesome mosquito. He wondered if they were playing opossum—hoping he'd stray to the line. Some said they got a weekend furlough for shooting a Yankee. Could that be true? One thing for sure, he wasn't gonna wander over and ask.

He leaned forward and drank, standing knee deep in water. The camp was quiet, save for snoring, coughing, and other night sounds. Low hanging clouds started thinning. They rolled and swirled overhead, like smoke from a forest fire, but the sun would soon replace them with sweltering heat and humidity. He couldn't stay here. Couldn't live like this. He'd rather be dead. But what if he could escape? Wirtz called for carpenters to work outside every day. If he ran, he'd violate his word of honor. Honor? What was honorable about dying here?

As the morning sun baked the fog away, the camp came alive—men moving everywhere, like ants scurrying over their mounds. By mid-morning, the gates opened and carpenters were called for. "I'll go!" shouted Ed.

"Me, too!" said another.

Day frowned at Ed. "What you wanna do that for? The sun is gonna be hot today. Hotter than yesterday."

Ed whispered, "I know, but if I get work around the cookhouse, I'll be closer to the woods. Then I'm home free."

"Home free?" whispered Day, blue eyes wide. "You've seen what happens to runaways—locked up in stocks under the hot sun. You wanna die or something?"

"Might just as well die out there as in here."

Sergeant Dowd stepped between them, stubbled face hard. "What's going on?" he asked softly.

Ed ran his fingers through his hair. "I was just going for carpentry."

Dowd looked closely at Best, then at Day, then at Best again. He lifted his hand and stuck a thick finger in Ed's face. "You better not be thinking what I think you're thinking. 'Cause if you are, I've got to tell you, you won't make it. They've doubled the guards and brought in dogs since the last time you were outside." He looked at the lines of men volunteering to go outside, looked back at Ed, tilted his head. "Help me get Darrow to the shed. He deserves a decent burial, and if we wait any longer, he'll stink."

Ed sneered at the sergeant. Darrow had died from scurvy and diarrhea. The same conditions that were killing Ed and everyone else. He shook his head hard. "What's wrong with Gilbert? He and Webster can help you with Jones. I've got work to do."

"Gilbert's come down with fever and won't wake up. Jack's got the cramps and is down at the slough. Ed, we need you to help us with Darrow. Okay?"

Ed felt conviction weigh on his shoulders. He didn't want to die here, but he didn't want to seem like he didn't care about Darrow's body either. He nodded slowly. "All right, Sarge. I'll help you, but if I get onto carpentry afterward, I won't be coming back. I'm getting out by hook or by crook."

The sergeant nodded, turned and walked toward the place where Darrow's corpse lay. Ed followed Dowd to the tent, where he found Ole Gilbert laying on his side buckled up with cramps. Webster hadn't returned yet, and Ed figured he would be at the slough all day. Such thoughts only strengthened his resolve to get away fast. Dowd grabbed the dead man's arms, and looked at Best. Ed stared at the cold blue face of Wallace Darrow, whose hair and beard were disheveled and covered with lice. He hated touching dead bodies, so cold and hard. Stone cold was the term the men used. Having touched, held, and carried corpses, there could be no better words to describe the feeling of once warm, supple flesh, now frozen hard in death. Ed couldn't stand to see Wallace like this, and he turned to face away from the corpse, before taking the legs in his hands. With a grunt, he pulled and lifted, then started walking. The two carried the corpse to the gate, where a guard lifted Darrow's head by the hair, checking to see that he was indeed deceased. Satisfied, he waved them through to the outside. The two carried the corpse out and laid it in front of a lean-to, where two prisoners built coffins, while another wrote in a book.

"Another?" asked a skinny coffin maker. He stepped back, wiped his forehead with his sleeve, took a deep breath, and sighed with disgust. "We'll be driving nails all day. Put him at the end of the line."

The scribe motioned with his pen toward a row of six bodies lying side by side beneath the lean-to. "Name? I said name!"

Best surveyed the woods as he turned. "Wallace. His name is Wallace Darrow."

The man put his head down and scribbled in the book. "Rank and unit?"

"Private. Wisconsin Tenth Infantry."

"That'll do," said the scribe. He looked at Darrow, then Ed. "Want his shoes?"

Ed shook his head.

Dowd put his right hand on Ed's shoulder. "No one leaves shoes on a dead man while others go barefoot. Wally doesn't need them anymore. Take 'em. Give you something to trade."

Ed shook his head." Damn! Rob the dead? He already lost everything."

"Suit yourself," said the scribe. "Next one to come along will take them anyway. Don't you think he'd prefer you have them?"

"That's all right," said Dowd, "I'll take them." He bent over Darrow's feet, removed the shoes, tied the strings together and threw them over his shoulder. Rifles fired from behind the cookhouse. Several Confederate soldiers sprinted past the guards toward the woods where three blue-uniformed men ran from the carpentry detail. One, already wounded, limped along, trying desperately to move forward. Three more muskets fired. The two lead men dropped to the ground. The third man continued limping toward the woods. A man on horseback galloped out, blocking the aim of the infantrymen with his horse. Within seconds, he cut the wounded prisoner off, moving constantly to block his path, toying with him. Finally, the prisoner turned and hobbled toward the prison gates.

Before he made it that far, Captain Wirtz came out of his office and walked alongside the limping prisoner. All the nervous tension normally displayed in Wirtz' hazel eyes now exploded from his mouth and face. "What you do this for, you stupid Yankees? You know you can't get away. Want to make me look bad? I'll show you. Into the stocks for three hours—and no more outside work for you. That's what you get when you cross me."

Dowd leaned forward, whispering into Ed's ear, "That'd be you if I'd let you go on detail. Come with me. I'll show you a better way." He turned and headed back into prison.

They walked through the sea of tents until they came to a group of unfamiliar men crowded together in a circle. The men had their backs to him. "Stay here!" said Dowd. "I'll be right back."

Ed stood alone and watched the sergeant move toward the men. The crowd parted, revealing men playing marbles in a circle with some smooth round stones. One man stood and talked to Dowd, then took him inside a nearby tent. A few minutes later, another came out and took Ed in. Inside he found strips of lumber forming walls, at least three to four feet below ground level.

Dowd sat beside Sergeant Major Lowry. "Look!" said Dowd, taking the shoes from around his neck. "If you'll take Best and me, I'll give you these shoes. If you don't, your man'll have to go barefoot out there. We can help you dig the tunnel. What do you say? Is it a deal?"

Lowry's cleanliness stood in stark contrast to three others within the tent. The man sitting beside him was filthy from digging, and his shoes separated in front, leaving his toes exposed. Couldn't run far in those, at least not through the forest. Pinecones and nettles would chew him to pieces. "All right," said Lowry. "Give us the shoes and you can both run with us, but you stay in the tent, where we can keep an eye on you. If you talk to any of the guards, my men will slit your throats. Understood?"

They nodded. The three disappeared in the tunnel. Before long, one reappeared with two crudely made canvass bags filled with dirt. Ed handed them out to a man outside, who dumped it into the area where a crowd watched the marble game. Feet moved in concert, spreading it evenly as the empty bags returned.

"It's done, Sergeant Major," said the dirty man with Darrow's shoes. "We're right under the sod and ready to go. If anyone walks or rides over that spot, we'll be found out. Have to go tonight!"

The sergeant major grinned. "Well, Dowd, looks like you came on board at the right time. Sit back and relax. We won't go until dark."

Swift sat on the davenport beside Marianne, a warm fire dancing in the marble-framed fireplace. A plaid blanket extended across their laps and covered their lower legs. The temperature outside had dipped below freezing, making the parlor even more homely than normal on this Saturday afternoon. Mr. Horde was in Madison, and Adrian had gone to shop. "Marianne, I need to talk to you."

Her bright blue eyes sparkled as the flames reflected off them. "Yes."

"What would you think if I gave up law?"

She smiled wide. "Don't be silly, Eusebius. You're just getting started in practice. Daddy says you're doing wonderful—that you'll even be a partner some day. Maybe even Congressman."

Swift looked away. "But I don't know if I can do it. The courts—"

Her hand slid under the blanket and up his thigh, gently rubbing. "Now there you go talking silly again. How are we going to have a nice house like this if you don't practice law? There are so many things we'll need after we're married. Of course, Mommy and Daddy will help us at first, but then it will be up to us."

Swift shook his head. "I don't care about those things. I'm not happy practicing law."

Marianne pulled her hands to her sides. "Why, Eusebius Best, you stop talking that way right now. We're going to have a nice big house and two children. You'll be Daddy's partner, and that's all there is to it. You'll just have to get over those silly ideals of yours."

She went back to rubbing his thigh. Oh, how he loved that. It made him want her so, to agree with anything she said. But there were two opposing fires burning within, and one was crossing out the other, leaving him empty and afraid. "One thing I learned in the war—"

"Eusebius! You aren't going to start on that, are you? Why, you are plum wearing me out. I think it's time you went home. You can return when you've chased all that silliness from your head." She leaned forward and squeezed his hand. "But don't be long."

Swift felt a different fire blaze through him, felt himself blushing. He wanted to apologize, wanted to sit right here with her by the warm fire. But something inside him rose up against it. "No, Marianne, I won't be coming back here if you don't want to hear my *silly* ideals."

"Now look at you. You're angry—and for what? What is wrong with you? I've been perfectly willing to look past your physical limitations."

Swift snatched his coat and cane on the way out, welcoming the cold blast of air as he stepped outside. He wanted his rifle, wanted to shoot Horde and his whole family. How he hated them. How he wanted her.

The door slammed as he entered the back of his house. He dropped his coat on a peg and stepped into the kitchen, where he found his father seated, staring out the window. "What's the matter, Pa?"

Doc turned slowly, eyes gazing afar off. "Just came from the Hansons."

"Velma have her baby?"

"Twins."

Swift smiled. "That's wonderful! So what's the matter?"

"Board of deacons wants to meet with you. About your drinking."

Swift blushed. "Nothing wrong with a drink once in a while."

"Swift, you've been coming home drunk. Drop your jacket and kick your boots on the floor wherever, not to mention the hours you keep. Whole town's talking about Radigan. Your mother is beside herself."

"I'm a man, Pa."

Doc's stare burrowed through Swift. "But are you a *good* man?"

Swift's stomach knotted and he looked away.

"What is it, Swift, and why won't you let us help you?"

"You can't help me. No one can."

Doc stood and put his hands on Swift's shoulders. "At least let us try."

Swift shrugged and looked away. "I can't. Lost too much."

Doc squeezed Swift's shoulders. "What have you lost?"

"I don't know."

"You must."

Swift watched his father's silver-streaked black beard pull up as his face wrinkled in anguish. "Remember Origen?"

Doc's dark eyes flashed. "Of course. Early church father, teacher, historian."

Swift leaned back. "Remember how he read the Scriptures literally? Some willingly became eunuchs for Christ?"

"Good Lord," said Doc, dropping his hands to his side. "I'd completely forgotten that. My God, you mean you—"

"No, but that's exactly how I feel. In my zeal for Christ, I've—How can I face the world?"

Doc's hands moved again to Swift's shoulders. "No, you haven't. Your leg is getting stronger."

Swift threw his hands up and knocked his father's hands away. "I'm not talking about my leg!"

"What then?"

Swift pulled out his St. George medallion and studied it. "My soul, Pa. I've defiled my soul, and all of the crying and praying in the world can't wash it clean."

May 5th, 1864, Andersonville, Georgia

Ed Best sat beside his sergeant, while six other men anxiously waited. The only light in the tent emanated from two candles, one at each end, mounted on small mounds of wax built up on scrap pieces of pine, wedged into the earth near the top of the pit. The gray hair of the sergeant major's head appeared at the opening of the tent. "It's dark enough. Guards look tired. Send the first man out, count to twenty, then send another. Keep the intervals, or you'll attract the attention of the guards."

Ed's heart raced, as the sergeant major turned to the dirty fellow with Darrow's shoes. "Randy," he said, "you go first, since you were the one to break through. Best, follow Randy, but wait 'til he's across the field before you make a run. In the tunnel there's a wooden strut every few feet. Don't hit any or you'll be buried alive, and everyone else's chance will be ruined. Understand?" Ed nodded. "Good. Then you two get going and we'll follow. Just remember, once you're out, you'll be on your own. Don't stop for nothing."

Ed followed Randy into the dark hole. It was so tight, he could barely pull his body along in an alligator crawl. With elbows bent, knees alternately bending and straightening, and trunk just high enough to be dragged forward, he slowly and methodically began his escape. Dirt dropped in clumps every time he lifted himself too high. Twice he bumped the wooden supports, sending dirt and sand into his eyes, burning and stinging them. He was terrified but determined. Stopping momentarily, he rubbed his eyelids, only to find the backs of his hands so dirty, they only made it worse. He squeezed his eyes shut, and crawled forward for what seemed like an eternity, before his hands finally landed on Randy's shoes. Without opening his eyes, Ed stopped and waited until he heard a harsh whisper. "I've pushed the sod back, and the field is clear all the way to the woods. Count to twenty, then follow. Once I'm in the woods, I'm as good as home, so don't bother looking for me. Ready— count."

Randy's feet pulled away, kicking more sand and dirt down. Ed held his eyelids shut hard, keeping his face down until the stuff stopped falling. About the time he reached ten, someone bumped against his feet. The next man was in place. At fifteen, he opened his eyes and lifted his head to see the star-lit sky above. Nineteen. He shot into the opening, looking for any sign of the guards. Twenty. The saliva in his mouth disappeared. Twenty-one. He crawled on hands and knees before drawing up into a crouch. Twenty-five. What was he doing? Only supposed to count to twenty. He surveyed the area. The guard stations and prison walls stretched behind him, the forest in front. No voices of alarm sounded, and no guards looked his way. He took off running in a half crouch.

What if one of the guards saw him? What if they caught him before he got away? One second terror engulfed him, envisioning Rebel guards shooting him in the back as he ran. The next second he was exhilarated, imagining himself walking down the road to his own house, running and leaping in unbounded freedom. The dark woods opened before him. Prickers tore at his clothing, piercing hands and face. Pine bows slapped him, but nothing slowed him. Onward he ran, down a gully and up the other side, all the time riding a burst of energy. Aching belly and sore gums mattered no more, nor did his lack of food. Freedom.

A shot sounded somewhere in the distance. He couldn't stop now no matter what happened. He had to get away. God, please. The ground dropped off suddenly, driving him recklessly downhill until his foot caught a rock, and he tumbled head over heels. Over and over he rolled through a maze of thickets, rocks, and roots until his body landed hard on a flat rock bed at the bottom of the valley.

He lay motionless. Every muscle in his body cried for rest. Every bone screamed in pain. His beating heart and panting breath were all he could hear until the night air was rent by a more hellish noise. Ahooow! Ahoow! The wail of hounds baying in the darkness. Sheer terror drove new strength into his legs, bouncing him to his feet. Across the moonlit riverbed that glowed ghost-white in the darkness, he spotted the water that wound its way around the bend. Over loose rock and gravel he ran toward the cauldron, where dark eddies and deep whirlpools cried *beware*. The water ran nearly fifty yards across. Could he swim it? The current might be too strong. The sound of the hounds grew closer.

He flipped off his shoes, tied the laces together, and wrapped them around his neck; then stepped into the river. The water gave a renewed sense of vigor as he waded to his waist. The current was strong, much stronger than he'd expected, but he couldn't turn back. Digging bare feet into the sandy river bottom, he pushed with all the force his legs could muster, and dived face first into the dark liquid. The water was cool, but the current pushed him down river too fast. He flailed his arms like a sick bird trying to fly. Had to get air. His head broke the surface and he gasped loudly. The river gripped him, pulling him along, dunking him at will. Panic raced through him, but he was too weak to fight the current. Something inside of him gave way, and he yielded to the force, expecting it to claim him. But rather than drown him, the water buoyed him, pushing him along while he rested. He slowly regained his strength. Something hard struck his feet. Big rocks or sunken trunks could do him in. He pulled up his feet in front of him, and rode the chair of water.

A small pine tree appeared, trunk partially rooted in the high bank, stem sloping into the river. Ed padded downward with his hands, legs straight, body bent at the hips. That's it. Use those feet like a rudder. Careful, just a little bit further. At the last second, he reached up and caught a branch, only to feel the current drag him down. Scaly pine bark slid through his weakened fingers as he lost his hold, and found himself submerged in watery darkness again. One foot struck a large boulder beneath him. He pushed hard against it, driving his body upward until his face broke the river's surface. Deep gasping breaths brought quick relief amidst the terror.

He floated for several minutes with no escape in view. Twenty yards down river, he spotted another pine extending from the shore, this one much bigger. He worked toward the submerged section. The river carried him straight to it, and he managed to drape his shoulder over the sunken end. Water rushed around his torso, pressing him hard against it. That's it, he told himself. Can't get off balance. Current will throw me off this thing. Use it. Don't fight it. He leaned into the current, pulled his left leg up until he straddled the trunk. His muscles ached, head pounded with exhaustion. But he could not be swayed.

Like an inchworm, he dragged himself up the thing. Its sappy bark was easy to grip, and incline gradual enough to allow him a rest every few seconds. Exhausted, he pulled his waterlogged body over the ground, and rolled off the tree trunk. All that time, the water babbled on in some unknown language. A hound howled excitedly, giving notice that the hunters had tracked him to the river. By the sound, he guessed the water had carried him a half mile. Once the dogs crossed they'd pick up his scent all too soon.

Steadily he worked up a ravine to the plain above. It was a gradual slope, which helped greatly. Onward he ran until his feet dragged on the ground and his head pounded harder and harder. Valuable distance had been gained, and the dogs could no longer be heard, when he finally stopped. Amidst a stand of young pines, he collapsed on a bed of dry needles and fell fast asleep.

How long he'd slept he had no idea, but the morning sunlight and the singing of a bluebird overhead, welcomed him back to the land of the living. Ed spied a small quail sitting on a low branch. He snatched it in his right hand, catching it before it could even spread its wings. Holding its neck in one hand, he snapped the little bones, then plucked the feathers wildly, before eating half the bird raw. The other half he put into his pocket, but before he could rise, he fell asleep again.

In his sleep, Ed found himself chased through darkness, men and dogs calling after him as he ran. Every few feet he would fall, then get up and run, only to fall again. Finally, he fell to the ground and stayed put, unable to get up again.

The dream dissolved at the distant sound of baying hounds. He opened his eyes and realized where he was. Above that of his beating heart was a second sound, one he didn't recognize at first. It sounded like a man's heavy breathing, but was loud and forced. Slowly lifting his head, he spied a large hound standing at his feet. The sagging jowls and sad brown eyes stared at him. Prison dog? Had to be. Why wasn't it barking? Tired? Hungry? Hey. He reached into his pocket, and handed the remainder of the bird to the hound. The dog snatched it up in one gulp, licked his lips, and looked back.

Ed had wasted valuable time resting, and should get moving, but wasn't sure what the dog's reaction might be. Of one thing he was sure, he didn't want the hound barking to alert the others. Reaching out with his hand, he let the dog smell him, which it did without reaction. Drawing the animal closer, he petted it, first gently, then with vigor. "Wanna come with me, pooch? Come on. I'll see if we can get something else to eat."

Ed stood and started to walk away, but the dog remained in place, as if uncertain what to do next. "Come on, boy. Come with me. You don't want to go back to those Rebels, do you?" The dog looked back the way he had come, then walked forward to his new found friend, who bent over and petted him hard. "That's a boy. You belong with me and you know it. Don't you?"

Throughout the morning, the pair followed a northerly direction, determined by the movement of the sun. Around midday, they found a cool spring where they drank. Not far away was a farm, where several women slaves were doing their wash. Hiding behind some holly bushes, Ed made sure no whites were around. Psst! He shook the bush until one of the Negroes turned and looked in his direction. The whites of her ebony eyes and her silver hair stood in sharp contrast to her dark face. Psst! he repeated, and the lady walked toward him, ringing her hands in the white apron that covered the front of her black dress. "Who dat? Who's sneakin' 'round dem bushes? You get out b'fo I get da massuh. He got a big gun. Don't like nobody sneakin' 'round his place." The other two women stopped working at their tubs, and looked in his direction. He stepped halfway out so she could see him, but remained partially hidden. "I say who dat? You ansa, or I's gonna get da massuh."

Ed lowered his head in submission, squinted, raised his trembling hands. "Please don't get your master. I'm only one man. Need to eat. Don't have money, but if you get me some food, promise I'll go away. Won't come back."

"Why, you's a Yankee! What you doin' hangin' 'round my massuh's bushes, Yankee? And why should I feed you? You's fixing' to bring a heap a trouble on me."

Ed raised his head enough to see her face, saying, "Don't want trouble. Escaped from prison. Just want to go home. All I need is a little food, so I can keep running." He raised his head all the way, felt genuine tears forming. "Please don't let them take me back. Fifty men die there every day. Water's bad, and our food isn't even cooked half the time. There's no firewood inside, and the captain won't let us go out and gather any, 'cause some of the men who did ran away. Can't go back. *Please* help me!"

The woman shrugged her narrow shoulders and rolled her round eyes. "I is gonna get in trouble dis time fo' sho', but I ain't gonna let no Yankee starve." She lifted her hand and pointed her finger at him. "You wait behind dem bushes 'til I come back."

Ed nodded, then waited nervously while the woman talked to the others. The three had a spirited discussion.

A short time later, she returned with a gunnysack and handed it to Ed. "You take dis food and get. If anybody catches you, you says you stole it. 'Cause I ain't gettin' no whoopin' fo' no run-way Yankee. Now get!"

Ed wanted to say thank you, but the faster he left the area the better everyone would feel. Disappearing behind the bushes, he turned and ran around the farm, sticking to the wooded areas. Once satisfied no one was in pursuit, he stopped and reached into the gunnysack. It contained a loaf of bread and some green beans, but the sweetest sight of all was a small ham bone, with a big hunk of meat on it. He chomped hard until his teeth and gums were sore. The hound sat with sad eyes pleading. Ed smiled and patted his head. "You want some?"

He handed over the bone and the dog's long jaws snatched and gnawed at it. Turning his attention away from the dog, Ed broke the loaf of bread and took a bite. It was soft and moistened into a ball. He swallowed it lustfully. When he'd had enough, he ate some green beans, then put the remainder of the bread into the sack, and threw it over his shoulder.

From there he continued north until nightfall. Exhausted, he sat down with his back against an old sycamore tree. Lots of wood here. Good. Couldn't see far, but no one could see him, either. Taking the remaining piece of bread, he swallowed half, and placed the rest into his pocket before falling asleep. Morning was breaking when Ed felt something nudge him, poking playfully at his ribs. He reached to pat the hound on the head, only to feel cold steel where he expected a warm furry snout. He sat up to see a woodsman standing over him.

The man had cold, dark eyes, a neatly trimmed brown beard, and a braided lock of hair that hung along one side of his face. His vest was rawhide, crossed by a bandolier of shotgun shells, and his double barreled shotgun pointed directly at Ed's belly. "Don't move too quick, boy. Done a heap a trackin' to find your sorry butt. Patience is about used up."

Ed looked over at the dog. The woodsman shook his head, smiled a smile that revealed dark brown, tobacco-stained teeth. "Don't blame him for you gettin' caught. That dog hardly ever barks. If'n he did, reckon I'd-a-caught you some time yesterday." He dropped into a crouch, shifted the gun into his right hand. His left hand moved into a vest pocket, came back with a plug of tobacco, that he bit hard and fast. After a couple bites, his cheeks swelled out like a chipmunk in the fall. "Name's Harris, Ben Harris. Cap'n Wirtz hired me to track you boys down and drag your skinny assess home." He smiled again. "Them's my dogs you been hearin' since other night. This one's mine too. Reckon he ain't good for much, 'cept maybe company. Anyway, least he finds what I send him for. And it's prob'ly easier to track six legs than two, so he does help some." Harris turned and spit on a pinecone, watched the juice drip onto the pine-needle bed. "One-a-my hands said I should put him down. Don't go for that sort of thing. Like them damned dogs too much." He slowly straightened until standing, put both hands on the shotgun again. "Reckon you'd better get up. Still got one skinny ass to track."

Ed rose to his feet, his mind in confusion. "Everyone caught?"

"Damn near. Two a you was the only ones to make it 'cross the river. Dogs chewed up a couple b'fore they got to water. Reminds me of hunting coons, 'cept coons are smarter."

Ed shook his head, felt his eyebrows rise. "Bad?"

Harris spit. "S'pose they'll be all right." He motioned with his rifle, and Ed started walking. Randy must be the only one left. The thought was so disheartening that his countenance dropped. With each step he felt every scratch, cut, and bruise from his flight through the woods. Even his knees and ankles ached. Corporal Ed Best was suddenly very old and very tired.

EIGHTEEN

"God has left all men free;
Nature has made none a slave."
—Alcidamas

Early June, 1864, Andersonville, Georgia

E D LIFTED HIS PICK AND SWUNG IT TO THE GROUND, STICKING IT HARD IN the red Georgia clay. The pick clicked loudly, stinging his hands and arms. "Damned rocks!" he shouted.

"Stop your miserable cursing," said a nearby guard. "You Yankees are a bunch of heathen, spawn of Satan, comin' down here and ruinin' our beloved South."

Ed felt his anger surge. He chipped the clay from around the rock, and rolled it out of the hole. This guard troubled the workmen daily, calling them "sloths" and "heathen," and Ed was about full up with it. But he couldn't do much without getting himself shot in the process, so he just kept working. The stone took two hands to lift, and he pulled it crotch high before starting around the hole to where he could deposit it, but the Rebel stepped in front of him, rifle across his chest, blocking the path. "Any God-fearin' man what knows the voice of his spirit wouldn't be fightin' against us. We're only doin' what God called us to do."

Ed's, biceps strained. "Bible say you should keep slaves?"

The guard waved his rifle. "Well. If you'd ever read it, you'd know about old Noah. Went to drinkin' wine and got himself drunk, he did. Ended up all bare naked too. His two sons, Shem and Japheth, they respected their daddy and covered him, but young Ham, he goes off to laughin' and the like. When old Noah woke up, cursed the boy black. Said he and his chillun'd be servant to the others forever. And that's what they is today, nigra slaves."

Ed's knees shook, hands growing weak from the weight of the rock. He looked at it intently, wanting to get by the guard to put it down, but he couldn't help asking one more question. "And Jesus, *his* death didn't change anything?"

The guard smiled wide. "Nope, couldn't change that. Nothin' could. They's still black, ain't they?" He pointed the barrel of his rifle aside, leaned forward. "'Cause they ain't got no soul. That's why we's right and you's wrong. See?" Ed tried to shake his head, but he couldn't. He needed all his strength to keep the rock from falling. "Hey!" the man shouted. "I'm talking to you, Yankee. Put that rock down and answer me!" Ed let the rock roll off his fingers, steering it with a little extra oomph directly onto the man's foot. The bone crunched. "Shhheeeiit!" the man shouted, as he dropped to the ground in agony, clutching his foot.

"Guess you fine Christian Rebels cuss a little yourselves," said Ed, and he turned and went back to his pick. Several guards came and helped the man away. Tears flowed over his darkly tanned cheeks as he screamed in anguish. A Rebel sergeant came up to Ed, rifle and bayonet pointed at his sweating chest. "What happened here?"

"Nothing," said Ed. "Guard wanted me to put the rock down, but didn't bother to get out of the way. Serves him right, I guess."

The sergeant's forehead wrinkled. "Get back to work."

"Nice work," whispered Gaffney. "Bastard had it coming."

"That's it, Yankees!" a guard hollered from the top of the hill. "Time 's up. Back to the compound."

Ed left the pick where he'd stuck it. He was too tired and hungry to pull it out anyway. Turning with the other prisoners, he fell into a haphazard column that marched back toward the prison gates, Sergeant Gaffney beside him. "You sure we should be doing this, Sarge?"

Gaffney wiped the sweat from his forehead. "Uh huh."

Ed shook his head. "Don't seem right, us making earthworks for the Rebels to defend against our own."

Gaffney's squinty eyes narrowed, brows furrowed. "I know, Best. But it's the only way to get the extra rations we need. Way they're feeding us, we won't make it. We've got to stay alive."

Ed looked at the clear sky above. "Still don't seem right."

"Isn't right that a hundred men get buried every day neither. With the well Bill Day dug, and with the extra rations we get from this work, at least we've got a chance. Those of us who can, got to work to feed our sick tent mates. Either that or they die."

Ed shrugged. The extra rations were bringing back his strength, and slowly improving his sick tent mates' health. He marched through the gate where some of the sick men waited. Hundreds coughing, standing with their heads down, or supported by a couple friends. Even if they did get to the hospital, what would they have? Medicine? No, just Raiders, and maybe a clean bed to die in. He worked his way past them to a large bulletin board, where Wirtz posted his messages. Ed's name was recorded on a list of people with packages to pick up. He walked over to a guard near the gates. "There's a package for me, Ed Best."

The guard smiled. "What did you do? Write home for a rifle?"

Ed shrugged. "Wouldn't matter if I did. Your people take whatever they want anyway. Letters say our folks send stamps or money, but there's never anything in there."

The guard laughed. "You're right, Yank. Some do. But what did you expect when your people started sending knives and shovels in the mail? Now we have to go through everything. Can't help it if some of our people steal. You have the same problems with your own. Don't you?"

The guard walked away and came back a short time later with a parcel wrapped in paper and string. Ed took it beneath his arm, and walked away. Barrel rims and tops lay neatly stacked beside a wood pile not far away. He stepped over and grabbed one before heading down the street toward his tent. That's what they called it, a street, an avenue for the men to come through to report for muster and ration distributions. But so many new prisoners had arrived by this time that it was becoming crowded with haphazard tents and sick men. Along this street, various tents and lean-tos stood, where prisoners who had extra rations, onions, or eggs to trade, called out prices to passers-by. Ed stopped near a familiar tent, where a tall, bald fellow with a fringe of curly brown hair around the sides smiled openly.

"Hey, Ephraim," said Ed, "Got any onions?"

Ephraim nodded. "Five dollars apiece."

Ed almost dropped the barrel top. "*Five dollars*!"

Ephraim pulled out two onions and placed them on the counter. "Yep. These here are expensive onions, 'cause they're practically the only ones around."

Ed shook his head and put the barrel top and package down, before reaching into his pocket for some crumpled bills. "Here, give me one."

Ephraim stared hard. "Don't let anyone see that many bills. Raiders have spies everywhere. They're not satisfied just to bilk you of your money, they'll beat and kill you for it."

Ed shook his head, ran his sweaty fingers back through his thick brown hair. "Got two full tents of friends and we stick together. Raiders won't step into a pack like that."

Ephraim shook his head, wide-eyed. "Yeah? And how many are sick? Raiders run in numbers—bigger numbers every day—and they're all healthy." He pointed toward the hospital tent outside the prison walls. "Dammed parasites oughta be. Even suck the life from our sick and dying. Watch what you say or they'll call when you least expect it."

Ed nodded. "Thanks. I'll remember that."

Ephraim leaned forward and looked down. "What's the barrel top for? Thought you had a well."

"I'm digging another. Want to sell water instead of working outside. The heat is killing me. Besides, I don't like helping the Rebels none."

"Just make sure the Raiders don't find out."

"I'm not worried about them. Like I said, my tent mates stick together."

Ephraim shook his head again. "Maybe so, but they've been getting bolder, hiring spies to tell them who's got money." He leaned over his elbows on the counter, looked over both shoulders before whispering, "Even offered to *pay* me. Told them I would, but I don't." He looked over his shoulders again, eyes darting wildly. "Can't trust anyone farther than you can fling a bull. Day before yesterday, they killed a man in broad daylight, right under the guards' noses. Rebs didn't lift one finger to stop it."

Ed narrowed his eyes. "You sure? Didn't hear about that."

Ephraim nodded. "Saw it with my own eyes."

"Thanks again," said Ed.

Ephraim pointed toward the gates. "Looks like another Bible thumper."

A well-dressed man stood on a wooden crate in the middle of the assembly area, holding his Bible in the air and shouting. At this distance, Ed couldn't hear a word, but it didn't matter. The few preachers who'd entered the prison always repeated the same message: "Repent and join the Confederacy, if you hope to escape the wrath of God."

"I don't see how they can think God is on their side," Ed said dryly.

"Funny you should say that," said Ephraim. "One of the guards said the same thing about us the other day."

Ed remembered his chaplain handing out New Testaments to him and the other men before they left Wisconsin. He'd taken great pride in that, knowing that God was on his side.

Ephraim smiled. "Look, Ed, ministers are flesh and blood. They can be as mistaken in their beliefs as anyone, no matter how loud they shout, or how high they hold their bibles. Look at that Catholic priest, I don't hold to his doctrines, so don't get me wrong, but he's the only one who comes in here regular, and he doesn't shove his words down anybody's throat. Just ministers the sacraments like he believes in them, before praying with anyone who asks him to. Always leaves as quiet as he came. Right doctrine or wrong, I'd put money on him making it past St. Peter."

Ed nodded. His eyes fell upon the front page of a yellow-faded, heavily worn newspaper setting upon the end of the counter top. It had a lithograph of an officer in uniform. "That who I think it is?"

Ephraim carefully unfolded the tattered paper. Big bold print across the top read: "October 10, 1863 Harpers Weekly Journal of Civilization: Maj. Gen. Thomas, U.S.A., Hero of Chickamauga." The general was pictured in dress uniform, from head to toe. "Know him?"

"Went to the wall for him at Chickamauga," said Ed.

Ephraim, crudely ripped the front page along the center crease, and said, "In that case, you can have this free of charge."

Ed felt the soft paper in his fingers, read so many times it was nearly worn through in places. He folded it neatly and stuck it in his pocket. "Thanks, Ephraim. I've got just the place for it."

"Gonna hang it in your tent?"

A wicked grin worked its way across Ed's face. "Nope. Gonna use it to wipe my butt. See ya later." He tightened his unopened package under his arm, and strode toward the sea of canvas spread out over the stockade grounds. At his tent, he placed the barrel top on the ground and turned his attention to the package from home. It was wrapped in brown paper and secured with string, which appeared untampered. "Boys," he shouted. "If there's any bristles on my back, pull them out. Looky here! Mama's made bread, Mama's made cake, Mama's made butter in the box. Come get a bite."

Bill Day's smiling face popped out of the tent, with Rouse, Webster, Dowd, and Gaffney close on his heels. Their faces filled with earnest anticipation as Ed showed them a piece of bread which he eagerly bit into. Though stale, it was the finest he'd tasted in prison, and it melted beneath his hungry palate. The others passed the box around until everyone had some, and by the time it came back to Ed, only one small piece remained. He lifted and shoved it into his mouth to the cheers of his friends.

When the party was over, Ed retrieved his shovel from the tent, to resume working on his well. Sergeant Dowd was inside, sewing money into the waistband of his trousers. "How much have we saved now?" said Ed.

"Nearly two hundred and a half," said Dowd.

Ed picked up the shovel. "Really? Didn't think we'd done that much digging." As he stepped out, he ran head first into a prisoner who fell off balance, landing flat on his behind. It was one of the Raiders. "Hey! What you doing here?" demanded Ed, but before he could get an answer, the little fellow jumped to his feet and ran away. Ed called to the retreating figure, "Don't come back. You hear?"

Dismissing the collision as a freak accident, he picked up his shovel and headed for the sight he had chosen for his well. His own tent was pitched on heavy clay, which made digging difficult, so he had made a deal with Sergeant Major Lowry to work in the sandy area near Lowry's tent. Ed did the digging, but Lowry's Ohio men hauled out the buckets of sand, and provided security. Upon arriving at the deep hole, he set down the barrel parts, took off his shoes, and jumped nearly ten feet to the bottom of the well. The impact of his bare feet on the cool ground felt different from the other times he had entered. The sand was wetter and thicker here, and he guessed it wouldn't be long before he struck water.

Shoveling in the narrow space was difficult, but with practice he had developed a system that worked. The Ohio men dropped a bucket on a rope whenever he asked, and pulled out the loose dirt on command. The first few shovel loads were wet and heavy, but by the time he cleared away two feet of dirt, water seeped into the dirt floor. Before long, he shoveled thick mud, striving to obtain a depth for a bucket to be easily filled with water. He was knee deep in water and mud when he quit. Calling for an extraction rope, he thrilled at the cool water covering his feet and lower legs. On level ground, he placed the barrel rim into the dirt around the opening, and set the top into place above it.

Lowry smiled at Ed's muddy feet and lower pants. "Looks like you hit it this time."

"Yeah," said Ed, brushing off the sand from his arms. "She's filling in. Just need to let her settle, then I'll taste it and see what she's got."

Lowry put his arm on Ed's shoulder. "Why don't you clean up while we wait?"

Ed frowned down at his muddy lower body. "Good idea, Sergeant Major. Be back in a bit."

At the creek, he removed his dirty pants and cleaned them. Squatting in the shallow water, he rubbed lye soap over the pant legs, then scoured them over each other. Satisfied the trousers were as clean as they would get, he turned his attention to his arms and legs. Feels good, he thought, better than sitting in the sun, but not as cool as his well water was gonna be. His gaze wandered over the water. Must've been two or three hundred bathing now.

Half of the prisoners were too sick to even bother anymore. He couldn't let himself get like that, no matter what happened. He stared at the water. It was brown from the men kicking up the bottom as they walked, but it couldn't compare with the slew down stream. A spot of blue, yellow, and red floated by, shining in the sunlight, runoff grease from the cookhouse. He now knew the Rebel's used the creek for washing their stuff. He'd seen it.

That thought spurred an even more bitter memory, the sight of a Rebel recruiter standing in their midst, calling them to join the Confederacy. "Union has forgot you," he said. "But don't die here. You don't have to starve. Could be eating regular meals and riding free. All you gotta do is take the oath." And maybe a hundred men came forward, just enough to add acrimonious insult to the God forsaken experience of living and dying here. Ed ran his fingers back through his hair. Thought, just like those dammed Rebels. Starving him and blaming it on the Union.

The late afternoon sun, together with his steaming hatred for the Rebels, had him in a rare mood when he finished bathing and walked to the shore. Finding his clothes already dry, he dressed and went to his well. At the site, he secured a little wooden bucket, tied it fast to a piece of rope, opened the barrel cover, and dropped it gently, being careful not to knock any dirt from the side walls. Once the bucket was in his hands, he took a ladle and dipped it in, then saw Lowry and his men approaching. "Just in time to taste the water from my well," Ed said, smiling. "Still some sand in it, but I'd wager it'll settle in another hour. Who wants first taste?"

Two of the men backed away, but Lowry stepped forward. "I'll take the first." He tipped the metal dipper up and swallowed every drop. A broad grin spread across his square jaw. "This is good. Fresh and cool. Not bitter like the creek water."

Ed took the dipper, extracted more water from the bucket and tasted it himself. It was indeed cool and soothing. Others eagerly took their turns. Numerous buckets were drawn from the well, and placed in the Ohioans' tents for later use. Ed was about to replace the cover, when a few men nervously approached him, buckets in hand. "Sorry, boys," he said. "This here's a private well. Have to get yours from the creek or dig your own."

A big man at the front of the group shook his head. "Heard a man tell this water's cool and clear, not bitter. Give you two bits for a bucket full." Others chimed in, agreeing to pay for the water, and Ed looked to Lowry who nodded. Word spread around the camp, and other men soon came bearing money, pocket knives, watches, or anything else of value they thought might buy them fresh water. Ed spent the afternoon hauling water up from the well, being relieved at intervals by his Ohio friends, with whom he split the take. Look at them. Just wanting good water. Maybe he should dig another. Toying with the idea, he heard someone call his name. "Who's calling Ed Best? I'm over here! You men over there, let that man through."

The crowd parted, and the troubled face of Jack Webster appeared. "Ed. Glad I found you. Raiders came to our tent and jumped Dowd. When I got there, they'd beaten him to a pulp. Tried to help him but he wasn't breathing. Raiders *killed* him!"

Ed felt his stomach fall out. He stared at Jack and asked in a wavering voice, "Where is he now?"

Webster's head tipped to one side. "Tent. Left him at the tent."

Ed pushed through the crowd. From behind him Sergeant Major Lowry shouted, "We're coming with you, Best."

They rolled like a flood around the little islands of canvas, as they made their way back to the Wisconsin tents. When they arrived, Sergeants Gaffney and Gilbert came from the other direction, their faces grim. "What's this about Dowd?" said Gaffney.

"Raiders got him," said Ed, as he threw open the flap. The tent was empty. He blinked a couple times, looking in every direction. "Did they come back and take his body?"

Webster shook his head, looking equally baffled. "When I left him he wasn't moving. Wasn't breathing. Chest wasn't moving. Had to be dead!" Looking down at the ground, Ed spotted a sparse blood trail, that he followed down the path toward Market Street. Along the way, other men who heard about Dowd's beating joined their party. Sergeant Leroy Key, a long, lanky, Illinois Cavalryman who had recently organized companies of men to resist the Raiders, joined them. His dark beady eyes leered beneath his dark, black hair. "What's this?" he scowled. "Raiders so sure of themselves, they attack in broad daylight again? Can't let this go on!"

"But we're not strong enough yet," said Lowry without slowing his pace.

"Maybe so," said Key shaking his head, "but we get weaker as we wait."

The blood trail led to a point where a sick man sat helpless at his tent. "Did you see the body of a beaten man carried by here?" asked Ed. The man squinted in the sunlight, sighed, and looked away. He, like so many others, was blind from lack of vegetables. Ed stepped around the fellow and walked over to a second sick man, seated outside another tent, and fired the same question.

"Nope," the man replied through a toothless mouth. "Saw a man stagger by though. Looked pretty near dead. Face punched in, shins raw, bleeding bad." Ed's mouth fell open.

Gaffney's eyes went wide. "He's alive."

Lowry stepped up and bent over the man. "You see where he went?" The man pointed up Market Street, and everyone hurried in that direction. By the time they reached the assembly area, Dowd was being helped out the front gate by one of the officers of the guard.

Gaffney, pointed. "There he goes."

"What will they do with him?" asked Gilbert.

"Take him to the hospital, I suppose," said Lowry.

Ed shrugged. "Lot of good that'll be. Raiders'll probably finish him there."

"Maybe he'll go to Wirtz," said Key.

Ed put his hands on his hips, turned and looked at Key. "What for?"

"Might ask for help," said Key.

"Ha!" said Gaffney. "He's probably hoping we'll *all* kill each other."

Lowry shook his head and pointed to Key. "He has a point. No one's asked Wirtz to help."

Key nodded. "I talked to Wirtz this morning while he walked the deadline. Told him what the Raiders were doing."

Gaffney glared. "Like he didn't know."

Key shook his dark-haired head and raised his hand for silence. "He can't understand how twenty thousand prisoners could allow a bunch of trouble makers to dominate them. I told him they have clubs and knives—asked if we could be supplied with the same, but he was doubtful. Seems to think it would be too dangerous for his guards. Maybe when he sees Sergeant Dowd he'll think differently."

Webster threw his hands in the air and shook his head. "Wirtz doesn't give a tinker's damn about our problems."

Key stepped in front of him, beady eyes glaring. "Then why did he provide the supplies and plans to better our sinks at the creek?"

The group argued for nearly an hour, before the gate opened and Dowd limped back through the entrance. He was accompanied by a Confederate officer and an escort of armed guards. His face was black and blue, left eye swollen shut, right eye nearly as bad. His lip was swollen and broken, blood dripping from one side. Dried blood caked over his hair. His pants were torn wide open below the knees, revealing bloody shins where the Raiders had beaten him to the ground. It was a wonder he could walk at all.

The procession marched through the assembly area, down Market Street, past the waiting crowd and on toward the creek. Ed and his friends followed, curious. After marching over the creek bridge to the other side of the compound, Dowd pointed toward the most notorious Raiders, whom the guards approached with bayonets. More than a dozen of the most hated men in camp fell into line.

"This is it!" said Key. "Wirtz is finally going to do something about those criminals."

"Aye," added Lowry. "And if Wirtz gives us the authority and some clubs, we can rid ourselves of the rest of those murderers once and for all."

NINETEEN

"What is being?"
—Thales

June, 1864, Portage Wisconsin

SWIFT RAPPED THREE QUICK KNOCKS AT THE DOORWAY TO ALAN HORDE'S office. Extensive research on the particular case in his hands had paid off, and he was zealous to share his findings, despite his misgivings about what Marianne might have said to her father about their little fight.

Horde was reading something, but his glistening bald head raised to reveal a broad smile. "Eusebius," he said in that musical bass voice of his, "come in. Had a couple of things I wanted to speak to you about."

Swift entered and sat down in front of Horde's desk. This chair, like the other two beside it, had shorter legs than normal, and a somewhat narrower seat too. It had been custom made that way, for the specific purpose of making anyone who sat across from this senior law partner, feel much shorter than the big fellow. But Swift was too excited for such things to have any effect on him at the moment. "Sir, I've been going over the widow Brotko's morgage deed, her husband's will, and important land contracts filed at the county office. These men have no case. As a matter of fact, I believe we can show they've been systematically working to defraud her of her property."

Horde nodded, his smile still broad and inviting. "Well. That was one of the things I wanted to speak to you about. You don't have to worry about the Brotko case any longer. Fortunately, the claimant's legal counsel is an old school chum. The case is in the process of settlement."

"Settlement," said Swift with a gasp. "What do you mean, settlement?"

"Just what I said. An agreement has been reached between the senior partners of the firms representing both clients. Mrs. Brotko will get a fair price for her land, minus legal expenses of course, and the land company will get what it is looking for. Everyone wins."

Swift rocked in his chair, trying to control himself. "But they have *no*

317

case! I can prove it to you. Just look at these—" Horde waved the files away, his smile unwavering. "*Not* necessary. Like I said, this thing is settled. Now you can move on to more fruitful matters."

Swift felt anger burning his throat. "How much did she get?"

"This is not *your* concern."

"But she hasn't seen these papers."

Horde shook his head, the smile slightly shrinking. "No matter. Just leave them with me."

Swift felt like a cornered animal. He was sure that if he gave the papers to Horde, Mrs. Brotko would never see them. On the other hand, the files and all documents they contained were the property of Horde's law firm. "Why are you doing this? We can *win* this case."

"Eusebius, I know your intentions are good, as is your work, but trust me in this. If we win in the lower courts, it could be appealed all the way to the state. Values she has in her property could be completely lost by dragged out court costs and attorney's fees."

"Not if we can show it was a *frivolous* lawsuit, accompanied by *blatant* acts of fraud!"

"Fraud? I think you might be stretching it a bit there."

"Mr. Horde, I have considerable evidence that the New Valley Land Company has attempted to gain possession of and alter county records. Bribes have been offered—"

Horde's smile vanished. "Forget it, Eusebius. Winning a case of fraud, or any sort of tort claim is far more difficult than a simple land case, and much too involved for what we are interested in here."

Swift felt ready to explode. He held up the files again. "Just read —"

"Not *that* again! How many times do I have to tell you? The case is closed!"

"But—"

"I mean it, Eusebius. I want no further discussion on the matter."

Blood rushed to Swift's face. His hands began to shake and sweat. He could feel saline drips pooling at the ends of his fingertips. A buzzing sound filled the back of his head. He remembered the fingering of his musket, taking careful aim, feeling the charges explode, watching his enemies fall.

"I'm really concerned about you Eusebius. From what my daughter tells, you haven't been treating her very well. One small spat and you haven't seen her for weeks. Do you realize what is at stake here—what you could lose?"

Swift felt his jaw tighten, his hands forming into fists. How easily he could kill Horde. Bare hands. Didn't matter.

"Think, Eusebius. Think about what a wonderful wife and mother Marianne could be!"

Swift leered at the man, wishing eyes could kill. "Ah, yes," he said with a course laugh. "Let us *not* forget. Me fighting on the field, Marianne commanding from the heights!"

Horde pounded his fist on the desk. "You just stepped over the line."

"I did?" said Swift with a sneer. "And what line would that be? The one where you and your family control my life—or the one where widows are sold out by old school chums?"

Horde's face flushed bright red, anger tightening every muscle. "You're through! I'll see to it that you never again practice law in this state."

Swift's stomach was churning with fire, but he smiled, somehow amused at seeing Horde finally lose control. "And how will you do that, sir? Will you take these files down to Madison and show our good magistrates how you covered up criminal actions, just to maintain good relations with an old school chum?"

"This had *nothing* to do with friendship."

"So what was it about? Money? Did they *pay* you off?"

The blood vessels in Horde's scarlet forehead looked as though they were about to explode. "Get out!" he shouted. "Get out and don't ever come back."

Swift exited the little office, barely noticing that every eye in the outside room was upon him. Snatching his cane, leather satchel, and cap from his desk, he marched out onto Wisconsin Street. It was late afternoon, and the streets were growing quiet. The rage of battle was still in him. How he wanted to kill! Wanted to curse Horde to a godless grave. But the Scriptures kept interfering. If he kept unforgiveness in his heart, he could destroy himself. The Scriptures were clear: "Forgive us our trespasses as we forgive those who have trespassed against us." Even so, he didn't care. All he cared for was seeing Horde suffer for the injustices such men as he allowed. Widows. Orphans. Such a man should suffer. There was spiritual power in forgiveness, but equal power in unforgiveness. "Whoever sins you shall forgive they are forgiven, and whoever's sins you shall retain, they are retained." Swift could hold Horde in an eternity of suffering, the power was within him. Oh, how he wanted to curse the man straight to Hell—call upon the Angel of Death to gather him— like those who had fallen at Bull Run—those innocent boys who had never defrauded anyone. All he had do so was say it, but no, the Scriptures would not allow it, declaring: "Do not return reviling for reviling or curse for curse, but blessing instead, for you were called for this purpose, that you might be a blessing." Blessing! A blessing? He didn't want to be a blessing. He wanted to kill Horde—wanted the man to suffer. Good God, what was Swift becoming? How could he hate with such unbridled passion?

He stopped, suddenly realizing he was on the edge of town, walking on the bridge that spanned the Wisconsin River. He stepped to the side, watching the water rush beneath. "Throw yourself down," something said within. "You are not worthy of bearing the name of Christ. Hater—hypocrite—murderer!" But he would lose his life, he countered. "What life?" said the voice. The only life he had, came the answer. "So what? What is worth living for in this life anyway? One simple decision and you will be with old friends again." He stepped closer to the edge.

"Swift," said a gentle, female voice.

He turned to see a soft white complexion framed by brown curls.

"Oh, hello, Bitsy."

Bitsy placed her hand on his shoulder. "Don't do it."

"Do what?"

"Don't jump."

Swift felt his face flush. "That's ridiculous."

Bitsy squeezed his deltoid. "Is it?"

Swift looked away. He suddenly felt so empty and ashamed.

"What happened?" she asked.

"I just got fired."

"There'll be other jobs."

"I know."

"So what made this so bad?"

He turned and looked her in the eyes. She seemed so compassionate, so interested. But how could he tell her? How could he tell anyone—what it is to kill—what it is to want to kill—what it is to not want to stop killing? His parents were spiritual leaders in the community, and he—he was a hypocrite—a disgrace to their Christian name.

"Come on," she said. "I'll walk you home."

Swift turned and walked with her, though he said nothing the entire way, and Bitsy seemed content just to be there. When they finally stopped in front of his house, he turned and looked her in the eye again. "How did you know?"

"I think there's a spirit on that bridge."

He laughed, then felt suddenly ashamed, as he realized she had told him something intimate, something very private. "I'm sorry," he said. "What makes you think there's a spirit there?"

Bitsy shrugged. "I don't know. Just a feeling I've had when I've been there and everything seemed topsy-turvy. Always seemed as though it could end right there."

"What could end?"

Bitsy looked away. "All the pain."

Swift was set back for a moment. What pain could such a young girl as Bitsy know? Why, she'd never even been out of Portage. Then he remembered the deaths of his infant brothers and sister, and all the torment his family had gone through. John Best had reached a reasonable age in comparison, but even his death had left some open chasm in Aunt Sarah. It was then Swift realized that pain knows no bounds. A faint spark worked its way into his heart, as he grasped hard the straw of hope. "May I see you again?"

Bitsy smiled. "I'd like that."

August, 1864, Fort Smith, Arkansas

Cavalrymen, ladies, businessman, and farmers scurried up and down the street of Fort Smith with the regularity of a city who's summer economy prospered in the midst of war. Socrates was on his way to the barber shop when someone called his name. At first he didn't recognize the man for the Union uniform and clean-shaven face. But as the man approached, Socrates recognized the short dark hair, and grass-green eyes of Jacob Mueller. "Thought you were in Texas, Jacob, helping the Union League."

The smile drained from Jacob's face. "Couldn't stay. Not with the hangings."

Socrates took off his hat. "Sorry about Gustaf."

Jacob's face went ashen. "You know?"

"My son found him. Guess someone wanted to make a statement. Wasn't any mistake he was hung on my land."

Jacob's mouth was open. "I never knew, Herr Best."

Socrates felt suddenly embarrassed. He turned his hat over, looked into it. "Thought your cousin would've told you."

"Why, I haven't spoken with him for long over a year." He tipped his head and lifted his hands, palms up. "With martial law and all the hangings—"

Socrates felt his stomach tighten. "You mean there were more?"

Jacob nodded. "First the army was sent to Kerr County. Colonel Duffy vowed to hang every man unloyal to the Confederacy. Some of my countrymen

321

tried to leave for Mexico—not to fight, but to find a place to live in peace." Jacob's voice dropped into a harsh whisper, "Fritz Tegener lead them to the border. They were camped there when Duffy's lieutenant caught them. Opened up while they slept. Those who surrendered, they hanged. Sixty five innocent men."

Socrates stopped twirling his hat and stared at Jacob. "I had no idea."

Jacob's green eyes seemed suddenly hollow. "That was just the beginning. Mobs ran wild at Gainesville, arresting everyone they thought might be a Unionist. Tried them without counsel and without authority." He looked away, pounded his fist into his hand. "The jury hung two, but that wasn't enough, so the men, they go and start hanging everyone. Hung sixteen at Pecan Creek, more in Cook County. Fifty, maybe sixty. Even hung men in Grayson County." Jacob shook his head, looked at Socrates again, but seemed to stare straight through him. "Left my family to fight those bastards."

Socrates remembered leaving his wife behind. Understood the turmoil of Jacob's heart and why he'd joined the cavalry. No words could describe it. But in Jacob's eyes where Socrates had once seen such purity of heart, only blazing tears of hatred remained.

Socrates put his hand on Jacob's shoulder. "I understand."

Jacob stood trembling, then turned and walked away.

At the end of town a wagon rode with its horses straining at such a hot gallop that it practically overturned as it cornered the main street. The dark-tanned complexions and lengthy, tobacco-stained whiskers of the sinewy scouts, Silas and Delbert, flashed in the afternoon sun as the wagon pulled up to the sidewalk. Silas stood a head shorter than Delbert, otherwise the two could have been twins. Seated behind them, on the flat bed of the wagon, were two young women, their long brown hair hanging in long curls beneath tightly bound bonnets. A crowd of inquisitive onlookers gathered, and Socrates found himself drawn along.

"What happened?" asked a silver-haired man. "Bushwhackers raid another town?"

Silas stood up to answer the question, while Delbert turned to help the ladies from the wagon.

"No, sir. No such thing at all," he said happily. "Why me and my pard here's gettin' married—that is if Colonel Cloud'll tie the knot. Yer all invited!"

Everyone congratulated the two couples. Cavalrymen joked and hooted, while the women chatted happily. Socrates worked his way back through the town with a sense of relief. With more and more reports of Anderson's and

Quantrill's murderous raids coming out of Missouri, there hadn't seemed to be much good news lately.

Ellen was working in the kitchen when he walked through the door.

"Good news, Ellen. Delbert and Silas are getting married."

"Really? I've never seen either with a woman."

"That's no surprise, since they're out scouting most of the time." He scratched his head and grinned. "Maybe they've been doing more than just scouting." Ellen threw a reproving glance, and Socrates laughed. "Anyway. They've got two pretty ladies, and they want us to come to their wedding tomorrow."

Ellen wrinkled her forehead. "How *long* have they known each other?"

"Don't know. Probably a while. Oh. By the way, there's a measles epidemic at the hospital."

Ellen shook her head. "So much illness everywhere."

Socrates caught the top of her apron and gently pulled her toward him. "As Hesiod once said: 'First came Chaos, then broad-bosomed Earth, the everlasting seat of all that is—and love.'"

She pushed him away. "Not *now*, Socrates. Can't you see I'm busy? And the baby will be awake soon."

After Friday evening dinner, Socrates and Ellen came to the chapel. Colonel Cloud looked pleasant and relaxed in his best dress-uniform. Socrates tugged gently on Ellen's sleeve and whispered, "Look how sharp Colonel Cloud dresses. Wouldn't guess he'd been a Methodist minister before the war. Seems like a military man in every way, except for that long black hair of his."

Ellen smiled. "Ministers and military officers both practice a lot of self-discipline. You'd *know* that if *you'd* finished seminary."

Socrates frowned and turned his gaze upon the two hopeful grooms. Nothing military about them.

Ellen glanced around the room. "Does everyone know these girls?"

"On the contrary," said Socrates. "I think everyone's as curious as we are."

A small organ played, and the people stood to watch two brides walking side by side down the aisle of the little church. Both were fair in complexion, with light brown hair held back with wooden combs, and could easily be sisters. Their dresses were of a light cotton fabric, the kind worn by simple country folk. The organ stopped when the girls reached the front of the church.

Colonel Cloud cleared his voice. "Uhhum. Dearly beloved, we are gathered together in the sight of God and man, to join these two couples in holy matrimony." Turning to the taller of the two scouts, he said, "Delbert, which of these two ladies is to be your bride?"

A long moment of silence fell upon the chapel as the scout blushed crimson. "I—I reckon—I don't rightly know!"

Murmuring filled the air. "Well," said Colonel Cloud. "Certainly you've *asked* one of them to marry you."

Delbert cracked a big smile. "Sure! Me and Silas asked them if they'd like to marry us, and they said they did. Brought 'em here the minute they said so. Guess we never settled who was gonna get who."

The colonel smirked. "Delbert, how long have you *known* these ladies?"

Delbert smiled wider, nodded. "Met 'em yesterday."

"Yesterday? And you're getting married today?"

"Yep!"

"Are you sure?"

Delbert nodded, smiling bigger than ever. "Yep. Ya see, we've been lookin' for wives all over the place, and these are the *only* ones who said yes. We ain't 'bout to let them get away neither." He puffed out his chest.

The colonel's dark eyes sparkled in the candlelight. "But you don't even know who you're marrying!"

"That's okay. We'll let *them* choose." He turned and looked at Silas, then smiled at the girls before turning back to Cloud. "Silas and me don't care—so long as we each gets one."

Colonel Cloud turned to the two ladies, a look of stunned embarrassment on his face. One of them turned to the other, and the two held a quick-whispered conference. When they finished, one stepped forward. "Colonel, Ruth will marry Delbert, and I'll marry Silas."

Cloud's dark eyes were bigger than ever. "And *your* name is?"

The young lady curtsied, offering a coy smile. "I'm Jane."

"All right, Jane," said Colonel Cloud, cocking his dark-haired head. "If that's how you want it, let's proceed."

The crowd cheered as the two couples kissed and walked out the back door. Everyone seemed genuinely happy. But Socrates couldn't get over the look on his commander's face. He walked Ellen home, laughing with happiness and excitement. The babysitter was paid and sent home before Socrates looked in on Gus and Willie, who were sound asleep. Satisfied, he retreated to the parlor where Ellen slipped baby Frances's white cotton gown off.

Everything Socrates and Ellen had lost was slowly coming back, and once again he felt as though his life was making headway. She lifted the baby's feet and removed the diaper revealing a red-speckled rash that flamed across her lower belly. The sharply defined pinpoints extended across her tummy and lower chest. Ellen laid her hand across baby's face, and turned to Socrates, dark-blue eyes wide and questioning.

"Looks like measles," said Socrates. "I'll get Dr. Root." Ellen's eyes widened. Socrates gave her a reassuring kiss and bolted out the door. Nearly an hour later, he returned with Dr. Root who examined the baby for a few minutes. Slowly, deliberately, he said "You're right, Socrates. It is measles."

"But—but how?" stammered Socrates.

"Who knows? Maybe you carried it here from the hospital. Maybe someone you or Ellen sat next to in church or spoke with on the street had it. The possibilities are endless. How it got here isn't important. Your baby is sick and needs your care. That's all that matters. Keep her wrapped so she doesn't get a chill, but apply cold wet towels to her forehead and feet when her fever rises. Try to get her to drink as much as you can. I'll stop in every day around lunch to check on her."

For two solid weeks Socrates and Ellen traded shifts in the night to care for the infant. By the end of the second week, the baby stopped feeding and drinking, becoming more and more listless. On the fifteenth day, Ellen sent Socrates to ask Colonel Cloud to baptize the baby. The Colonel arrived with Dr. Root late that afternoon. The physician cradled the baby gently in his arms as Colonel Cloud sprinkled water from the end of his fingers onto her forehead. A solitary teardrop rolled down Socrates' right cheek. He thought of the words of Leucippus:

"Nothing comes into existence at random, but there is an explanation for everything, and everything is brought into being by necessity."

If everything came into being by necessity, then they could only leave by necessity. That was a clear logical deduction. But life wasn't logical. The best fighters didn't always survive the battles. Captain Lines would be alive if that were true. Where could one turn for peace among such confusion? The words of Paul floated through his mind:

"And we know that all things work together for good to them that love God, to them who are the called according to His purpose."

The words held a certain comfort, but not the promise he was seeking. Ellen's face paled. The spark of life that had always glowed from her countenance suddenly vanished—like a candle flame snuffed between unseen fingers.

Socrates followed the two officers out the door. "Dr. Root, is there *any* hope?"

The physician shook his shiny head. "You *know* the answer to that. We've seen it before. Haven't we?"

Socrates nodded. "But those were grown up folks, not babies. You said that the younger you are, the quicker you bounce back from sickness."

Root took Socrates' arm, squeezed it. "I *did* say that. And I believe it is an accurate statement. But infants don't always have the ability to fight these illnesses like grown-ups. If they can overcome an infection, they often recover quickly. Unfortunately, your little girl can't fight this, and I don't think she'll last much longer. I'm sorry. I've done all that I can." The doctor lowered his head, turned, and slowly walked away.

"Socrates," said Colonel Cloud softly, "perhaps we should pray."

"Pray?" asked Socrates through swollen eyes. "Will God heal my baby girl?"

Cloud lowered his dark-tanned face, put both hands around his prayer book. His dark eyes seemed to focus inward before he raised them. "I don't know, Socrates. Maybe. Maybe not. I can't answer for God. I do believe that his ways are greater than ours. Whatever happens, we must trust in *his* goodness."

Socrates looked away, then back at the colonel. Tears flowed freely down his cheeks. "But—I've done everything I'm supposed to. Haven't I? I've taken my family to church. Taught my children to pray. Even read from the Bible every night. How could God do this to me?"

Cloud slowly shook his head, long black hair brushing his thick shoulders. "Many people in the Bible suffered loss, Socrates. Job did. David did. Even the Israelites suffered terribly under the Egyptians. Paul wrote that now we see through a glass darkly. We don't have all those answers—can't understand everything from here. Someday we will—when we stand before him."

"I don't want to understand then," said Socrates, throwing up his hands. "I need to understand now. Can't you see this is killing Ellen? What will I say to her? That we've done everything right, but God doesn't care?"

"You know better, Socrates. You've studied the Scriptures nearly as much as I. Sometimes we just don't want to accept God's decisions for us—can't see all the good we have to give thanks for. Pain does that to us. But through that pain we must find and cling to *him*. He has broken us, but he will *surely* heal us."

Colonel Cloud ran his fingers through the prayer book.

Socrates couldn't look at him.

The Colonel's finger pointed to a verse in Scripture. "We endure testing on this Earth so the trying of our faith might produce eternal endurance, and somehow that endurance makes us more perfect and complete."

Socrates hands knotted into hard fists. "My baby dies and it's supposed to make us better?"

"I can't answer for God," said Cloud, lifting one hand from his prayer book and placing it firmly on Socrates' right shoulder. "I only know we *must* believe in the goodness of God, no matter *what* we see happen around us. That's what faith *is*."

Socrates looked away. He couldn't bear the colonel's forthrightness, his steadfast faith. After all, it wasn't his child dying. But Cloud loved each man as his own. Every soldier knew that. They'd witnessed his pain every time he placed one of his boys in the ground. That's why they fought so hard for him. Knowing he cared, and that he had already buried too many. Socrates lifted and opened his hands, palms up. "I just want my baby well—for my wife's sake if not for my own. If our baby dies, and God has the power of life and death in his hands, how can anyone believe God is good?"

Cloud stared straight into Socrates, not with a vindictive or reproving look, but with that of a concerned father. "We have only one assurance," he said, letting his hands slide off the shoulder and onto Socrates' hands. "He gave us his *only* son."

October, 1864, Andersonville, Georgia

Word spread fast through the ranks of Union prisoners gathered for morning roll, and Sergeant Gaffney quickly returned to Ed, sitting outside his tent. At first, Ed refused to believe the reports, shaking his head angrily at his smiling sergeant. "I don't care what you say, Sarge. How many times've they told us we'd be exchanged in a few days? And how many soldiers've gone out that gate? Like I told you, those Rebs are twisted in the head. They just tell us that to get our hopes up, and keep us from trying to escape. It's not gonna work. I'm not falling for it this time."

"Look!" said Gaffney with a hard grimace. "I don't know how to get through that thick skull of yours, but maybe if I talk real slow, you'll understand. They haven't counted us out into divisions since we got here, but they are *now*, and if you're not ready when they call your name, someone else will take your place. If that happens, you'll die here. You want *that* to happen?"

Ed stared at the blurred image before him. He knew it was Sergeant Gaffney but couldn't get his eyes focused. With the fall of Atlanta, food had become even scarcer than before, leaving no fruits or fresh vegetables to fight off the scurvy, and this deprivation clouded his thoughts, swelled his joints, almost blinded him. Black flies swarmed about his head. "Where we going?"

"Home," said Gaffney.

Ed looked around in a daze. "Can't go. Everybody's—too sick." Why was Gaffney getting his hopes up? Dowd was outside the walls since he fingered those Raiders. Wasn't right in the head either. Burk was sick. Webster and Hull. Day could hardly walk. Neither could he. He focused on a wide weeping sore in his arm. "Thought we would once, Sarge, but Atlanta fell. Sherman never came."

"I know," said Gaffney. "Sent Stoneman's cavalry though."

Ed rolled his eyes, "Ha! In here with us now."

Gaffney bent forward, gripped Ed's shirt and shook him. "Listen to me, Best."

Feeling as if his brains were coming out his ears, Ed raised a hand in surrender. "I hear ya. But even if I believed you, my legs couldn't carry me."

Gaffney leaned up close, said, "I'll help you."

Ed looked over his shoulder at the tent. "Who's gonna help *them*?"

"Listen, Corporal," hissed Gaffney. "I don't care if I have to carry you out to formation myself, but you're getting down there for roll, and so is everyone else. Got that, Corporal?"

Ed pictured his mother pouring apple preserves over a freshly baked pie crust. His stomach rumbled. "You sure it's for real?"

"It's real all right, and I'm not leaving you behind. Already lost too many. Now get your sorry two stripes up, and help me get Webster out of the tent."

Must, Ed told himself. Get up. Swollen knees and ankles screamed in pain, but he refused to acknowledge them, willing himself up to a crouch. Every joint ached as muscles stretched like steel wire. Everything within him said stop, but he forced himself to stand and follow Gaffney to the next tent. Jack Webster was there, weak and listless.

Jack could barely shake his head. "I'm too weak."

Gaffney bent over and looked in his face. "Nope. Not leaving anyone."

A head appeared at the tent entrance. It was Ole Gilbert. "What's going on?"

Gaffney turned his head. "Jack's too weak to go on the train."

"Can we carry him?" asked Ole.

Gaffney shrugged. "Let's get him to his feet and see."

The three men pulled Jack to his feet. His arms were strong, stronger than Ed's, but his feet wouldn't flatten out on the ground. The two sergeants held him there, his feet bowing so much that he resembled a ballerina. He had barely straightened his back, when Ed fell to the ground.

"Oh. Great," said Gaffney. "Grab those sticks over there, and give one to Webster and one to Best."

Ole propped one stick under Jack, then pulled Ed up, and stuck one under him. The four meandered at a snail's pace through the sea of tents, and out to the assembly area. Ed felt his muscles gradually loosening, but every movement brought more pain. At the assembly, roll was called and the men counted off. After that, the sergeants went to a briefing. "Is it true, Sarge?" asked Ed. "Is it really true? We goin' home?"

Gaffney smiled and whispered, "Sergeant of the guard says we're to form ten divisions and be ready to go. Ours will be the second division to board the trains, so if anyone is gonna get out of here, it's us. I'm not sure where we're going, but *any* place would be better than *this*."

October 20th, 1864, Fort Smith, Arkansas

Socrates stood hunched over a kitchen basin, splashing water onto his face. Exhausted and in desperate need of rest, he couldn't allow himself to sleep. The last three months had sapped every ounce of emotional and physical strength he possessed. After the baby died, the love of life completely left Ellen. She came down with the measles herself, started to recover, then developed a bad case of dysentery, which made her weaker and weaker every day.

Doctor Root stepped into the kitchen beside Socrates. "She's resting."

Socrates peered through a hollow cloud. "Any improvement?"

The doctor shook his head. "She has the bloody flux now."

"Is there any hope at all—anything we can do?"

"I'm sorry. She hasn't long. Best you can do is make her comfortable. I'd stay longer, but I must get back to the hospital."

Socrates dipped his head. No one could make it through this without a will to live. Ellen, Ellen, Ellen, Oh, how he loved her. But all hope had fled. What would he tell the boys?

He shook his limbs, pumping blood in an effort to drive out the fatigue.

As he did, he caught his image in the mirror. An unrecognizable person stared back at him. The face was drawn with thick, dark circles beneath sad, gray eyes that sunk deep into his skull. The hair was disheveled and unkempt, while the gray-streaked beard was rough and uneven. Who are you? he wondered, as he turned to walk into the other room. Words of his namesake pressed upon his mind:

"So long as we keep to the body and our soul is contaminated with this imperfection, there is no chance of our ever attaining satisfactorily to our object, which we assert to be truth . . . ."

What comfort could such words bring? Certainly they wouldn't stop what was about to happen here. They provided no salve for this horrible pain. Plato would say that death is bliss, but that from it also must come new life. Was that the eternal life Christ spoke of? The words of Isaiah came to mind:

"He was a man of sorrows and acquainted with grief."

Socrates was angry with God for a time, but like Ellen, the fight had gone out of him. He desperately needed something, someone more powerful to hold on to. He needed God, whether he could understand him or not. Socrates thought about this verse in light of the image he'd seen in the mirror, stopped in front of the door and whispered, "Bible says you were tempted, Jesus, that you suffered like us. Give me strength."

A sense of peace swept over him. He stepped into the room where his wife sat in her bed, propped up by several pillows. He remembered her soft, slender body as he'd first seen it on their wedding night—the milk-white, firm, round breasts—long dark hair draped over naked shoulders—how her shapely hips had excited him. The woman now before him was an emaciated mask of death. Her skin was devoid of all natural color, the once pink cheeks pale gray. Her eyes were hollow, cheek and jaw bones carved deep, and far too prominent. Long dark hair spread out over the shoulders of her white cotton nightgown. He had combed it for her earlier, fearing this might be her last day. Stepping to her side, he lifted her hands and held them.

"Socrates," she began in a soft, raspy voice, "been thinking—boys will need a mother when I'm gone." She paused and breathed deep.

Socrates desperately wanted to interrupt. But he said nothing.

"Lord will bring you another wife," said Ellen, but her words were so soft, he barely heard them. He bent closer. "You must love her as completely as you've loved me. I want an oak casket, not pine, and put me in my best Sunday dress—one with ruffles." She stopped for a moment, fighting to get the air she needed. "Lay Ben next to me." Again she stopped, gasping. "Take care of our boys—brought up right—I—love you." A rush of air came out of her and she was silent.

Socrates wrapped his arms around her and cried. At first he wept for the loss of the only woman he had ever loved, then he cried for his boys who had lost their mother. Finally he cried for the three baby girls they had buried on Southern soil. Why would God take away this frail lady, this fragile frame of gentle kindness? Grief swallowed him, revealing all he'd lost since leaving Wisconsin. The entire country was caught up in some giant whirlpool that consumed everything one dared to love.

TWENTY

What am I? —Socrates

November, 1864, Portage, Wisconsin

SWIFT SAT ON THE DAVENPORT BESIDE BITSY HYDE, HER PRESENCE EMANATING a certain blissful aura. The house was a modest two-bedroom cottage where the Hydes had raised six children, Bitsy being the youngest. Her mother sat on an old rocker at the other end of the room, knitting a sweater from black and blue yarn. She acted as if no one was around, but her presence was always a distraction. The three had enjoyed a pleasant lunch, Bitsy's mother doing most of the talking, chatting about her church group, the war, and other small talk.

"How is your practice going?" asked Bitsy.

Swift's stared into her soft complexion and pretty round face. She possessed neither the elegance of Marianne, nor the pretentiousness, and he had a hard time identifying her with the skinny little girl that used to follow him around school. "You mean the *Divine* Calling of justice?"

"Why do you do that?"

"What?"

Bitsy put her hand upon her hip. "Put your profession down."

"Because it seems that those who should know better do the least to improve this world."

"Maybe so, but you don't have to be so negative about it. Just makes you a sour puss."

"And what *should* I say, Miss Hyde?"

Bitsy shook her head. "Not what you *say*, but what you *think*. Whatsoever things are *good*, whatsoever things are *lovely*, whatsoever things—"

Swift threw his hands out at his side. "Of good report, yeah, yeah, I know all that."

Her eyes sparkled when she was angry, and right now they were a spectacular green. "Knowing it and practicing it are two different things, Swift Best."

Why was it he liked to see her so angry? Was it the innocent sincerity of her faith? He'd once believed like that. His gaze turned toward the window.

Bitsy placed a large brown album before him and opened it. "Wisconsin River Times," was printed in bold black ink across the top of a newspaper clipping dated May 4th, 1861.

Swift blushed. "Why'd you make this?"

Bitsy offered a thin-lipped smile. "To think of you while you were away. Always knew you'd come back, but I couldn't stop praying—even when you were in prison."

Swift flipped the pages. There were articles from camp at Washington, Centerville, Germantown, Bull Run, even a copy of his letter home from prison. He'd never expected it to be published in the paper. "Why?"

"Why what?"

"Why'd you keep these after I was home?"

Bitsy's soft green eyes narrowed, and her mouth pulled up into a frown. "Because, Swift Best, I've loved you since I was thirteen. Though you didn't even known I was alive."

A cold wind swept through him. "I'm sorry, I never realized."

Bitsy glanced toward her mother and put her hand on Swift's. "I knew God would bring you back. Always knew. Only hard part was you never seemed to care."

Swift blushed again. He busied himself with the album, spotted Mrs. Hyde glancing toward him from the corner of her eye. He flipped more pages. There were articles about the Tenth Infantry at Perryville, Stones River, and Chickamauga. Everywhere the Bests had fought. On the last page he found something he hadn't seen before.

"Florence, SC, Oct. 8th, 1864. Secretary of Wisconsin State Sanitary Commission. Sir: There are six members of the Tenth Wisconsin Infantry here together, who were captured at the Battle of Chickamauga. We are destitute of clothing, and as defenders of our country, we apply to you for aid, hoping you will be firm in relieving, in a measure, our necessities. Please send us a box containing blankets, undergarments, shirts and socks in particular, and we stand very much in need of shoes; but I don't know as they are in your line of business.

We would also like stationery, combs, knives, forks, tin spoons, tin cups, plates and a small sized camp kettle, as our rations are issued to us raw; also thread and needles. We all have the scurvy more or less and I think dried fruit would help us very much by the acid it contains—you cannot send us medicine as that is contraband. We would like some reading matter. If there is anything more that you can send, it will be very acceptable.

We should not apply to you were we not compelled, and did we not know that you are the destitute soldiers' friend. You will please receive this in the same spirit in which it is sent, and answer accordingly, and you will have the satisfaction of feeling that you have done something to relieve the wants of those who went out at the commencement of the war to defend the rights of our country. Direct to Wm. W. Day and Joseph Eaton, prisoners of war, Florence, SC, via Flag of Truce, Hilton Head. Yours and etc. Wm. W. Day. P.S. I've forgotten to mention soap—a very essential article."

Swift recognized the name of Bill Day as one of cousin Ed's tent mates. The letter induced a flood of memories, lice, bug soup, armed guards, scurvy, painful hip bones on hardwood floors, the hospital with bloody limbs stacked into neat piles. He felt suddenly nauseated and leaned forward as the room spun.

Bitsy's gentle fingers stroked his spine. "You all right?"

Swift took a deep breath and straightened up. "I'm fine."

"Sure? You look awfully pale. Want some water?"

Swift shook his head. "No thanks. Think it's time to get back to work."

He arose and nodded toward Bitsy's mother. "Thanks Mrs. Hyde. Lunch was great."

She flashed a quick smile. "You're welcome, Swift, and please come again. You're always welcome here."

Bitsy walked him to the door, and her presence was suddenly overwhelming, almost imposing. He rolled his fingers and pushed his jaw forward. "Thank you, Bitsy. Not just for lunch, for sharing."

Bitsy opened his hand and placed hers in it, fingers looking so diminutive and childlike. "You can talk to *me*, Swift."

Swift looked away. "I know."

Her emerald eyes flashed. "No, you don't. I mean it. You can talk to me anytime, about anything."

Swift nodded but felt she was expecting something more. He turned, walked out the door, and down the street, mind filled with pictures of sick and starving men. He wished he hadn't eaten so much lunch, but the fresh air soon revived him. Upon reaching the downtown area, he stepped off the sidewalk and started across the street where Tom Ramsey strode in Union blues and infantry cap from the direction of the railroad station. "Hey! Tom, didn't know you were coming home."

"Hello," Tom said with a wave. "Didn't know myself until I got a weekend pass this morning. Thought it would be a good idea to surprise my wife." He looked around, smiling. "Good old Portage. Always growing. Never quite the same."

Swift laughed. "You've *only* been gone a month."

"I know. Seems longer though." He turned and looked down the street. "I suppose I should go home and see Ma and Pa, but you're house is just down the street. Maybe I'll go see Aunt Emily first."

"She'd like that," said Swift, pulling out his pocket watch. "I've got a few minutes before I have to be back at court. I'll walk with you.

They turned toward Doc's and quickly fell into step. Just a few weeks of training, and Tom was tramping in time. The sounds of marching music and cadence songs rolled into Swift's brain. Out of nowhere came the thunder of cannons, that awful hail of bullets, the sights of men strewn around a field like so much litter.

"You all right?" asked Tom.

Swift pulled out a handkerchief and wiped the sweat from his brow. "Yeah."

"Sure? Look white as a sheet."

"Said so, didn't I?"

Tom nodded, then shrugged.

They crossed the street, and spotted Curge riding toward them on a brown gelding. He lead two pack mules with five antlered bucks stretched over their backs. A wide grin stretched across his skinny, full-bearded face. "Well, I'll be. Tom, what you doing back so soon? Thought you'd be chasing Lee back to Richmond by now."

Tom beamed as he stared at the bucks. "I will. Soon as my unit heads out. Looks like your usual luck."

Curge glanced over his shoulder at the pack mules. "When I sell these, we'll be set for the winter."

Few in the county could match Curge's skill in hunting. He could keep on a trail for days, weeks if necessary; and his aim was sure. His small build, combined with the illness that had thinned his frame to the bone, may have given the impression he was frail and weak. But to those who knew him, he was a hearty and determined hunter, one who understood the ways of the wilderness.

"Anything happen while I was gone?" asked Tom. "Or you been off in the woods so much you lost all touch with civilization?"

"Now that you mention it," said Curge with a sly grin, "I hear there's a lonely lady out near Big Spring. Let me see now. Edna? Nah, that's not it. Etta? Not that either. Emma? Emma Ramsey—that's her name."

"Heard about her," said Swift with a sly grin. "The one all the boys been stopping over to see."

"Heard about her myself," Tom replied with a laugh. "Husband went off and left her for the army. That's why I'm here—looking for a lonely woman to pass some time with. One that won't throw me out when her mood changes."

Swift frowned at Curge and shrugged.

"Hey!" said Curge. "You hear Hub and Ellen had a baby girl? Named her Minnie. Maybe you and that lonely lady you're gonna see can stop by and see her."

A devilish grin crept across Tom's face. "What makes you think I'm going anywhere with my lady? After living in barracks with a bunch of men for a month, I might just latch the door and close the curtains. Don't be surprised if I don't come out 'til I'm A-W-O-L."

Curge smiled. "Feel the same way when I come home from hunting, and look how many years Angie and I've been married."

Thomas looked at Curge, then at Swift. "Heard anything from Ed? Any prisoner exchange?"

Curge grew sullen and turned in his saddle to look around. Then he leaned toward Tom and spoke in a low tone. "Ed writes Ma often enough. Says there's always talk of exchange; but listen, Swift, Tom, and don't go blabbing this to your ladies, he doesn't believe a word of it. Ed's written me things he doesn't want Ma to know—like how bad it really is—tens of thousands of prisoners in tents, sickness and disease everywhere. Says the prisoners hate the government—even said a hundred joined the Rebs rather than rotting in that stinking place. Others have become thieves and murderers. Worst of them the prisoners hanged."

"Just read a letter from the Milwaukee Journal," Swift said slowly, still trying to comprehend what Curge had just reported. "Was written from Florence, South Carolina, by Bill Day and Joe Eaton. If Ed is still with *them*, he can't be far from release one way or another. Charleston Harbor is under a full blockade and naval bombardment, and Sherman is at the sea in Georgia, ready to march north through the Carolinas."

Tom flashed a quick smile. "Guess I better get back on time after all, if I'm gonna get any chance to help win this war."

January 17th, 1865, Fort Smith, Arkansas

Socrates was content to work in the hospital ward well after most of the regiment left for Little Rock. And all that time he was fully aware that once he received orders to follow, he would have to send his boys home to Wisconsin. With most of the regiment gone, and a large portion of it mustering out, he felt an overwhelming sense of loneliness. The needs of his two boys and the sick men he tended gave him something to focus on. He threw himself into his work, losing his pain in helping those worse off than himself. He was carrying a wicker basket of used bandages to burn when he saw Colonel Bassett. "Anything I can do for you, sir?"

Bassett nodded. "Colonel Cloud says to gather everyone on detached service, and have them prepare to leave this afternoon for Clarksville. We'll be traveling by river boat, and I'll need every man present on the docks in three hours."

Socrates hadn't expected such short notice. The boys would have to go with him to Little Rock before he could send them home. "Are we to bring our belongings, sir?"

Bassett nodded. "Rifles, blankets, everything. Pass the word. No one shows up without their basic issue. I'm not sure when we'll return to Fort Smith, if at all."

"Yes, sir. I'll get to it right away." Socrates informed Dr. Root and the hospital personnel of the new order, then went to the adjutant's office. He took an early lunch with his sons before gathering their belongings and walking to the docks, where he found Colonel Bassett with about twenty men. A short time later, Captain Gunther showed up with the remainder of Company H. That brought them up to nearly fifty soldiers and officers. The steamboat *Annie Jacobs* awaited them, its two tall smoke stacks spitting black plumes as it prepared to move out. Gus's and Willie's faces glowed with excitement.

With everyone accounted for, Bassett ordered the men up the gangplanks, where they joined two hundred other passengers. Socrates took his boys to the main cabin, and stored his belongings under the watchful eye of an appointed guard. Satisfied, he took the boys out on deck. Willie rode on his shoulders and Gus stood under his right arm as they watched the Arkansas River roll by, its current plowing millions of gallons of water past them every minute. The leafless trees on the opposite bank looked gray and dead next to the vibrant waters. Farther down the docks, other soldiers climbed the gangplanks of two other boats. At least two hundred blacks gathered on one deck.

"Look, Pa," said Willie. "What's them folk about?"

"Those are Negro soldiers and their families, Willie. You know, the people we're fighting to free."

"Soldiers?"

"Why not? It's their fight too."

"Different looking soldiers."

"Yeah. They do look different from us. But they feel joy and pain, just like you and me."

"They slaves once?"

"Probably."

Gus turned bright blue eyes toward his father. "Why?"

"Wrong thinking, Gus. The great Socrates once said, 'God has left all men free. Nature has made none a slave.'"

"Some are soldiers?"

He nodded. "Must be at least a hundred of those. I suppose they've more reason to fight than any of us."

"That's a big ship," said Gus.

"Quite a bit bigger than ours," said Socrates.

In a few minutes the shrill whistle of the *Annie Jacobs* sounded, followed by blasts from the other two vessels. The big paddle wheels rolled over and over, pushing their boat out into the river, the others following in line. His boys wiggled with enthusiasm. The cool January wind brought a hard chill, and he led the boys inside where he was confronted by the familiar faces of Friendly Reuben and Vince Osborne.

After Ellen's death, Socrates had become so sick and depressed that he couldn't take proper care of his boys. Then the church people had begun stopping in, making sure there was always something good and warm to eat. They were like kinfolk, holding him and his boys up, when there was no strength to go on. Colonel Cloud eventually lured him back into church, and it was there that Socrates made a decision. There hadn't been a clap of thunder or anything like that. He just whispered under his breath, "Lord, I don't know what I'm living for anymore. Take my life, if you will, and use it." Then he'd met with Colonel Cloud after church, who'd led him in a prayer of dedication, which seemed to seal the bond.

After that, he started looking at Vince, Friendly, and all those church people in a different light. When Ellen was alive, he had always thought of them as thinking they were holier or better than he, despite his education.

But now he saw something different. He saw women who'd lost their husbands, and men far away from their wives and families. These folks were neither prideful nor arrogant, but were bruised and bleeding from a war that had broken their hearts. They had come together to comfort, encourage, and help one another through their pain. They were simply a family. The family of God. But why couldn't he see that until Ellen was gone? The thought shamed him.

"What you think of her, Socrates?" asked Friendly, as he spread his arms wide and smiled. "Isn't she grand?"

Osborne grinned agreeably.

Socrates nodded. "Always a wonder to me. Looks like you're as excited as my boys."

Friendly slapped his rear and laughed. "Beats pounding your thighs into saddle sores any day."

Socrates surveyed the golden wood interior of the cabin. "Haven't ridden a vessel like this for a long time, not since Ellen and I came to Texas. Never would've guessed I'd be going home without her. We were young then—eager to start a school and build a new home." He smelled her fragrance like sweet lilacs, felt her leaning against his chest, remembered forgotten conversations full of broken dreams. Turning toward his boys, he saw their drawn cheeks, puppy dog eyes, brows turned inward.

Socrates turned away and stared across the river. "When we get to Little Rock, I'm sending the boys home. They'll be safe there until my enlistment is up. I don't think I *ever* want to see Texas again."

"Don't blame you," said Osborne. "You darn near lost everything."

"I'm not sure what I thought I'd find. Wasn't anything there but the gold of Tolosa."

Friendly smiled. "At least you've got your boys."

Osborne nodded. "I hear we'll be mustered for pay at Clarksville. It'll be good to have money again. I suppose you'll be sending most of yours to care for the boys."

Socrates looked away. How hollow his life would seem without them. "If we muster before they leave, I'll send it with them. I don't need much to get by." He turned and looked at Friendly. "My brothers are having a hard time keeping up. With teaching and farming, there's hardly enough hands to work all the land now. Guess when the younger ones joined the army, they never thought Pa would die like he did. Always had good health."

He put Willie down on the deck and continued talking, while the boat stopped to take on wood. Socrates felt himself relaxing for the first time in months. He talked freely about Wisconsin, Ohio, his folks, their lives, practically anything that came to mind. And it felt good, so good that he didn't want to stop. And all the while, Vince nodded and stared intensely, while Friendly just stood like a dish rag, soaking it all in and affirming Socrates with that easy smile of his.

They finished refueling and headed down river again. The riverbank was suddenly dwarfed by tall steeples, roofs, and gables. "Look," Socrates said.

"That there's Roseville," said Friendly. "About as nice a place as I've ever been."

Vince flexed his neck and stood on tiptoes. "How come there's nobody walking around."

"Yeah," said Friendly wrinkling his brow. "Should be hopping with business this time of day."

"Maybe Quantrill's been through," said Socrates.

"Nope," said Vince. "You'd see smoke for sure. He'd have Johnson taking scalps and burning down their houses."

Socrates shivered. Anderson was said to have destroyed Centuria while butchering an entire Missouri militia company the previous fall. The guerillas now had the reputation of being untouchable. "Wouldn't want to cross paths with the likes of *those* bushwhackers."

"Me, neither," said Vince. "But I wouldn't mind meeting them on an open field with the Second. We'd show them the difference between warring against women, children and old men, and warring against real men. God knows I'd like the chance."

Socrates tipped his hat. "I'm content with hospital work."

Friendly frowned. "Bushwhackers are bad for sure. But what the Union did in Georgia doesn't sound much better."

"Whose side you on?" Vince asked.

Friendly lifted his arm and pointed. "Look! What happened *there?*"

Toward shore, a steamboat had run aground, a thick cloud of smoke drifting away from it. "I don't know," said Vince.

"Me, neither," added Socrates. Then he spotted yellow flames beneath the smoke. "Look! She's on fire." As the *Annie Jacobs* came closer, Socrates watched the soldiers on the deck of the other ship fighting the fire. "How do you suppose that started?"

A number of men climbed off the boat, ran up the bank, and waved frantically. It looked as though they were shouting, but the wind swallowed their words. "What do you suppose they're saying?" asked Vince.

Reuben shook his head. "Maybe they want us to pick 'em up."

"Can't do that without running aground," said Socrates. Suddenly the *Annie Jacobs* surged forward, its engines churning. The main channel at this point in the river changed from the north to the south bank, directly into which the boat was being steered. The boom of an artillery piece shattered the cold January air, followed a moment later by a huge fountain of water that rose up from the river alongside the boat before splashing down upon Socrates and his shipmates. He grabbed his boys and pulled them close, shielding them with his body. Gus and Willie turned huge round eyes toward him, and he hugged them to his breast, craning his neck to see. Above the river banks sat an entire artillery battery, and just below them, gray-shirted infantrymen ran to form firing lines. The river was driving the boat directly into their line of fire. "Looks like you two won't have to worry about Quantrill," said Friendly wincing. "We've got the whole Rebel army."

Socrates chewed his lower lip and tightened his hold on Willie. He prayed in a soft whisper, "Lord, take me if you will, but these boys never hurt anyone." The boat veered, pressing him against Gus and Willie—pinning them hard against the wall. They trembled. Men shifted toward the other side of the boat, striving to keep their balance. The vessel fought across the current, its rudder bending the river hard. Water bubbled and splashed against the side of the boat. Was it possible? Could this be the end after everything they'd endured?

Another cannon fired. A shell ripped into the upper cabin. More shells came in rapid succession and new fountains appeared everywhere, drenching the helpless soldiers who could do nothing as they watched the ship close to within a quarter mile of their enemies. Socrates prayed aloud. Death had stalked him for years, consuming everything he had ever loved, and now it stood like a dark shadow in a child's room, a specter in the night awaiting its final lunge.

Water streamed against the bow, resisting the engine's drive, disputing its power to turn. A cannon shell struck the side of the boat, ripping through its wooden walls as though it were made of twigs. Then the boat shifted, its bow finally past the turning point. A series of shells slammed the outside walls. Others landed in the water nearby, washing more water over the deck. A shell exploded somewhere behind, showering Socrates' hair with splinters. The boat stopped dead, propelling men into walls and over rails. Hard iron strained, squealing as the engine's gears reversed against heavy resistance. It sounded as though the engine would blow and kill them all.

A shell crashed into the cabin—ripping in one side and out the other—

splashing into the river before exploding. Another shell ripped through the engine room. But the ship was responding, pulling them out of the current. Two more shells struck the engine room. Socrates held his breath, convinced his boat was powerless against the current, but the engines kept pumping. Maybe twenty shells had struck, most tearing through the vessel without exploding. But at least five had erupted, rocking every fiber of the boat.

Free of the current, the steamboat plunged headlong toward the north shore. Socrates could no longer see the Rebels, but their shells threw more and more water all around him. Two more exploded on board, shaking the wounded vessel like a patient in death rales. Willie cried and Socrates tried to comfort him, but felt like crying too. Then the *Annie Jacobs* plowed straight into the sandy shoreline, spilling men all over the deck. One of the crew threw a cable ashore. Vince Osborne jumped into the shallow water after it. He mounted the riverbank and secured the line to a tree, while other men scrambled to evacuate the floating target.

Vince turned and waved to his friends. His grin of victory turned to a grimace of pain when a musket ball smashed his thigh. He winced and gripped the leg as he hit the ground, but was soon dragged to cover. Bullets popped and zinged all over the river bluff. Reuben jumped over the side and hollered up to Socrates, who handed down his boys one at a time before following them. One man turned his ankle as he landed, and Socrates helped him limp to shore. They walked slowly, without fear, the boat providing ample cover from the rifle fire. The cannons stopped firing altogether, as someone shouted, "Go back! Didn't you see what happened to us? Go back!"

The third boat ran under a full head of steam straight down the path the *Annie Jacobs* had just abandoned. The faces of the Negro soldiers on board shined black as night in the midday sun, heads bent, as if questioning. Cannons boomed on the distant bluff where white puffs of smoke appeared. The third boat responded quickly, turning faster than the *Annie Jacobs*, but the artillerymen fired without mercy. A bomb exploded in the center of her deck as the ship sprinted past Socrates and his friends. It surged another fifty yards and plowed into a sandbar up river. Three Negroes jumped off and ran to secure a cable thrown from her deck. Others handed down the injured.

Socrates looked at his boys. "Stay here. And don't step out where you'll make a target for those rifles. Understand?" The boys nodded. He walked over to the colonel who was talking to some officers. Socrates waited rather than interrupt.

Colonel Bassett threw a questioning glance.

"Any wounded I can help with, sir?"

"Only one injury here, Vince Osborne."

"I saw him get it, sir."

Bassett nodded. "Could lose a leg." Socrates closed his eyelids tight, felt Bassett's hand on his shoulder. "Why don't you go and see if you can help the Negro troops. Looks like that boat took some bad hits."

Socrates turned and jogged down the beach to where the last ship had run aground. Its wounded passengers were being laid on the sand. He stopped, leaned over the first man he came upon, and placed his fingers on the jugular. Nothing. He went to another and another, each the same as the first. The fourth man had a big piece of shrapnel protruding from a hole in his right shoulder. Bone was showing. "I'm not gonna lose it, am I, Doc?"

"I don't think so," said Socrates, "but I'm not a doctor, just a steward. If we can get this piece of metal out and clean the wound, you'll have a chance." Socrates tore off his shirt and made a compress to stop the bleeding. Pressing hard, he saw red blood on black skin. Why did the blood look so red on a black man? And why were they so hated? Bled the same as us. Hurt the same as us. Was it just easier to hate someone different?

"Here, I'll take that," said a voice from behind. Turning, Socrates saw Dr. Root lean forward to look at the man's wounds. "I'll need some cleaner bandages and some boiled water." Before Socrates could answer, one of the Negroes behind Dr. Root said, "I'll get that. You jus' he'p my friend."

Socrates nodded and turned to check on the others. Five dead and a number wounded. Strange. His ship was fired on over forty times with a half dozen explosions on board, and only suffered one injury. This ship was struck once, yet suffered so much more.

TWENTY-ONE

"The unexamined life is not worth living."

—Socrates

January 18th, 1865, Portage, Wisconsin

THE FROZEN STREETS OF PORTAGE MADE WALKING DIFFICULT FOR SWIFT, but he was determined to make it to Bitsy's without falling. Twenty yards from her front door, he watched her hurry down the steps. She wore a long brown coat, muff, and mittens, and was on the last step when she slipped and slid down the walk on her rear. Snow piled high on each side of the walk, kept her straight for ten feet before she stopped. Swift couldn't help laughing.

"Hey!" she said. "Wouldn't be laughing if *you'd* fallen."

He reached down to pull her up, but his cane slipped on the ice and he fell on top of her.

"Ah! Your squashing me."

"Sorry," he said as he pushed himself up. He was almost straight when he slipped and fell flat on his back. Now she was standing over him and laughing harder than he had. Swift frowned. "You going to help me?"

"And fall again? Not a chance."

He slowly pulled himself erect and took her arm before they started down the path again. The snow was getting old and had many yellow stains and brown droppings in it. He wished it would snow again.

Bitsy squeezed his arm. "Still upset about your father?"

Swift's stomach tightened. "Don't want to talk about it."

She squeezed his arm again. "Can't keep blaming yourself for everything. And you *need* to talk about it."

"Says who?"

"Says *me.*"

He shrugged. "Just wish he hadn't joined the Army. He's nearly sixty."

344

Bitsy squeezed his arm again. "He's a *good* doctor. Can *help* a lot of our boys."

Swift's stomach rolled into a knot. "Thinks he'll find what I lost."

Bitsy stopped and turned, soft green eyes glowing amidst the afternoon sun and snow shine. "Maybe he *will*."

"Some things you can't change."

"Well at least *he's* trying. Sometimes I don't think *you* are."

Swift shrugged, and walked on. They passed the iron-gated Horde mansion where Swift stopped and surveyed the beautiful home. "You know, I once read where Antisthenes said the Athenians should vote that asses are horses."

Bitsy's shoulders hunched up. "*That's* what I mean. You can't keep blaming yourself for everything this country does wrong, can't keep blaming *them* either. If it bothers you so much, *change* it."

Anger flashed in him as he turned to her. "In the courts? *That's* a joke."

She thrust her mittened-hands out. "So? Find some other way to change it, but stop making everybody else's life miserable. If I didn't love you, I don't think I could stand to be with you. What happened to the gentlemen you were, the one who always helped anyone in need. Was that really you, or just something you made up to fool everybody?"

Swift felt a burning in the back of his scalp. He concentrated on walking without falling, but her words buzzed in his brain as they approached the depot. The inside walls were coated with a rich pine stained golden-brown. Aunt Sarah stood beside Hub and flashed a warm smile. "So glad you both could come. Ed should be here soon."

The Gaffneys of Lewiston huddled together on the far side of the room. In the middle of the scuffed wood floor stood a black, potbellied stove that rumbled a steady fire. The families didn't speak to each other, reminding Swift of his homecoming, the band, the fall, the embarrassment. Late afternoon shadows stretched across the tracks, and the station master came out of his office and lit several kerosene lamps mounted along the walls. The last train of the day appeared in the distance, its lamp barely glowing over the black iron cow catcher. It chugged slowly into the station, venting streams of steam as it came to a halt. Various individuals climbed off the train, wrapped in warm winter jackets. In the midst of those ten or twelve passengers, several Union soldiers wearing clean blue uniforms, hats, and winter jackets with capes walked toward them.

Sarah ran past the men and embraced the pale, skinny figure of Ed.

"Oh, Ed, so *glad* you're home." She stepped back and eyed his gaunt cheeks, and he smiled wide, revealing several missing teeth.

The image reminded Swift of bloody gums and swollen joints. But Ed looked worse than anyone Swift could remember. He stood tall, yet bent, face so thin that his cheek bones protruded above a long thin jaw. And at that moment, Swift realized what the Union's policies of stalling prisoner exchanges had cost his cousin. Anger flamed in his belly.

Hub stood open-mouthed, eyes like saucers.

Sarah took a deep breath and slowly put her arms around Ed. "It's *so* good to have you home. And look at you, son. You're a *man*."

"No. Mama, I'm *still* your boy."

Sarah shook her head and looked nervously about. "You've lost so much weight."

"I'm fine, Mama."

Sarah eyed him. "You *sure?*"

"Had a steak dinner for New Years!"

Sarah eyed him closely.

"Well, I'm a little stiff from the scurvy, but vinegar and onions work wonders. Imagine that—vinegar and onions!" His mouth puckered up in one corner, and his eyes rolled back and around.

Sarah laughed through tears that streamed down her cheeks.

Ed turned to the others. "Hey, Hub, Swift, did ya come down here just to see *me?*"

"You bet I did!" shouted Hub. He stepped forward and hugged Ed into his portly frame.

Ed pushed Hub away. "What you doin', trying to spoon with me? Hey, Swift, who's the girly?"

Swift put his hand on Bitsy's back. "This is Bitsy Hyde."

Ed's blue eyes went wide. "*Same* girl as always followed you around school?"

Swift nodded.

Ed smiled wide, showing his missing teeth again. "Well, fancy *that*! Looks like I got here just in time to save you from a fate worse than death, Bitsy."

Swift and Bitsy looked at each other and laughed.

The group walked to the carriage, where Hub and Swift had to help Ed into his seat. Those legs were nearly as straight as boards, and Swift remembered the pain of those joints, the constant bone ache that never went away, day or night.

346

Hub sat in the driver's seat and jumped up even faster. "Hey! What the—" he eyed a cold rock in the center of the seat. "Where'd *that* come from?"

Sarah's gray eyes turned toward Ed. A smile spread across her face. "You're home, Ed. You're *really* home."

"*You*," said Hub. "It was *always* you. Wasn't it?"

Ed's eyes bugged as he feigned innocence. Everyone laughed. Then he turned and called to Sergeant Gaffney, walking out of the station, "Hey! Sarge, you were right. We did make it home."

Gaffney stopped and stared hard. "That's right, Best. Just think what would've happened if Gilbert and I'd left your miserable butt at Andersonville. That's why sergeants get paid more than corporals."

Ed smiled and turned to his mother. "Heard from Nels or Solon?"

"Still both in Ontario."

"You wrote me that."

"Then you *did* get my letters!"

"Caught up with me in Washington. But how are they?"

"Sol says his innards aren't right, and Nels can't stand in the sun for long. Once that steel plate gets heated, he loses his head. Can't be too bad though. Wrote last month to say he's in love.

A jagged grin spread across Ed's face. "Gotta get *me* one of those. Hey, Bitsy! Come up here and ride on my lap."

Swift pulled Bitsy away and put his arm around her shoulders. "Sorry, this one's taken."

Curge rode up on his horse and flashed a smile toward Ed, but when he got close, his eyebrows went up. "Shoot! You all right?"

Ed grinned. "Sure. Know where we can find some pretty girls?"

Curge shook his head.

Swift pulled Bitsy away and walked her home without a word. When they stopped outside her door, the sunset splashed orange over the front windows of her parent's house. "Do you love me?"

Bitsy looked aside. "Oh, Swift, I loved the person you were. I even love the person I believe you're going to be. But right now, I'm—not sure."

Swift took her chin and turned her face until he looked straight into her green eyes. "I'm going to quit law."

"What will you do?"

"I want to write—for a newspaper. And not a small town one either. One big enough to print the truth."

Bitsy's eyes widened. "But what made you?"

"The newspapers haven't been telling the truth. Ed looks like he does because the Union stalled the prisoner exchanges. Most papers said it was hooey, but I felt it in my gut. Knew something was wrong."

Bitsy shook her head. "But, where will you go?"

"Chicago." He took her hands in his, pulled her closer to him. "If you'll wait, I'll come for you, as soon as I get a job."

Bitsy nodded. "Swift, you're the only man I've ever loved."

April 25th, 1865, Little Rock, Arkansas

The long thin line of blue uniformed soldiers was at least one hundred strong, as Socrates awaited his turn to muster out of the army. A spirit of joyous revelry had taken over the streets since word of Lee's surrender at Appomatox Court House. Cavalryman raced their steeds through the streets, while people stood on the sidewalks cheering, arguing, and betting on the fastest horse. Every once in awhile, someone pulled out a pistol and shot it into the air. Bottles of liquor passed freely from mouth to mouth, and everyone smiled. The celebration ran for ten days, growing hot and violent after Lincoln's assassination. But now it was quiet again, as the regiment disbanded its few remaining companies. Many were already released with the termination of their three-year enlistments. Even Colonel Cloud was let go when the regiment was reduced. With no enemy, those who remained were no longer needed. Socrates stood with his hands in his pockets, as the men around him talked excitedly about their families and homes. His own thoughts turned to Gus and Willie. They were good boys. Too bad they'd seen so much trouble. Blood rushed to his face as he thought about their trip home. He'd entrusted them and his money to the care of an Indiana chaplain, but how those boys ended up abandoned in Springfield, Illinois, was beyond Socrates' understanding.

There were over four hundred refugees on that train, so it could have been a mistake. But why hadn't Parsons Leard tried to contact him to let him know the boys were lost? Hadn't even tried to get Socrates' money back to him. Of course, seventy-five dollars didn't matter as much as Gus and Willie, but Socrates smelled a rat. It was a good thing D.P. Brandwell took the boys in and saw to it that they got safely home to Wisconsin. Socrates didn't know who Brandwell was, but would surely stop to thank him on the way home.

Socrates kicked at the dirt. He'd make it up to the boys, take them fishing, teach them to ride. But somehow his reassurance couldn't seem to break the sadness clutching his heart, squeezing the life out of him. It seemed improper to regret going home, but he did. What was it? He ought to be happy as the rest of these men. What was bothering him? The school in Texas? Maybe. He'd never left anything unfinished before. Or could it be Ellen's last request to bury Ben's remains at Fort Smith?

Friendly Reuben grinned wide as ever. "*There* you are, Best. Heading home? With all these fellas leaving post, won't be long before I'll be down right lonely."

"What do you mean?" asked Socrates. "Thought everyone was mustering out. You mean to tell me you're staying in?"

Reuben nodded. "Root said he needs stewards to stay and help with the sick and wounded. Can't just pack 'em up and ship 'em home in *their* condition. Someone has to take care 'til the War Department decides what to do. That's why I'm here. Doc says I should see if I can talk you into staying an extra month or two. The pay'd be the same, and there's no extra duties outside the hospital. What do you think?"

"What do *I* think?" said Socrates throwing his hands out. "I think I have a couple boys back home with no mother or father. *That's* what I think! How could I stay here when they need me? Absolutely *out* of the question. I'm drawing my pay and going home."

Reuben tipped his head, smiled as if he were the happiest man in the world. "That's what I figured you'd say. Told Doc, but he said I should try." Reuben leaned forward, whispering, "He's short handed—needs help. Hardly makes sense to work hard at keeping someone alive and then just say adios."

Socrates stared hard, trying not to be angry. The words of Aristotle:

"Friends and truths are both here, but it is a sacred duty to prefer the truth."

He shook his head. "Sorry, Friendly, 'can't step in the same river twice.'"

Friendly's eyes narrowed. "Hercules?"

Socrates laughed. "Heroclitus."

Friendly scratched his head. "The way up is the same as the way down."

"Hey! You messed that up. Besides that's *my* line."

Friendly laughed. "It's what you get for teaching me philosophy."

Socrates rolled his eyes, but Friendly just stood there grinning. Socrates shifted his feet. "Stop that darned grinning, Reuben!"

"The war may be over for us, Socrates, but not for them. Not by a long shot. Well. Anyway. It's been good knowing you. Good luck."

Shoot! thought Socrates as his face tightened. He's doing it again. "Stop being so friendly, Friendly. Darn it anyway! You know what I mean. Knock it off!"

Friendly offered empty hands.

"I *know* what you're trying to do," said Socrates, "making me think about our boys, so I feel guilty, but I'm not gonna fall for it." His words were strong, convincing, yet even as he spoke, something registered in his brain. That's what had been bothering him. Never could leave a crop in mid harvest, and it was killing him to just up and leave his patients. But he couldn't stay, he had his own boys to think of."

Friendly stood before him, face painted with this unflappable grin.

"I *can't* go!" said Socrates. "I've *got* to see my boys."

"No one's twistin' yer arm."

Socrates jeered. "Quit smiling. You're killing me." He turned and looked away. A big oak tree stood there, just like the one Vince Osborne tied the *Annie Jacobs* to. The tree reminded him of Vince, still in the hospital, minus one leg. Socrates couldn't think of Vince now. Had to get it out of his head. "Thanks, Friendly, I appreciate that." Did Friendly know what he was *really* thinking? "I'm sure you and Dr. Root will get along fine without me. It takes committed men to work together, and with my mind on my boys at home, I probably wouldn't be much help anyway."

Friendly stuck his pointer finger beneath his chin and smiled again. "May be true, but I doubt it. Been gettin' along fine since they left. Don't think it's a performance problem. Anyway, if you don't want to, you don't have to. Like I said, no one's twistin' yer arm." He looked down the line of men, turned and shook Socrates' hand. "Hope we meet again. Really. You've been a good friend—good worker too. That's why Root wanted you to stay. Oh, well. Shouldn't be going on and on. Already have your mind made up. Don't want to sway you. Like I said, Hope we meet again. Oh, almost forgot. Presbyters want to meet with you before you leave. Said your testimony has so touched everyone in the community, they're having a dinner in your honor."

Socrates stared into the sky. "Strange. He couldn't understand his father's hard-line faith until he'd lost nearly everything he held dear. Through a dense cloud of despair, the Bible's words had taken on fresh meaning, causing him to read it in a whole new way. Those words were now as alive to him as anything the Greeks had ever written, and he found himself relating his entire life's experiences through the writings of John, Peter, and Paul. And though he still didn't agree with his father's decision regarding Ellen, he finally understood and respected it."

Friendly smiled one last time, turned, and walked away.

The next half hour dragged along until Socrates finally stood before the payroll officer. His mind replayed Friendly's words. Dr. Root needed assistants and so did the sick and injured. They needed him, but so did his boys. What was a body to do? And why did they have to ask him? Him! With everything he'd lost, they wanted him to give up going home. He had every right to go home.

"Name—I said, name!" The payroll officer's words commanded his attention. "What's the matter with you, soldier? Don't you have a name?"

"Best, sir. Socrates Best."

"All right, Socrates Best, pay attention now, and don't be daydreaming on me, 'cause I've already had a hard day. Now, let's see when you were last paid." Searching his rolls, he found a line and followed his finger across to the side of the page. "Here you are. I see you were last paid on February twenty-eighth, you provide and take care of your own horse, and your uniform allowance was taken care of at last pay. That means you're owed one hundred dollars. If you'll sign here, you'll be officially mustered out of the service."

Socrates chewed his lip, took the paper money, folded it neatly into his billfold, and slipped it into his pocket. Turning to the books, he took the pen in hand and started signing his name. He stopped and looked at the officer. "What do I have to do if I want to stay in?"

The officer's mouth dropped open. "You *want* to stay in? All day long I've been mustering people out, 'cause no one wants to *stay* in! Fact is, you're the first one to concoct such a notion. Why you want to stay in? There's no enemy. Heck! There isn't even a regiment."

"I know that," Socrates said slowly, "but I've been working under special orders at the hospital, and all of the boys can't go home yet. They need someone to tend them for now. Dr. Root sent one of my coworkers to ask me to stay on, and I've decided that's what I want to do."

The officer's scowl softened. Turning to the books again, he slid his finger up the page. "I see you've been an acting hospital steward since August of '63, under Special Order No. 26. Yes, if you want to stay and help at the hospital, I'm sure there's need there." Turning back to the scroll, the officer crossed off the words, mustered out, and scribbled, "Remarks: retained in service under provision of Circular 36, War Dept. Series of 1864—recruit." "There. That should do it. I was told the hospital personnel and patients will be transferred to Fort Gibson. You'll have to report to Dr. Root, but remember—you're still in the army, so don't be late."

Socrates smiled at the officer. The irony of the situation was not lost on him. One moment he felt like laughing and dancing, while the next he wanted to cry, scream, or yell. He wandered slowly toward the little cemetery, where his wife's body lay, until he knelt beside the stone. The warmth of her body, the thickness of her dark hair enveloped him. "I'm sorry, Ellen," he whispered. "All is lost, save honor. Forgive me. Please forgive me." The words of his namesake came to mind:

"True philosophers make dying their profession, and to them of all men death is least alarming . . . surely there are many who have chosen their own free will to follow their dead beloveds to the next world . . . ."

Socrates wished he were with her, wanted it with all his heart. He *could* be with her. But what about the boys? Could he simply trust his mother and brothers to take care of them? There would be no more pain, no more sorrow. Paul's words swept through his mind:

"Death, oh death, where is thy sting?"

But her death *did* sting, and with the most *searing* of pains. Why? Sweet Jesus, why?

Consumed with guilt and sickening grief, he lay down on his back in the green grass and cried. Wave upon wave wracked him until his ribs ached as bad as his heart, and he couldn't summon another tear. Then he lay silent. Empty.

Large white clouds passed overhead in swirls of white on blue, and he remembered the game he used to play, when he was a boy growing up in Ohio. *Faces in the Clouds* his teacher Robert Campbell called it. And within a minute or so, the taut lower jaw and thick, white brows of the man appeared. Socrates could see him there, clearly painted in the clouds. His image gave way to the faces of Washington and Lincoln, then a ship, perhaps Columbus's *Pinta* or *Santa Maria*. Mother's face was there, so kind and compassionate. His father's angry face appeared, then softened into an approving smile. The faces of Socrates' wife and infant daughters followed, and he grew sullen until they too smiled. The face of the young, blond-haired boy he'd killed crowded the sky for a moment, before fading into amorphous streaks of white. Buck Malneck floated momentarily overhead, his raging face contorting until it too dissolved. Socrates' boys' faces appeared briefly, just long enough to spur the thought that they were in good hands with his mother.

Then came other thoughts. Friendly's words that these boys in blue, whom he had served with for nearly two and one-half years, were sick, hurt, and alone. They needed someone they could trust to take care of them until they too would be well enough to go home. Sadly, some never would, but would have to wait until permanent facilities were prepared. And maybe, just maybe, Socrates might be able to get Ben's body shipped to Fort Smith, where his bones could rest beside those of his sister.

Time's never ending stream had flowed by him as surely as the air above, shaping and twisting things with invisible, incomprehensible forces. Its next moment would never be the same, could never be the same, for it was as eternally changing as the clouds in the sky. He could never alter the past, could never make up with his father, or stop himself from going to Texas. But somehow, it was all right. All he could possess was here and now. So much remained to be done, before the cool blue streams of time could take him home again.

He rolled onto his side to look at Ellen's stone one last time. It was then it dawned on him, something like the sun bursts rays of gold over green pastures following a violent summer storm. His father hadn't driven him to education to fulfill some lost paternal opportunity, but in preparation for Socrates' own. John Best had somehow divined the future, preparing his son to live when men would contend for the very heart and soul of the nation—when paupers and princes would battle side by side—those days when philosophers were kings.

AFTERWARD

Thomas Ramsey died from typhoid fever before ever seeing the enemy.

Dr. Thomas Best was forced out of the army with chronic dysentery and kidney failure, not long after the close of the war. He later died from complications of these conditions.

Following two years of practice, Swift left law forever. He married Betsy (Bitsy) Hyde, and the couple had four children. Betsy passed away after only fifteen years of marriage, and Swift remained a widower. He worked on the Chicago daily newspapers, and the Burlington, Iowa paper, before joining his brothers in their newspaper at Neligh, Nebraska. He was known as an avid reporter and outdoorsman, who traveled to every state in the continental U.S. before his death in Superior, Wisconsin, in 1924. He was eighty-one.

Solon returned from Canada with Elizabeth after the war, and pioneered into northwest Wisconsin, settling in Best Valley. He died at the age of fifty-one of stomach cancer.

Ed married after returning home to Big Spring, and also pioneered into northwest Wisconsin, where he taught at the Best Valley schoolhouse and developed his first homestead farm. Around a decade later he pioneered again, this time with his brother Hub and some of Nels' children. They moved to Idaho and settled near Coeur d'Alene. He died there in 1924 at the age of eighty-two.

Nels returned from Canada with a bride, Jane McCormick. They, too, pioneered with the family into northwest Wisconsin, at Downing. He was plagued for years with severe headaches and could not tolerate heat, which ultimately forced him to retire on a military pension. He lived to the age of eighty and had eight children—a far better outcome than the doctors must have hoped for.

It is not known today if Socrates was ever able to retrieve Ben's body and have it placed next to Ellen at Fort Smith. He finally returned to Big Spring in July 1865, where he remarried and raised a blended family of eight. Later he pioneered into northwest Wisconsin with his brothers. He never returned to teaching. He farmed and became chaplain of the G.A.R. (a precursor to the VFW) in Dunn County, Wisconsin, until his death in 1896 at the age of seventy-one.

EPILOGUE

I N THE COURSE OF THE CIVIL WAR, THE STATE OF WISCONSIN PROVIDED EIGHTY thousand five hundred ninety-five soldiers to fight for the preservation of the Union and the abolition of slavery. Of those volunteers and draftees, approximately eleven thousand died, and fifteen thousand were permanently disabled (a casualty rate of about thirty-one percent). Sickness and disease killed nearly two-thirds of the dead as camp life exposed large numbers of these American men and boys to illnesses they might never have encountered otherwise. Unsanitary living conditions led to diphtheria, typhus, and typhoid fevers running rampant through the camps.

Prison camps in both the North and the South became overcrowded by senseless political arguments, which the North used to stymie prisoner exchanges. At the same time, Sherman and Sheridan went to great efforts to destroy Confederate supplies, and all their means of delivery, thus placing further burden on the South. Between February of 1864 and April of the following year, approximately forty-one thousand prisoners were brought to Andersonville Prison, near Americus, Georgia. Of those, nearly thirteen thousand died from lack of food, unsanitary living conditions, illnesses, and sadly enough, from the attacks of fellow prisoners.

While the war ultimately preserved the Union and abolished slavery, it also killed about six percent of the nation's population (comparable to about fifteen million of today's populace), arguably the youngest and most virile elements of its future. The late Archie Crothers, a local historian and grandson of Sally Best-Ramsey, made this astute observation in his memoirs:

"The Civil War took a heavy toll from this area. So many of the young men were killed, or permanently disabled, the area never regained a population equal to that attained prior to the war. The effects of such upheavals were, in my opinion, much more keenly felt in a community such as Big Spring, than in the larger centers of population."

Today, Portage remains a substantial Wisconsin community and county seat; and though residents of Big Spring still retain a close knit, rural farming community, there are few buildings left of what once offered the promise of a growing little town. Residents of this community now shop for groceries and other household needs about seven miles down the road, at the town previously called Kilbourne, and presently known as Wisconsin Dells.

For further information regarding truth vs. fiction,
bibliography of reference materials, index of names,
and a complete photo library of characters and places, see:
www.smbest.com